# CRUSADERS

## Also by Barnaby Williams

*Death Before Dishonour*
*Revolution*
*Anno Domini*

# CRUSADERS

*Barnaby Williams*

POCKET
BOOKS

LONDON · SYDNEY · NEW YORK · TOKYO · SINGAPORE · TORONTO

First published by Simon & Schuster, 1996
First published in paperback by Pocket Books, 1997
An imprint of Simon & Schuster Ltd
A Viacom Company

Copyright © Barnaby Williams, 1996

This book is copyright under the Berne Convention
No reproduction without permission
All rights reserved

The right of Barnaby Williams be identified as author of this
work has been asserted in accordance with sections 77 and 78 of
the Copyright Designs and Patents Act 1988

Simon & Schuster
West Garden Place
Kendal Street
London W2 2AQ

Simon & Schuster of Australia Pty Ltd Sydney

A CIP catalogue record for this book is available
from the British Library.

0-671-51643-4

This book is a work of fiction. Names, characters, places
and incidents either are products of the author's imagination or
are used fictitiously.

Printed and bound by
Caledonian International Book Manufacturing Ltd, Glasgow

For my darling wife, ANNE.

With all thanks to:

The prince of publishers, Nick Webb, as always.
My editors Jenny Olivier, who began it, and Jaquie Clare who
finished it, for much hard work and great ideas.
My marvellous agent Anne Dewe.
My mother, as always.
My daughters Abbey and Philippa, who light up my life.

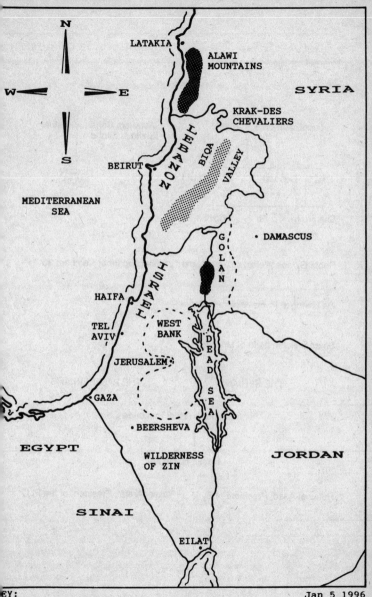

## THE ISRAELIS.

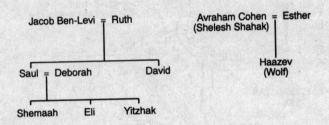

Jacob Ben-Levi = Ruth

Avraham Cohen = Esther
(Shelesh Shahak)

Saul = Deborah     David

Haazev
(Wolf)

Shemaah     Eli     Yitzhak

Rabbi Gideon Weiss, self-proclaimed prophet, leader of Numbers 33

Zvi Levinger, Prime Minister of Israel

Shaul Shiloah, head of Mossad

## THE SYRIANS          THE PALESTINIANS

Bushra = Hadj Hamouda

Hasan Hamouda

Hafez al-Asad, President of Syria     Yasser Arafat, President of the PLO

**Israel** ancient homeland of the Jews, a twentieth-century miracle, a phoenix risen from the ashes of history

**Filastin** ancient homeland of the Palestinians, a twentieth-century horror, a land under foreign rule

**Bilad al-Sham** ancient belonging of the great Syrian Empire, seaward edge of the lands of Damascus

**The same place**

**The Palestinians** Yasser Arafat, leader of the PLO, and Abu Hataf, aka Hadj Hamouda. Blood-drenched murderers, terrorists – or keepers of the flame, freedom-fighters in a greater cause against totalitarian tyranny

**The Syrians** President Asad and his closest adviser, Hasan Hamouda, son of Hadj. Patriots and peacemakers – or inheritors of the mantle of the great Salah el-Din, victor of the Battle of Hattin, twelfth-century conqueror of the Crusaders

**The Israelis** Holocaust-survivor Jacob Ben-Levi, *sabra* General Shahak, American-born Rabbi Gideon Weiss. Members of a once-scattered, holy race reunited by God – or men of the last imperial nation, twentieth-century Crusaders, aliens and oppressors in a foreign land

Jacob Ben-Levi knew them all. He escaped from the Nazi V2 rocket factory at Dora to fight *with* them and *against* them, from the devastating War of Independence to the day he became Foreign Minister of Israel. For his country he was gun-runner, commando, spy, envoy and diplomat, a survivor of an endless war. Finally all he wanted for his country was peace. Because he wanted peace he started the most terrible war of all . . .

# PART I

## The Vistula River, Poland, September 1944

THEY walked along the river path in the early autumn sunshine, the water gurgling pleasingly, the children's feet pattering on the yellow leaves, while the adults made their way through the grass along the verge. Scarlet and blue berries hung on bushes, and birds clung to their branches as they twisted them off, undisturbed as the column of families and guards went by.

A natural meadow led down to the water's edge. There the ground was soft. The guards issued spades to the men and the bigger boys, and they began to dig. The sun rose in the sky and looked down on the pit as it took shape. Different birds arrived to feast on the worms that the men were turning up.

Jacob worked next to his father and his younger brother, David, flinging the earth from his shovel up onto the growing rampart above them. When he paused to wipe away the sweat running down into his eyes he could see his mother, huddled with the other women and the younger children, under the gaze of the heavy machine-guns and the guards.

The guards broke out the schnapps mid-morning, drinking from tin mugs, staring balefully down at the Jews digging the long grave. When Jacob next looked up he saw the women and the little ones being lined up along the edge of the pit. The guards summoned the men up; the spades they carried were of value, far too good to be left down there.

In that brief frame of frozen sunlight a terrible agony shot through Jacob. After all they had done, after all they had gone through it had come to this; after all the escapes from murder, they were here. His whole being screamed with protest.

The pistols began to go off, like popping fireworks.

As Jacob climbed out of the trench he saw the man behind his mother. The gun barrel jerked as he pulled the trigger. *No.* She tumbled in the air as she fell, the blood from her head spraying the air scarlet behind her. It drifted against the sun. His brother saw too and cried out, just in front of him. Jacob felt numb. It all seemed unreal. *Mama.*

There was a pause as they stood in line and a guard went past with the sack of quicklime. It fell white onto the tumbled bodies below, and became stained red. Here and there a hand, an arm moved feebly. There was the smell of chemical, of blood, of tobacco smoke as the executioners enjoyed a cigarette in the break. From somewhere came the smell of forest and grass sweeter than the stench from the freshly turned earth.

The man had reached the end of the trench, the killers were feeding the little bullets into their clips. They shone, silver and gold in the sun. They slapped them home into the grips of their pistols, and stepped forward once more – men with a job of work to be done. The line of Jews stepped obediently forward, and the guns began to pop again.

A little girl was lying below Jacob. Somehow she had fallen so that she lay gazing up at the sun. Jacob knew her. She was Hilda, the little daughter of Moishe, the baker. Her eyes were open, looking up as though wondering what the rivulet of blood flowing down out of her hair was.

He was gripping his brother by the shoulder as he looked along the row. When the executioner turned his head away, looking for the man with the quicklime, he gave David a sudden, violent shove. He toppled over, landing with a squelch on the dead girl below. Jacob caught a momentary flash of his terrified eyes, and then he lay still, just like the dead.

There was a flat bang next to Jacob and Yechiel Katz, the beadle, stumbled forward. Jacob felt that he should say something. He wanted to talk to the man with the gun. Reason with him. There was so much that still had to be done. Golda, Moishe's older daughter, had returned his smile when he had gone for the bread, he had wanted to walk with her one more time. There was the return match of draughts to play with Saul, the unfinished fight with Joshua. What of the birthday of Levon? He felt the light tap of the muzzle against the back of his skull as his killer lined up his weapon, he smelled alcohol on his breath. Now he must do something. He felt very strongly that he must do something – it was wrong to simply stand there like a beast awaiting slaughter. But he stood, like all the others.

There was an empty click as the pistol hammer fell. The executioner clucked his tongue, and Jacob heard the metallic noises as he changed clips.

The muzzle tapped his head once again.

'*Yitgadal veyitkadach . . .*'

The chant was so sudden, so loud he jerked his head. The executioner fired, and Jacob tumbled into the trench, blood streaming from him. It seemed to him as he fell, as it became dark, that he could still hear his father singing the Kaddish, the prayer for the dead, above him.

'*Veyitkadach shme raba . . .*'

A pop, and all was quiet.

He was very cold, and yet his skin burned. It was very dark, and heaviness weighed upon him like a thick black blanket. His nostrils were filled with the stench of death. Someone was pulling at him; he struggled, feebly at first, then more frantically, as earth cascaded around him. He pushed himself up, and sunshine burst into his eyes. He was kneeling in the middle of a long rectangle of earth, freshly dug and raked, like a sown field. David was pulling at him, lifting him free of the earth's grip; and in the hole he had made Jacob saw Hilda, the daughter of Moishe the baker, still staring up at him.

His head was on fire – a terrible gouge ran through his scalp from the back to above his temple. His hair was stiff with congealed blood, his skin burned, red patches and weals showing where the quicklime was eating into it.

'Come on, Jacob,' David urged desperately.

He staggered across the empty meadow towards the river, his brother helping him, and they fell into the shallows.

He could hear voices on the path. A log, almost the whole of a tree, lay caught in some rocks. The boys seized it and pushed it out into the flow, holding on tight as it bore them away to safety.

When they were washed ashore the sun was low over the trees bordering the river. The log came to rest against the sloping bank, and they crawled onto the land. Some mean village occupied the bend in the river, two lines of wooden houses with a muddy road between them. The boys staggered towards it. Although his clothes were sodden and the day becoming cold Jacob burned with fever. The ground was light under his feet and he saw it all as though from high up, through clear air.

Some peasant boys little older than himself were lounging by a gate. When they saw the yellow stars on their jackets, they called out, 'Yids! Stinking yids!'

One of them threw a stone at them; Jacob felt it hit his leg, but there was no pain.

The yellow star. As he trudged along he heard his father's voice telling all the others in the little ghetto, 'It won't kill us, after all.' And they all sewed them on.

A man was sitting up on his wagon, piled high with vegetables, potatoes, beets, cabbages, his horse waiting patiently between the shafts. He looked down at them.

'You, boys. You Jews?'

He could see the yellow star, too, tinged red from the blood that had flowed from Jacob's head. But he spoke politely, not using any of the nasty expressions there were for his race. For him, the Jew. Jacob paused, peering through his fever at the man, who asked, 'Where are you going?'

'To Palestine,' Jacob replied without hesitation. He could see it, green trees and sun-drenched rocks, and no one trying to kill him.

'It's a long way to Palestine from here,' said the man, smiling slightly.

'We're late, that's all,' said Jacob. 'I wanted us to go, but my father said it would get better. He's dead now, so I'm going myself with my brother. We're going to see Cousin Avraham.'

'Dead, hey?'

'They took us from the little ghetto. Took us all out this morning. The others, they're lying in the grave they had us dig, so we must go to Palestine without them.'

'Well, get up on the cart then.' The man repeated thoughtfully, 'It's a long way to Palestine.'

It took the last of the boys' energy to climb up amongst the vegetables. And the vegetables smelled of the earth that now covered the grave.

He was there. In his fevered sleep he was there, in the warm sunshine, and among the fruit trees, laden with sweet blossom. Palestine, the land of the Jews, where people did not want to kill you.

The creaking and bumping of the cart had stopped and someone was pulling at his leg.

'Here. You. We're here.'

It was the man. Dazed, Jacob sat up in the pile of beets. It was dark, but all was lit up by the giant flames leaping from tall chimneys into the black sky. A terrible smell was in the air.

'Where?' he muttered. 'This is not Palestine.'

They all roared with laughter. Others were there, men in uniform.

'*This* is where the Jews live. In the *kazett*,' said the man, and he grinned cruelly at the success of his joke. David ran off in the dark, but one of the men caught him easily.

They hustled them through an iron door – above it were the words *Arbeit Macht Frei*, work is liberty. The chimneys roared above them, and a dreadful ash drifted down to settle on their skin.

## The Haifa–Safed Road, Palestine, October 1944

The five men were hidden from view in the ditch. At the bottom ran a trickle of water from the autumn rains which flowed off the hill, but they bore the discomfort of their wet feet stoically and kept their Lee-Enfield rifles up and dry. The day had become warm since they had first taken up their places just before dawn, and now they were thirsty in its heat. But this too they bore. They were waiting for something which made the aches of the body insignificant. Agents of the Devil were coming; today the forces of God would tilt the scales a little in His favour.

Hadj Hamouda cocked his ear. He was the leader and they all looked to him for their instruction. The Devil and his disciples would be wearing the clothes of the people; it was necessary to have someone who knew who they were. The noise of an engine came up the hill. On the road lay a boulder, looking as if it had rolled down the slope from the nearby village of Sajur, loosened by the rains. Any vehicle that came by had to slow down and manoeuvre around it.

'Prepare yourselves,' Hamouda ordered; safety catches made a soft metallic click in the ditch, and the men's feet shifted in the muddy water, as they positioned themselves for action. There was a sudden aroma of sweat, garlic and wet earth, and on the breeze came the sound of the approaching vehicle.

It was a taxi, he could see that. It carried the name of a Tel Aviv firm. Within were people in all their finery, going to a wedding, just as though they were decent people. These evil ones, they had pretended to be friendly, and yet all the while they had reached out with the Devil's claws, stealing the land of those who were good. As the van came closer, the men in the ditch could hear voices raised

in song, they recognized the foreign language, the tongue of Hell.
In the ditch, dark eyes shone, white teeth flashed in olive faces. It
was all worth a little discomfort.

They heard the whine of the gearbox as the driver changed down
to negotiate the boulder. Hamouda was on his feet, balancing himself
in the ditch. His first shot was expertly placed, shattering first the
windscreen then the face of the driver. The van lurched and crashed
straight into the boulder, immobilizing itself in the middle of the road.
The others were on their feet too. A continuous volley of fire tore into
the van, punching holes in its blue metal sides, spraying the windows
scarlet as the victims inside thrashed about in death's agony.

Then all was quiet, just smoke in the air and the ringing of the
explosions in their ears. Blood and petrol dripped mingling onto the
macadam. Their triumphant rifles high in their fists the men capered
around the wreck.

They tore open the twin rear doors, the torn metal shrieking in
protest. Inside was the smell of the slaughterhouse, hot blood and
offal. They inhaled it as though it were perfume.

Hamouda pulled at a bloody foot, and a middle-aged man in a
dark suit slithered from the pile of dead and dying to fall wetly on
the road. A blood-stained white flower in his lapel. His eyes still
moved; Hamouda opened the fly of his trousers and urinated in his
face as he died.

Gaily-wrapped boxes, wedding gifts, now spattered with blood,
their wrappings torn by the bullets lay amongst the carnage. And
from beneath came an involuntary moan of terror. With a howl of
triumph the assassins dragged out a young woman.

She was unharmed; they hustled her screaming onto the stony
hillside. They ripped off her clothes and held her down as they
raped her, one after the other.

Hamouda stood to one side, smoking a cigarette as his men took
what they believed was their due. Out on the hills nobody stirred,
although he knew a hundred eyes looked down upon what they did
– and approved. It was good to see Satan humbled, torn, just for a
day, from his throne where he oppressed them, dragged down into
the dirt and made to feel pain.

When the men were finished the woman lay bloody and broken
on the hard hillside. She was olive-skinned, as they were. She had
glossy, black hair, as they had. Hamouda took a machete from his
belt and hacked her to pieces.

When the shrieking had faded to echoes, he led his men away
through the groves of gnarled, indifferent grey olive trees.

In the bloody van, where the flies had arrived to feast, something stirred amongst the dead. A boy crawled out, standing shaking on the slippery road. Avraham Cohen looked at the savaged corpse of his mother on the hill, and at the retreating forms of her killers, disappearing into the trees and vowed his revenge.

## *Konzentrationslager Dora*, Kohnstein Mountain, Germany, December 1944

It had snowed again during the night. On the slopes of the mountain the pine trees sparkled, green needles dusted with fresh white powder, shining in the early sunlight. The shivering column of men and boys came shuffling out of the gate, their breath frosting in the air. Their wooden clogs thumped softly on the new snow, their striped clothes hung from their bodies.

The scar on Jacob's head throbbed. It was livid red on his shaved scalp, disappearing under a greasy cap. Behind him was David. Next, Baruch. The three Jews stuck together. *Kazett* Dora was different, it contained men from all the conquered lands – Frenchmen, Czechs, Poles, Italians, British, Dutch, Norwegians, Danes and many more. It didn't mean they weren't to be worked until they died, but simply that they had to be good with their hands while they did it.

They crunched through the barracks where the SS men lived. The man next to Baruch was beginning to stagger already, his breath rattling in his throat. He began to cough, bringing up great gobs of bloody phlegm. From the smell of his clothes and the toxic purple rash of his skin it was clear he worked in the paint shop. They didn't last long in there.

As they came down the slope, the mouth of the tunnel opened square in front of them and they trudged towards it, following the railway line. From inside they heard the shriek of the whistle, the first grunt of the pistons, and the locomotive came into view, staining the clear air with belching grey smoke. It went past them, the driver looking down at them indifferently as the train hauled a line of big, boxy trucks containing the things that they had made.

The huge tunnel filled with smoke, which set the man from the paint shop coughing again. In the glare from the overhead bulbs, his blood seemed purple.

The guards marched them in. The man from the paint shop

staggered on down the tunnel. Jacob, David and Baruch joined the others in the deep, cathedral-like gallery of the final assembly, where they put together all the parts the others had made, galvanized and painted, and assembled them into a whole, to be taken away by the train outside.

He was waiting for them on the platform outside the engineer's office, the one whose mother had christened him Karl, but whom they all knew as the Butcher's Boy. He grinned to see them come in. The yellow hair under his black cap shone white in the powerful light of the lamps. He was probably no older than they were, certainly not yet twenty.

The assembly line began at the far end of the gallery, where it met the second of the two tunnels that pierced the small Kohnstein mountain from side to side. Here they brought in all the component parts, made on the lathes and cut, shaped and welded in the vices. Empty wheeled transporters were being pushed back along one of the lines in the gallery, their wheels groaning on the rails. The noise was beginning to increase as the belts of the lathes started to slap, as the men in the striped clothes fitted metal to the chuck and the blades began to bite, as the compressors cut in, pumping the air for the men in the paint shop to spray, the generators thumping ever harder to cope with the rising demand for electricity in the subterranean factory.

The men knew better than to delay and took up where they had left off. Jacob, David and Baruch worked in the same team; the gas turbine fuel pump was ready on its bench. They went over to it, taking spanners for checking each nut was secure on each bolt. You would be flogged, for certain, for a loose nut, or if it was the Butcher's Boy that found it, as he prowled through the giant workshop, even killed.

By Engineer Ibach's office stood the crane. Items such as the fuel pump could be lifted by hand and fitted into the alloy skeletons lying on their sides in the transporters. Other parts were too heavy and too bulky. The two fuel tanks, one for the alcohol and water mix, the other for the liquid oxygen, had to be lifted in by the crane; the amatol warhead certainly did too, as it weighed one ton and was wheeled in on special trolleys.

Everything checked, they carefully carried the pump over to the frame, and began to bolt it in place in front of the combustion chamber itself, which had already been fitted. Others in the team were carrying over the long, galvanized shaped tubes that carried the fuels from the tanks. At the front of the transporter Baruch began to fit the various boxes that held the component parts of the guidance system. What exactly was inside was a mystery, as the boxes arrived already assembled, and only needed to be put into place. This was Engineer Ibach's domain – what he did in his office governed the way in which the incredible machine was guided to its target, where its job was to make people dead, by the hundred, within a fraction of a second. It was known by the slaves who fitted the boxes that they were both extremely important to the functioning of the weapon and delicate. When van Koop the Dutchman had dropped one, Engineer Ibach had seen him do it, so Karl Franz the Butcher's Boy had hung him from the crane by the ankles and whipped him until he was dead.

They worked in silence. Communication beyond the exchanging of signs was considered planning for sabotage. Baruch was bolting one of the boxes into place, while Jacob held the complicated wiring loom that connected it all. David climbed up, leaning over the frame to begin screwing the various wires of the loom into place. There was a hole in the box where the multi-pin plug fitted. Below the frame Jacob held the loom. His brother's trousers were against the box, hidden from sight by Baruch's body, Jacob reached inside the fly above him and held David to the hole in the box. He urinated swiftly. Then Jacob took his screwdriver and fixed the plug firmly in place. Another bomb would miss its target he thought with satisfaction.

They worked on throughout the morning. Jacob imagined what it was like above ground. Outside the pale sun would be climbing up over the mountain, the fresh air would be warming up a little. It was too early for the spring flowers to push green and white through the softening snow. Inside the black rock caverns it was always the same, whatever the hour.

The weapon was starting to take shape, less a strange collection of parts bolted into a frame, more an entity, a creature. Its clothes were waiting for it – the light alloy panels that dressed it from needle nose tip to four-finned tail. When they were on, it was complete, just requiring its fuels to fly.

Twice in the morning they all had to stand back, away from it, as their work was checked, once by a civilian engineer under Ibach, once by the Butcher's Boy in his long leather SS coat. They were all warmly clad. The slaves wore the same thin striped clothing, summer and winter.

The work passed. It was near noon, they guessed, when the man came, with his escort all around him. He swept in and up the steps to the office, and they saw Ibach standing at attention while the man shouted at him. He was angry, the man, he had come all the way from Peenemünde on the Baltic coast where he designed what they were building, here in the galleries under the mountain – he had *not* come to congratulate them.

When he came out he glared at them all as he strode through with his escort, and they prepared themselves. They did not have to wait long. It was, Jacob thought detachedly, a circular process. When they managed to leave a bolt loose, or cut a cable, or urinate into a guidance box, the man in Peenemünde become very angry. When he was very angry he came down to the caverns and vented his anger upon Engineer Ibach. That anger was then transferred to the SS guards, who then returned it, with a correct amount of interest, to the slaves who had initiated the trouble. But at least they were doing something to stop these bastards, thought Jacob. The risk was worth it

Jacob stood with the others and waited to see what form the interest on the anger would take. Since the day of his parents shooting he had felt little if any emotion. So far David and he had been lucky. If they survived he would have his revenge.

'We are winning the war,' shouted Ibach. He was young, like the man from Peenemünde, only a few years older than they were.

'Our *Vergeltungs-Waffe 2*, our rockets of reprisal, are turning the tide in our favour. The British have no defence against them. These V2 rockets have been designed by Chief von Braun to be perfect. If they do not perform perfectly, it is because they have not been constructed properly. It is you who make these weapons – therefore, if they do not work, it is you who are to blame!'

He paused, and allowed his gaze to travel slowly over them, as they stood next to the partly-completed, 46-feet-long rockets. Beside him, Karl Franz looked down upon them too.

'A rocket was fired at London yesterday. It disintegrated shortly after take-off, like others before it. We intend that this sabotage shall stop. Each time a rocket fails, we shall hang ten of you. We shall begin now.'

He turned and went inside his office, and Karl Franz the Butcher's Boy came down the steps.

The slaves knew what to do; others had been hanged before, although not ten at a time. They stood immobile, faces blank, and waited as Franz came down the line, pulling one of them out from each team. He began at the far end.

Those chosen stood forward quietly. Only the sag of their shoulders gave them away.

The Butcher's Boy had eaten sausage. Jacob smelled it on his breath as he came by, very close, looking into their faces. His gloved hand reached out, and David stumbled forward turning to look helplessly at Jacob as he did so.

There were nine teams, making the rockets. One man still to go. The Butcher's Boy teetered deliberately from toe to heel on his knee-high boots. They all waited, holding in their breath as they stared straight ahead, willing themselves to be strong.

'*Du.*'

The gloved hand landed on his shoulder, pulling him forward with an expert jerk.

'Jacob.'

Jacob wearily slapped forward next to his brother, and Karl Franz turned, striding across the stone floor to the crane by the office. He started it up, the smoke of the engine very blue in the lights, and manoeuvered it so that the jib stuck out over the office platform. He got out of the driver's seat and went back up the stairs, to where he kept the rope. With the jack-knife he used to slice his sausage, he cut off lengths from the rope, tying slip-knots and fashioning the nooses, fastening the ropes to the jib, whistling through his teeth as he worked.

He attached them one after the other, spaced evenly along the jib, until they met with his satisfaction; he went along the row, pulling down on each with all his weight to check his work.

'*Komm,*' he beckoned, smiling down at them. Jacob took David's hand and they went up the steps, their wooden shoes clattering.

The Butcher's Boy tied their hands behind them, and slipped the nooses over their heads, pulling them tight with a tug. It is not right, to die like this, Jacob thought. But they would kill them anyway. At least by destroying the V2s they were fighting back in their own way. He had to be strong, dignified.

He stood next to David, looking straight ahead. The rope was rough against his skin.

Franz knocked politely on the door of the office.

'*Herr Direktor!*' he called. '*Alles in Ordnung.*'

Jacob heard the creak of the door behind him, and Ibach came along the line, with Franz at his side. He went from one end to the other, and then back. He stopped by Jacob. He has green eyes, thought Jacob. I did not know.

Ibach stood looking at Jacob and David for long seconds, Franz standing respectfully next to him. He reached out suddenly, feeling Jacob's muscles like a dealer testing cattle at the market. He did the same for David. Of all the emaciated men in the cavern, the two brothers had survived best. With Baruch they pooled their food, helped each other – and it showed.

'These two,' Ibach said without expression. 'Take them out. Take two others.'

Franz looked at his master in surprise.

'Take them out!'

The noose was off, Franz's knife blade was cold at Jacob's wrist. His hands were suddenly loose. He went down the steps with David as two others came stumbling up, pushed by Franz, their eyes suddenly wide with horror and shock. He stood back with the team as Franz fitted the nooses round their necks, before going down the row, stuffing rough chunks of wood into their mouths, so that they would not scream. Jacob's heart began to pound.

Ibach was back inside his office, where it was warm, and they could see him standing at the window, looking out at the row in front of him. In the seat of the crane, Franz started the engine, and smoke blew out once again. He moved the lever and the jib rose. Those standing on the floor flinched as the jib creaked and and the ten victims were lifted up, and strangled. After a while, it was quiet and the bodies were still. Ibach came out of his office and went down the row, pushing the feet so that they swung. Franz was at the end, smiling; they saw Ibach reach out to caress his bottom.

In the end, it was time to go, to return to the barracks. It would be dark outside. They took the dead men down. In the office, Ibach and Franz were laughing, sharing a bottle before they went to Ibach's quarters. They carried the bodies down the steps to the tunnel, where the dying men from the paint shop were carrying their own dead. Jacob saw that the man who had coughed his way there that morning was among these, his face purple and blue.

Jacob found himself carrying the man who had replaced him on the gallows. His eyes were still open and there was congealed blood around the chunk of wood jammed in his mouth.

'Why?' Baruch whispered, holding his feet. 'Why did he spare you?'

'I don't know,' said Jacob.

As they began to march, he heard Ibach and Franz coming down the steps together, laughing, their arms about each other's waist.

'I don't know.'

*Konzentrationslager Dora*, March 1945

At night, lying on the filthy straw that covered the concrete hut floor, they could hear thunder. Not the kind that crashed overhead and shook the windows, but the menacing kind that rumbled in the distance. It was louder each night than the one before, and when they pressed against the wood shutter to peer out, the dark was lit up by far-off red flashes, like sudden flames.

The Russians were coming.

And they went on making the rockets. But the trains did not always come to collect them, and when they did, the crews wore a look the slaves knew well. People wanted to kill them. They glanced nervously at the sky as they pulled out with their trucks.

The Americans and the British were coming. Their fighter-bombers roamed the skies, looking for things to loose their rockets on, to fire their cannon at. The Germans in the trains were afraid. The slaves found it quite pleasant.

They marched out every morning and back again in the evening, usually carrying some dead.

The March morning had been blustery, with lumpy grey clouds like porridge scudding low overhead, but yellow and white flowers had started to appear on the hillside. The ground had been sodden, their clogs had filled with mud.

In the cavern the long day had ended and the slaves were standing in line ready to march back to the SS camp, dwarfed by the giant rockets on their wheeled cradles. The lamps shone down on them, acrid paint drifted by them from the shop, tinging it blood-orange, when Karl Franz came clattering down the steps from the office in his long black coat. He came directly over to Jacob and David, who were standing together.

'*Komm*,' he said, indicating with a jerk of his thumb that they were to wait by the steps. The guard got impatient at the head of the column, so Franz nodded to him.

'*Ja, ja.*'

They shambled out and Jacob saw Baruch glance back at them before he vanished into the great tunnel, his face full of fear for his comrades. It was the last time that they would see him in Dora.

What you could be sure of in Dora was that being selected was *never* for your own good.

The cavern was empty, it was quiet. Franz looked about him like a fox judging whether the coast was clear or not, almost sniffing the air. Whatever he sensed satisfied him and the brothers watched as he loped away over the stone floor, jumping nimbly over the sleepers of the railway line and vanishing like the column of slaves into the tunnel.

They stood and waited, shivering slightly. Above them they could hear Engineer Ibach moving about in the rooms of his office. He seemed to be moving things, pulling them, dragging them, opening and shutting doors, sliding drawers, rolling cabinets. From the corner of their eyes they looked warily at each other. In Dora, changes were *never* for the slaves' benefit.

Something was coming, they could hear the popping and thudding of an engine. A lorry, one of the Czech ones they had bumped over the railway track, stopped near the entrance, its passage blocked by the assembly line of rockets. When the driver jumped down from the cab, they could see it was the Butcher's Boy. He came over, his coat flapping, and indicated up the stairs.

'What are you waiting for?' he demanded, and they propelled themselves up the steps as quickly as they could. Ibach glanced up as they came in. The office was a kind of orderly shambles. Wooden crates were piled everywhere. Some they recognized, for they held many of the thousands of parts that went into the construction of the rocket. Others had been emptied, and refilled with stack upon stack of papers, type-written ones and hand-written ones, ones filled with calculations and formulae, ones covered in complex and detailed drawings. Ibach was engaged in tapping down a lid, nailing it shut with a little hammer, and writing some description of his own devising upon it.

'I want these put into the lorry,' he said. 'Pile them up carefully.'

Franz kicked the brothers into action with a boot.

'You heard the Engineer!'

David and Jacob sprang into action, seizing the first case, taking it out and down the steps with care. Franz accompanied them, directing them on each trip as the back of the Czech lorry with its hooped and covered bed began to fill up with the wooden cases. After a while, he seemed satisfied with their performance, and went away.

When he returned, he was carrying black bread and cheese. He put it on a flat fin together with a jug of hot, dark tea.

'Here,' he said to them. 'Eat.'

The SS were expert in knowing how much effort could be wrung out of the human beasts under their command. Few had much reserve left, if they wanted a lot of work out of them, they had to put fuel in.

Jacob and David fell on the food, chewing as best their loose teeth would let them, washing it down with the sweet hot tea, feeling the numbness of their bodies recede. In a corner, by the office there was a big iron stove where the guards used to keep their coffee pots hot and to stand beside to keep warm.

As the brothers ate they saw a strange sight, that of Karl Franz coming down the steps having changed into civilian clothes. A pair of high-waisted brown suit trousers hung by a pair of braces from his shoulders, swinging baggily about his legs. He was also wearing a white shirt with a sober blue tie. His SS clothes he carried over his arm, and as they watched he opened the door of the stove and began to stuff the uniform into its glowing maw.

Membership of the SS was what Franz got up for every morning; he delighted in the duties it required of him. For him to burn his uniform meant that something was very wrong. And anything being wrong would without fail, rebound upon the slaves. Franz straightened up, shutting the door upon his blazing black cap. He turned and looked at Jacob with his cold blue eyes.

'*Ja?*' he demanded menacingly. Jacob and David hurried for the steps.

They were tired when the last box was loaded to the satisfaction of the Germans. Engineer Ibach came to check himself. There was a small space left in the lorry, and Franz indicated that they should climb up into it. Very wearily they pulled themselves up with painful, splinter-stung hands. Franz fastened the tailboard carefully on his cargo, so that it would not slip out onto the road. The brothers felt the truck rock a little on its stiff springs as the men got into the cab. Then the engine rattled into life. There was a crunch as Franz selected a gear and the vehicle began to move, very carefully, out of the cavern. The brothers peered out from under the canvas flap. The office was brightly illuminated.

'Ibach hasn't switched out the lights,' David said.

'He's not coming back,' said Jacob, as they went into the gloom of the tunnel. 'The Russians are coming.'

'Where are they taking this lot?'

'Berlin?' Jacob suggested. 'They want us to unload when they get there.'

'The war's finished for them,' David objected. 'What's the point? Dragging off all these boxes.'

Rain suddenly began to rattle on the canvas roof and cold air blew in, draughty fingers seeking them out in the pile of boxes. Arc lights briefly limned the patches in the roof, then it was dark. The lorry gained speed, its tyres slicing through the running water on the road. The brothers huddled together for warmth, terminal weariness sweeping them away, and they slept.

When Jacob awoke a grey light was seeping in. He felt cold and hungry. Looking out of the back he could see that they were coming out of the mountains, the land was widening out. Standing up on a box he could just make out through the grille at the back of the cab the voices of the Germans talking. Franz was driving and he saw him peer anxiously up at the sky.

'Don't worry,' said Ibach. '*Jäger* can't fly in this weather. Von Braun knew what he was doing, choosing a day like this.'

Jacob saw that he had a map, which he soon looked at more and more often. They rounded a bend and he pulled off the road and stopped. They had been following a river, which now lay below them down a steep slope, rushing grey and swollen with the melt water from the mountains. David awoke. The canvas flap was pulled back and they saw the Butcher's Boy.

'You can get out,' he said. 'Stretch your legs. Make water.'

The rain had stopped. They climbed out and saw immediately why Ibach had stopped. Several more lorries stood under some trees by the roadside and Ibach was walking across to them. David and Jacob saw the man from Peenemünde, Von Braun, get down from a cab.

The two stood talking for a few moments. The brothers in their striped uniforms stood surreptitiously watching them. Von Braun pointed towards the road ahead.

'*Amerikaner*,' David whispered. 'The Americans are ahead?'

'I think he's *meeting* the Americans,' Jacob muttered.

Ibach was asking Von Braun something, pointing to the lorry. The man from Peenemünde answered with a question, and Ibach nodded.

'He's saying the lorry's running well.'

'Von Braun says not to unload it then.'

Not far away, Franz had been listening to the conversation too, in the patient, dedicated manner of a guard dog. Now he turned and looked at them with a look of curious assessment in his eyes.

They knew Karl Franz. 'He's going to kill us,' said David, very quietly.

They stood still for a moment.

'He's going to kill us,' Jacob echoed. Down the slope was the river, rushing down the hill faster than any man could travel. Franz was by the cab of the lorry, they saw him reach in, almost casually, they saw the glimmer of the morning light on the oiled metal of his Schmeisser and they moved as one.

The slope was steep, grass and shrubs and weeds whipped wet on his skin as Jacob bounced and crashed down the slope. He landed at the bottom in a heap, winded, and forced himself upright. A burst of gunfire screamed about him and he ran for the water. At the edge, he turned. David was staggering, hopping on one leg. Karl Franz was picking himself up at the bottom of the slope. The gun was in his arms.

David glanced behind him.

'*Jump, Jacob*,' he screamed.

Jacob was standing on a rock, slippery with wetted slime, when his legs suddenly went from under him. The roaring grey current seized him with powerful, icy hands, rolling him over and over. He struck out against them, gasping for air, and they swept him away. In his ears a flat bang echoed, what it was he could not say. *David, David.*

Where the valley flattened out into farmland again the icy river relaxed its grip. On a bend by a meadow Jacob floundered towards the shore and came to rest in a bed of reeds. He was very cold, shivering uncontrollably. Some cattle were tearing steadily at the green grasses of the meadow, while in the distance were some simple farm buildings. He scrambled up the low riverbank and slunk along a muddy lane towards them, keeping low.

He did not dare enter the house, but there was a barn nearby, which he slipped inside. In the loft he could see piles of straw, so he went up the wood ladder and hid himself, slowly drying out and becoming warm. Exhausted, he slept.

The mooing of cows awoke him, and the pinched voice of a woman. He thrust a hand into his mouth, biting down on his bone to stop himself crying out. What strange hell was this? Morning sunshine . . . What had happened to the camp?

The memories of the previous day slowly filtered through into his tired, weak brain. David, how had he lost David? A warm tear trickled down his cheek. How could he have lost David, after so long . . . ?

He wiped the tear away, quickly. In the *kazett*, in the camp, a tear was a death sentence.

He pushed himself up in the straw and made himself think. He felt weak, yes, but it was a good day. He was free. Why should David not be free too? They could not have escaped death so many times to be caught now. No. The sun was shining. He had escaped the camp, and the guarantee of death. Yes, here it was, a good day. And if there were cows, might there not be some milk?

The door closed and in the gloom he could see three of the beasts tethered to stalls. He took an enamelled jug he had found on a window ledge and crept down the ladder with it.

Milk hissed warm and foaming into the jug. He filled it and went quietly into a corner to drink it. It was wonderful. He filled it again, and carried it up the ladder to the loft. He tried to think what he must do next but, still tired, fell back to sleep.

He was awakened by the noise of a motorcycle outside. Quickly, he reached for his jug of milk. It had a skin on it, which he ate ravenously, then he drank the rest. A man started yelling, and a woman began screeching. He went warily out of the barn and into the farmhouse. In the kitchen a Mongolian soldier in calf-length boots and baggy trousers and tunic was slapping a peasant woman, shouting at her in Russian. A sub-machine gun was strapped around his shoulders. Jacob knew then that he was safe. It was going to be OK. He stepped forward into the kitchen.

'He wants a wrist-watch,' Jacob said, in German.

As the soldier turned, he spoke in Russian.

'Welcome, comrade.'

The soldier stared curiously at the strange, skeletal figure in its flapping striped uniform.

'A zombie,' he said, speaking in Russian with an atrocious foreign accent.

Jacob felt a sudden sting of indignation, the first stirrings of a free man.

'I am not a zombie,' he objected. 'I am Jacob.'

'A zombie that speaks Russian,' the Mongolian observed.

'There were Russians in the camp. I learned a little.'

The soldier spat. '*Germania kaput*. You speak German.'

'Yes. Polish, Yiddish, German, Russian.'

The Mongolian beamed, displaying gold teeth.

'You a good zombie to have around. Not like the other. The other no speak at all. I am Ali. You come with *me*.'

Jacob reached down to help the farm woman to her feet, and she pulled her arm away roughly.

'Jewish filth,' she muttered.

Ali understood the intonation. He kicked her, knocking her across the kitchen.

'I'd get him a wrist-watch if I were you,' Jacob observed.

The woman scuttled away, and returned with an old, but serviceable watch. Ali strapped it on, and held it out on his wrist to admire it.

There was the sound of a truck in the distance.

Ali stared at the woman and she cringed.

'No,' he said. 'She's too ugly to fuck. I have fucked twenty-six German women so far.' He beamed. 'Plenty left!'

They went outside, where a Ford lorry was pulling up.

'You get in. You can translate for us.'

The American lorry was soft on its springs and Jacob luxuriated on the canvas seat as it gained speed down the road.

'What other zombie?' he demanded, thinking of David.

'Hah?' Ali asked, admiring his wrist-watch.

'You said there was another zombie. What, someone that looks like me?'

'*Da.*'

Hope flared suddenly within him.

'I have lost my brother David,' he said.

'We found this one hiding. In a place where they made weapons. It come with us. Is like a dog. No speak.'

Hope died.

'Is it a man or a woman?'

'Who knows?' Ali replied, expansively. 'Is a zombie, like you.'

'I am a human being,' Jacob insisted, fiercely clinging to his new identity. 'I am a man. I am Jacob.'

'Okay,' said Ali. 'If you say so. Where are you going, friend Jacob?'

'I'm going to see my Cousin Avraham,' Jacob said, and a prickle of fear ran through his stomach and up into his eyes, for David should have been there to say it with him. Ali looked at him with some amusement.

'You have a cousin around here?'

'Not here. In Palestine.'

'I do not know this Palestine.'

'It is the land of the Jews,' explained Jacob. 'It is where the Jews live.'

'Not so,' Ali objected. 'Jews everywhere. They scattered, like corn.'

He made the gesture of a farmer flinging a handful of seed over a field.

'No more!' Jacob cried, with a sudden, blinding certainty. 'We are going home!'

Ali jumped down from the lorry, Jacob followed him more slowly. Ali laughed behind his pink sunglasses as Jacob looked up the valley. It was filled with men and tanks and lorries, with horses and tents and piles of equipment; the air was filled with the clanging of metal, the roaring of engines, with men banging tank tracks and heaving shells.

'The Germans they say we are a steamroller. Is not so,' Ali boasted. He suddenly bounded about in great leaps, his sub-machine gun swinging about. 'We are a great monster. We jump on the enemy, we eat flesh.'

'What is the monster doing?'

'We rest before we do it again.'

Ali paused, frowning. Jacob's striped jacket had come loose, its wire fastening pulled through the rotten fabric. Purple, swollen skin protruded through the gap. The Mongolian's nose wrinkled at the sight of an enormous boil.

'That we fix,' he said. He spoke Russian less well than Jacob. He led the way through an orchard.

'You good to have,' he said. 'We good at killing Germans, yah, but sometimes you got to talk to the bastards, and none of us good at that. You do that for us.'

The woods and orchards were filled with men, tanks, guns, lorries, rockets. Some soldiers had caught and killed a horse, the marks of its death struggle had churned up the earth. They were expertly butchering it with long knives they kept in their boots. The day had turned to spring sunshine. With the split mind of the KZnik he enjoyed its warmth and light while wondering where his brother was.

They came to a farmhouse, where there was the smell of disinfectant in the air. Ali took him inside to a young Slav doctor with a nurse, also young, dark-haired, attractive. It had been a long time since Jacob had seen a woman. Ali took off his jacket.

'Another one. You were a strong boy,' the doctor, Pimenov, said wonderingly. They were looking at his arms, like sticks, his ribs, as visible as the slats in a washboard. In the company of these strong, healthy young people Jacob realized just how emaciated he was.

They looked at the vast boil, purple and red, that throbbed in his chest.

'That we must lance,' said Pimenov. 'We must get the poison out. But ... I have a problem, we are out of anaesthetic. Nothing ... I am waiting for supplies to come up from the rear. And I dare not give you vodka to numb the pain. You have not had normal food or drink for so long, it might kill you. You must be careful what you eat for a while, you know. Some bread in milk, milk puddings ...'

The nurse, who was called Ludmilla, stepped forward.

'He is a hero,' she said. 'And a good-looking boy. We only need to have his mind on other things while the boil is lanced.'

Pimenov sterilized his instruments, while Ludmilla brought disinfectant and dressings. While Pimenov was preparing she came close up to Jacob. She wore a Russian *rubashka* blouse, which she began to unbutton. Taking his hand, skin on bone, she put it inside. She smiled at him, and sitting by the door, Ali yelled approval. Jacob gritted his teeth. In the corner of the room, a heap of rags moved.

Jacob suddenly felt enormous relief, and realized that Pimenov had done his work. The pus gushed into the bowl he held.

Jacob slid his hand out from inside the young nurse's blouse.

'Thank you,' he said gratefully. The bundle of rags in the corner sat up.

Ludmilla buttoned herself up, smiling, and began to prepare a dressing.

'You get to do a lot of things in this job,' she joked.

'You can do that for me too!' Ali bawled happily. 'Any time!'

'He is a hero,' Ludmilla said with dignity. 'You are a common fellow.'

Ali laughed. The rags in the corner pushed themselves up and two huge eyes stared out at Jacob. Ali glanced over.

'Is the zombie,' he observed.

Thin as a stick insect, its shaven skull seemingly huge, the thing walked towards him.

'See,' said Ali. 'Is same as you.'

Jacob had held an image of himself in his mind as he had been. Even in Dora, he had thought of himself as he had once been.

'Do I look like that?' he said, and they looked at him strangely. The skeleton came and stood silently by him.

Pimenov gave Jacob a brown glass bottle of pills.

'Vitamins and minerals. You'll be short of everything. This one
. . .' he indicated the creature at his side '. . . this one we have given
them to.'

'You'll need all the help you can get when Ludmilla gets her hands
on you!' Ali bawled.

The nurse sniffed, and finished binding a bandage over the deflated
boil. Jacob felt something like a claw, dry as biscuit grip his hand. On
reflex he squeezed, and felt in return the faintest pressure. He glanced
down, and saw that the skin of the hand holding his was marked with
criss-crossed scars.

'Say, friend Jacob,' Ali asked. 'You need a woman? I get you a
German.'

The claw seemed to hold on to him.

'No,' he said. He stood up. Outside there was a commotion, Ali
turned and opened the door to talk to some comrades. Ludmilla
cleared up her equipment and Jacob saw the emaciated creature at
his side following her with its eyes. They rested on her round chest,
her femininity.

The voice was as faint as dry leaves rustling in the wind. It spoke
Yiddish.

'I want you to do that to me, when I am a woman again.'

'Who are you?' Jacob murmured.

'I am Ruth,' the girl whispered.

By the door, Ali turned back.

'Friend Jacob,' he said, with a curious look on his face. 'Come
speak for us.'

Jacob followed Ali back across the fields and through the little
woods and orchards, with Ruth at his side. The soldiers had lit a fire
a little way from the dismembered horse and were cooking enormous
steaks together with mushrooms in a great skillet over three stones.
They beamed at him with uncomplicated broad peasant faces, already
part-full of good horseflesh, and laughed.

'They say is like you looking in a mirror,' Ali explained. 'Two
zombies the same.'

'We are human beings,' Jacob insisted.

'Is a zombie,' Ali objected, pointing to Ruth. 'Does not speak.'

They were going through a copse of trees, all gaily decked out in
their fresh young leaves and blossom; their scent all around.

'I got some Germans for you.'

In a clearing a group of soldiers were gathered around a large,
old tree. Beneath one of its outstretched branches huddled a small
group of Germans in SS uniform, a young woman and two men.

The woman was half-naked, clad in the tatters of her black and white clothes.

A chair stood beneath the branch, from which dangled thin, shiny lengths of wire.

'Igor,' Ali called to a big Russian standing by the group. 'Here is Jacob, who can speak to these bastards.'

The man beamed. 'Tell that bitch to tie up the others' hands,' he said.

Automatically Jacob translated for him. 'He wants you to tie them up. The hands.' Frantically, with bleeding fingers, she began to do so.

'My little sister was a partisan in Minsk in 1941,' said Igor. 'Get the first one up on the chair.'

The man climbed up.

'Have the bitch put the noose around his neck.'

'You must get him ready to be hanged,' said Jacob, and the girl scrambled up and put the thin wire around his neck.

'My sister was brave, and fought for the Motherland,' said Igor. 'Have her pull the chair away.'

'Take the chair from under his feet,' said Jacob. Terrified, the girl did as she was bid, and the man dropped with a hideous gurgle, thrashing about as he was strangled. Beside Jacob Ruth stood still and silent, staring expressionlessly at the execution.

'Can't you stop them?' pleaded the young woman.

Jacob felt he was standing at the edge of the pit, watching the Germans shoot them all, one after the other, in rows. He was standing with the men beneath the cruel jib with the Butcher's Boy smiling down at him. He was running with David and the guards were shooting at them.

He looked at the terrified face of the SS girl, white and pinched. It all ought to be different.

'My sister blew up a troop train,' said Igor. 'Next.'

The second man climbed up.

'She was caught, and they tortured her for two days. Kick the chair away.'

The Russians cheered as the two men thrashed in the air together.

'They hanged her and her comrades like this, from wire.'

Then there was just the girl left who had been forced to be hangman.

'Save me,' she whispered to Jacob.

'Your people hanged a young Russian girl your age in Minsk, four years ago. It was that man's sister,' Jacob tried to explain.

'*It was not me.*'

Jacob tried to explain to her; 'He wants you to pay,' he said.

The girl climbed up on the chair shaking, and put the wire round her own neck.

'Please don't . . .' she begged.

'*You did not spare us!*'

The scream from Ruth at Jacob's side was sudden and shocking. She sprang forward and the claws of hands seized the back of the chair, tipping it forward.

With a terrible shriek that rang out round the clearing the girl slipped from the chair, and the Russians all cheered.

'Is not a zombie,' Ali observed approvingly. 'Is a person. It speaks.'

Then they went back through the wood, leaving the bodies turning and twisting in the air. The girl was clawing at the wire with bloody hands that slowly fell to her sides and were still. The sun pierced the budding branches of the trees in golden bundles, and the smell of moss and blossom was in their nostrils.

Down by the river some soldiers were washing clothes on flat rocks. As Ali, Jacob and Ruth walked along they heard one of them call out. Something like a log had drifted into the shore, and he pushed at it with his foot.

They were all used to dead bodies. The Red soldiers had seen them all the way from Stalingrad. Jacob had seen them every day since he had put on the uniform of a slave.

But it was the colours, sodden though they were . . . He ran across the grass and splashed into the water, catching the corpse by its foot as the current tried to carry it away again.

The river had washed it clean; now it floated, face down, its head was shaved – the bullet hole in the back of the neck seemed small and almost insignificant.

'That is how we were shot,' Ruth said to Ali. Jacob bent down in the cold water and gently turned the body over. It was cold, very cold. The hole in the throat was larger than the one in the back of the neck. Jacob sat down in the water, holding the icy body.

'It is not right,' he said, looking up at the Mongolian. 'It should not be this way.'

Ruth knelt down with him in the icy water, and held his head in her chest of bones as he wept.

He woke because someone was shaking his shoulder, gently but insistently. He had slept because he had eaten bread softened by warm milk and because those in the KZ learned to sleep whenever they could, and he had not been free from it for long enough to lose that habit.

It was Ruth.

'Come,' she insisted, pulling him. 'Come with me.'

The voice was less dry. He followed her and saw that light was still filtering in from the spring evening.

They were in the farmhouse that had become a field hospital. As she went down a little stone corridor and opened a door, he saw that she looked different. She wore Russian army clothes, baggy, green and mud-coloured trousers and a shirt that hung on her like a badly put up tent. But she exuded a fresh smell, and when he followed her into a little scullery, he saw a fire burning in the hearth, and steam rising from a big round tin bath. The air was filled with this very good fresh smell, and he realized that it was soap. A splendid, bright yellow chunk of it lay on a plate by the bath, and there was a real towel hanging from the back of a chair near the fire.

'Take these things off,' she said, undoing the horrid twists of wire that held his tunic together. 'I have burned my own, now that I am a human again.'

'But what shall I wear?'

He saw a simple cot by the wall, and on it were more new army clothes.

'Ali, the Mongolian, gave them to me.'

She pulled the striped rags from his back and threw them onto the fire. They burned with a spiteful hissing of charring dirt. She tugged at the ghastly plait of filthy rags that was the belt he had made to hold up his trousers, and he clutched at them in sudden alarm as they fell towards his knees.

What was undoubtedly a smile lit up the skull-like face.

'You cannot be shy?' she asked mockingly.

'I am not used to being bathed by women,' he said, with as much dignity as he could muster, and stepped into the warm, soapy protective water. He heard her toss the ragged trousers onto the flames, and then the sound of a sponge being soaped. She rubbed his back with it and he moaned quietly with joy.

'Is it a long time since you had a bath?' she asked sympathetically.

'Since ... since I was with Mama and Papa, in the ghetto,' he said. 'I have been in Auschwitz, and then Dora, since then.'

'I can tell. The water, it is becoming very dirty.'

He found her practicality very comforting. She soaped his stubbly skull, and he closed his eyes as warm water flowed over him, putting his face up in pleasure.

'The ghetto, it will not be there when this war is over,' she observed. 'But you will go home?'

'Those who betrayed us to the Germans will still be there,' he replied. 'Those who hate us for being Jews. No, I shall not go home. You, you will go home?'

'Where I come from they . . . ,' she began.

There was a short silence and she tried again.

'In the synagogue . . . they b . . .'

Ruth choked on her words once more. He turned to look at her and around her eyes she was flushed.

'It is no good,' she said. 'I cannot talk of these things. Leave me be. But you, if you may not go home, where will you go?'

He smiled then, seated in his tin bath with warm water all about him, for it was there, bright and shining, in his heart.

'Me, I shall go and stay with my Cousin Avraham.'

'How do you know where your Cousin Avraham is? This war has scattered us all, like ashes in the wind.'

'I know where Cousin Avraham is. He is in the golden land, the Promised Land. He is in Palestine.'

'Palestine . . . ,' she echoed wonderingly. 'I have heard of Palestine . . . It is the Holy Land. But we Jews were expelled from there so many centuries ago.'

'Almost two thousand years ago!' he cried. 'But this is the time of the Jewish miracle. Here they have tried to kill us all, but we have survived, and now, *now* we are going home. This war is almost over, and these Russians, and those *Amerikaners*, and the British, all of them may do what they will, but we Jews, we people of Israel, we are going home!'

She was silent, impressed by his sudden, blazing passion.

'It is allowed?' she asked full of doubt.

'Allowed?' he shouted back. 'We are the Jews, we have survived, there is nothing we are not allowed! And we wish to go home! There over the sea our empty land awaits its children, and we say, we come, we come!'

She began again to soap away the dirt.

'What is it like, Palestine?'

'A land flowing with milk and honey. A land of sparkling streams, and green orchards,' he promised.

'Then I shall come with you,' she said firmly. She paused in thought a moment.

'What of those ... the ones here ... the ones who would kill us?'

He laughed.

'We shall leave all of that behind. When we are in Palestine we shall be at peace. There we shall have no enemies.'

'Then I shall come with you,' she said again. 'Now. The top of you is clean. We must do the rest of you. Stand up.'

'I said I was not used to being bathed by women,' he protested.

'Is it so bad?' she demanded. 'Many would like this treatment, but I am offering it to you only. So stand up like a man and be soaped.'

He stood up in the water and felt the warm, slightly scratchy sponge working away at the encrusted grime on his body. As it moved around to his groin he felt a most unexpected sensation in a region which had stayed quite dead all the time he had been in the KZ. It was so sudden and he was so unused to it that he gasped and put his hands protectively around himself.

She tapped on them with the sponge.

'I cannot wash you like this.'

'It is not the washing that concerns me.'

'You must think of me as a nurse,' she giggled. She pulled his hands away. 'Now let me get about my business.'

'Nurses do not do this,' he said, unable to protest any more.

'The one with the big breasts let you feel them,' she pointed out. 'I have nice breasts too,' she went on, in a small voice. 'You will see, when they grow back.'

'I shall like that,' he promised.

She sat back on her heels, admiring her handiwork.

'Did it do this to you, when the one with the big breasts put your hand inside her blouse?' she demanded.

'No,' he said truthfully. 'I did not think it would do it again.'

'See how good I am for you,' she said.

She stood up, and reached for the towel.

'Now I shall dry you.'

The light from the window had darkened to night, there was just the yellow flickering glow of the fire. She reached to her waist and unclasped her belt, and the baggy trousers fell into a crumpled heap on the floor.

'I will have my good legs back too, soon,' she promised. 'But lie with me on the bed anyway.'

'Yes,' he said. 'I would like that.'

She kept her loose shirt on. It was as baggy as a tent over her thin frame of bones. It fell off one shoulder quite completely as they embraced on the rough wool blanket. In the gold light of the fire the overlapping criss-cross of the savage scars of the whip shone a fading red over her shoulders, her back, her chest.

Where her breasts would be when they grew back, the skin was smooth and unmarked, and he understood why the backs of her hands were slashed and scarred.

'Palestine!' she cried.

'We are going home,' he promised. 'We shall be safe, in Palestine.'

He woke in the night, and put more logs onto the glowing embers. He climbed back under the blanket with her, and watched as the golden flames licked into life, lighting up the room like the sun rising over the Promised Land.

'Palestine,' he whispered to himself, like a lucky charm, and slept.

# PART II

## Jerusalem, March 1946

CORPORAL Pete Ball didn't like Palestine. It was hot, dusty, fly-infested and one half of the inhabitants hated the other half. As for Jerusalem, they could keep it. Jesus, the Prophet Mohammed, the lot. All he wanted was to get home, put on his demob suit, collect on the NORWICH with which he sealed his letters to his wife and see West Ham win at home. But first of all he wanted a beer, and as he was off duty, he was on his way to the NAAFI to get one. It would be warm, weak and flat, but it would taste of home and be served in a tankard. It wasn't much to ask for.

The boy came running out of the alley. He saw Pete Ball and sprinted frantically up to him.

'Oh, I say!' he blurted out. 'Do come quick, my pal's had the most frightful accident, he's caught under something . . .'

The boy was about thirteen; he wore a striped school tie over his white shirt and his shorts were held up by an elasticated belt with an S-shaped snake buckle. He had a public schoolboy's short back and sides haircut and looked just like the Colonel's son. Pete Ball ran with him down the alley, his hobnailed army boots pounding on the cobbles.

'In here,' the boy gasped, and dived through a small, low doorway. It was dark in there, and the corporal's eyes were used to the glare of the street. He felt the hard hands of the men waiting for him before he saw them. Then they put a sack over his head, and he could see nothing at all.

They hustled him deep into the ancient building, set in the very rock of the city. Where the ancients had once stored jars of oil a beam ran across the room, and they stood him up on a chair beneath it with his hands tied while they adjusted the rope.

'You going to hang me?' asked Pete Ball, inside the sack.

'You keep quiet,' said the man with the rope.

'Yer Jews, ain't yer? I can tell from yer voice. What you got against me? I ain't done nothing to yer.'

There was a silence, just the harsh breathing of men getting ready to kill another.

'I got a wife and two kiddies at home. It ain't right to do this to them.'

The rope was tight against his neck, it ran taut over the beam, and was tied fast to the peg on the wall. The hangman got down off his chair, his hand ready on the one the British soldier was standing upon. One of his companions put out his hand.

'Giddy. Wait.'

He motioned towards the stone doorway.

'The boy.'

The schoolboy stood there, his eyes burning with hate.

'You go next door,' said Giddy, the hangman. 'This is not for you.'

'I brought him here for you,' said Avraham Cohen. 'I have the right to see justice done.'

'What have I done to you?' cried Pete Ball, inside the sack. 'I ain't never hurt you.'

'The Arabs murdered my family. They raped my mother and slaughtered her on the hillside.'

'Well, that was the Arabs. You go get the Arabs.'

'Oh, we will,' shouted the boy. 'But you British are giving our land to the Arabs, so we shall hang you first.'

He jumped forward and heaved at the chair, tipping the soldier off balance.

With a terrible cry, he slipped from the chair, his shout cut off as the rope bit into his neck.

The beam creaked as the body swayed back and forth. The clawing fingers became limp. There was just the rumble of the distant traffic along the street.


## Haifa, May 1946


In the thin blue light of the dawn sodden people, aflame with joy, scrambled into lorries, aboard trailers, squashed into rickety old Morris and Citroen taxis. On the path that led up from the beach Jacob counted them as they panted by, while by the straggling pines Ruth directed them to the waiting vehicles, and one by one in clouds of acrid blue smoke they rattled off up the road.

'One hundred and thirty two!' Jacob cried, as an old woman came up the sandy track, half-carried by a young boy and a woman.

'Come on, Geula, the taxi awaits!'

Down on the shore a boxy landing craft unlike a ship lay grounded on the hard sand fifty yards from land. Further out a minesweeper blew angry white smoke from its funnel. A lean young man in an army cap came running from a small lorry as the old woman was helped into the taxi.

'Jacob? I am Captain Zvi. Don't hang about! The British will be here.'

Jacob and Ruth scrambled into the front of the little Austin and the captain squeezed into the little canvas seat, setting the engine turning with a rattle of gears. As they went bouncing up the dry, sandy road, he put his head back and laughed.

'A landing craft!' he chuckled. 'We are coming in on everything now!'

'We shall swim if we have to,' Ruth cried.

'You might have had to, on that!'

He turned towards her.

'I am Captain Zvi. Zvi Levinger of the *Haganah*. That is our army.'

'A Jewish army,' she breathed in wonder. 'When has the world ever seen such a thing?'

'Not since the days of Bar-Kochba, to be sure,' said Levinger, sweeping recklessly onto a macadamed road. He peered into his mirror. 'They shall not get us now.'

'Are there many, in this army?' asked Jacob.

'More every day! We are the new Maccabees, none shall withstand us.'

Ruth looked at the tough young soldier in wide-eyed amazement.

'I have never met Jews like you. Only Jacob.'

'We are the new Jews,' Levinger said, almost savagely. 'Nobody will come and take us away. We shall not walk meekly to be gassed. Those who hate us shall stay silent when we pass by, for they shall know how we can defend ourselves.'

There was silence in the little rattling lorry as it hummed down the road and then Levinger smiled again, his fit of anger passed.

'A *landing craft!*' he said again, quite joyfully. 'How did you manage that?'

'We found it,' said Jacob. 'In Italy. Where there had been an invasion. We had come down from the north. We met with a Russian army, and when the war was stopped we went south. We knew enough of camps, so didn't want to go to the displaced persons camps. In Naples we made contact with an agent of the Yishuv. In turn, he put us in touch with other Jews.'

'All those who burned for Palestine!' laughed Ruth.

'We found the landing craft and there were those amongst us who knew how to work the machinery, so we refloated it, and repaired the engines. And when the sea was calm, we set off.'

'You were nearly caught.'

'We had charts of the shore. We went into the shallow water where the British could not go. It was just as well, only one engine was working by then.'

Jacob looked back on the fearsome journey, one of overworked pumps, of choked engine filters, cracked cylinder blocks, seasick people and overheated engines. Then he put it away. In the scale of things it was a tiny footnote to the birth of a nation.

'The British,' he said. 'They are trying to stop us getting in?'

'All the time,' Levinger said shortly. 'But they may as well try to stop the wind! In we flood, all soldiers of Zion. That is what we need, more and more Jews, first to fight, and then to people this empty land.'

They passed by some fields where people in loose, dun clothes were working, some tending the plants, others driving goats.

'Who are they?' asked Ruth.

'Oh, just some Arabs.'

'We heard that the British have killed some people who tried to get in,' said Jacob.

'They are trying to stand in the way of history. They will not succeed.'

'The British Empire?'

'If Adolf Hitler could not win against us, how can the British?' Levinger asked.

'I heard that we too have killed some of them.'

Levinger was silent for a moment.

'You should know,' he then said slowly, 'that we are all not of the *Haganah*. We of the *Haganah* are men of honour, we are soldiers who preach the purity of arms. You will learn that when you train with us in the *kibbutz*. But there are others, who are not men of honour, but men of terror. They are those of the Stern gang, of the Irgun. Their weapons are the noose and the bomb. Their method is murder.'

A small dusty town was gaining in size through the windscreen. Levinger slowed down, pulling into the side of the road.

'In a moment you shall have food and drink, fresh clothes, a bath, as do your comrades, those that you brought in on your craft. You shall join us in the *Haganah*, you shall be trained. But first, I have to ask you something.'

'No,' Ruth said with a grin. 'First *we* wish to ask *you* something.'

'Yes, certainly . . .'

'*Can we get married?*' Jacob and Ruth chorused together.

'We would not do it until we came to Palestine,' Ruth explained.

'Yes, yes,' Levinger laughed. 'A thousand times yes! It shall be arranged!'

'Perhaps even time for a small honeymoon?' Jacob suggested.

Ruth gestured at Jacob mischievously.

'It's not because of me. He wants to look for Cousin Avraham.'

'Cousin Avraham?' Levinger said, puzzled. 'You have relatives here?'

'I *had*,' Jacob explained. 'The most famous member of my family, he left our land when hard times made the making of jewellery hard, and he travelled all the way to Jerusalem.'

'To Jerusalem?' Levinger said, interested. 'When was this?'

'In the twelfth century. He became a wealthy man at the court of King Guy of Jerusalem, for his jewellery was beyond compare.'

'The twelfth century!' Levinger burst out laughing. 'Truly the old Yishuv! What happened to this jewelling Jew of antiquity?'

'We are not certain. For he was captured by Salah el-Din, the great Saracen leader the Crusaders called Saladin.'

'He was? How was that?'

'He was with the army of King Guy at the Battle of Hattin,' Jacob said simply.

A strange glaze came over Levinger's eyes.

'The battle of what . . . Hattin?' he said indifferently. 'I do not think I have heard of it.'

'But surely you must have,' Jacob said, surprised. 'When they lost the battle of Hattin, the Crusaders lost all. Although they remained – here, here in these very parts – for some time after, the battle proved fatal. Where are the Crusaders today?'

'Where indeed?' asked Levinger. 'But these parts have seen so many battles, and it is the present that concerns me, not the dusty past.'

'That cannot be so,' Ruth remonstrated. 'For we Jews are returning here because of history.'

Levinger chuckled.

'See?' he said to Jacob. 'She is a good Jewish wife to you already. She is already willing to put us foolish men right. So be it. We are all here because of history.'

The smile died slowly from his face as he sat in the little worn seat, gripping the wire-spoked wheel.

'But I am right to think about the present. A war is coming,' he said quietly. 'The British, they are tired of fighting. The war has made them poor. Their empire weighs upon them. Like Titan, they stagger under its load. Soon, maybe next year, they will begin to depart from here, for they do not want Palestine. And when they are gone, the Arab countries all about us will fall upon us like wolves, should we let them.'

'We shall fight,' Jacob said certainly.

'To be sure,' said Levinger. 'But what *with*? A war is fought with arms, and we only have a few.'

He turned and pointed through the little, dirty window of the lorry. Across the scrub, the blue sea glittered.

'Out *there* are arms. Out there are Jews. We need both. We have men and women of enterprise out there, gathering them in.'

He looked them both in the eyes, searchingly.

'You have come here with great difficulty. Now I have to ask you. For the people of Zion, will you go back, and bring us arms?'

'No,' said Ruth, and Levinger's face twisted in disappointment, in disillusion.

'Not until you let us get married!'


## Naples, Italy, May 1947


Service abroad meant more than being shot at by foreigners, it meant foreign food, and the British soldier was not fond of foreign food, little more than he was of foreigners shooting at him. So when an Italian grandmother and her pretty granddaughter moved into a deserted farmhouse on the Salerno road and opened a cafe offering egg and chips and English bitter, the soldiers of the British army did not ask where the hens that laid the eggs came from, nor the potatoes, and certainly not the beer.

Corporal Symes and his mucker Corporal Miller had two piping hot platefuls on their way to Bari and washed it down with two pints of bitter apiece. They were served by the granddaughter, a charming, raven-haired beauty who wore a blouse that could have been one of Dorothy Lamour's cast-offs. She enquired in charming, broken English where they were going in their empty lorry and they told her to the arms depot. She insisted they come back again, and the combination of the food, the beer and the bosom concealed beneath the blouse made them determined to pay a return visit.

The girl, Sophia, was delighted to see them as they pulled up in the big Bedford.

'Oh, boys,' she said, in her seductively accented English. 'Will you help me?'

In the rude kitchen stood a hogshead of beer. The grandmother stood peeling potatoes, and there was a chip pan on the flame, a frying pan next to it.

Sophia bent down to illustrate how difficult it was for her to move the barrel and Corporals Symes and Miller's collective hearts turned over.

'I have to get this down into the cellar, and it is so heavy.'

'We'll help you, miss,' said Symes. 'Won't we, Dusty?'

As she stood to one side he saw that her pretty hands were marked over their backs by faint, whitening scars. She saw his eyes on them.

'The war,' she said, with a small, strange smile. 'Bad things happened in the war.'

The cellar was down some steep wooden steps, and they had to be very careful. When they had it down there they set it up for the girl, and waited while she poured them two foaming mugs.

'Drink,' she said. 'Then I can give you another to take upstairs.'

It was very pleasant, standing in the dimly lit, cool cellar, drinking bitter and watching the young Italian tidying up, something that seemed to involve a lot of bending over. They were there for a quarter of an hour, at least. That was what they told the adjutant, anyway.

When they emerged, the grandmother was in the hen run, collecting eggs. The chips were in the pan. The road outside was empty.

They thought that they might as well be hanged for a sheep as a lamb, so they sat down and ate the eggs, and the chips, and drank the beer. Then they began to walk down the road, looking for a lift.

When Privates Symes and Miller came back with the adjutant and the Military Police that afternoon, they found no one there. Not grandmother, not Sophia, not hens, not beer.

The sign outside the gate said 32nd Signals Company, Polish 2nd

Corps. The soldier on guard swung up the barrier and Jacob turned in, driving down the lane of olive trees to the farmhouse. The barn doors were open, and he guided the Bedford straight inside. Three of his men were waiting, and one of them set to removing all the British Army insignia before painting in the markings of their signal company while Jacob and the others began unloading their haul. It was a good one. Olive-painted metal boxes of .303 ammunition, brass agleam, boxes of Mills 36M grenades and several boxes of .455 Webley ammunition, together with a dozen of the heavy revolvers.

While they were unloading a light Austin lorry came down the lane. In it was Baruch Bashan, reunited with Jacob now as a free man and as a fellow soldier of Israel. With him was the girl whom Corporals Symes and Miller had known as Sophia, together with her 'grandmother', who came from the *kibbutz* Beit Zera. In the back of the truck were twenty-eight chickens, which they put into the farm's chicken run.

'Well done, well done,' Jacob congratulated them. He kissed Ruth. 'See what we've got.'

While the paint was drying on the Bedford, they drove out in the Austin, heading for the coast near Sorrento. The lorries made their way along the winding road leading down the steep hillside. In a little bay a fishing boat was drawn up on the beach, and men were unloading. Out to sea another craft was anchored. Equipped with a trawler's winch, it was hauling a harvest from the sea. The head of a diver appeared briefly in the water by its hull, and then disappeared.

On the beach were artillery shells and .5 calibre machine guns, still thickly coated in their Cosmolene protection. A man in swimming trunks came splashing through the water, the marks of his goggles, flippers and acqualung still on him.

'There's five Sherman tanks in her,' he grinned.

'Those we will have to leave,' Jacob said regretfully. 'Here is the lorry. Baruch will start moving the supplies now. Baruch, I'll see you back at the camp this evening. There's a little village up the road, and someone told me a Messerschmitt 109 crash-landed there in '44.'

The peasant looked at Jacob in the cunning, uncommunicative way of peasants everywhere, as he sat at his little wooden table, a cheap glass of his own *vino rosso* before him, silver stubble on his chin, dressed in a singlet that had once been white and some faded blue trousers. Cicadas were chirping among the olives and grape vines spreading their fresh leaves in curving rows.

Jacob took a ten-dollar bill from a fatly stocked wallet and rolling it up, poked it between the cracks of the planking on the table.

'I wished to see the aircraft, that was all.'

The scars were gone, and fresh vines planted. The propeller was still twisted, but morning glory had climbed up it in search of the sunlight, and cow parsley poked through the holes in the wings where the inspection panels had been. Along its side the savage holes told why it was there, and not far away there was a simple wooden cross.

'He died not long after we got him out,' grunted the old farmer.

Jacob looked at the wreck, noting the loose covers and panels.

'An aircraft such as this has guns. Cannon. One in the nose, and two in the wings. I cannot see them.'

He smiled at the old Italian, and once more took his wallet from his jacket.

'Shall we?' he began.


When he got back to the camp Ruth was waiting for him. She had changed into a suit of civilian clothes, and while Baruch and some others unloaded and packed the cannon ready for transit with the rest of the arms gathered, he did likewise. When he came out of the house she was sitting in the driver's seat of the truck. Her face was set and pale. He climbed in beside her.

'Are you sure you want to do this?' he asked. 'I . . . I must. For David, if not for all the others. But . . .'

'I shall try,' she said in a small but determined voice. 'I know it would be best if I try, so I shall.'

She gestured at herself.

'Everything else has come back to me,' she said, forcing cheerfulness into her voice. Jacob leaned over and kissed her. Her lips were full and springy, her breath sweet.

'You were beautiful to me from the moment I laid eyes on you,' he said.

She laughed in a sudden stab of real happiness.

'Truly, you will have to become a politician when this is all over!' she admonished. 'I was a ghastly skeleton, and you know it!'

'These things are relative,' he said. 'I too was a skeleton, and as one set of skin and bones to another, I tell you, you caught my eye.'

'A politician, as I said.'

Then she seized his hand in a sudden fit of nervousness.

'You will never leave me, Jacob, will you?'

'Never,' he promised. 'Never, never.'

She started the lorry, and they drove out and down the road into Naples. On the Via Appia they saw the signs of the US Army, slowed down, and turned in by a barrier guarding a large office building where an American military policeman in a helmet and shouldering an M1 carbine was manning a post.

'We are Jacob and Ruth Ben-Levi,' Ruth said. 'We have an appointment to see Captain Snow.'

He checked a list upon a clipboard.

'That is correct, Ma'am. Please leave your vehicle over there and report inside the yellow door.'

Inside the yellow door, in a room on the first floor they found Captain Snow of Army Intelligence, a young man in his twenties, with large spectacles perched on his nose. He offered them coffee, which they accepted.

'Okay,' he said, consulting a file. 'I want to say that we appreciate you both coming forward. You probably know that the allies are investigating war crimes committed by the Nazis. I'm sure you know about the Nuremberg Tribunal that sentenced Goering, Ribbentrop and the other top Nazis last year; well this is a process that will go on for some time. Those who committed war crimes – especially those involved in what Hitler called the "Final Solution" – we wish to bring to justice, and we can only do that with the help of those who were there, their victims who survived and can bear witness.'

He paused, and looked expectantly at them both.

'We thank you, Captain,' Jacob said politely. 'I . . . will say what I have to say in a moment. My wife here is also a survivor of the death camps, although we met when we were both free near the end of the war. My wife was in fact at Auschwitz as I was, but briefly, as I was, and we did not meet there. She was shipped out to the weapons factory at Radom as slave labour, and only released by the arrival of the Russian armies.'

The American officer's gaze moved to Ruth, who sat silent in her chair, her scarred hands clasped in her lap, her eyes down.

'My wife finds it very difficult to talk of those times,' Jacob said gently. 'She cannot talk about them even to me, and I do not press her to, for what memories are within her assail her with a dreadful terror. However, when I said that I was coming to see you myself she asked to accompany me. That is all I can really say.'

'Of course . . .,' Snow murmured sympathetically. 'Mrs Ben-Levi – may I call you Ruth? Ruth, we would appreciate any evidence you may want to give us, but I do understand if you find it very difficult to talk to me. Maybe you would like to sit at the table over here, if I give you some paper and a pencil? You could write down anything . . . ?'

Ruth nodded slowly.

'I will try . . .' she whispered.

Snow got up and led her to a table at the side of the room, where he furnished her with paper and a pencil, and carried her coffee over for her. Then he came back.

'I've been working on this side of things only nine months,' he said quietly, looking Jacob frankly in the eye. 'And *I* get nightmares from what I've been told. So I do understand, as well as anyone can who wasn't there. What is it you would like to tell me, Jacob? Is it about Auschwitz?'

'No,' Jacob said directly. 'Auschwitz was a terrible place, but I was not there long. However, others were, who have survived, and they can give you much better evidence on what happened there than I can. No, I wish to tell you about where I went, with my brother David, who is now dead, and I wish to have the men who killed my brother brought to justice.'

'Sure . . .,' Snow uncapped a pen and pulled a pad towards him. 'Where did you go when you left Auschwitz?'

'I went to Camp Dora.'

Snow's pen slowed in the writing of the date, and Jacob's name. 'Dora.'

'Yes. You have heard of it?'

'It doesn't come to mind . . .,' Snow said vaguely.

'The V2 rockets,' Jacob said sharply. 'You have heard of *them*, surely?'

'Of course, of course,' Snow said quickly. 'I just didn't know where they were made.'

'In caverns hewed from the inside of a mountain, by slaves. Slaves like me, and my brother David, who is dead.'

'Yes, you said . . .,' Snow murmured.

'He was murdered by a man called Karl Franz, who was in the SS. He did so at the instigation of another man who was in fact his boyfriend, although this is not important. The other man was an engineer at Dora, who was in charge of the special equipment that guided the rocket to its destination. These rockets were very accurate, they fell from the sky on London, and killed many people.'

'Yes, I know,' Snow said quietly.

'The engineer's name was Ibach . . . Captain Snow, you are not writing any of this down.'

'Perhaps it's best if I hear your story first.'

'Very well. I was with my brother David in a lorry, in the spring of 1945. Karl Franz and Engineer Ibach had bid us fill the bed of the lorry with boxes containing rocket parts, and many piles of paper filled with calculations and information regarding the rocket, especially the way in which it was guided to its destination. We did this one night as the Russians were advancing with their armies, and they drove the lorry from Dora with us aboard. In the morning they halted some way down the road, when they were out of the mountains. A river was running fast in the little ravine below, under some trees some other lorries were waiting. With them was the man in charge of the V2 rockets, a greater engineer than Ibach, called Von Braun. They were all headed west, I heard the word "*Amerikaner*" used.'

Snow had sat back in his chair, holding his pen between his hands as he listened. His eyes were very attentive, almost calculating behind the big glasses.

'It became clear to my brother and myself that we were only being held in reserve should it be necessary to unload the lorry on to another. When it was apparent that this was not required, it became equally clear that we were to be killed, right then and there. We attempted escape by jumping down the steep slope to the river below. I succeeded, but Karl Franz, whom we knew as the Butcher's Boy, pursued us. He shot my brother David in the back of the neck. I found his body washed up at the river bank the next day.'

Snow shook his head silently, his face puckered.

'I wish to find Karl Franz and Engineer Ibach. I wish them to stand trial. Not just for David. For others they killed,' Jacob continued.

'Of course,' Snow murmured. 'But let's see now . . . this camp Doris . . .'

'*Dora!*' Jacob snapped, suddenly angry.

'Yeah, sorry. Dora.'

'You *have* heard of it?' Jacob demanded.

'You know, Jacob, it doesn't spring to mind . . . you see, I know most of them . . . Belsen, Buchenwald, Birkenau . . . Aschersleben, Shonebeck, Flossenburg . . . I can tell you all about those. But Dora . . .'

He suddenly snapped his fingers.

'Yes, I think I have it. Wasn't it a test site for rocket equipment?'

'*It was a concentration camp!*' Jacob shouted.

'Hey, I'm sure you're right . . . um, say, where *was* it now . . . ?'

A large map of continental Europe hung on the wall. Jacob jerked from his chair, strode over to it and stabbed his finger unerringly at the site.

'Here. Here in the Harz mountains.'

Snow's face lit up in well-simulated relief.

'Why, of course. *That's* why I didn't know where it was. Your camp is in the Soviet sector, Jacob.'

'Does it make a difference? You said the *allies* are to charge former Nazis with their crimes.'

'That's true . . . but the Soviets are not our allies any more, Jacob.'

'It makes a difference?'

'Well, yes. It sure does. You may perhaps have heard of British war leader Churchill's speech in Fulton last year. "An Iron Curtain," he said, "has come down over Eastern Europe." One day, Jacob, we may find ourselves at war with the Soviets.'

He carefully put the cap back on his pen and stood up. The pad of paper remained empty but for the date and the beginning of Jacob's name.

'But say, there's nothing to stop *you* talking to the Soviets about it. They have a consulate here in Naples.'

'You may be sure I shall do that.'

Jacob went over to the table where Ruth sat, her head down. The pad in front of her was quite bare except for irregular splashes of tears wrinkling the paper.

'I cannot . . .,' she whispered.

Jacob helped her to her feet as Snow courteously pulled back her chair. The American said goodbye at the door.

'Best of luck,' he said, and in his eyes was a strange pity.

'Anybody here speak German?' Jacob demanded. '*Ja? Sprechen — Sie — Deutsch?*'

He stamped into the drab ante-room with its black and white photograph of Stalin looking gruesomely benevolent, and a middle-aged Russian woman with a nose like a boiled potato jerked her gaze up at him with instant hostility. He stared arrogantly at her as he had seen them do, in the camps.

'I – wish – to – speak – with – someone – in – authority.'

A man appeared through a doorway behind the woman. He wore a suit that appeared to be made from grey felt carpet underlay, and the indefinable, underlying air of meance that went with membership of the secret police.

'Then you must wish to speak to me,' he said smoothly, in passable German. 'Who are you?'

'My name is Ziegler,' Jacob lied.

'And what can I do for you?'

'A lot,' Jacob said boastfully. 'For I can do a lot for you.'

The secret policeman's eyebrows raised. Jacob tapped himself on the chest.

'I helped build the V2 rocket. *Ja?* You are familiar with this?'

Interest sparked immediately into the man's eyes.

'Yes, I am familiar with this. And you helped make the rocket?'

He reached into his inside pocket and took out a packet of cigarettes. He gestured to a table in a corner.

'Over here. A cigarette?'

'Thank you.'

They sat down at the table and the Russian lit the pale brown cigarettes with their hollow cardboard mouthpieces.

'My name is Ivanov. Now, where did you make them, these rockets?'

'In Dora, of course,' Jacob said, with well-simulated irritation. 'The factory inside the Harz mountains.'

'Yes, of course,' the Russian murmured. 'And on what part of the rocket did you work?'

'Guidance,' Jacob said blandly. 'I was a part of Engineer Ibach's team.'

Further interest grew in his eyes.

'Ah . . .'

'I lost contact with Engineer Ibach in the last days of the war. There was much chaos, you understand.'

'Much, yes.'

'I thought that you could put me back in touch with Engineer Ibach.'

'We?'

'Why, yes.'

Jacob looked at the Russian officer as though in mutual understanding.

'Well, of course, yes. Your armies overran Dora. I assumed you would know where he was.'

'*Herr* Ziegler, did we discover *you* in Dora? No. Neither did we discover Engineer Ibach or anyone else of scientific authority. They had all gone, of course. All we discovered were thousands of miserable *zeks*.'

'Slaves, yes? *Kazettniks*.'

'That what you call them? We call them *zeks*.'

'Yes ... The *zeks*, the slaves, the ones in the striped suits, the *kazettniks* who made the rockets. What about them?'

The Russian shrugged in incomprehension.

'What *about* them?'

'They were slaves. Many were murdered, tortured, died of disease, of neglect, of the working conditions.'

Ivanov nodded.

'Yes, yes, that is so, I am sure.'

'What about charges?' Jacob asked quietly.

The Russian looked puzzled.

'Charges? Explosive charges?'

'No. The slaves, the *zeks* in Dora, they suffered and died as a result of what they were made to do there. Those who made them do it were the people who were in charge. Like Engineer Ibach and the SS. What they did must come under the heading of war crimes, does it not? Like those at Nuremberg. They will face charges, if they are found. They too will be hanged.'

Ivanov's face cleared, and he patted Jacob jovially on the arm.

'Don't worry about a thing, friend Ziegler. We don't care about a few *zeks*. You help us, we'll help you.'

'I would like you to,' Jacob said. 'And Engineer Ibach, you don't know where he is?'

Ivanov shook his head regretfully.

'A pity. Because I want him.'

'Yes? Why?'

'I have not lied to you. I did work under Engineer Ibach. I was one of the *zeks*. I was a slave in Dora. I want Ibach hanged!'

A heavy shutter went down over Ivanov's eyes.

'I cannot help you,' he said coldly.

'You must have a file.'

Ivanov got up, he indicated the door.

'There is no file, Mr Whoeveryouare, Mr *Zek* from Dora. Not here, not anywhere,' he said, so quietly that only Jacob could hear him. 'You are wasting your time. Dora exists only in your mind.'

# PART III

## New York, September 1947

GIDEON Weiss paid no attention to the high coffered ceilings of the temple, its golden chandeliers or the beautiful carved wood pews where he was sitting. His father was the rabbi, the Brooklyn synagogue was as familiar to him as most kids' front yard. The fact that on this evening the oriental Sephardic Jews whom he little saw had come down from their upstairs chapel to join the European Askenazis, to hear the men from Palestine speak caused him little concern. Even being close to the men of the Irgun, who kept his neighbours open-mouthed as they told them of the struggle of the Jews to regain the ancient homeland, was little novelty. His father had supported Jabotinsky and was one of Menachem Begin's right-hand men in America. The pile of weapons on the floor of the temple was proof of that. Brought and bought, destined for the struggle, they were proof that no Jew would ever suffer the Holocaust again.

The weapons – brought in by Jewish ex-servicemen, bought by sympathizers – were no novelty. He had helped crate up hundreds like them, taken them down to the docks. What *was* new was the size of Rebecca Goldman's tits.

He could hardly believe it was her. He certainly couldn't take his eyes off them, filling the front of her demurely cut white blouse. It had only been last year that she had moved with her mother, over to Queens. She knew he was looking. He'd seen the glitter of her eyes, under the dark lashes. She was sitting with her cousin Libby, so maybe she was visiting. Mentally he tried to calculate her age. Certainly, no more than a couple of years younger than he was. He casually smoothed his curly black hair, sat nonchalantly with one leg outstretched – suitably muscled, he was a track man. The girls liked him at first sight, he knew that.

Rebecca sat up straight in the pew and breathed in. The crisp cloth went taut and Gideon could feel himself getting stiff. With an effort, he dragged his eyes away. On the platform a boy was standing alone under the Israeli flag, symbol of a nation that did not exist.

There was something about the boy that managed to wrest his attention from Rebecca Goldman's chest. He was younger than Gideon's seventeen years, but his face looked much older. It seemed as though it had been a long time since it smiled. It was, somehow, a frightening face.

'My name is Avraham Cohen. I am a soldier of Israel.'

It should have been ludicrous, a boy speaking that way, but nobody laughed. They sat in rapt attention.

'I killed a man a little while ago. I killed a British soldier.'

His eyes swept the congregation, looking for those who would not meet his gaze.

'I killed him because the British want to give our land to the Arabs. I will kill anyone who tries to give the Holy Land of Israel to the Arabs. It is ours, God wills it so.'

A rumble of agreement, of approval, went through the temple.

'I did not always think this way.'

There was a creaking as they sat back, waiting to be told. Like them, Gideon's eyes were on the boy, his attention seized.

'My parents did not think this way. My grandparents did not think this way. And yet we lived all together in Tel Aviv. We had made *aliyah*, we had come to build the nation of Israel once again, in our historic homeland.'

Avraham Cohen stood up straight.

'My parents, my grandparents worked with the Jewish Agency. They believed in *havlaga*, in restraint. The worked on the land, helped drain swamps, built settlements. They believed in partnership with the Arabs, in negotiation, in buying from the Arabs the land that was their own, given to them by God. They believed, may God help them, in being friends with the Arabs.'

He looked out over them.

'One day we went to a wedding. We hired a taxi. On the Haifa –Safed road we had to slow down, for a boulder on the road. As we did so an Arab gang leaped from the ditch, firing rifles.'

A growl of anger went through the temple.

'My grandmother died immediately. She was shot in the head. My aunts, my grandfather died too. My father was dying. The leader of the killers dragged him out on to the road, and relieved himself in his face. They looked in the van for the presents we were carrying, and found my mother, still alive. They dragged her out onto the hillside.

She was young and beautiful, they tore off her clothes. They felt her body with their hands. They did hideous things to her.'

The boy's face was like stone, now they knew why he never smiled.

'I was there too, under the dead, under the blood, the brains and the bone and the hair. I saw the leader stand by and smoke a cigarette as his men did these things, I saw him hack my mother to death when they were finished. One day, I shall hack him into pieces. That is why I joined the Irgun. We are the new Maccabees. Our war is *milchemet shel mitzvah*. A holy war, a war of liberation. Forget *havlaga*. Forget restraint. Forget talking, negotiation, friendship. *No more six million dead. Make your choice. Us or them. Kill or be killed! Conquer or die!*'

The congregation sprang its feet yelling. The men from the Irgun had spread an Israeli flag on the floor of the temple, the people of the synagogue were reaching into their pockets, pulling out great handfuls of *gelt*, flinging it onto the pile. Alert as hawks, the men from the Irgun were moving among the crowd, looking out for GI veterans, for young men, looking for soldiers for the coming war.

Gideon did not see them. Sitting in the pew he had a vision of a dry hillside, dark figures clustered around a white woman. They tore at her clothes. A white blouse, a skirt, underclothes, scattered on the rock. Feeling her body. Throwing her down, mounting her one after the other.

In the synagogue he looked about him, at the milling people, with his mouth dry, his heart thumping. The vision hid at the back of his mind, strangely thrilling.

The doors opened and he saw Rebecca going outside with her cousin. He followed and caught up with them as they paused in the doorway.

'Hi, girls. Hi, Rebecca.'

He gave her an extra nice smile, showing off his even white teeth, smoothing back his curly black hair. Libby was a bitch who wore cast-iron underpants, he wasn't interested in her.

'Hey, Gideon.'

She smiled prettily at him, innocently, as though she hadn't been showing her tits to him all evening.

'What do you say, feel like a drive down Ocean Parkway?' he said boldly.

'You have a car, Gideon?'

'Sure,' he said casually. He dropped his voice. 'Me, I take the guns down to the docks for my dad. I use the car whenever I want.'

'We mustn't be late,' said Libby and sniffed.

'I wasn't asking you,' said Gideon, without looking at her. 'I want to hear all Rebecca's news. I want to talk to her about Israel.'

Rebecca smiled dazzlingly.

'I feel like talking about Israel,' she said. 'I'll be back in an hour, Libby. Gideon'll drop me off home, won't you, Gideon?'

'Sure will,' he said and slipped back inside. The keys were in his dad's jacket pocket. With the men from the Irgun there, he could have them back and his dad not even know they'd been gone. He was back outside within a minute, showing Rebecca and her chest to the blue Dodge parked outside the synagogue.

He gunned the engine, making the big V8 rumble through the mufflers, and cut through towards the parkway.

'You gonna do it, Gideon?'

He grinned in the dark.

'I'm always ready to do it, Rebecca.'

'You're so smart. No, you going to fight for Israel?'

'Sure. But we got to get the guns there first.'

'When are you going?'

'Soon. Hey, listen, I'm not called Gideon for nothing. I'll be a real warrior, I'll slaughter those Arabs.'

He pulled over by the liquor store, by the drive-thru window. From the fund-raising money in his pocket, he passed over a ten-dollar bill and got some beer and a half bottle of Jack Daniels. He passed a beer to the girl and she giggled, enjoying the forbidden fruit.

'What do Arabs look like anyway?' she asked.

'Sort of like niggers,' he said vaguely. 'Just the same as niggers, always wanting to get into our girls' pants.'

She giggled again.

'Isn't that what you want to do, Gideon?' she asked, teasing him.

'I'm going to be a warrior,' he said, and they turned on to the parkway. 'I'm descended from King David.'

'How do you know that?' she scoffed. 'Nobody knows that, it was too long ago.'

He thumped his chest with his fist.

'I know it here. I'm called Gideon, and I'm descended from King David,' he said seriously. 'You know why? I'm going to be the saviour of Israel, one day. God'll give me a sign, and I'll know.'

'You take all that stuff really seriously. I guess you being the rabbi's son and all. My family, we only really get Jewish at Passover. I guess I'm more American than Jewish.'

'That's wrong to say that,' he said seriously. 'We're God's chosen people, nobody else in the world matters but us. No one else exists but us. That's why God's sent us Israel again.'

There was the point where the road curved away from the water, it was quiet there, you could park, and he swung the Dodge into the lot. They went under the street light and it illuminated her blouse, white and crisp. He wondered if the woman on the hillside had been like that. Hands, tearing, squeezing. He felt his breath quicken, she saw him looking at her, and smiled.

In the sudden quiet the crack as he unscrewed the liquor bottle was loud. He held it out.

'Want a pull?'

'Sure,' she said boldly and took a careful sip. When she gave it back he chugged down some real swallows and the liquor rushed into his mind. On a hillside a woman was running, they pulled her down, ripping at her clothes.

On the bench seat he slid over to her, putting his arm about her. She put up her face to be kissed, and his free hand caressed her chest.

'Hey . . .,' she said, but she didn't stop him.

The buttons of the blouse came undone, he slid his hand inside her bra, feeling her round and smooth and warm. She giggled, innocently pleased with the effect of her new shape. She did nothing to stop him.

They were both free, he saw her rise in the cool air, he bent to put his mouth round her. On the hillside, the woman lay with her breasts exposed.

His breath was very fast.

'Hey, Gideon,' she chuckled. 'You sound like you're about to come in your pants or something.'

He put his hand up her skirt, but she kept her knees firmly together, and kept his hand on her thigh.

'Uh-huh,' she said.

The woman on the hill would have screamed at them to stop.

She filled his mouth. Suddenly, he bit into her flesh.

She shrieked in pain, staring at him in shock, blood spilling from her beautiful round breast.

'Bitch,' he snarled. He punched her in the stomach and she begged him to stop with a voice that had no air. He tore at the blouse in a frenzy, he ripped off her white pants and stuffed them in her mouth to stop her screaming. He had her on the seat in a swift sudden attack, just like the Arabs on the hillside.

She was sobbing, she crawled up against the door, trying to gather

her torn clothes about her. The other bitch had done that. The one he'd got in Queens. Filthy little slut.

'It was your fault,' he said. 'You wanted me to do it.'

He took another drink from the bottle. The door was suddenly swinging open, he saw her running away across the lot in the half light.

Shit.

He sat, slightly drunk, slightly dazed with pleasure, the sweat cooling on him. He reached over, and pulled the door to.

Damn. He fired up the engine. They were all bitches. Wanted to get you hot, wanted you to do it, then said they didn't.

He turned in the lot, the tyres squealing. He'd have to catch up with her. That other little bitch had wanted to run off too, the one from Queens, only he'd explained how everyone would think she was a whore, and no other boy would want her anyway, not to marry, a slut like her, if she said anything. Let him just find Rebecca, cool her off. She'd see it his way.

Where the hell was she?

Who was that? The figure walking along was familiar, he pulled over, winding down the window. He recognized the boy from the synagogue, Cohen, Avraham Cohen.

'Hey, Avraham. It's Gideon. Where are you going?'

The boy peered in, with his unsmiling face.

'The docks,' he said. 'I'm going back to Israel for the war. The ship sails at midnight.'

The war. He'd have a chestful of medals. Nobody would believe a bitch like Rebecca. Not about a hero.

'Get in,' he said. 'I'll take you there. I'm coming too.'


## Tel Aviv, April 1948

Jacob had forgotten. Where the sea met the land, lines of flat roofs rose from an expanse of sand, grey cement enlivened by the occasional splash of green. The light was harsh, breaking on the choppy water into a myriad of glittering needles. They were waiting on the jetty, women in sandals and khaki bloomers, their heads covered with faded scarves of coarse blue cotton, they swarmed aboard and perspiring, began hauling the heavy boxes on to the quay.

There was one standing aside; Jacob cried out to her, saw her

smile, the flash of her teeth, it lit him up inside, he hurried down
the plank, his arms outstretched for her.

'Ruth . . . Ruth my darling . . .'

He held her for a long time, and she him. Then he stepped back,
still clasping her hands, and looked at her.

'So soon?' he said.

Ruth smoothed her shirt over her wonderfully rounded stomach,
and laughed happily. The drab port seemed suddenly alive with
colour, Jacob found himself laughing too.

'You arrived just in time,' she said. 'Next month we shall
be three.'

The women were piling the olive boxes about them, the air filled
with bursts of Hebrew.

'We laugh in Hebrew,' said Ruth, 'and then at night you hear
people cry out in so many different languages.'

'Where are the men?'

'At the fighting,' she said. 'Now, see, I have become one of them,
I see my husband for the first time in months and I must hustle him
off. Your Captain Zvi is waiting where the men from the refugee ship
are. He says to bring enough guns and arms for a squad of ten.'

'Here,' Jacob called to the women. 'Load these boxes for me
and these.'

They piled them on a waiting trolley, and Ruth led Jacob by the
hand along the quay towards some rough sheds. They moved with
the energy of youth, squeezing each other's hands and laughing
into each other's eyes. Behind them the women smiled, one to the
other, and made female jokes about young love. Beyond the wire
that kept the city out old brown buses with dirty windows behind
their protective wire netting ground along dusty streets.

In the shed were men straight off a refugee ship, some still in
their striped Displaced Persons clothing. Levinger was there, in army
uniform. The *Haganah* was out in the open.

His face lit up when he saw Jacob coming through the door and
embraced him.

'Well done, well done. I wish I had time to thank you for all
the stuff you've got through. When this is all over we'll go to
Ben-Yehuda Street and have the best dinner they can serve up.'

'I'll keep you to it. You said you wanted arms for a squad of
ten. Sten guns and 500 rounds per man. Mills grenades, eight per
man. Fairbairn commando knives. One Bren gun. Where are we to
use them?'

'The British are pulling out. The Mandate ends on the fifteenth of next month. They aren't going to risk their soldiers now. The Arabs know it. They have Jerusalem sealed off. The last convoy got through two weeks ago. The one that followed it was wiped out. On both sides of the road our dead lie piled up. Your wife was one of the last to get out, she was bringing information.'

Ruth patted her stomach. 'I've been working for intelligence. Some of the British soldiers were willing to sell information – for example, when key buildings were going to be evacuated. A pregnant woman can go anywhere.'

'There're one hundred thousand Jews under siege in Jerusalem. They are slowly starving. Boys and girls are carrying in food at night. The "Primus plane" – it's just a Piper Cub – makes a run once a day bringing in milk powder for the youngest babies. It has to land in a wadi by the Monastery of the Cross and gets shot at coming and going. We're going to break the siege. How can there be a Jewish state without Jerusalem? It's like a body without a head. We're throwing in everything we have. The plan is called "Nachshon".'

'The first Hebrew to take the challenge of Moses to plunge into the Red Sea during the exodus,' said Ruth.

Jacob smiled, and reached out to ruffle her hair.

'Where is that good Polish girl I married?'

'Where are the Jews?' she said, waving a hand about her. 'We are all Hebrews now.'

'Yes.'

The memory stabbed into him, as it did, every day. She knew him so well, she saw his face crease in remembered pain, she reached out and held him, quickly, squeezing him.

'David should have been here,' he said, his voice muffled. 'It is not right.'

'You will find him,' she assured him, her voice intense and fierce. 'You will find Ibach, justice *will* be done.'

Ibach.

'Yes,' he said sombrely. 'I will see to him.'

Then he smiled fiercely too, and kissed her.

'I do love you. I do, I do. But first, we have a country to win!'

The men off the refugee ship smiled at each other.

'Bring up the other boxes, and we can divide them up like this,' Levinger said to the women acting as stevedores. 'Three 500-man battalions are going to seize all the villages and strategic heights that overlook the road above Bab el Wad. The fighting will be very heavy indeed, they're going to need all the reinforcements they can get. That's you.'

He looked over the waiting men. 'You must think it's mad, getting off the ship and going straight into combat.'

'You do not have to mad to be a Zionist, commander,' a tall man in DP clothing called out, thick black curly hair framing his face. 'But it helps!'

'This is Jacob – Jacob, . . . Jacob Ben-Levi. He's your *mef-kaf*, your combat sergeant. Do as he says, and you'll be all right.'

Two boys in their teens were standing near the men in DP clothes.

'Jacob, you'll be fighting at night, it won't be easy to find your way. I have a guide for you. Avraham, come here.'

One of the boys came over, leaving his companion. He was about sixteen, stone-faced.

'This is Avraham Cohen. He knows the area like his own back yard.'

'I had relatives there, commander. I can get you where you need to go.'

'Are they still there?'

'Their bodies, commander,' said the boy. 'Only their bodies.'

Jacob glanced over at the other boy. He had dark curly hair, and the physique of one who had eaten good food for all of his life. He was very pale and uneasy.

'Who's your friend?'

'He's from New York,' said Cohen. 'Rabbi's son, come to fight. Gideon. Gideon Weiss.'

'We need everyone we can get,' said Levinger.

'He looks nervous.'

'I'll look after him,' said Cohen.

A motley collection of requisitioned lorries waited outside to take them up to the fighting. They pulled on webbing over their clothes that they had come in, and loaded it with their arms.

'Magazines on the left, and grenades on the right, if you are right-handed.' Jacob called. 'Don't forget your water-bottles.'

As he was about to get on board, Ruth called to him.

'Jacob, quickly!'

He went to her and she placed his hand over her stomach. Through the wall came the inquisitive tapping of life.

He beamed with joy. 'It's your papa,' he said.

The lorry smelled of ammonium nitrate, and its grit ground under their boots, ten of them squeezed together along its sides.

'Okay,' said Jacob. 'Anyone here been a soldier?'

Three of the nine held up their hands.

'I was in the Polish army,' said the dark-haired man who had claimed that madness helped, if you were a Zionist. 'My name is Zenon.'

'Infantry?' Jacob said hopefully.

'I was a cavalryman.'

'Zenon, we'll find a horse for you.'

The men laughed at the small joke.

'What about you?'

'I am Luigi, sir. I was in the Italian Army.'

'Recently?'

'No, I was a corporal in the Wolves of Tuscany. I was captured in 1941, in the desert. I have been working on a farm in England since then.'

'Farmers we need, Luigi.'

The little Italian shook his head. 'You need soldiers today, sergeant. I will try my best.'

Jacob turned to the last man, who sat comfortably in a corner, well-covered, in American fatigues. His trousers were held up by a big pair of red braces.

'Ah'm Abner Goldstein,' he announced in a southern accent.

'I thought you looked like you'd seen good food too recently to have been a DP, Abner. US Army?'

'Yassuh. I'm just a volunteer. I was a machine gunner.'

'Great. You can have the Bren.'

'I make a good machine gunner, I'm too fat to run away,' he chuckled and they all laughed.

'None of us can run here, Abner,' said Zenon. 'We run, we have to run a thousand miles.'

The six others comprised Avraham Cohen and Gideon Weiss, another American, Shmuel, who had been at Hebrew Union College studying to be a Rabbi, Leonard, a bespectacled tailor from London, a young man whose orange hair blazed against the side of the truck and a very quiet boy who looked about twelve.

'What's your name?' asked Jacob.

'Elie, sir.'

'You call me Jacob. And where are you from?'

'Buchenwald.'

'How old are you?'

'Eighteen.'

'*Really how old?*'

'Sixteen . . ., Jacob.'

'What can you do?'

'I can pick your pocket so you wouldn't know it. That's how I stayed alive.'

'We need money, we'll send you out, Elie. Listen to me, you stay close to me when the fighting starts.'

Outside there was rock and dust and harsh sunlight. For thousands of years, a battleground. Zenon was humming the *Hatikvah* the Zionist song of hope.

Jacob turned to the young man with orange hair. It was truly the colour of a carrot, he thought. A generous band of freckles ran over a snub nose. Green eyes and a wide, cheerful mouth grinned at him and he grinned back.

'I have to say this,' he told him. 'If you are a Jew my name is Winston Churchill.'

'Oh, to be sure, no, sergeant,' the young man said in a broad Irish brogue. 'Seamus Flynn at your service.'

'If you aren't a *Jew*, why are you *here?*'

'Well, you see, I'm one of the Fighting Flynns. That's what they call us, back home. We're ones for the girls and for a good fight. We like a fight, we Flynns.'

'You've come here for a fight?'

'And the girls, sergeant. To be sure, yes. You see, my brothers, they got to fight with the British in the war, but I was too young. I missed it, and I simply cannot hold my head up. Listening to my brothers talking in the bar how they shot the Germans and won the war is just more than a boy's stomach can stand. So here I am, sir, at your service.'

'*With* the British? I thought the Irish fought *against* the British.'

'To be sure we do, sir. When there is nobody better.'

'Will the Arabs do?'

'They will indeed,' Seamus Flynn said cheerfully. He looked out at the arid land passing by. 'Though it's a strange place to be fighting over, to my mind. You'd not grow many potatoes here.'

Zenon sat up against the metal side of the lorry as though stung by a wasp.

'These rocks are holy!' he shouted.

'To be sure they are,' Seamus said pleasantly.

Gideon Weiss watched the land go by with his strange, chill eyes.

'I'm taking some home, when I go,' he said.

'Let me show you how to strip and use the Sten,' said Jacob. 'I know it looks like something someone threw together out of some gas pipe and bits of an oven, but it's a good effective weapon. These are Mark Vs, and new. To use you put the loaded magazine – bullets pointing forwards! – into the housing here. Push until it locks with a click. The cocking handle is here, and under the safety slot there is a button that passes through the gun from side to side. I suggest that unless any of you are expert with sub-machine guns you all push the button through on the left side, where it is marked R, for repetition. That means you fire once for each time you pull the trigger, as opposed to automatic fire. Okay. To shoot at someone, you line up the sights like this . . .'

Gideon Weiss held the gun up, tracking on an approaching rock.

'I'm descended from King David,' he said to nobody in particular.

'To be sure,' said Jacob. 'Here, we are all the descendants of that mighty king. We shall prove it today. Now, our Sten guns. To shoot at someone, you line up the sights like this . . .'

## Bab el Wad

'Vickers three nought three,' Abner muttered, trying to get his bulk further behind the rock. The steady stutter of the machine gun was blotted out by the sudden shattering of rock as a burst slammed into the hill around them.

Jacob wiped blood from his forehead where a rock splinter had opened his skin.

'Do you know how to use that, Abner?'

'Yassuh. I'd like that gun. Best heavy machine gun ever made.'

In the dark the village was lit up by the flames from the burning houses. Three companies were held down on the slope by the sustained fire from the machine gun in its fortified house. Their guide, Avraham, was at his place at Jacob's elbow. He turned to him.

'Avraham. I want to get up close to the machine gun. Is there any cover we can use to get there?'

'There's a gully, where the spring water runs.'

In the darkness Jacob could see his team, scattered and pressed into cover in the rock.

'Listen, everyone. Stick together. You get lost out here the Arabs will find you. They'll have your *schmuck* off for a necktie like that.'

He led them up the gully, following Avraham, climbing towards
the house. Firing was coming from the roof and some outbuildings
as well as the ground floor where the machine gun was. They crept
to within three hundred yards. Ahead was the plateau that overlooked
the gorge, a killing ground of rocks and dry dirt.

'I'll take the team in,' Jacob said to Abner. 'I want you to put
down suppressing fire on the house and outbuildings. When you
can see us going in keep your fire high.'

Jacob turned to Zenon. 'I'll take Elie, Leonard the tailor and
Avraham. I'll go in through the front, while you take Shmuel,
the rabbi, Luigi, Seamus and Gideon and go through the back.
Each group split into two teams. Now, one team moves while
the other covers. We have Abner giving us supporting fire with
the Bren as well. Use the cover we have here – go from rock to
rock, and move as quickly as possible. Once they have realized
we're here use aimed shots from the shoulder, and when you're
firing from cover, fire around the cover, not over it. If you actually
come up close to an enemy aim at the centre of his body and
pull the trigger. Not once, but several times. You fire first, you
laugh longer.'

'When this is over, sergeant, I will teach you to make a suit in
ten seconds too,' said Leonard, is round spectacles glinting in the
firelight.

Jacob grinned. 'Okay, Abner, move across to the right so that we
get a reasonable angle between us.'

The fat man moved off, keeping the edge of the wadi between
him and the enemy. Jacob paused for a last word with Zenon.

'The kid Gideon is jumpy. Watch out for him.'

'He is a Jew,' Zenon said simply. 'He will be a hero.'

Zenon led his team across, to bring them round to the back of
the farmhouse, and they began to move.

From the edge of the wadi they heard the first three and four
round bursts of fire from the Bren. They were close now, within
fifty feet. Jacob had lost sight of Zenon's group in the darkness.
The Arabs were firing on a broad front, trying to find the Bren.
Machine-gun fire came from a window in the farmhouse and a man
screamed as Abner returned the compliment into the walls below
each side of the window.

Jacob gathered his team of three in a fold of ground.

'Okay. Now I want you to push your selectors through to the
other side. Automatic fire. In bursts. I'm going to crawl along here.
When I give the signal I want you to pop up and hose the farmhouse.

I'll go in and post some grenades through their firing hole. If I'm hit, Avraham, you take over.'

Jacob crawled along the little ridge of dead ground. Dust rose up, and coated his teeth. He slung his Sten gun over his back and took two grenades from his webbing, holding them in each hand with the pins out.

The noise of the battle had changed. The steady stuttering of the Vickers had ceased. It seemed as good an omen as any. He gave the signal and began to run across the ground. The Sten guns were firing and he could see powdered stone puffing out from the walls of the house. An orchard lay on the other side of the building. He thought it would be wonderful to eat an orange and feel the fresh juice filling his mouth. He seemed to be moving so slowly. A man was looking at him from an upstairs window, he saw him bringing a rifle to aim, and he zigged and zagged across the ground to upset him. Things began going crack-thump past his ears, and there was a scream from the window. He thudded into the wall and lobbed the grenades in, one after the other.

The double crash of the explosives was followed by intense firing from behind the building. Avraham, Elie and Leonard were running up. Jacob kicked in the door and they piled inside. Someone came pounding through the back and Jacob yelled not to shoot, for it was Zenon and the red-haired Irishman, Seamus. They checked the house and threw the bodies outside.

Abner came puffing along, and took charge of the Vickers.

'Barrel change,' he said. 'And they were out of water. Damn. Okay, guys, who wants to take a pee? Line up and fill this coolant can.'

'The Arabs will counter-attack,' said Jacob. 'Set it up to cover the ground between us and the next village.'

'I'll need three guys to help,' said Abner. 'This thing's heavy.'

'Elie, Leonard, Avraham, help Abner. Zenon and your guys, *acharei*,' he said, using the motto of the Palmach, which he said twenty times a day. 'Follow me.'

Zenon was doing up the buttons of his trousers.

'In Israel we waste nothing,' he said, 'not even piss.'

'Get in among the trees of the orchard. Get ready when they come. And remember, if we have to pull back, I'll provide covering fire.'

A Very signal pistol was lying on the floor, with a box of flares. Jacob put them in his pack, took the Bren, and went out into the darkness. He took up a position that gave him a ninety-degree angle of fire to the slope facing the orchard and waited in the dark.

'Gideon,' said Zenon. 'You stick with me.'

The Pole had an entrenching tool. Where there was a natural dip in the ground he began to dig.

'Pile up the earth and rocks in front of us,' he ordered, and Gideon dropped his Sten down on the ground, helping build a parapet.

'Get in,' said Zenon. 'They'll be here any moment. We can't get it any deeper.'

They crouched in the little trench, and Zenon handed Gideon his Sten.

Suddenly the Arabs were upon them in a wave; there was yelling and firing with figures flitting through the darkness. From his position at the side Jacob fired a white flare over the fighting and in its light he saw the men fighting.

In the sudden brilliance Gideon saw the Arabs coming at him. Next to him he heard the stutter of the Sten as Zenon began to fire, and then his own gun too was jerking in his hands. He fired, and a man clutched at his stomach before falling. Suddenly, Gideon was possessed of an overwhelming joy. He had never killed before, and he found it wonderful.

As the flare floated down Jacob saw a man who stood out, a tall man, moustached, two bandoliers crossing his chest. He was at the forefront, leading the charge on the farmhouse. Jacob fired two four-round bursts into him from one hundred yards and blew his body over the dry stone wall.

In the trench the firing of Zenon's Sten suddenly stopped.

'*Gideon!*' he screamed. 'My gun is jammed.'

The attackers were all over the shallow trench. Gideon fired on automatic, and heard a man scream, then he saw the flash of a blade in Zenon's hand.

From the farmhouse the Vickers began its deadly, steady stutter. As suddenly as they had appeared, the Arabs vanished, slipping away into the darkness.

It was past midnight. In the gorge below Jacob saw a long train of little lights begin to move. Sixty lorries were down there, bumper to bumper, laden with food and supplies. Another three hundred were assembling behind them. They would arrive in time for Passover, and Jews would celebrate the Exodus, the freedom from the yoke of Egypt.

Gideon stood up, in the scraping of a trench. The Arab he had hit was crawling towards the darkness, his breath hissing agonizingly in his chest. He left a clotted streak of blood on the ground. Gideon's eyes swept over the little battlefield. The Arabs were gone, his hands trembled hot and sweating, eager on his weapon. His body was suffused with a feeling almost like sexual desire.

The Arab was still crawling towards safety. Gideon unsheathed his fighting knife and bounded towards him.

Jacob walked back to the orchard. Bodies lay scattered among the trees. Over the parapet of a little trench the body of Zenon lay entwined with three of his attackers. All were dead.

A deadly Fairbairn knife was in one of Zenon's clenched fists, dark with gore.

'He is holding something in his hand,' said Elie. 'What is it?'

Jacob reached down to prise the bloody fingers open. A cloud of the black flies that had been blown in by the hamsin rose were buzzing, already feasting. Ants crawled thick over the ground, voracious for the blood of the dead and the wounded. Clasped hard to his palm like gold Zenon had a handful of soil.

From the darkness there came a sudden, dreadful shriek, and Jacob whirled in alarm, bringing his Sten up, but he could only see Gideon bent over something on the ground. It writhed in agony and he saw that it was a man.

The howls of agony suddenly muted to a strangled gargling as he ran up. Gideon stared down at the Arab with shining eyes and teeth, his lips bared a rictus of the insane. In his hand he held in triumph his savage fighting knife. His arm was bloody to the elbow and Jacob could smell its stench.

The Arab soldier's trousers were loose and slashed about his knees. Between his thighs there was nothing but a hole that spouted blood. His mouth was filled with gory offal.

Jacob bent in sudden compassion and put the Sten to the man's temple. He fired once, and the body jerked. Then it lay still, its torment over.

He straightened up, and found Gideon staring at him in contempt. By his side, Flynn bent down and closed the man's eyes.

Gideon found Avraham at the roadside. He was sitting in the shade of a tree, and had a clean cloth spread out on a rock in front of him. On it was a sub-machine gun. It looked finely tooled, unlike the Stens they were using, which seemed to be made from left-over parts of gas ovens. He was folding a large red handkerchief into a blindfold. Gideon squatted down beside him.

'What're you doing?'

'I took this off one of the Arabs last night. I shot him in the fight in the orchard. It's German, an MP40. It's a very good gun.'

He bound the length of cloth about his eyes.

'What're you doing now?'

'I've stripped it and put it back together with my eyes open. Now I'm doing it with my eyes shut. You have to know your weapon. It's your best friend.'

With deft hands, the teenager extracted the long magazine, and felt for the bolt. He twisted the receiver lock and squeezed the trigger. Holding it down he rotated the pistol grip and pulled the entire frame free.

'That bastard Jacob is sending me back to Tel Aviv.'

'Ah?'

The recoil spring and firing pin emerged, to be placed on the clean cloth.

'I shot one of the Arabs in the battle. He wasn't dead. When the others ran away I went out to him. I cut his cock off, and his balls too, Avraham.'

Cohen laughed, humourlessly.

'Less of them to breed, you cut their cock and balls off.'

Gideon darted a calculating look at the young man, now beginning to reassemble his weapon.

'That's right. This is war, isn't it? I don't like that bastard Jacob. All that shit about purity of arms and taking prisoners. This is war. This is us or them. I say slice them up, so they know not to come back.'

Avraham nodded from behind his fold.

'You're the right sort, Gideon. What will you do?'

'Hell, I don't know. I just came here to fight for the Jews.'

Avraham slid the frame group back into the receiver, and twisted the pistol grip to lock them together.

'Yes, me too,' he said. 'I'm not one of them – the *Haganah*, Jacob's lot. But they needed guides, and I have relatives in Jerusalem. So I helped yesterday. But the *Haganah* don't understand who we're dealing with. They don't understand the Arabs. I understand the Arabs. The Irgun understand the Arabs. I understood them the day I saw my mother being hacked to death, Gideon. The *Haganah* think we can have an Israel with Arabs in it. You can't, Gideon, you can't.'

'No,' Gideon whispered softly. 'Israel is for Jews.'

'Nobody else.'

'It's God's will.'

Avraham slipped the magazine into its housing and pushed it until it went home with a click. He pulled the bandana from his eyes, and picked up the gun.

'Arabs have to know what happens to Arabs, in the land of the Jews,' he said. 'And we're going to show them.'

'What are you going to do?'

'Come and see. I'm waiting for the lorry.'

Gideon felt a strange prickle of anticipation run through his guts.

'Another battle?'

'Not another battle,' Avraham said patiently, his eyes looking down the road. 'Was my mother killed in a battle? No. She believed in co-operating with the Arabs. The Arabs are used to the old Jews. We're the new Jews. We'll see how they like it. When we're through, all you'll see is running Arabs. We're going to cleanse Israel.'

The anticipation became a real excitement.

'You sound like my people,' Gideon said. 'Oh yes, you do.'

Dust was coming up the road.

'You know,' said Avraham, 'I even know his name.'

'Whose name?'

They heard the driver going down through the gears. Avraham bent and picked up the cloth.

'The man who killed my mother. I'll get him, one day. He's called Hamouda. Hadj Hamouda.'

The driver threw open the door of the old lorry, and the two young men climbed inside.


# Jerusalem


The house was old with thick walls and heavy doors. It had an aura of respect, the other houses and their inhabitants pressed up against it. In the alley that ran along one side was a little window that let in a small draught of fresh night air. Hadj Hamouda lifted his young son Hasan up onto his shoulders, his hands about his ankles. The six-year-old was slim and flexible, his father propelled him upwards and he slid inside the tiny opening.

As he vanished Hamouda ran softly down the alley. Quiet, dark men were in the doorways. They gathered outside, and a creaking came from the big thick wooden door, and it opened. Hasan stood there in triumph, and the men flowed past him into the house.

They brought out the people who were inside. Children, both

older and younger than Hasan, the grandparents, old and trembling, the new wife, young and beautiful, the man, whom all respected.

They beat on the doors of the neighbouring houses with insistent fists, and made all those inside that respected the man come out.

They stuffed rags into the mouths of his family, and gagged them.

Hadj Hamouda turned to the silent crowd.

'This man, this Khalil Sourani, is a traitor. He was planning to betray you. There are those of you who already listened to him. You doubtless thought that what he asked you to do was but a small accommodation.'

He signalled with his hand, and his men brought forward a little girl of no more than three years, in a white nightshirt. There was a moan of outrage, of horror from the crowd as they saw what was to happen. Hamouda's eyes swept over them like a burning brand, and they fell silent, staring only with huge eyes.

He nodded, and they slashed her to pieces in the courtyard.

Hamouda raked the crowd again with his gaze, as the smell of blood filled the square, but none would withstand him. An old woman, a neighbour, stuffed her fist into her mouth to stifle her grief and averted her gaze.

'That is what would have happened to your little girls, if you had done what this Khalil Sourani asked,' Hamouda told them savagely. 'For the accommodation would have been bigger, the next time. You are all fortunate that I am here. Now you will know better.'

They cried out through their fear, wishing to appease him. A boy of twelve or thirteen, held up his head high, his eyes burning with hatred, before they cut him down.

'And bigger.'

They slaughtered the old people.

'And bigger.'

They killed the children.

'Until there was nothing left.'

They took the wife and opened her up like a beast, leaving her dying in the bloody abattoir.

'Khalil Sourani wanted you to treat with the devil, with Satan himself. And when Satan had taken all your possessions from you, your family, your house, your lands, he would strip you of even the chance to come back, to begin anew. What the devil holds, he holds forever.'

They tore the clothes from the sobbing man. Hamouda castrated him with one blow of his knife, took out his eyes, slashed his tendons and left him flopping in the gore.

Hamouda looked about at the crowd of people, very silent in their terror.

'You are most fortunate that we, who love God, have come to save you from treating with the devil. Should Satan return, we shall come back, to deal with him and his works.'

In the morning it was fine, and Hamouda took his little son Hasan for a walk. They went past the mosque with its high minaret, through the dusty streets, past the low, flat-roofed houses where squatting women baked bread in ovens of stone and baked mud. In the courtyards and on the roofs apricots, tomatoes and bunches of brightly-coloured peppers were drying in the sun.

It did not take long to get out of the city onto the hill. An Arab shepherd was tending a herd of goats among the wild oats that had blossomed there. The city was built high up, and they looked down through the clear air over the land below. Hamouda sat holding his son between his knees.

'All the land you see before you is the land of our people, and has been since a time long forgotten. It is called Filastin. It is a beautiful land, watered by the rains and by the dew. It is the land they say that flows with milk and honey, here our sun shines on green trees and flowing wheat, and the very rocks produce sweet water for us to drink.'

The little boy stared solemnly at the country spread out beneath them.

'Evil men have come to take our land away from us,' Hamouda continued quietly. 'At first they were few, and pretended to be our neighbours and our friends, now more and more have come, to seize what is rightfully ours. The man we killed last night was one who wished to betray us to these evil men, who worship Satan, who are his servants. What we did was for God.'

'I understand, papa,' said the boy.

'This man we killed, the evil ones seduced him with honeyed words, saying that there was no harm in our living together with them. You must know who the evil ones are, what they are called. They are *walad el-mita*, the Children of Death. You and I are Christians, we live in peace with our neighbours, who worship Allah. There is no living in peace with the Children of Death. The foolish man we killed, this Khalil Sourani, was taken in by them. He allowed them to give him gifts of friendship, he listened to their promises of equality. But you must never listen to their promises, for the words say one thing, but they come from the mouth of the Devil himself, and mean another. The *walad el-mita* say they wait for their God, who has commanded them to come here, but this is a lie, for they worship Satan in his black Hell. Many, many years ago, more than there are stars in the sky, our Lord, the Son of God who was Jesus Christ, came down to earth to be with us in this land we call Filastin. He lived among the evil ones, offering them salvation. Because they worship Satan they murdered the Son of God. For their punishment they were scattered to the four corners of the earth. Now, after so many years that we can not count them, they have regathered their strength, and return.'

'Who are they, Papa?' whispered the little boy.

'They call themselves Jews,' said Hamouda.


## Deir Yassin


The dawn was coming, the grey rocks were beginning to shine pink and the first rays of the sun lit up Jerusalem on the hill. The troops in their khaki waited the stone walls, hidden amongst the olives, crouched in the dry watercourse. Gideon gripped his Sten gun with hands that were slippery with sweat. He was breathing in quick, short gasps.

The commander was at their head, a few yards from the stone arch that led into the village. He stood up so that they could see him; the light of the sun fell on his face, shone on his oiled carbine. It was Avraham Cohen.

'We are in Judea,' he said, and they heard him clearly. 'We have come back to Judea. Now let us make it clean. There is vermin in these holy places. Let us make it clean.'

He led them in at a jog trot, and they fanned out through the narrow streets. Within seconds the screaming began. Gideon was at the back, he saw a half-naked Arab man come tumbling out of his door, dressed only in a pair of loose trousers. Avraham was behind him, as he struggled to get to his feet he let loose a terrible kick with his nailed army boot, and the man fell back, buckled over and clutching himself, groaning with agony. A woman and some children followed, Avraham flinging them against the wall. Gideon went through the open door, his Sten at the ready.

There was but one large room inside, four stone walls with a stair leading upwards, and a door outside to the yard. A clay oven was set in one corner, there was a table set and the smell of baking bread in the air. Gideon stood very quiet. From outside he could hear the crump of grenades, the rattle and pop of gunfire. Above him, on the brown floorboards, something moved.

He went up the stairs, his Sten cocked, his finger on the trigger. The man of the house was gone, he had seen him thrown into the street. He was breathing more steadily.

He stood in the open doorway. A pattering, like a mouse, came from under the wood-framed bed and he could see a hand, trembling on the board, small and pale.

He heaved the bed over with one hand, and she screamed in terror, scrabbling across the boards to crouch in the corner. She had black glossy hair and olive skin. Had she not been so frightened she would have been beautiful. Gideon pointed the Sten at her, trembling slightly with excitement.

'You Arab bitch,' he whispered, and she stuffed her knuckles into her mouth to stop from crying out in fear.

He hit her with the butt of the gun, and blood began to run down her face. From outside, a woman screamed. He was suddenly aware that he was aroused as never in his life. His fingers tore at the buttons of his trousers, his eyes never leaving the girl's face. He seized her by her long hair, ripped her clothes away so he could see her body, forced her onto her knees, entered her mouth. From outside the little room came the sounds of fear and beating.

Gideon yanked the girl up on to her feet, threw her down on the bed, tearing the last of her clothes away. She put her hands over her eyes and sobbed as he violated her. Fragmented visions of Rebecca Goldman in the car went through his mind like pieces of film.

As he got up he was swaying, drunk with emotion. The girl crawled across the floor, wailing, entreating him in her foreign tongue. Her tears wet his boots as she held on to them. He shot her twice in the back. Something gleamed about her neck. He bent down and took from her a slim gold necklace.

The door burst open with a crash. It was Avraham, gun in his hand, his eyes wide with adrenalin.

'What . . . ?

The two young men stared at each other over the body of the dead girl.

'I'm making it clean, just as you said,' Gideon said softly.

He casually buttoned up his army trousers. For a moment

Avraham was a child again, soaked in blood by the van, staring at his mother's killers. A man cried out from the street, the gun twitched in his hand.

'Not me, Avraham,' Gideon said urgently. '*Them.*'

The fixed glaze vanished from Avraham's eyes, they hurried down the stairs. The room was filled with the smell of baking. Gideon took the stick and pulled open the oven door. Some flat unleavened loaves were inside, a golden brown, and he took one. Some blood splashed down onto his army tunic from the holes in the floorboards above. He went outside, chewing on the hot fragrant bread.

Jacob moved cautiously up the dirt street, using the doorways as cover. Two men were coming down, one supporting the other, who was limping heavily, a hasty improvised dressing around his thigh already staining red. They wore Irgun markings.

There was indifference, hostility even, in the gaze of the young Irgun fighter as he went past, supported by his comrade.

'You stay out of it,' he called. 'We do not need the Palmach here. We know what we are doing.'

They had a field dressing station outside the town, which Jacob had seen as he drove up. He was puzzled. What was happening? Why was only the Irgun here? He moved on into the town.

Now he could hear the noise of gunfire from within houses, the cries and the wailing of Arab women and little children. A ghastly horror was sweeping over him. The sounds of killing from the past, from the Polish pit where the SS had slaughtered his village.

A door burst open in front of him, and an old woman fell into the street. She was bare-headed and dishevelled. The soldier who followed her lashed out with his boot and she tumbled onto her face in the dirt. He cocked his weapon. It was Gideon Weiss.

'*Don't,*' Jacob yelled. He hurled himself forward, pushing the soldier violently to upset his aim. The bullets from the gun ripped craters in the dirt. Jacob grabbed hold of Gideon, turning him. His eyes were glazed.

'*Stop it!*' Jacob shouted again.

Suddenly he was standing by the pit of dead, while SS men murdered old women and children, unarmed men, lovely girls.

'No, no!' he shouted. He had a grip of Gideon's gun, forcing it down.

'No, we are not Nazis!' he shrieked. 'We are *Jews.*'

Jacob received a terrific blow that knocked him to the ground.

There were other soldiers. Blood was in his eyes, but through it he could see Gideon aiming his weapon at him.

'*He's one of us.* Don't shoot him.'

He thought it was the voice of Avraham Cohen.

Shouting and screaming suddenly broke out from a house further along the street. The door burst open and a family of Arabs tumbled out, clinging on to each other in terror. A peasant farmer, his wife, three children, two old men and and an old woman. Bare feet, simple sandals. White trousers, knotted shirts.

They were against the wall. Through the blood streaming down his face Jacob saw Gideon turn laughing. Jacob struggled to get up.

Gideon fired in short bursts, his lips parted and his head back as he laughed, and the brass cases tumbled tinkling against the stone.

## Jerusalem, 14 May 1948

It was an old brown bakelite radio. The cloth over the speaker was dusty and torn, but the bulb behind the tuning dial was still intact. Elie had found it, but he was asleep, exhausted, leaning up against the bulk of Abner, also snoring by the wall. They had been fighting for four days. Their bodies ached, hallmarked with the myriad of small cuts and bruises acquired from fighting from doorways, around walls, among rubble, in the street. Levinger was there, it was he who was searching for the station.

They were singing the *Hatikvah*. As the voices died away they heard Ben-Gurion speak. He spoke of an exiled people, who had never ceased to hope and pray for their return to their homeland.

'They reclaimed the wilderness, revived their language, built cities and villages ... The state of Israel will be open to the immigration of Jews from all countries of their dispersion.'

'At last ...,' breathed Levinger.

Out of the applause came an old, trembling voice with the cadence of a rabbi. 'Blessed be Thou, O Lord, our God, King of the Universe, who has kept us alive and sustained us and brought us to this day. Amen.'

There were tears in Levinger's eyes. 'At last,' he said again. 'I was born here, Jacob. We have waited a long time for this.'

The Irishman, Flynn, leaned with his back against the wall, watching the Jews with a faint, amused curiosity. His carrot-coloured

hair had become dark with dirt, dust, smoke and propellant. Streaks
ran across his freckled face where he had scratched himself with
grubby hands.

Ben-Gurion spoke for the last time from the Art Museum on
Rothschild Boulevard, down the winding road from where they
listened, in Tel Aviv.

'The state of Israel has arisen!'

'One thousand eight hundred and eighty seven years since Batrar,'
said Levinger.

'We had better be sure the Arabs do not do to us now what the
Romans did to our ancestors then,' said Jacob. 'We have but thirty
thousand soldiers against five Arab armies. Let's see what the others
are saying about us.'

He turned the dial slowly, and out of the static and dance music
came an excitable, voluble howl.

'Azzam Pasha,' said Levinger. 'Secretary-general of the Arab
League.'

'What does he say?'

Levinger listened. 'He says the war will be over in ten days,' he said.
'He says it will be a war of extermination and momentous massacre
. . . the war of extermination of the Jews will be spoken of like the
Mongolian massacres and the Crusades.'

'Ibn Saud says that with 50 million Arabs, what does it matter if
they lose ten million to kill all the Jews. He says the price is worth
it. You might think we need a miracle to win this war. One of the
boys said that to Zenon – do you remember him? He died fighting
with me at Bab el Wad – as we were going up in the lorry, he gave
me a great grin and said, "In Israel, the man who does not believe
in miracles is not a realist." He died fighting with a commando
knife, gripping a handful of our soil. He had not been there for
one whole day.'

'We have a secret weapon they do not have. *Ain lanu derech acheret.*
No alternative.'

'When we've won the war we can make the peace,' Jacob said
certainly. 'In twenty years we'll meet up with these Arabs and
drink beer.'

'They're Muslims,' Flynn objected. 'They don't drink.'

'So they'll drink tea,' said Jacob. 'Does it matter?'

'There now, I've never trusted a man who wouldn't drink
wit' you.'

It was hot in the little room, it smelled of gun oil and sweat.
Flynn began loading a clip, slipping the bullets in against the

spring with a steady clicking sound. In the corner, Elie and Abner snored.

The door opened suddenly and the flat evening sunshine flooded into the room. Elie and Abner awoke, reaching for their guns. A young soldier stood there; Jacob recognized his guide, the *sabra*, Avraham Cohen, the one who had ordered Gideon not to kill him at Deir Yassin. The war seemed to be making him bigger and older. Again Jacob felt the prickle of loathing he felt for the Irgun, the killers in the village. He pushed it away as quickly as it come. Cohen had told Gideon not to shoot him.

'There's fighting by the monastery,' he shouted. 'We need reinforcements.'

The soldiers of the state of Israel went out into the street, casting long shadows across the ground, checking their webbing for arms, slipping fresh magazines into their weapons. They set off towards the sound of the guns.

They came in from the sides and the back. Abner slipped as they ran up the lane behind the building, and by the time he had clambered to his feet the others were in the building. Berating himself for being such a clumsy fool he hurried after them, taking the back entrance.

Jacob and Seamus Flynn came in from the side with Avraham, jumping through the window. Jacob was first in. In the doorway an Arab froze, coming the other way. Jacob was down on one knee as they both fumbled to bring their guns up to aim. A short burst of fire from behind him blew the Arab backwards into the corridor, and Elie jumped down behind him. Jacob ran across the room, pulling the pins from two grenades and threw them each way down the corridor.

After the explosions he led them at full tilt through the dust and smoke that filled the corridor. It was light at the end, where the main hallway met the stair well. He tripped on a body lying there, hidden by the billowing dust, and measured his length. The other two jumped over him and took the hallway. Sheltering by a pillar Flynn directed a whole clip up the stairs, firing in short, controlled bursts. They were all experts on the Sten by now. Elie dashed for the corner and a burst of fire from the hall caught him in the shoulder. He was bowled backwards, blood squirting high in the air. A body came tumbling down through the air from the stairs, and landed with a noise like a sack of wet sand being dropped from a height.

From his position at the entrance to the corridor Jacob lobbed
two grenades over the banisters into the hallway. After they went
off he heard someone screaming through the singing in his ears.
He ran round with Avraham at his side, and they saw two men
dragging a third away, a slim man with a shock of tight curly black
hair. At his side Avraham suddenly howled like an animal. He
sprayed the corridor with fire, holding the trigger down until the
gun was empty and caught one of the men as they hurried around
the corner.

From upstairs there came the shattering of glass and a rising
shriek as the defenestrated victim fell to earth. Then suddenly all
was quiet, just the singing in the ears, the pounding in the chest. Dust
entered the lungs, clinging to the sweat of the body and blackening
the dryness of the mouth.

Jacob vomited, his body arching in uncontrollable cramp. When
the pain left him he managed to straighten up, and found Flynn
binding a dressing over Elie's wound. Avraham had gone.

'You got the leader with the grenades,' said Elie. 'They've
run away.'

They went through the building, securing it. It was Shmuel who
found him, lying in the conference room. The head lay in a corner,
bloodied beyond recognition. The body was savaged with knives,
the genitals were missing.

'In the name of Jaysus . . .' Flynn whispered. 'Who is it?'

Jacob bent down and pulled at a strap running over the dead
man's shoulder.

'These were not red with his blood before. It is Abner. They
have massacred him.'

Shmuel, who had planned to be a rabbi, and wound up a
soldier, slipped his *kippa* onto his head and in a voice half-wail,
half sing-song, in the old manner, began to recite the *Kaddish*, the
prayer for the dead.

'*Yisgadal V'yiskadash shmay rabah* . . .'

Flynn took off his beret, and crossed himself.

As they were carrying the big man out they met Avraham.
Tears had cut channels into the caked grime and dust on his
face.

'He got away,' he whispered. 'They got him away.'

Jacob took him by the shoulder.

'Who?' he asked.

'Hamouda,' said Avraham, and his body shook with sobs. 'He
killed my mother.'

# Haifa, February 1949

Jacob, Seamus Flynn and Elie sat watching the battered old merchantman slowly enter Haifa harbour. Ruth sat next to them on the pine log half in the sand, gently rocking an elderly perambulator on its springs. It creaked in a pleasing manner as she did so. Two small heads stuck out of a woolly blanket, one at each end, snoozing under little white knitted caps.

The men had a large brown bottle of British beer sealed with an attached rubber, porcelain and wire cork, which they were democratically passing between them. The war was over, the blue star of David on the brand-new flag of Israel flew from the Red Sea at Eilat in the south to above Haifa in the north.

The decks of the ship were crowded with people.

'There she is, the *Atzmaut*,' said Jacob and raised the bottle in salute.

'Now that's a grand name for such an old ship,' said Flynn, taking his turn with the beer.

'The *Independence!*' Jacob cried triumphantly. 'The last of our people from the British camps.'

'They cannot keep our citizens, now we are a nation at last,' Ruth said joyfully. 'Now every Jew in the world can come in.'

Jacob caught her eye and they smiled with unspoken understanding at each other.

'Every Jew in the world . . .,' Flynn mused. 'That would be a lot of people in such a small place, to be sure.'

'We shall take them, every one,' Jacob promised, and passed the bottle. He bent forward to peer adoringly at his two sons.

'Real Israelites,' Flynn said amiably. 'Born here as well.'

'The first for many centuries,' Ruth said proudly. Jacob slid over to sit on the log beside her, and slipped his arm about her.

'The Germans didn't win,' he said suddenly. 'We won.'

'Of course y'did, Jacob,' Flynn said sympathetically. He knew his former commander, the way that memories from the past attacked him without warning.

'I am sorry,' Jacob muttered. 'I was thinking of David, my brother. He should be here.'

Ruth smoothed a woolly hat over a little head.

'He lives again in David, our son,' she said. 'All the dead live again, they live here in Israel. David has risen from the ashes of death, has defeated those would have killed us, just as the David of old slaughtered Goliath.'

They passed the bottle around again, and Franz and Ibach, who had killed David, retreated into the cave inside Jacob's head.

'What will you do now, Seamus?' young Elie asked. His arm was free from its sling. 'Will you be staying here, or going home, you being an Irishman?'

'I'll go back, just to see how idle and fat my brothers are becoming, and to have the pretty girls admire me for being one so brave, but whether I'll stay, now that's a different matter.'

'What's wrong with Ireland, then?' said Jacob.

'There's not much opportunity for a young fellow like me. I'm not ready to sit and grow potatoes. I'm one of the fighting Flynns, did you know that?'

'I heard,' Elie said gravely, and the Irishman gave him a friendly shove.

'I'm looking for the land of opportunity,' said Flynn. Down at the dock they could hear the band playing, see the people waving and dancing.

'And you won't find that in the old world,' he went on. 'I think I'm for the empire. I'll go to Rhodesia, I'm thinking. Rhodesia. One of my brothers now, he sent me a letter telling me how to do it . . . The British government, they want people out in their colonies, they'll help pay your way.'

He sat looking out over the grey water of the harbour, his thoughts on a different land.

'And what with me being a man fresh from the fighting, I might do well in their army.'

'This Rhodesia, Seamus,' Ruth said curiously. 'Where would that be, now?'

'Why in Africa, to be sure. The British own most of Africa, you see. This Rhodesia, there's a northern part and a southern part, and a bit on the side called Nyasaland.'

'Rhodesia . . .,' Elie mused. 'A funny name, that.

'Rhodes,' Jacob said suddenly. 'Cecil Rhodes, isn't that right, Seamus? He dreamed of an empire from the foot of Africa to the very tip, I think that's what I read. From the Cape to Cairo.'

'And that's what there is. There's South Africa at the bottom. And now not just Cairo but Tel Aviv!'

'Different countries, all the way,' Jacob countered. 'There's the French Empire too, don't forget.'

'All empire!' Flynn cried ebulliently. 'Here we are, sitting in the new Jewish Empire! Joshua, Saul and David would be proud of us, boys.'

'Saul and David!' Ruth laughed, looking at the two little boys. 'You see what happens when you come to Israel, Seamus, you don't have one child but two!'

'Grand wee fellows they are too,' Flynn said, smiling at them.

'What about you, Jacob?' Elie asked, turning to the older man. 'Will you stay in the army?'

'He will not,' Ruth said quickly. 'Why would he need to stay in the army? The fighting is done, they will probably disband it soon.'

'I would like to study,' said Jacob. 'But I will have to make some money first. Perhaps I will find the fabled hoard of Cousin Avraham.'

'He was a jeweller, this cousin?' said Seamus. 'That's what you said.'

'His fame was great in these parts, all those centuries ago. At the court of King Guy his work was greatly prized. But he was captured after the great Battle of Hattin by Saladin himself, and we, his ancestors, know no more of his fate.'

'How would you be knowing, then, if you found some of his pieces of jewellery?'

'He worked in gold, and used it to mount precious jewels. Always stamped upon the gold was his mark, the seven-stemmed *candelabra*, with the letter A for Avraham as its base.'

'And where would you go looking?'

'Among the ruins, where the Crusaders had their famous fortifications. The castle of Krak des Chevaliers, I should like to look there. And there is Jerusalem itself, of course, where King Guy ruled.'

'You will have to wait awhile then. The great castle is in Syria, is it not? And King Abdullah still has Old Jerusalem.'

'We are making peace with the Arabs now,' Ruth protested. 'Very soon, we shall all be free to visit each other. Jacob will be able to go to Jerusalem, and if he wishes, the King can come here. The war is over.'

In the pram one of the little boys opened his eyes and gave a great yawn. Down at the dock, the immigrants still flooded down the gang plank into the Promised Land.

Gideon and Avraham stood at the side of the road looking up at the ancient city set amongst the rock. They still wore their army fatigues, their Sten guns slung over their padded jackets.

'It shall be ours,' Avraham muttered malevolently.

'All the lands God gave to Israel, that are written down in the Torah, they shall be ours,' Gideon agreed. 'Yet even Joshua and David only took one city at a time.'

'It is true,' Avraham admitted. 'We can still learn from the great war leaders of old.'

He shuffled his feet in his army boots, and looked down the road. Nearby were some Arab peasants tending their land. The steady clack of mattocks was the only sound in the chilly air. The young soldier's face wrinkled with loathing as he looked at them.

'We should have made the land pure,' he muttered.

'Give us time,' said Gideon.

Avraham peered hopefully down the road.

'Where's that lorry? You know, I can smell those Arabs from here. They stink, Arabs do.'

A tremendous blow smacked him in the side, spun him round, sent his weapon flying across the road. In his ears was the flat crack of a rifle firing. He was lying on the tarmac, and his arm wouldn't move.

Gideon crouched down in fear and bewilderment, bringing his gun up, but he could see nobody. Avraham grabbed a hold of his leg, he reached down and seized him, dragged him to the ditch and fell in beside him. Avraham's mouth was opening and closing silently, his jacket was ripped and splashed with a great gout of sudden red blood.

Gideon peered through the brown scrub that marked the side of the road. Up on the hill a man moved, loping up towards the city. An Arab. He could see the head-dress and the long rifle. He brought up his short-barrelled sub-machine gun, but the marksman was already well out of range, perhaps half a mile away.

He poked his head up, hearing sudden, fearful voices. It was the Arab farmers in their field, gathered together, a little knot of four, peering about them to see where the shot had come from. Bending low, he was on his feet, leaving Avraham in the ditch, running for the field.

He burst through the hedge and there they were, still babbling at each other in their filthy language. They clasped their mattocks protectively as the young Jew advanced towards them, his weapon held up and pointed at them, their sun-seamed faces fearful as they saw the hate that possessed him.

'Get going!' Gideon screamed.

They did not understand the foreign language, or his American accent, but the ferocious gesture of his gun was unmistakeable. They stumbled forward over their turned earth, moving as quickly as they could.

He marched them down the road, to where Avraham was lying in the ditch, the blood spreading over his jacket. His eyes were closed, his breathing shallow.

'Aaii . . .,' said one of the farmers, and took off his head-dress to form a bandage.

'Don't bother,' Gideon said, from behind him.

The heavy spring of his weapon was back, the safety off. High up on the hill, the sniper vanished among the rocks. In the distance Gideon could hear a coming army lorry.

He squeezed the trigger, firing in short bursts as he knew how. The bullets blew the first farmer off the road and into the ditch. The red head-dress hung for a second in the air like a flower.

Two of the Arabs ran, and he cut them down with a joy in his heart. The fourth raised his mattock high, staggering forward towards him with a death cry in his throat and Gideon blew pieces off him at short range. The gun suddenly clattered and went silent in his hands. His ears sang in the silence.

He went forward and jumped down into the ditch next to Avraham. Heat radiated from his weapon, a little smoke drifted up from it like fragrant steam. A wonderful smell filled his nostrils, the smell of propellant and the blood of Arabs. From the ditch there came a sound of joy, the sound of an Arab gargling in the agony of death.

Avraham opened his eyes.

'They came to kill you,' Gideon told him, and Avraham nodded weakly. He knew that Arabs came to kill Jews.

'But I got them,' said Gideon. 'I got them dead.'

The lorry came grinding up the road. Gideon stood up, still holding the Sten, and flagged it down.


# Cairo, Egypt, April 1949


For the survivors of victorious wars the gratitude of those they fought for rarely lasted longer than the victory parade, or amounted to more than a few pennies, shekels or piastres in the tin cup of the man crouched by the wall with faded ribbons still on his chest. For the survivors of defeat there was nothing.

For the Egyptian *fellahin* walking out of the Negev desert from Faluja in his officers' wheel tracks, there would be little waiting on the other side of the Suez. The wounded were largely left to die where they were rather than taken home to die as there were no facilities left for them. What there was had already been taken up.

It was not much. Hadj Hamouda had a dirty pallet in the corridor of what was called a hospital, where the staff carried out the bodies of the dead and robbed the dying. Hamouda survived because he had a knife, some money and his son. The knife prevented him being robbed, the money enabled him to buy food and water, and his son went out in the street to get it. They shared the pitta and hummus together.

Hamouda wanted to get out. He already had dysentery, and recognized the place for what it was, a place where the sick died, not one where they recovered. However, for him it was a humiliating twenty-minute crawl along the corridor even to reach the noisome latrine. His torn legs suppurated from their wounds, the summer and the heat were coming, without proper medication they would become gangrenous. Hamouda had seen it happen to others.

Outside the air was fresh; through the dusty, half-opened windows he could hear the sounds of the *Ikhwan* Muslim Brotherhood as they rioted against the enfeebled rule of the *ancien régime*, corrupt and fat in its Nile-side salons. He longed to be out there with them, for there was a new world to be made, an old order to be overthrown and dispossessed, a new invader to be expelled. Like the pus that seeped from his legs, his hatred of the Jews that had done it to him and had taken his land, suppurated in his mind. He had to get out, to shed blood, to slaughter Jews.

Hamouda lay by two planks, one long, one short. He had sent his son to find them, him and his street urchin friends. In the long one he had carefully drilled a hole using his knife, at one end, and another through the centre of the short one.

Along the corridor came a squeaking. A crowd of dirty and ragged children, bright of eye and tooth, were pushing a bodyless perambulator, upon which rested the frayed seat of a cane chair. Hamouda embraced his son.

'Where did you find it?'

'There is a place by the big block, where the effendis throw out what they do not want,' said Hasan proudly. 'There I found it.'

'And the other thing I asked for?'

'Here, *ya sheikh*,' a dishevelled seven-year-old said, and produced a wooden-handled screwdriver from the folds of his dirty clothes.

'That was with the wheels too?'

'No, *sidi*, I stole it!'

They all laughed, and Hamouda reached in his pocket and gave him a couple of precious piastres. Then they crouched down on their heels and watched, fascinated, as Hamouda unscrewed the front axle of the pram, and affixed it to the short plank. The chassis of the pram supported one end of the long plank, and he lashed it into place. A precious bolt pierced both holes and joined the two planks, so that the vehicle under construction might steer. With the remainder of his rope Hamouda tied the seat of the cane chair into place.

'There,' he said, when it was done. 'A chariot, an Arab Rolls Royce. It is the way of the world, my children. The Jews who have stolen our land come from the West, they understand the ways of the West, its machines of war. But one day, it will be our turn. One day, we will not ride in Arab Rolls Royces. Now, lift me on, and with care, I beseech you.'

Hadj Hamouda was not out of place in the small gathering. Palms provided pleasant shade in the red-earth square, and an effigy of the Empress Victoria stared disapprovingly over the ragged crew of Arabs beneath her. All were poor, most young, and several, like Hamouda, injured or maimed from the recent fighting. It was the first anniversary of Palestinian Martyrs' Day. Hamouda's urchins stood around the carriage he had made.

There were speeches, in fiery, flowing Arabic, and poems read, embedding the wrongs that had been done into the very fibres of everyone there, promising the justice and revenge that was to come.

Hamouda had the boys push him forward, and a place was made for him, the men looking down at the crippled fighter. He pushed himself upright in his chair and held his fighting knife high. Blood had stained its blade, and run bright down the handle, the blood of Khalil Sourani, his wife, and his children. The blood of Abner Goldstein, whose head and genitals it had removed.

Hamouda held it high, and it glittered in the sun, just as bright as his eyes.

'Knives and guns make the blood gush in torrents.
Haifa and Jaffa are calling us.
*Fedai*, go ahead, do not worry:
Gunfire and screams break the silence of the night!'

There was a swell of approval as his voice died away. It was good
to think of such things happening to the Jews.

As the meeting broke up, a thin young man, with full lips and
prominent, bright eyes came over to Hamouda, and knelt down by
the carriage.

'I liked your poem,' he said. 'We must all become *fedai*, sacrifice
ourselves. Only with knives and guns will we take back our land.'

'You are a Palestinian?'

'My full name is Mohammed Abdel-Raouf Arafat al-Qudwa
al-Husseini. My family is of Abu Saoud, I was brought up in
Fakhriyya, in the Old City.'

His nostrils twitched, he could smell the infection in Hamouda's
legs.

'You are in pain,' he said. 'You received these wounds in the
fighting? You are yourself of Filastin?'

'My mother was Syrian, a great beauty. My father was of Palestine,
he owned much rich land around Ramlah. Land the Jews have taken
from us. I was with the Army of the Jihad under Kader el Husseini.
I was injured fighting not far from your home, not far from the
al-Aqsa mosque.'

The young man waved an extravagant hand around to include
the men in the square.

'Soon you will be back in your lands of Ramlah. We shall drive
the Jews out.'

'Not unless we do much better than last time,' the wounded
veteran said levelly. 'The Jews were formidable. They had trained
men with combat experience. They were efficient and ruthless. We
had fine words. At least Kader was brave. Kaukji was a buffoon.
The Jews are telling the world how the Israeli David slew the Arab
Goliath. Let me tell you, as one who was there, it was the other
way around.'

The young man looked at Hamouda thoughtfully with his intelligent, protruberant eyes.

'You are someone it is good to talk to,' he said. 'Are you receiving
treatment?'

'No,' said Hamouda. 'I need a woman, a nurse to dress the
wounds. And a doctor, with medicines to make the wounds heal.'

'But you came here,' the young man said admiringly. 'To be with us. Tell me, since you have fought them, if the Jews fight so well, how should we drive them from our land?'

'With terror. With men prepared to kill and burn. Make the land they have taken a place that no one can live in or bring up their family. Make the ones who now pour in look again when they wake up and find their neighbours dead in their beds, look again and leave the way they came.'

Hamouda ground his teeth together with hatred. He looked his fellow Arab straight in the eyes. Suddenly, he spoke in English, for Arabic was the language of hyperbole, of extravagance and fire. It was difficult to order coffee without a flight of rhetoric, but English, English was cold and exact, and meant what it said.

'We must slaughter them all,' he ground out. 'Each and every one, old, young and unborn.'

The other nodded soberly. He had understood.

'You will need to be well again if you are to accomplish such deeds. I am at the university. I am on the executive of the Palestinian Students' League,' he said grandly. 'I shall see to it that your wounds are healed. Come with me.'

The little procession set off along the dusty street towards King Fouad I University in the distance.

'I am Hadj Hamouda. How do they call you, from your many names?'

'My friends call me "Yasser" – the easygoing one. I am always late! I am called Arafat. Yasser Arafat.'


# New York, May 1949


Gideon Weiss sat in front of his father's wide wooden desk looking out at the street, while his father sat behind it looking at his medal. He fished inside his jacket, and tossed a folded square of paper next to it.

'They gave me that, too,' he said, casually.

His father put the Ott medal down reverently, and unfolded the paper. There at the top was the blue six-pointed star of David, and beneath the brief citation. His father the rabbi looked at it in wonder, his eyes filling with sudden tears. He looked old to Gideon, worn

before his time. In the fullness of his youth, Gideon felt contempt
for him.

'At last,' he whispered, and he stroked the blue star. 'After all
this time.'

He wiped his eyes with the back of his hand and read the
citation.

'Four armed Arabs . . .,' he marvelled.

'It was nothing,' said Gideon. 'We were battling all the time.'

The rabbi peered at the signatures at the bottom.

'David Ben-Gurion . . .'

'I was in the Irgun to start with. Good people, father . . . but they
had that trouble and I went with Zahal. That's the regular army.'

'And you won this . . .'

The colour and wealth of the Brooklyn street below still swamped
Gideon, after the drab dun-and-dust, the worn poverty and coarse
clothing, the sweat and the striving he had left behind. Below people
swaggered in bright clothes, huge shining cars glided by, the air was
filled with the scents of spices and perfume, it rang to the vibrant
sound of car radios playing dance music. Gideon smiled to himself.
He looked good, he knew it, the hard physical effort of soldiering had
made him fit and lithe, his white teeth showed up against his tan.

In his mind he saw an Arab girl on her knees, begging him for life.
His fingers, casually resting on his knee twitched as they relived the
moment. Blood splashed across olive skin and a tingle of excitement
ran across his back. Below on the street a young black girl in a
tight red dress sashayed across the street with a girlfriend, dodging
between two long cars, their teeth very white in their very black
faces. He watched them with a sudden lust, a vision of spattering
blood jumping in his mind. Niggers were like Arabs.

Gideon brought his attention back inside the room, and found
his father watching him.

'I'll want to borrow these,' he said, indicating the medal and the
citation. 'I want to show them to the people round here.'

'Fine, dad,' Gideon said agreeably. He hid his contempt. He still
needed his father.

'There was a bit of trouble round here when you left all of a
sudden.'

'I had to fight for Israel, dad!' Gideon protested, open-eyed. 'I
couldn't wait any more.'

'Yes, *I* know that, son. It was Rebecca Goldman. She . . . she was
in one heck of a state. That night you left. Hysterical and screaming
. . . she claimed you raped her, son.'

His father looked at him with penetrating gaze, and Gideon looked him straight back, shaking his head in disbelief.

'Rebecca . . . she kind of thought she was my sweetheart, you see, dad. When I made up my mind to go that night I took her for a drive and told her. You just wouldn't have believed it, dad, she started screaming at me, saying I'd get killed, and she wasn't going to let me go. I had quite a struggle with her, I had to get her out of the car, and I drove off. She almost made me miss the ship . . .'

'There were . . . some teeth marks in her breast, they say. Her mother saw them . . .'

Gideon shook his head again in disbelief.

'Like I say, dad, she was acting real crazy. I just hadn't realized she had this thing about me . . . I guess she just did it herself, to get me into some kind of trouble. I tell you, she was that mad . . .'

'Yeah . . .,' his father said thoughtfully. 'She got quite a few people round here fooled, I guess . . .'

He looked up again from the desk.

'What you got planned, then, son?'

'I'm going to be a rabbi.'

Meir Weiss nodded.

'Have to go to Yeshiva,' he said.

'Yeshiva Mirrer's here in Brooklyn.'

'Ultra-Orthodox?' the rabbi asked doubtfully.

'I've been where Israel is born again,' Gideon said, his voice suddenly cold. 'God wants it only one way.'

'Okay . . .'

Meir looked at his son curiously.

'You're going to have a synagogue, like me? I never had you down as that patient. You settle for something, Gideon, if you do that.'

'I'm not settling for anything . . .,' Gideon said softly, his eyes suddenly glowing. 'Nothing but the most.'

'Most?'

'I'm going into politics.'

'Yes . . . I think I could see you there, son,' Meir said, enigmatically.

He carefully folded up the citation, put the Ott medal into its little case and gathered them up in his hands.

'In that case, son, I think I had better do a little politicking of my own. These will help.'

'You going to see Rebecca and Mrs Goldman?' Gideon asked blandly.

'They will be first on my list,' Meir agreed.

'I'm real sorry Rebecca got so hysterical, made up all those lies about me,' Gideon said sincerely. 'I know she'll have seen the error of what she did, by now.'

'We don't have so many genuine heroes who've fought for Israel,' Meir said, and there was a certain steel in his voice. 'I believe I can get her to revoke her story.'

'The Goldmans are not that devout. But maybe she can be straightened out.'

'Maybe,' Meir agreed.

'Best for her not to see me. Might light those fires in her heart again.'

'Yes . . .'

Meir paused by the door.

'Gideon.'

'Yes, dad.'

'Don't get any other girls getting so passionate about you, like Rebecca did.'

Gideon smiled his wide-eyed smile.

'Hey, dad, all the girls love a hero.'

'Hero all you want to,' his father said quietly. 'That wasn't what I meant.'

A jumble of feelings, of memories that were unpleasant suddenly rose up in his mind, and the rabbi made a great effort to push them back.

'You . . . you've been quite wild, as a kid. I'm not saying you're not a good son, and a good Jew. You just proved that here. But your mom and me, we've had to get you out of quite a few scrapes . . .'

He paused, his mind in the past.

'More than scrapes, some . . . and what I'm saying, son, is that problems have a way of getting bigger as you get older. If there was anything like Rebecca Goldman again . . . or something worse than that . . .'

Gideon smiled disarmingly.

'Dad, dad. Don't worry. And I can solve my own problems now.'

He pointed a finger at his father like a pistol, and the smile widened into a grin.

'All four, in one go . . .'

'Okay, son. You remember what I said though. Especially, you want to go into politics. They look for dirt on a man . . .'

'I know . . . don't worry, I'll stay clean.'

He stared at his father with a look of utter certainty.

'I'm going all the way, you see. I'll be president one day.'

Rabbi Meir Weiss went downstairs and out into the sunny street to drive over to Queens, where Mrs Goldman lived with her daughter Rebecca, who couldn't go out alone any more. He shook his head, trying to get rid of the image of the cat. He had had to get it off the wall, it had screamed when he tried to lever out the nails.

He remembered Gideon coming round the corner, asking wide-eyed what the noise was.

# PART IV

## Beit Hakerem, Jerusalem, August 1953

JACOB came through the pretty garden. By the wall was what looked like a converted chicken coop. It had a door, however, and he knocked on it. It opened immediately and a burly young man poked his head out.

'Ariel Sharon?'

'That's me. Don't I know you?'

'Jacob Ben-Levi. I was in the attack on Latrun when you were shot.'

'I remember you! Come in.'

Going in, Jacob could see how Sharon had opened the door so quickly. There was little room for anything else other than the bed, a table and some chairs, one of which he had been sitting on. There was another person there, a young man, with thick black hair and a strong set to his jaw.

'Avi, this is Jacob Ben-Levi. He was in the Palmach in the war.'

Avraham Cohen stood up and held out his hand.

'Jacob and I know each other,' he said. 'We fought together, here and there, in the war.'

Jacob looked at him thoughtfully as he shook his hand, then turned to Sharon.

'You're recovered from the wound?' said Jacob.

'Yes,' Sharon patted his lower abdomen. 'It went in here and came out at the top of my thigh. Just missed what was important. When the doctor saw me he said if I had been feeling amorous instead of fighting it would have been entirely different! So what can I do for you, Jacob?'

'Somebody threw a grenade through my bedroom window last night.'

'Anyone get hit?' Sharon said sombrely.

'We were out on the porch. Me, my wife and two little children.

I am a man of peace, I do not want to live in a country where
people throw grenades into other people's houses. You and I and
a few thousand others won the war, we beat our enemies, and now
the army can't stop a bunch of Arabs from coming over the border
and bombing anyone they want. What the hell is going on?'

'There were six hundred thousand of us in forty-eight. Now there's
one and a half million. From the point of view of Zahal all their energy
is taken up simply trying to organize an army. They can't cope with
the terrorists. The men who could, who fought in forty-eight, were
a people's army, and when it was over they all went home.'

'Well, one of them has come back. I heard that you were the
person to see, if you wanted to do something about it. What are
we called?'

'Unit 101.'

Avraham Cohen loved the land, he knew every wrinkle of it, could
move through it without being seen. He had walked from the Dead
Sea to Jerusalem through the land controlled by the Jordanians and
not been caught by the Bedouin, who would, after some while, have
killed him. That was the year the war was won. The following one
he made a trip alone across the desert to the ancient city of Petra,
to see where Moses had struck the rock, once again without being
caught. It was this feel for the land, his ability to move through it
while always knowing where he was that had made Sharon give him
the lead of the group approaching the Palestinian village. There were
twenty of them, Cohen, Jacob and three other Unit 101 commandos,
and fifteen paratroopers. All were heavily laden with arms and packs
of TNT. They paused on the stone-walled terrace.

Cohen pointed back the way they had come.

'That is the way home. To the left of the lights of the farms is
the path over the hill. Beyond that, the woods of Ben Shemen.'

He turned again.

'Here, the village through which the terrorists who killed the
mother and her two little children came.'

Jacob took a deep breath. There was no escaping it. Sudden
memories of the dead in Deir Yassin flickered through his mind
and he forced them away. This was different. The State of Israel
had to protect itself. Cohen was not a killer, but a patriot.

'Let's go,' he said thickly.

They slipped through the olive trees and the orange trees, heavy
with the scent of citrus. They dropped their packs silently at the edge
of the wall and waited. From the position above them that looked

down over the hillside of orchards came the occasional clink of a
rifle, the shuffle of a shoe.

From the other side of the village came the sudden rattle of Sten
guns, and the bang of grenades going off in the stone streets. There
was a startled muttering from the handful of Arab home guard
soldiers, and they saw dark figures running to peer down the street
in the direction of the fighting.

They came over the wall and massacred them all in one fusil-
lade of fire.

The runner said the villagers were pouring past the roadblock by the
score. From a deserted cafe an Arab radio was spilling quarter notes
into the empty square. They began setting the TNT charges against
the foundations of the big stone buildings.

It took a long time. Before they blew each one a paratrooper went
into the house, shouting out a warning. The reprisal was to destroy
the village through which the killers had come, not to murder the
occupants.

Jacob lit the fuse, and heard Cohen shout a warning. Then they
ran out into the dust-filled air. There was a roar from the end of
the street as a charge went off, and as the house crashed into the
road Jacob heard a terrified sobbing.

He ran inside the building, into the kitchen where food lay
abandoned on the table, chairs kicked over. The noise was coming
from under the sink. He pulled open the door, and a little girl was
hidden in the tiny space, biting her finger in an attempt to muffle
her fear.

The TNT went off as he was coming through the doorway, it blew
him across the street and into the square. A rain of dust and plaster
fell down on him. He felt something gripping tight to his neck, and
opening his eyes, he saw the little girl in his arms.

He had a good bed in Hadassah, by the window, so he could look
out and see the cars and people moving on Balfour Street. It was
well enough to be entertained, while you waited for it all to mend.
Cohen stood by him, with some sweet white grapes he'd brought
from the Bezalel market.

'What went wrong?' said Jacob.

'They weren't used to us being any good,' said Cohen. 'For years
our idea of a reprisal raid was to sneak in, blow up a couple of outlying
buildings and run away. So when we came this time some of them
just hid in the cellars, or the back rooms. Those stone houses are

big, they have three generations in there. They hid, and waited for us to go away.'

'How many?'

'Some seventy, they say.'

The young man's face was cold.

'They're casualties, just as the young mother and her two children were. Like my mother was.'

Cohen looked out over Balfour Street. He took one of the grapes he had brought, and crushed it between his teeth.

'It was stupid of you,' he said. 'There's so many of them, so few of us. We can't afford to lose soldiers.'

Jacob saw the slope again, on the river bank, heard David's voice calling out for him.

'I heard a voice from the past,' he said. 'From the KZ. An SS man was trying to kill me and my brother. I escaped, he didn't. I heard him cry out for me to help him.'

'I hear my mother scream,' he said stonily. 'But she isn't telling me to spare Arabs.'

'You and I have both lost those we loved,' Jacob tried to explain. 'But I do not want to kill all the Germans. If Karl Franz and Engineer Ibach were in front of me, yes, I would kill them. But not all Arabs.'

'You don't seem to understand where you are,' Cohen said, his eyes focused on a different world. 'They outnumber us, hundreds to one. They hate us. When they can, they kill us. Your lot, the Jews in Europe, the Ashkenazi, they walked like a lot of sheep into the gas chambers, so I hear. Well, no more. We are *Giborei Israel*, we are the heroes of Israel, we are the descendants of David's warriors, we are the Maccabees. When an Israeli walks by, Arabs should be afraid to step on his shadow.'


## Kirya, Tel Aviv, December 1954


The peace, what there was of it, seemed to have aged Levinger worse than the war. His once curly hair had thinned, his face had taken on a lean look. He stared at Jacob as intently as ever.

'How long has this been going on?' said Jacob.

'Did not Moses say to the twelve heads of the children of Israel: ". . . spy out the land of Canaan . . . see the people that dwelleth

therin, whether they be strong or weak . . . and the land, whether
it be good or bad, fat or lean . . . be ye of good courage and bring
of the fruit of the land"?'

'They came back within forty days, with reports of a land flowing
with milk and honey,' said Jacob.

'But even more important, with warnings as to what the Israelites
would face if they went in there. Ignoring warnings of enemy strength
leads to disaster.'

Levinger stared at the picture of the two young people, one man,
one woman, hanging from the gibbet.

'We need to know,' he said. 'We need to know, just as much
as Moses did. What's happened to the Nazis? Will they rise again?
What are the Arabs doing? What friends are they making?'

He put the grisly image on his desk.

'Poor children. We didn't get much from them, and now we'll get
nothing. The whole network blown, and poor Max dead. The one
person who *did* give us what we wanted, caught up with the others.
Dead. Suicided for fear he'd talk under further torture. Our best
man. General Neguib's personal friend. One of the last things he
told us was that Nasser is arranging an arms deal with the Soviets.
But now we don't know any more.'

He looked one last time at the two young Egyptian Jews hanging
strangled from an Alexandrian hook, and then turned the photograph
over. Outside, it was dark in Kirya. Nearby the prime minister had his
office, a modest three-storey, red-tiled house surrounded by trees and
a garden. In similar buildings the general staff were to be found, as
well as the offices of the growing intelligence community. The three
most important elements of the new state lived side by side. Over
the sea the *goyim* were preparing to celebrate the birth of the son of
their god, but for Levinger it was one more working day that did
not end until late.

'I do not know what Moses called his spy service,' said Jacob.
'What do we call ours? What is this?'

'*Ha Mossad, le Modiyn ve le Tafkidim Mayuhadim.* The Institute
for Intelligence and Special Operations. The Institute, or Mossad,
for short.'

'So this is where you went, once the old man got rid of the
Palmach. But why am I called here from my studies of Middle East
History?'

Levinger smiled in a friendly fashion.

'Jacob the historian! What are you doing?'

'I wish to write the history of this land. From before we were thrown out by the Romans, to when we returned in triumph. All of it. These rivers, this sea, those forests, deserts, plains. The people who came and went. Everything.'

'That's some project,' Levinger said admiringly. 'Real research. It'll take you a while.'

'It will,' Jacob agreed. 'So why are you dragging me from this congenial task to talk about spies?'

'We have to get someone into the top echelons of Arab society. It's a small world up there. We need to know, and we need to put the fear of Israeli intelligence into the Arabs. Get in and you get to know. When they see that we always know they will feel fear.'

'I know a young soldier who talks like you. Avraham Cohen.'

'Avraham Cohen cannot pass for an Arab.'

'He would be delighted to hear you say that,' Jacob said dryly.

'Fortunately we do have those who can pass. Do we not come from 62 different countries? We even have blue-eyed blonds who could have served in the *Liebstandarte*. At the other end we have the dark-skinned, aquiline types who can pass for Arabs. We need one such. One who has a flair for language. Who is quick witted, able to think on his feet. A commando. Trained in the hardest school of all. Who survived the KZ, the *kazett*.'

'You seem to be describing me,' said Jacob. 'But I could not pass for an Egyptian.'

'The Egyptians are not Arabs, they are Africans. Poor, miserable and backward, old King Abdullah used to say, and spit into the corner of his tent as he did so. He was wrong, though, for it is the Egyptians who are likely to cause us the most problems in the not too distant future. No, Jacob, you could not pass for an Egyptian. I would never ask you to try. But you could pass for a Syrian. An expatriate businessman, with a fortune made in America. A Ba'thist patriot, returning home to participate in the great national revival. The Arab affairs section has an identity prepared as foolproof as is possible. We have such a man. Salem a-Din is his name.'

'How does that help us to know what Nasser is doing?'

'The Syrians are edging into the Egyptian orbit. There is talk of a defence treaty, even a kind of merger, a united republic. With our man in among the Syrian leaders we would know.'

'I am circumcised.'

'Frank had his reversed. It can be done. If they get around to pulling your pants down it is all over anyway.'

'Even for the State of Israel I will not have my dick carved up by a surgeon. And I am tattooed, with a number.'

'Plastic surgery. Your arm, not your prick.'

'I am married, with two sons.'

'The most perfect cover. Who would suspect? David and Saul are six, and old enough to be instructed in the new role they are to play. They speak American English. Perfect.'

'Children too must become spies?'

'We live in a terrible world, Jacob. We are surrounded by our enemies, who wish nothing more than to kill us. Your sons are not circumcised.'

'I would not allow it. It sent me to the KZ. My wife Ruth said I was a poor Jew, something I have never denied. I am a poor Jew but a good Israeli.'

'A good Israeli is what we need in Damascus.'

Jacob pointed to the face-down photograph. 'You had good Israelis in Cairo.'

'We are a young state. We've had to do so much in a hurry. But do it we must.'

'You organised that fuck-up in Cairo.' Jacob pointed out. 'Asking me to get involved with them in something similar comes under the heading of *chutzpah*.'

Levinger smiled. 'Everyone's got their own version. What's yours?'

'The man who murders his own parents and asks the court for leniency on account of his being an orphan. That fits with what you want from me.'

'The guys who screwed up are gone, Jacob. And it wasn't all bad, you know. Our agents were good. They were dedicated, they improvised under pressure, they kept their heads. You can do these things too. *And* we're getting more professional. I'll be running things. We go back a long way, don't we?'

'These emotional strings do not work with me,' Jacob said coldly.

He sat for a few moments, deep in thought, while Levinger watched him calculatingly.

'No,' he said. 'I will not do it. I must think of my wife and sons. It is not right that I expose them to such danger.'

Levinger gave a small shrug.

'Are you not exposing them to danger by *not* doing it? Do you not expose us all to danger, if we are made weak by not knowing the war plans of the Arabs?'

'You will get someone else!' Jacob burst out. 'You yourself said there are many of us who can pass for Arabs. Get someone who has yet to pay.'

He tapped his chest violently with finger and thumb.

'Me, I have paid. Have I not brought in immigrants under threat for my country, have I not run arms for my country, have I not fought for my country? I have done enough, I am tired. I wish to go back to my study of our history at the university.'

Levinger looked calculatingly at him.

'I bumped into Ruth, the other day,' he said casually.

'You did?' Jacob said in surprise. 'She did not say anything about it to me.'

'I asked her not to, until I had talked to you. *She* no longer thinks you should retire to academia just yet.'

'I know what my wife thinks,' Jacob said stiffly.

'She wants the best for all us Israelis,' Levinger urged. 'You study history, you know that nations must protect themselves by whatever means possible. Ruth understands that. Look how fine the country is! Just a few years ago, we were a bunch of immigrants and concentration camp survivors fighting for our land – now we are a nation. Crops grow, children are born, we prosper! The cities are expanding to take in the Jews who come to us from all over the world. We build roads, plant orchards, create reservoirs, begin industries. We are a part of the great host of nations once more. You, Jacob Ben-Levi, have played your part in that. You cannot give up now, because what you have helped make still needs protection. And you, you aren't quite as impartial as you are making out. Haven't you been in America recently with your family?'

'I may holiday where I choose,' Jacob said stonily.

'To be sure. But you have been trying to find Ibach.'

'It is not right . . .,' Jacob muttered. 'My brother David is dead, and so many others . . . and he and his have not been brought to trial! No, no, worse than that! It is not even acknowledged that they were murdered in Dora!'

'How's that?' Levinger said quietly.

'Dora does not exist. Not officially. I have been to the Army and the Air Force, I have been to the State Department. I have talked to a senator. You may ask the American government all you like, but they will tell you they have no record of it. I can go to London and still show you a bomb site created by a V2 rocket! Where did it come from, that rocket? Dora, which does not exist. Like my brother David does not exist. Like Engineer Ibach does not exist. What of me, do I exist, and my memories, my pain?'

'Jacob,' Levinger said softly. 'I need you.'

'Get someone else.'

'I want the best. I want you. Ruth thinks you should go.'

Jacob folded his arms across his chest.

'My wife does not make my decisions for me,' he said resentfully. 'I shall not go.'

'You have to,' Levinger said softly. '*They* insist that you go.'

'Who does?' Jacob cried indignantly. 'Who makes these demands on me?'

'*They* do. Those who didn't survive. The six million that stand behind your very shoulder.'

The two men stared at each other in silence, and then Levinger spoke again.

'Hear their voices, Jacob. They cry out, you must hear them, for no one heard when they lived. What are they saying to you?'

Jacob spoke slowly and wearily.

'They say I survived.'

## Damascus, Syria, September 1955

The long green Cadillac had become something to be remarked on, to be shown to visiting relatives from the country if seen gliding past the mosaic pavements on its way to or from the luxurious Abu-Ramana quarter of the city. There goes Salem a-Din, they would say, who has so much money you could not count it all in a week. He made his fortune in America, dealing in liquor, tobacco and women, and has come home.

Jacob's neighbours included the top officers of the regime, who had spent the past few years playing musical villas as *coup* succeeded *coup*, the wealthy merchants and fledgling industrialists, the diplomatic representatives of the foreign legations. The Syrian Army Headquarters was not far away. Jacob's villa was well-situated. Its owner landlord had demanded an outrageous rent for it, and a year in advance, and Jacob had simply reached into the pocket of his suit and paid him in Syrian pounds on the spot, thus beginning the legend of the fabulously wealthy Salem a-Din, whose riches one could not count in a whole week. Given the garrulity of the Arabs, Jacob had estimated the story would have passed through the neighbourhood like contagion.

So it had proved. In the shaky, faction-ridden city it was men like Salem a-Din, wealthy, ardently patriotic, well-connected and generous that everyone who mattered wanted to know.

The golden light from his villa gleamed on the polished paintwork of the Cadillac, and on the lesser vehicles of his guests and the teeth of their chauffeurs as they elaborated upon the delights their masters enjoyed inside. The evening air was filled with pleasing scents from the garden, for Salem a-Din had imported a wondrous machine from America that sprayed his exotic plants with water, not simply once, but twice a day. They could hear it, the drivers swore, swishing to itself in the dark.

Jacob's guests inside could not hear it, for the buzz of voices, both deep and soft, the chuckles and silvery laughter drowned it out. Along one wall dishes of food, highly coloured and spiced were arranged, and the men who talked together, and to the attractive, curvaceous girls that circulated in the rooms came from time to time to help themselves.

The brass, the top army men, the ones who ran the place liked to be informal after working hours. Fine surroundings, soft rugs on the floor, imported hard liquor, good food, attractive young women circulating, these were the ingredients for success. Jacob knew it, you could usually find present, future and sometimes past members of the governing elite present at his cocktail parties.

Jacob drank orange juice. Stupid Muslims, he thought, as he always did, while sucking on his non-alcoholic beverage. Jacob kept the girls at his parties well-supplied with scarce and unobtainable luxuries, and in return encouraged them to make the high-ranking officers boast of their exploits, connections, secrets, all of which they reported to him. It was a simple formula which worked. Its products were transmitted to Tel Aviv on Jacob's small secret radio transmitter every week.

Jacob circulated through the shoal of men in dress uniforms and dark business suits. The air smelled of liquor and perfume. Through a partly opened door he could see the huge oak table was already set with dishes. They were indifferent to the temperature of food, provided it was highly spiced, oily and plentiful. On salvers was a whole roast lamb, a brace of turkeys, a coop of chickens, a flock of stuffed pigeons and a small regiment of side dishes with everything from rice and almonds through tehina to salad.

'*Ahalen wa-Sahalen, ya* Sheikh!'

A tall, imposing man in high-ranking military uniform came through the throng, which parted for him. He was beaming at Jacob, who smiled back with unabashed enthusiasm.

'General Saif! You came after all!'

'A man does not lightly miss one of *your* parties, Salem,' the officer assured him.

Jacob snapped his fingers and the waiter who observed him at all times was at their elbow with a loaded silver tray. Jacob held up his orange juice ironically.

'Can I tempt you, General?'

A huge smile enveloped the man's face.

'I am not one of you Muslims!' he boasted. 'I am an Alawi, my faith allows me to drink what I please.'

So saying he helped himself to a tumbler of the finest Scotch whisky, and took a good gulp.

'Stand there, my man,' he ordered the waiter. 'I have been out on the borders, and have a thirst.'

'How goes it, on the border?' Jacob asked casually.

'Well,' said the general, tossing back the remainder of his drink and helping himself to another. He had, as Jacob knew, a great capacity for alcohol.

'I saw the land they call Israel, those who have taken it for their own,' General Saif went on. 'She was spread out like a lovely green carpet below us. Through the binoculars I saw the girls working in the fields of the Tel-Katsir *kibbutz*, and Lake Kinneret. A beautiful land, waiting there to be suitably ravished by us Syrians.'

'To be sure!' Jacob cried. 'It shall be ours. Living space, access to the sea, fine agricultural land.'

'It is all ours anyway,' Saif agreed. 'All *bilad al-Sham*, the lands of Damascus, that run from the Taurus Mountains to the desert, from the Euphrates to the sea. And one day we shall drive the bastard Israelis into that sea.'

'Why do we not do it? Are we afraid of the Israeli army?'

Saif shook his head as around them men came and went, and liquid-eyed girls led them on.

'No, the Israeli army is good, but with fifty million Arabs, what matter if we lose ten million, provided the Jews are expelled. No, what protects Israel is public opinion in the West. The Israelis created their state on a wave of public sentiment because Hitler tried to eliminate them. A pity he didn't do a better job. They won the War of Independence against the odds. The Western public sees it as . . . Hollywood. You will know about this, Salem. You have lived among the bastard Americans. They wouldn't allow the Israelis to be massacred, any more than they would . . . what is this dog that is a film star, Salem?'

'Lassie the Wonder Dog.'

Saif nodded his head in a kind of amazed disgust, that there existed a race so base that they made sentimental films of dogs.

'That's it. The Americans think the Israelis are . . . pure in heart. That they are . . . Snow White, and that we Arabs are the wicked stepmother. One day, they will know differently, they will know the Jews for what they are, and on that day, we shall fall upon them like wolves, as we once did, so many centuries ago.'

A handsome young man in slacks and a white blouson shirt stood casually by the wall, keeping his eye on Jacob.

'I was hoping you'd make it to the party. There's someone I'd like you to meet.'

General Saif's gaze flicked up and followed Jacob's.

'Yes,' he said quietly, approvingly. 'I will meet with him.'

He bent confidentially towards Jacob.

'Colonel Adnan al-Malki was shot dead through the efforts of Egyptian intelligence, working through Akram al-Dayri, the Military Police Chief.'

'Yes . . .,' Jacob said slowly, thinking about this nugget of news. 'That would make sense. Malki was the leading Ba'thist officer in the army. Al-Rahim who shot him was SSNP.'

'Which has given the Ba'th the opportunity to destroy the SSNP,' said General Saif. 'And who benefits? Egypt. The SSNP was pro-West, and anti-Arab nationalist. The Ba'th wants to unite all Arabs against Israel and the West. The United Arab Republic they're talking about may emerge after all.'

His dark eyes regarded Jacob carefully.

'*Shu dinak* . . . where do we stand? That is what we must all ask ourselves in these times.'

'You know you can count on me . . .,' Jacob murmured. He motioned with his hand, and the young man was at his elbow.

'Kamel, I'd like you to meet General Saif.'

Kamel bowed from the waist, his teeth gleaming.

'The honour is mine, General . . .'

Jacob murmured a couple of pleasantries and moved on through his guests. He went out of the rooms containing his party, and along one of his marbled, colonial corridors. He slipped a key from his pocket and opened a door, closing it behind him as he went inside.

He was in a little room, not much bigger than a cupboard. A chair was there, facing one wall that was glassed. On the other side of the wall was a small but luxurious bedroom, tastefully lit by a few small lamps placed about the walls.

Jacob sat down behind the mirror, and waited patiently.

A few minutes later the door opened in the bedroom opposite, and General Saif came in with Kamel. He paused to lock the door behind him. When he turned round Kamel was hanging his blue slacks over a chair. Saif went forward, and ran his hands lustingly over the young man's long bare legs. They embraced, and Kamel's quick fingers undid the general's belt, so that his own trousers fell to the floor.

In the little room, Jacob watched expressionlessly. At intervals, he pressed the shiny silver button of the cable release, and the Hasselblad camera mounted in front of the special mirror recorded the scene.

General Saif fell on his knees, taking Kamel in his mouth, and again Jacob pressed the cable release.

He bent over the arm of the sofa, and on the film every detail of the joy on his face was recorded as Kamel buggered him.

When they had left, Jacob wound the film on. He wrote down the time and place, and the names of the participants on a small section of sticky paper, which he affixed to the film before putting it away in its little container. He reloaded the camera, ready for the next time.

It was late by the time he saw the last of his guests to their cars. Most, even the Muslims, were staggering. He saw to it that the girls were paid, and gave Kamel an extra sweetener. He knew he would be needing the young man again. Then he went through to the family quarters at the back of the house. He peeped in at the boys' bedroom, where David and Saul were sleeping without care. He was unable to resist creeping in and kissing each softly on the cheek.

'I love you,' he whispered and they, his future, slept serenely on.

Ruth was in their living room overlooking the garden. The curtains were drawn. She was clad in a fine striped gown, suitable for the wife of a prominent Arab millionaire. She had been waiting for him, but at some stage of the long night had sat down to rest and was now asleep on the sofa.

He stood looking at her for a few moments, at first with simple affection, and then with a certain alarm. Tiny beads of sweat shone on her forehead, rimed her upper lip; she made feeble movements of her arms, as though pushing something away, moaning quietly. Jacob went quickly, sitting by her and taking her hands.

'Ruth ... Ruth darling, it is me, Jacob,' he said kindly, firmly. 'Wake up, darling, you are dreaming.'

Her eyes opened and stared without recognition at him.

'*Wstawach*,' she whispered fearfully. An atavistic terror stabbed into his own heart. '*Wstawach*, get up, get up. *Wstawach* . . .'

'No,' he insisted. 'Not *wstawach*. No get up. Ruth, this is me, Jacob, your husband . . . we are in Damascus, not in the *kazett*. We are free, Ruth. No *wstawach*, no get up, get up.'

'It is dark,' she persisted. 'They will beat us if we are late for the factory.'

Her hands slipped from his and cradled her shoulders against the blows she knew were coming.

'The whip, it hurts so . . .'

'No whip, no *wstawach*,' Jacob repeated. 'We are free . . .'

The beginnings of recognition came into her eyes.

'Jacob . . .?'

'It is me, Jacob,' he reaffirmed comfortingly. 'We are free . . .'

He held her in his arms as she burned with a sudden fever.

'Why are we here?' she whispered.

'We are fighting for Israel.'

She clutched on to him with hands as wet as though she had been under water.

'Who made us come to this place?'

'We came because we must.'

'Who made us come?'

She managed to sit up. Sweat was running down her face in rivulets, her glossy hair was soaked.

'I know now,' she muttered. 'It was the dead . . .'

She looked at him without the glimmer of a smile.

'The dead bade us come,' she said. She staggered to her feet.

'I shall take a shower,' she muttered. 'Come and talk to me, that I may know what it is I am doing here in Damascus.'

She pulled ineffectually at the striped gown that stuck to her body, dark with sweat.

'Help me, Jacob.'

He stood behind her and undid the zip, peeling the wet silk from her. The white scars shone in the light, he could see her ribs, she had lost weight.

She went into the bathroom, dropping her clothes on the floor, and stepped into the bath, pulling the shower curtain around it.

'How did it go? There was a party.'

The water hissed inside the curtain, and Jacob bent to pick up the clothes and put them in the wicker basket.

'Well,' he said. 'I suppose. Yes, well.'

'You sound doubtful.'

'I got Saif on film. Now I must blackmail him.'

'What did you get?'

'He's queer.'

'So what? Aren't most of these Arab men buggers? "There is a boy over the water with a bottom like a peach, but alas, I cannot swim." Isn't that right?'

'Saif is the one with the bottom,' Jacob said, sounding depressed. 'He likes it done to *him*.'

'Nail him to the wall,' she said savagely. 'He'd do it to *us*.'

'He would,' Jacob admitted. 'He thinks Israel is a part of *bilad al-Sham*. The lands of Damascus, the ancient Syrian empire.'

'We were there first. It is ours by right.'

'Were we?' Jacob said doubtfully. 'What of Sargon the great?'

The water ceased to hiss, and the curtain was whipped back.

'Never question our right to our land!' Ruth shouted angrily.

'No,' he said placatingly.

'Who cares what some Syrian barbarian did three thousand years ago!'

Jacob handed her a towel and she began to dry herself. She was a handsome woman, thought Jacob. He wondered why she had lost weight. Perhaps the stress of this double life they led. It was enough to wear anyone down. Perhaps if things had been different they would have had more children. Perhaps she was right, one had to guarantee the future.

'He was a very great general and a great king,' Jacob said mildly. 'Well before David.'

Ruth peered at him over the furry edge of her towel.

'Let us save history for when you are back at the university,' she suggested, more quietly. 'I am glad you have this pederast Saif. Is he not an important man?'

'Commander of the border defences.'

'So squeeze him like a lemon,' she said coldly. 'Then nobody will come for *our* children in the night, and take them away.'

She got out of the bath, and finished drying her feet.

'You have a kind heart, Jacob,' she said warningly. 'You think maybe you can change the nature of people. *I* know you cannot. Let us just make our land safe. This Saif would have us all strung up like chickens, if he knew.'

'You're right,' Jacob admitted. 'I'll tie him up, next week. I'll go out to the castle tomorrow with the boys, and I'll do it when I get back.'

'Good.'

'Will you be all right?'

'Yes. Don't worry about me. I am all right now.'

She went through to the bedroom, where a nightdress was lying on the bed, and pulled it over her head. She sat on the edge of the embroidered counterpane as Jacob undressed, staring at the rugs on the floor.

'You know ... when we escaped, when I met you, I thought it was all over, all in the past, all the terrible ...'

'I know.'

'But it does not go away,' she whispered. 'It comes back. Tonight I was back ... *there*. And in my mind I knew it was a dream, that if only I could wake up it would be all right. There was a voice, it said *wstawach*, get up, get up, and I knew if I could wake I would not be there. And I awoke, and I was still there.'

'You are here now,' Jacob said. 'Not there.'

'It is difficult,' she said, very wearily. 'It is very difficult to leave *there*, and come here.'

Jacob got into bed next to her, leaving the light on.

'You have to promise me something,' she said, gripping his hand fiercely.

'What?'

'You must promise. Say you promise.'

'I do not know what it is you ...' Jacob protested.

'If you love me you will promise,' she insisted.

'Very well,' he said slowly. 'Then I promise.'

'If one day I am back in the *kazett*,' she said clearly, 'and I cannot leave – do you understand? If I am awake, if the voice says, *wstawach*, get up, get up, and I am awake, but I cannot leave, if I cannot come back into the world where my body is, if my mind stays in the *kazett*, if you cannot summon me to be with you, I do not want to stay.'

'No.'

'So you must not let me stay there. You have promised not to let me stay there.'

'I don't ...'

'You must kill me,' she said clearly. 'You must not leave me at their mercy. If you cannot rescue me, you will kill me. You have promised.'

Jacob put his hands under the thin nightdress and held her.

'I am with you always,' he assured her. He began to stroke her to soothe the memories.

'We all have our memories. I think of Ibach, I remember David ...'

In her turn she began to run her hands over his body as well.

'Never leave me, Jacob.'

'Never, never,' he assured her. Why was she so thin? Her full breasts were small, he could feel the ribs. He must try to feed her up.

'Remember your promise,' she said, as she pulled him to her.

'We shall not need that,' he said. It was the strain of this life they led, he was sure of it.


## Krak Des Chevaliers, Syria


'Beat you to the top!'

Jacob watched in amusement as his two sons raced up the ancient stone steps where once the Knights' Hospitallers had moved about their tasks of subjugating an alien land.

'You take care,' he called as they managed a dead heat at the top. 'I'm going to poke about some more for Cousin Avraham. Shout if you want me.'

'We will,' they yelled. 'When can we have something else to eat?'

'We've just had lunch.'

'We're still hungry.'

'Soon, then. Don't go near the edge.'

He left them, identical in grey flannel short trousers and white shirts about to become grubby devising some game that involved lobbing pebbles. Jacob entered the shade of a long cloister, broken up by arches and coffered ceilings, his eyes scanning the stone walls and windows. Over on the hills the morning mist was rising to hang in curtains of cloud. From the vast castle one could see for miles. Once, the fierce men within it had dominated that land, but they were long gone. They had left on their brightly caparisoned horses, armed with the highest technology of the day and with their god, both of which they had been sure would never let them down. They were men of iron, armed cap-à-pie they rode horses equipped with stirrups; they could charge with their lances *couched*, as they crouched behind their large, teardrop-shaped shields. Those they did not spear in their terrifying armoured charge they hacked to death with their fine swords. They carried the holy cross of their salvation in their midst, accompanied by its bishop. They were invincible.

In fact, as Jacob knew, they were not. Both their god *and* their technology had failed them in the fearsome arid heat of the desert. Their cross had been captured and its bishop put to the sword. Those left alive at the end of the battle had been marched into captivity and never saw the great castle of Krak again.

Jacob wandered about the great ruins, imagining the presence of its ghosts. A cool breeze blew on him from an ancient window in one vast round tower and he peered out. Below he could see his Cadillac, in which he and the boys had ridden all the way from Damascus.

Next to it was a Citroen.

He frowned. The ruined castle was normally deserted except for the wild animals that made their home there, the birds that nested in its cliffs. The only signs of human life he had found was an empty round cigarette tin left by some British soldier from the days of occupation.

He moved back from the window in a soldier's reflex, and stood for a moment, gazing at the wall as he thought.

Who could it be?

Had somebody followed him?

Suddenly, something broke in on his mental queries. He was staring at something carved on the wall.

It was a menorah, a branched candlestick, with a capital letter A taken from an illuminated manuscript for its base.

'Avraham . . .?' he whispered.

Then he turned, for he could hear footsteps. He came out of the round room of the tower. A young Arab man in a white *keffiyeh* was coming briskly along the ruined rampart. He beamed as he saw Jacob, and waved enthusiastically.

'Hello, hello!' he called.

Jacob smiled back in greeting.

'Hello. Is that Citroen down there yours?'

'For my sins! I would rather have your Cadillac, Mr a-Din.'

The young man stopped in front of him, still smiling.

Bright, protruding eyes as sharp as a squirrel's looked at Jacob from under the folds of the white *keffiyeh*.

'I have heard of the wondrous car of Salem a-Din as far away as Gaza,' the young man beamed.

'You are a Palestinian?'

'More than just a Palestinian,' he boasted. 'But about the car. Myself, I covet a Thunderbird. Did you buy it in America itself?'

'Why yes. That was where my business interests were – and are. I like your head-dress, by the way.'

It was unusual to see a Palestinian so clad. The young man was scruffily dressed except for the *keffiyeh*, which was pure white linen, held to his head by twin black rings.

'It is my battle dress!' he said gleefully. 'The fighters who struggled against the British and the Zionists in Palestine in the revolt twenty years ago wore it as a part of their uniform. Now that we Palestinians fight to regain our land I wear mine. I have just started doing so, it will become everyone's fashion, now.'

He grinned. This one's worth watching, thought Jacob.

'You have the advantage of me, Mr . . .'

'Arafat, Yasser Arafat.'

They shook hands warmly.

'How are things in Gaza?' Jacob asked. The tiny strip of land was crammed with Palestinian refugees. 'Do the Egyptians give you trouble?'

'In Gaza we may shout out loud, I am a Palestinian. There we are organizing ourselves for the liberation of Filastin.'

He looked intently at Jacob.

'I have heard that Salem a-Din has returned to his native land because he is a patriot. Does his concern extend to the dispossessed of Filastin?'

'I am not a pan-Arabist like Nasser. I believe that Syria must become strong in order to help the Palestinians help themselves. But tell me, what brings you to this remote place?'

'I am President of the Palestinian Students' League. I travel widely, seeking to knit together those who have been scattered. We have to learn from the Jews themselves, our enemies. That is something I have learned. Know your enemy.'

'And when you know him, what will the Palestinians do?'

'We will fight!'

Arafat dropped his voice.

'The struggle is beginning. There are those among us who are *fedai*, ready to offer up their lives. The first commando raids into Israel have begun.'

'I have heard.'

'We need money,' said Arafat. 'Money from wealthy men.'

'We must meet again,' promised Jacob. 'I would like to know more about these commando raids.'

'Perhaps you would like to come to Gaza . . .,' suggested Arafat.

'To be sure . . .,' Jacob murmured. He waved a hand about him, indicating the ruins. 'You are expecting a gathering of the students of Filastin here, perhaps?'

Arafat chuckled.

'No, no.'

He bent towards Jacob.

'I have come that the ghosts of the past may talk to me.'

'Which ghosts? The crusaders, the Knights of the Hospital of St John in Jerusalem?'

Arafat looked into Jacob's eyes with his own liquid ones, which were suddenly completely without humour.

'The crusaders are back, Salem a-Din.'

He waved a hand towards the south, where Israel lay.

'They have returned, so I am asking the shade of the great Saladin how to drive them away again.'

There was a clattering of shoes coming up a stair.

'Ah, that will be Hadj . . .,' Arafat murmured. 'Hadj is one of us, he fought in the war against the filthy Jews.'

A well-set man a little older than Jacob came up out of the stairway. He had curly black hair, he looked at them both with inquiring, intelligent dark eyes. As he came over, Jacob saw that he walked with a limp.

'Hadj!' Arafat called ebulliently. 'Come meet the famous Salem a-Din, he of the great green Cadillac!'

Hadj Hamouda stared at Jacob for several seconds. Then he reached inside his jacket and took a heavy blue revolver from his belt.

'I do not see Salem a-Din,' he said grimly. 'I see the man who threw a grenade at me in Jerusalem.'

He pointed the gun at Jacob. Arafat threw up his hands in alarm.

'Hadj! What are you doing?' he cried in horror.

'I assure you . . .,' Jacob began.

'You assure me nothing!' Hamouda snarled. 'Yasser, I *know* this man is not one of us. He is a Jew.'

'A Jew . . .,' Arafat repeated, bewildered by the alleged sudden change in Jacob's persona.

'In the war I led my men into a house the British had abandoned,' Hamouda explained. 'We went in from the front and unbeknown to us the Jews came in from the back and the sides. Inside the house, we met and fought. The Jews were led by a sergeant – in the hallway he threw a grenade at me. I was wounded with the wounds you found me with, in Cairo. My companions dragged me out. For me the war was over. But I remember the face of that sergeant as though it were but yesterday.'

Hamouda stabbed the thick blue barrel of the British Webley revolver at Jacob.

'It is this man,' he insisted.

He did not take his eyes off Jacob and was standing far enough away to make it impossible for Jacob to disarm him.

'Who did you say he claims to be?' he demanded.

'Salem a-Din,' said Arafat. 'I assure you, he is famous in Damascus.'

'Famous? Famous for what?'

'He is immensely wealthy, he has returned from America. But Hadj, he is known as a patriot . . .'

'I assure you it is . . .'

'Assure me nothing,' Hamouda snapped. 'And this recently – returned, very wealthy citizen Salem a-Din, he consorts with the upper levels of society?'

'Of course,' said Arafat. 'He knows everybody.'

'Everybody . . .,' Hamouda said softly. 'Everybody who matters.'

He nodded to himself in satisfaction, his dark, unwinking eyes never leaving Jacob.

Fifteen feet above him, two small faces silently and carefully peeped down from an empty, teardrop-shaped window. Jacob forced himself to keep his eyes on Hamouda. The impassive faces of his sons vanished.

'He is a spy!' Hamouda spat. 'A Jewish spy.'

Arafat looked at him calculatingly, and nodded in agreement.

'We shall take him to Damascus, where the proper authorities will reward us with power and influence.'

From somewhere above, Jacob heard the faintest scratching, as of mice.

'I am Salem a-Din, as I say I am!' he boomed suddenly. 'By all means let us go to Damascus, where you will apologize to me for ever having doubted my word.'

Hamouda smiled, very thinly.

'No, we shall not.'

He bent down and patted his maimed leg.

'It remembers you, Mister Jew, and so do I.'

The heads of David and Saul appeared above Hamouda. They looked down on him, each holding a large rock high in their small hands.

At an unheard, rehearsed signal, the rocks flew. Hamouda, as alert as a cat, was twisting to meet the threat as the ancient lump of stone crashed into the side of his head. The second caught Arafat on the thigh, knocking him sideways, and Jacob dived for the revolver as it clattered across the stone floor.

He clasped it, on his knees, and pointed it at Arafat. Hamouda lay unconscious on the flags, blood oozing from a gash in his scalp.

'Attend to your companion,' he ordered, and wincing in pain, Arafat crawled over to him. Jacob looked up at his sons and they cheered in triumph.

'Come down,' he said and he heard their feet slapping on the stone.

'Quickly now,' he ordered. 'Down to the car.'

He glanced back at the two Arabs as David and Saul raced ahead. Hamouda's eyes were open, he looked at Jacob.

'I will remember you yet,' he whispered.

Jacob caught his sons up as they piled into the Cadillac. Jacob wrenched open the bonnet of the Citroen, flinging it open on its long hinge. He held the muzzle of the revolver against the distributor and pulled the trigger. In a colossal bang shards of bakelite and metal flew everywhere.

He jumped into the Cadillac, bringing the giant eight-cylinder engine to life. As he gunned the throttle, and the whitewall tyres squealed, high above he saw Hamouda and Arafat staring angrily down at him from a window like the eyesocket of a skull.

'I got him, I got him!' Saul crowed, bouncing up and down on the wide bench seat. 'Whack!'

He turned to his brother, next to him.

'You missed,' he said accusingly.

'I did not!' David protested. 'I knocked him down. He was further away, too.'

'You both did well,' Jacob reassured them. 'Without you I should be a prisoner now.'

Saul looked up at his father assessingly.

'Are we going home now? I mean, back to where we belong?'

'Yes.'

'Goodygoodygood. No more filthy Arabs.'

'Do you hate them so?' Jacob asked, without taking his eyes off the dusty track. The heavy, strong tyres of the Cadillac rolled over the stones without problem.

'I don't like them. *He* does.'

'Do you, David?'

'I like playing with them,' his son said quietly. 'They're the same as us.'

'They are not!' Saul cried. 'He's so silly.'

'But if you hate them so, how did *you* play with them, Saul?' Jacob asked.

The small face looked up at him, deadly serious.

'Mum talked to us, before we came. She said we were going somewhere we'd live in a big house and have lots of nice things, but we must never never tell anyone that we were Jews. We had to be like the Arabs, 'cause if we didn't they'd come and take us away like they did with all our aunts and uncles and grandmothers and grandpas, and stick us all in a great hot oven and die.'

In the mirror the great castle was small.

'Did you do that for Mama?'

'Yes. I . . . love my mummy.'

'Do you love me, Saul?'

'Of course we do!' David shouted.

'You never told me about it,' said Jacob.

'Mum said you were busy, beating the Arabs. So I played with their sons.'

'Was it very bad?'

'I pretended,' the little boy said coldly. 'But now I don't have to pretend any more. And I hit the Arab with the gun with my rock, whack!'

'How are we going home, Dad?' David asked.

'In the aeroplane. Like I promised.'

Both brothers cheered, and bounced on the seat.

The wadi floor was smooth and dry, only ten miles from the Damascus suburbs. Jacob drove all along its length, and then stopped the car. Opening the vast trunk he took out two powerful black flashlights. Their lenses were fitted with red and green filters. He set them up, one each side, pointing up, and back down the wadi. Then he got back in, turning the car around to drive back the way they had come.

A third of a mile along it going by the milometer, Jacob stopped again.

'David, this will be your one. Saul, yours is the other.'

'I know, Papa,' they chorused.

'I know,' he said patiently. 'I know that we have practised this many times. Now, listen to me. I want you two boys to stay here, for I must go and get Mama. The aeroplane will come, when it is dark.'

The boys capered in joy, making zooming noses and running about the wadi with arms outstretched.

'Listen, listen. If Mama and I are late, you are to get into the

aeroplane anyway, and fly off in it. You understand? Mama and I
will come another way, then.'

The two boys stopped capering, and eyed him thoughtfully.

'You promise?'

'I promise. When it is dark and you hear the engine, you are to
light the torches. Not before. And whatever you do, wait until the
aeroplane has stopped.'

'*And don't walk across the front!*' they choroused.

'And don't walk across the front,' he agreed. He went to the huge
rear of the Cadillac, opened it and took out bottles of water, a large
umbrella and some packets of biscuits. He added a bag of Dinky
toys, and some paper and pencils. They had just discovered how to
play battleships and hangman.

'Here. Remember to drink plenty of water.'

'We will!'

He bent to kiss them both.

'This is super!' David grinned.

'Very super,' Jacob agreed. In the mirror, he saw them making
the umbrella into a den, anchoring it amongst the rocks.

Jacob came off the desert onto the road, and the setting sun glowed
golden in his wide rear-view mirror. Soon he was in the straggling
edges of the shantytown. Small children waved in delight to see the
vast green car rocket by, old men eyed it in bemusement.

A store, festooned with French and English enamelled advertising
signs, for cooking oil, soap and cigarettes came into view. A thin
black cable travelling to a pole. A telephone.

He slowed, swinging in onto the dirt front. A crowd of ragged
urchins and barking dogs appeared from nowhere. When Jacob got
out of the car they surged about him. He chose the two largest
and most villainous of the children, and dashed some paistres into
their palms.

'See to it that nobody touches the car,' he ordered, and his small
guards burst into action, shouting and pushing the others away from
the immense vehicle. They formed a ring about it, staring in awestruck
delight at its gleaming form.

Jacob pushed back the flyscreened door and a man in an old shirt
and baggy brown trousers came scurrying over.

'I need to talk on the telephone,' Jacob ordered regally, and the
proprietor ushered him to it. He inserted the jeton, and dialled his
number, the circular ring clicking rythmically as it went around.

'Hallo?'

It was Ruth. She was home.

'Darling. Jacob.'

'Yes, Jacob.'

He could sense the sudden alarm in her voice.

'I met friends,' he said. 'They wanted us to get together later.'

It was a rehearsed drill.

'Of course,' she said, trying to keep her voice steady.

'So I should call our other friends and make the appointment for tonight?'

'That's right. I'm on the edge of town. I should be with you in half an hour.'

'Yes,' she said. 'I understand.'

She put the telephone down and ran into the bedroom. Concealed behind tiles in their bathroom was the morse transmitting set they used to send their messages to Levinger. She took it out, set the aerial, donned her headphones and began to tap the key.

What she sent was a prearranged code, only to be used when all was lost. She waited, her hand hovering anxiously on the key, the earphones silent. She was beginning to sweat, she wiped her hand nervously on her loose trousers. As she went to transmit her message again, bursts of morse came squeaking through. The aeroplane would be coming.

She acknowledged, and stuffed the radio set back into its hiding place. Half running, she dashed into the bedroom, looking about her in a half-panic, wondering what to pack and take.

She looked out of the window, and an army truck was drawing up at the gate. It halted, and troops began to pile out. Throwing down the dress she had picked out of the wardrobe, she ran for the stairs.

The automatic watering system was bathing the back garden in water, as she ran through the waving arcs of spray. There was a wall, covered with an ancient fig tree, which she scrambled up like a tomboy, the huge leaves swaying madly; then she jumped down into the lane behind.

Jacob would be coming in from the west. She knew the road and she ran. Dusk was beginning to fall, urchins ran alongside her yelling with delight. The air was scented with the spices of cooking, the aroma of lamb and flat bread.

She stumbled onto the edge of the road, her chest heaving, her clothes stuck to her as if coated with glue. In the gloom something huge hissed by, lit up with great lights.

'*Jacob!*' she screamed.

The Cadillac swayed on its great soft springs, the tyres squealing and she ran towards it, jumping in beside him.

'Troops!' she gasped, heaving air into her lungs. 'Troops at the gate.'

The tyres howled as Jacob turned the car, wheeling on its springs. The huge headlights illuminated a concourse of amazed humanity staring at them from the sides of the road, and Jacob gunned the throttle back the way he had come.

'*Where are the boys?*' she shrieked in terror.

'At the wadi,' he said reassuringly. 'At the wadi, as we practised.'

'Yes . . . of course. Jacob, *what happened?*'

'Just real bad luck. A couple of Palestinians came by the castle, just like a pair of tourists. One was the leader of an Arab fighting platoon in Jerusalem. The one who killed Avraham Cohen's mother, the one Avraham was so upset I didn't manage to kill. I got him with a grenade, and it seems to have fixed my face in his mind. *He knew who I was.*'

'How did you get away?'

Jacob smiled.

'The boys dropped a rock on his head.'

She turned to look behind her for pursuit.

'They managed to raise the alarm,' she said bitterly. 'Why didn't you kill them?'

'It isn't easy to shoot people in cold blood,' he observed. 'I thought they would be marooned out there for a couple of days at least.'

'It is us or them,' she said viciously. 'Will you never learn?'

'I have killed enough people!' he shouted. 'It is not something one grows to enjoy.'

She turned away from him. In the huge headlights the shanties were flicking past, lessening in number. Scrub and rock lined the road.

'Listen!' he said, wanting to bring her back to him. 'Just before they appeared, I saw, carved on a wall, Cousin Avraham's menorah!'

Something faintly resembling a smile flashed across her face. It was not a happy expression.

'My husband, the historian,' she said quietly. 'Well, you will have to wait a while before you see it again.'

'I wonder if he went to Jerusalem . . .,' Jacob said thoughtfully.

He looked across at her in the soft light of the instruments, as the great car boomed down the centre of the road. She was staring at nothing, her face slick with water and sweat.

'You won't let them take me,' she said. 'Will you?'

'No,' he said.

'They have come for me once.'

\*     \*     \*

On the still night air, he heard the sound of engines.

'Is that the plane?' Saul asked.

'No,' said Jacob. 'It's the sound of trucks. Wait here.'

He climbed up the side of the wadi. Across the plain lights were moving. In the city and for miles around, people knew of the great green limousine of Salem a-Din, whose wealth it was not possible to count, not in a whole week.

He looked down, and saw the shining red and green lights, bright enough to catch the eye of a pilot in the sky. He scrambled back down. From the car he gave his two sons two more flashlights.

'I have to move the car,' he said. 'When you hear the noise of the plane you stand here, like this, and wave the torches. If I am not back, you get yourselves and mama into the plane. Do it the way we have practised. Get in from the side.'

'We don't walk at the front of the plane,' said Saul certainly. 'Because it would hurt us.'

'That's right, darling. It would hurt us. I must move the car, so you stay with mama.'

Jacob got into the car, and drove back along the wadi. The lights gleamed bright, red and green. He passed them, and went on in the dark, driving cautiously by the dim starlight. The floor rose and through the rocks he could see the lights of the lorries in the distance.

A mile from the landing strip by the milometer he stopped, switching off his engine. In a land where a man could drive a long way between filling stations it was wise to carry fuel, and the capacious trunk contained two large five gallon jerry cans. He stripped off his shirt, and soaked it in petrol. Then he opened the filler cap and stuffed one arm in as far as he could.

He stood in the cool night air. Amid the grinding of engines and gearboxes came the shouts of sergeants and corporals.

Through the air came a hum, a pleasant, deep-throated thrumming.

Jacob flicked his lighter and the flame ran up his shirt. He began to run back along the wadi.

The fuel tank of the Cadillac went up like a bomb, turning night today. There was a ragged roar from the troops searching the plain.

The noise from the air ceased. The pilot was side-slipping into the threshold, marked by red and green lights, and two waving white torches. Jacob heard the rumble of the tyres on the rock-hard ground. As he came gasping past his first set of markers he saw it, the big Lysander, its nine-cylinder radial ticking rhythmically, swinging the great propeller effortlessly. Two little figures were hurrying to its side, pulling their mother with them.

Jacob ran around, avoiding the propeller, ducking under the wing strut and climbed aboard.

'We're all in,' he shouted to the pilot. He had his arm around Ruth, holding her tight, with the two boys between his legs. The pilot gave it the fuel and the cabin filled with the roar of the engine. The tail rose, the tyres tapped the wadi floor one last time and they were climbing out, away from the blazing Cadillac below, the pilot carefully shielding his eyes from the glare to protect his night vision. Then they were alone in the night sky.

The two boys grinned up at him.

'We're going home,' they chorused.

'Yes,' said Jacob. 'We're going home.'

'No more filthy Arabs,' Saul crowed exultantly.

# PART V

## Tel Aviv, August 1962

'I'VE changed my name,' said Avraham Cohen. 'And so has he.'
The four men sat in the darkened room, staring at the image projected on the screen. It was hot and they were all in shirtsleeves, sweating.

'What's his?' asked Jacob.

'Mohammed Akbar,' said Levinger.

Jacob looked at the photograph on the screen.

'He doesn't look like an Arab.'

'He's not. He's former SS Lieutenant Ulrich Kraus.'

Jacob turned to Avraham Cohen, sitting in his brigadier-general's uniform. Age had not softened him at all, his face looked as though it were made from rock.

'And who are you now?'

'Shahak,' he said, and the short, ugly Ivrit words fell like stones. 'Shelesh Shahak.'

'Strength, pulverize,' said Jacob, and Shahak, who had been Cohen, nodded. Jacob shook his head to himself. Strength, Pulverize. Levinger pressed the switch and the drum rotated to bring a fresh face to the screen.

'Professor Omar Amin,' said the fourth man, a thin, alert figure with a face like an intelligent weasel. His name was Shaul Shiloah.

Jacob looked at the bleak, European face on the screen.

'Dr Johannes von Leers,' said Shiloah. 'Chief Assistant to Dr Goebbels in the Propaganda Ministry of the Third Reich.'

Levinger thumbed the advance of the slide projector and a series of faces clicked across the screen.

'General Wilhelm Farmbacher.'

Click.

'Leopold Gleim. Chief of the Gestapo in Warsaw.'

'Any more of these bastards?'

'Plenty,' Levinger said softly. 'As many as you want.'

'And where are they, with their new names and old hatreds?'

'Cairo. Back in business.'

Jacob felt the thrill of horror in his spine, sure as a knee-jerk, property of all the Jews, the thought of a Nazi phoenix.

'All those that won the world war, they're not angry any more.' Shahak who had been Cohen spat. 'They don't mind doing business with Nazi murderers. *We* mind. We remember, and we do something about it.'

'They're all the same,' Levinger agreed. 'The Americans, the British, the French. They tried a few like Goering but then it all stopped. Bastards.'

The memory of Ibach came out of its cave in Jacob's mind. It was true. All the time he had spent, all the American government departments he had tried. Dora. No such place.

'Bastards,' he agreed.

'Well, these ones are working for Nasser,' said Levinger.

'Jew-hating is becoming respectable again,' Jacob observed. 'We did well to get Eichmann and remind everyone what happened.'

Shaul Shiloah stirred. 'I was on that team,' he said.

'We're going to capture some others? Put them on trial?'

'Perhaps not this time,' Levinger said smoothly. 'Let's have a look at some more.'

He thumbed the advance on the slide projector and two new faces appeared.

'Paul Goercke. Once a top scientist on the V1 rocket programme.'

Shahak, who had been Cohen, was staring at the screen with a peculiar ferocity.

'I know who the other one is, the Arab,' Jacob said quietly. 'That's Hadj Hamouda. The Syrians are in on this too?'

'They hate us,' said Shahak. 'But that is all right, because we hate them more.'

He seemed unable to take his eyes from the screen.

'I'll make him settle, yet,' he said, almost to himself. Jacob indicated to Levinger that he should press the advance button.

Click.

'Ferdinand Brandner. Former Colonel in the SS. An aeronautical construction expert. To our certain knowledge, Brandner has recruited, on behalf of Voss and his deputy Goercke, over 200 other German scientific experts.'

'To do what?'

Click.

'To make these.' Shahak broke in. 'The one on the left is called "Al Zafir", or "Victory", the one on the right "Al Kahir", or "Conqueror".'

Jacob looked at the missiles.

'The one has a range of 175 miles, the other 350.'

'So they can hit any part of Israel they want. But a rocket is only a big firework without a warhead. What do they carry?'

'Some of the scientists are involved with the design and construction of the missiles, the others with what they will deliver. We know of two major programmes, one called "Ibis" and the other "Cleopatra". "Ibis" has a warhead of strontium 90 and cobalt 60. It is a very "dirty" nuclear weapon that if it were used, would pollute the very land with radioactivity for hundreds of years. "Cleopatra" is a cheap, small, but nuclear weapon. Now, we do not know whether the Germans are able to produce such things. We *do* know that the two delivery systems have been successfully test fired.

'Nasser has cottoned on to something. In conventional terms he cannot fight a war against us at the moment with a sure chance of winning. But what of that elusive and transitory thing, technological superiority? These weapons are potentially war-winning. Nasser appears to be dealing himself a full hand, for there are men working for him now whose expertise is not in the fields of nuclear physics.'

Click.

There he was, come out of the cave, onto the screen.

Jacob realized that they were looking at him, all of them.

'Yes,' he said quietly. 'I know him. Ibach. Engineer Ibach. He was in charge of the guidance systems for the V2 rockets at Dora.'

Jacob stared at the image of the man. He did not look very evil. Balding, with glasses. Studious.

'So what are we going to do with this grisly crew President Nasser has assembled?'

'We'd like them to go home and take up gardening.'

'Sure . . .'

'But they're all very well paid, and have been given magnificent villas in which to live. Here, I can show you Ibach's. We think we will have to make the attractions of growing fresh vegetables back in Stammheim clear to all.'

Click.

'This is where Ibach lives. That's him. Jacob, are you all right?'

Jacob was staring at the screen, very pale, his face slick

with a sudden sweat. Levinger moved quickly, offering him water.

'Yes . . .'

He looked at the other three men.

'Ibach and another man, Karl Franz, an SS guard . . . they shot my brother David. We had loaded a truck with documents and parts of the V2 rocket under their orders. They were escaping West and met up with others of the team. When they saw they did not need us any more they prepared to kill me and my brother. We tried to escape and I succeeded . . . David was shot. I found his body the next day washed up in the river. Not a day goes by but I wonder where Ibach and Franz are now.'

'We don't know where Franz is,' Levinger said quietly. 'But Ibach is in Cairo.'

'Yes,' Jacob looked at Shiloah. 'You may kidnap him for me any time you like.'

He looked at the three men in turn.

'Is that why I am here? To help kidnap Ibach?'

'You can pass for an Arab. You've done it before,' said Levinger.

'You want me to spy on Ibach?'

'Spy, no,' said Levinger. 'We thought you might kill him for us.'


## Cairo


The villa was situated on the outskirts of Heliopolis, a smart address. From inside you could hear the finely machined purr of the Mercedes as it pulled up in the hibiscus-lined driveway, the clunk of the well-fitting door. No, *two* clunks. His thudding heart beat a little faster.

Ibach did not lock the villa when he left for work, for his Sudanese cook-cum-butler lived in, and oversaw the cleaning maids, took deliveries, did the shopping and was waiting when his master came home.

'*Fouad.*'

That's him, thought Jacob. But who's with him?

'*Fouad.* I'm late today.'

You are, thought Jacob. I thought you were never coming.

'When I've changed I must get on to the Gezira Club.'

Ibach liked the riding and tennis out at the old British imperial club near the pyramids, and he enjoyed going out there after work for a few drinks among convivial company before dinner. He made the rounds of the Gezira, the Heliopolis, the Cavalry Club. The rich Egyptians had taken to the lifestyle of their former British masters with a will, and having experienced ruin in the years following the fall of Hitler's Third Reich his former servants found it most congenial as well.

'*Fouad.*'

Fouad was in a cupboard in the kitchen, gagged and trussed like a chicken.

Jacob was Aleph, to do the job. Outside were Beth, after the second letter of the Hebrew alphabet, there to guard the killer. Two of them, in the dusty Volkswagen parked along the street. Elsewhere in Cairo were the Heth, Ayin and Qoph teams who organized cover, central support and communications, and whom Jacob would never see – the parts that made up the whole, the *kidon*, the bayonet that eliminated the enemies of Israel.

He came in, a balding, bespectacled scientist, carrying a green Samsonite suitcase filled with papers. The elegant sitting room was decorated with vases of flowers, their scent filling the air. Ibach liked flowers, Jacob remembered. He had liked to wear a buttonhole of something in season. Jacob had a sudden, terrible image of the slaves rising in their nooses as the jib of the crane lifted them. The gargling, purpling faces. Ibach behind the glass of his office, sniffing at the flower in his lapel.

There was a man with him, an Arab.

Jacob got out of the straight-backed dining chair in which he had been sitting, tucked out of sight behind the archway, as he waited for Ibach to return home.

'You won't be going to the Club today, Herr Engineer,' he said quietly.

Ibach whirled in alarm, losing his balance and half-falling against his long, polished dining table, the briefcase slipping from his hand. The Arab turned too, and froze when he saw the Skorpion machine pistol in Jacob's hand. It was essential to use non-Israeli materials, and the efficient Czech weapon had been provided, together with its long, baffled moderator, which while it would not completely silence the shot that was to end Ibach's life, would ensure that no one not inside the villa heard it.

The Arab was Hamouda.

'Down on the floor, both of you,' said Jacob, and motioned with the gun. Hamouda lowered himself carefully down, watching Jacob all the while.

'He is a Jew,' he said to Ibach. 'I know him.'

'Engineer Ibach should know me too,' Jacob observed. 'For I helped build his rockets in Dora.'

Ibach let out a wail of terror. He fell on his knees, and held out his palms beseechingly.

'*Please* . . . please do not kill me.'

'You probably do not read the Bible, Herr Ibach,' Jacob remarked. 'But if you did, you would find in it a saying, that some men are marked to die.'

He pulled back the domed cocking button on the side of the receiver. The .32 ACP rounds of the gun were modified, containing light powder loadings. They made little more noise than a small firecracker.

'By coming here to kill Jews, you have become one of them.'

'*No* . . .'

Ibach's voice was a coloratura shriek of agony.

He fell with his face on the floor, and crawled on his belly to Jacob.

'*Please, please* . . .'

He banged his head on Jacob's boots, and his hands grasped his legs.

Jacob pointed the pistol down at his back and tried to visualise his victim's green eyes.


## Kirya, Tel Aviv


'He didn't know me,' Jacob said to Levinger. 'Hamouda did, but Ibach did not, although I stood as close to him as I am to you, many times, in the gallery where we made the V2. It is always the same, of course. The slave knows the master, but to the master all the slaves look the same. We were not people, to Ibach, only things that made the rockets. And also, we *did* all look the same, we were skeletons.'

Jacob paused a moment. He was holding a green briefcase.

'That's almost true. Not always. Karl Franz, who we called the Butcher's Boy, he knew us. But he was SS, and Ibach was an engineer. The SS types, they *liked* their jobs . . .'

Jacob took an envelope from his jacket pocket. He gave it to Levinger.

'It's my resignation,' he said absently. 'I didn't kill Ibach. Or Hamouda.'

'No,' said Levinger. 'Why not?'

'Karl Franz liked his job,' Jacob went on, as though he had not heard. 'He liked every bit of it. It was, I think, for him, almost a sexual thing . . . having total control over us, being able to beat us, to kill us . . . Franz was something like that. The humiliation of a slave, the beating, that was like foreplay, and when he got to hang one, that was just like sex. I think I realized it when he was going to hang the young French boy, Marcel. He dropped a pump, Franz saw him do it. Marcel cracked, he fell to the ground, he held on to Franz's boots, and banged his head against them, begging him not to kill him. I was watching Franz's face, he looked like a man with a woman, you know, on her knees, he was watching him begging, and it excited him.

'He hanged Marcel from the crane, he lifted him up and let him hang there gargling, then he let him down. He had him beg again before lifting him up. He kept it going a number of times . . .

'Klaus Ibach crawled across the floor of his house, and begged for his life. He grasped my legs and beat his head on my boots. I did not just remember Karl Franz murdering Marcel, *I was there, I was back in the KZ*. I do not know how long I stood over Ibach with the pistol in my hand but when I came back to the room he had very, very cautiously moved his head to look up at me.'

Jacob got up, still holding the briefcase.

'I tied them up. I told them that it was a warning, that we Jews of Israel would strike at any who threatened us. And I left. I could not become Karl Franz, not even for Israel.'

He put the case on the desk.

'Ibach had this, so I took it. It's got some interesting material on what he was up to. I've brought it for you.'

Levinger nodded. 'Klaus Ibach flew out yesterday, on the very first flight.'

'Where did he go?'

'America. He has American citizenship, you know. He went to Cairo for the money. It was a very lucrative contract.'

'What about Hamouda?'

'Back with his rag-bag comrades in *Fatah*.'

Levinger's face twisted with a mixture of dislike and contempt. '*Fatah* . . . Conquest, indeed. That's your friend Arafat's outfit.'

'He's not my friend,' Jacob said mildly. 'I met him just the once. In the ruined crusaders' castle.'

'You have an annoying habit of not killing people we would like dead when you have the opportunity,' Levinger complained. 'Arafat's just a shifty Egyptian windbag, but Hamouda's bad news. I'd have liked him dead and buried.'

'Hamouda is a frightening man,' Jacob agreed. 'When I tied him up he just stared at me, like a wolf calculating the distance between it and its next meal ... But don't underestimate Arafat, there's something about him. He's very quick on the uptake.'

'He's quick on the take!' Levinger jeered. 'He goes around the Arab capitals with his hand out like a Jerusalem beggar. To buy arms for this pathetic guerrilla army of his. *Al-Asifa*, the Storm. The Storm! Just let them wander across the border and we'll show them what a storm is ...'

Levinger picked up a report on his desk and glanced at it, clearly not for the first time, before tossing it back.

'Hamouda now ... He's a man steeped in terror. Where do we find him before Cairo? With the FLN in Algeria. *The FLN has just won, Jacob!* The *Front de Libération Nationale* has finally beaten the might of France. The French are leaving Algeria ...'

Levinger stared out of the window.

'In grand strategy terms, it is getting lonely out here, Jacob. The imperial powers are leaving. Our allies are going home ...'

His head swung back to look at Jacob.

'The Palestinians are a joke, but even jokes can become serious. We do not need them gaining the services of someone as trained in the arts of terror as Hamouda. Do you know where *Fatah* has set up shop? Algiers.'

Levinger's mouth twisted in contempt.

'Self-styled centre for the liberation movements of the world! But the FLN *won*. And Arafat was invited to their independence junket. And has his own mission there. *And* has made friends with Asad in Syria.'

'Who?'

'Asad. Air Force general, now part of the new leadership there after the *coup*.'

Levinger tapped his fingers irritably on his desk.

'My job is to stop this kind of thing gathering momentum,' he remarked. 'Eight years ago nobody would have believed that the FLN could kick the French out of Algeria. Now it's happened. That shifty old bastard Macmillan must have sensed it ... all that guff about the "Wind of Change" just masked the British getting out at any cost. They're scuttling home like rabbits before it happens to them.'

'We are the Jews! We shall never leave.'

'I wish you had remembered that when you had our enemies at your mercy,' Levinger said sourly. 'Do you know what Hamouda's doing in Algiers for *Fatah?*'

'No.'

'He's started a training camp for them, to pass on the fruits of his experience.'

'One training camp . . .'

Levinger waved an angry hand about them.

'Here we are! In the state of Israel. *We too* started with one camp. One *moshavot* called Mikveh Israel, in 1870. *I do not want the Palestinians starting camps.*'

On his way to the door, Levinger spoke again to Jacob.

'He's changed his name, by the way.'

'Who?'

'Hamouda. He's become an Abu. Abu Hataf is what he is. Hataf. That's *Fatah*, spelled backwards.'

'It's also death, in Arabic,' Jacob remarked. 'Him and Cohen, what a pair. Hataf and Shahak. Death and Pulverize. Life would be a lot simpler if we all just went down to the beach and got drunk.'

'Jacob?' Levinger called from the door.

'Yes?'

'Aren't you . . . I don't know, disappointed would be too mild a word . . . I mean, this man, you've wanted him for years . . .'

'I do not yet know what I think about Ibach. I still hate him, still feel that he must, in some way, make restitution. Perhaps fate will direct me that way. It is not over. I simply know that I cannot kill him. Not without dying myself.'

'The war is over for you,' Levinger observed.

'I have done my part for Israel. Should she still need strong young men I have two sons.'

Jacob went out and into the office outside. Shahak himself was waiting there to come in. He got off his chair.

'You gutless bastard,' he whispered. 'You let him go, when you had him right there for the killing.'

Jacob moved to go past, and Shahak seized him with a powerful hand.

'What happened?' he demanded. 'You were a good soldier, once.

We should have sent your wife, she would have done the job. Just tell me. What turns a man into a coward?'

'I was not prepared to commit murder,' Jacob said steadily, looking up into Shahak's eyes that were so filled with hate. Shahak threw him back against the wall.

'Murder?' he cried. 'War *is* murder. If you cannot commit murder for your people you should not be here. Read the Talmud. Does it not command us? "If one comes to kill you, make haste and kill him first." That's what we must do. Kill them, before they kill us.'

Jacob was walking away down the corridor, but turned as he went.

'Reading the Talmud was what got us into this trouble in the first place,' he called acidly. 'Simeon bar-Kochba's rabbis knew their Talmud. The Romans nailed them all up in front of a giant stone pig not very far from here, about two thousand years ago. Then they kicked us all out. *That's* what reading the Talmud does for you.'

'Run away then.' Shahak called furiously. 'We shall fight without you. We don't need your kind.'

'Nor I yours,' said Jacob. 'My fighting is done.'

# PART VI

## Egypt, June 1966

THE early morning sun was up, and in the powder-blue sky the fighter aircraft in the aerodrome circuit coming into land were shining silver and gold. The *fellahin* was pushing his cart of yellow and green melons to market in the cool. A polished white BMW came past, the sun's rays glinting on its bodywork. The peasant spat onto the side of the road, and the dust raised as the car passed coated his teeth. As it disappeared into the best part of town, he spat again.

Ahmed Barghouti, setting out the little round tables of his cafe, waved to the driver of the white car as it turned into the road to park. As he got out, the young man in his cream linen trousers and shirt waved back cheerfully. He was clutching his shiny blue American transistor radio, an earplug running up to the side of his head, and he bounced to the music as he went into his apartment block. Ahmed, middle-aged and fat, shook his head in amusement at the antics of the young. Playboy Walid Ayesh, vanished from sight. He would soon be down, he liked to have coffee and a sweet roll after his night out in the Cairo fleshpots. Walid was popular, always ready to listen to the local news, free with his money. Ah, the young weren't all bad, thought Ahmed.

The windows of the cafe rattled as one of the pilots at the aerodrome applied afterburner and went around. The early morning was the time of alert, when the pilots of the squadron were up before dawn, practising their skills for the day when they would drive the Israeli enemy from the skies. Soon it would be quiet, as they landed for their breakfast. Later on, some might come by the cafe, smart in their Air Force uniforms. Walid hung out with some of them. They had the glamour, he had the money.

From his apartment on the eighth floor, the young man they knew as Walid could see the airfield in the distance, see the last of the squadron rolling in along the perimeter taxiway to line up along the hard standing. The earplug was still firmly in his ear, through it he could hear the pilots communicating with ground control. The tiny jets in the distance stopped moving, they were lined up like toys. The radio in his ear went quiet. Tiny lorries were moving along the perimeter, taking the pilots to breakfast. He knew them all, knew them by name, could recognize their voices over the air.

Saul Ben-Levi slipped the earplug from his ear. He carefully turned the dial to tune into a music station, then turned off the volume control to conserve his batteries.

Putting it away he went downstairs and out into the fresh morning, across the road to Ahmed's cafe. He'd have a roll and coffee before going up for a nap. Some of the pilots had the afternoon off, they were going down to the beach. Their friend Walid was giving them a lift in his shiny white BMW.

Saul Ben-Levi grinned to himself, his curly black hair bouncing. Ahmed watched him come in with a sudden pang of envy. Young kids like him had it all. Money, good looks, hot young women. He cast a glance at his own wife, spreading around the cash till. She had been slim and voluptuous, once.

Saul sat casually down at a table, shaking open his paper, and lighting an American cigarette. Ahmed brushed his hands on the apron covering his capacious belly, and went out to serve him.


## May 1967


'We're up against it,' said Levinger. 'It's 1948 again. Only this time they're better prepared.'

Knesset member Jacob Ben-Levi reached for the cup of coffee opposite him. Grounds were floating in it, but he sipped it anyway. He felt very tired.

'Nasser has got his ducks lined up this time. He's got the UN peace-keeping force out. They've been there since Suez, eleven years ago. No need to ask why. His armour and troops are in the Sinai, facing Israel, right up to the border. His troops have occupied Sharm al-Shaykh, and the Straits have been closed to our ships.'

Levinger looked up from the dossier on his desk. Jacob was rubbing the corner of his eye in an attempt to rid himself of a jumping muscle. He looked older than he should, Levinger thought.

'You all right, Jacob? You look terrible. It's not Ruth is it? I

know the boys are doing well. Law and journalism is it? As well
as fighting for us.'

'Yes they're doing well. Ruth's OK. I've been sitting *shiva*. Baruch
... You maybe remember him. No? He came in early. He survived
Dora with me. I escaped, he got released by the Russians ...'

'I'm sorry ... What happened to him?'

'He threw himself out of a window. That's not what the coroner
said, but that's what he did. He was with me in Dora, in the tunnels,
where we made the rockets ...'

'That's terrible ... Was he depressed?'

'He was a KZnik,' Jacob said simply. 'We are damaged goods,
all of us.'

He paused, staring into nothing.

'He had been watching television,' he said suddenly. 'One of the
American rockets going into space ...'

'Oh ... the rockets.' Levinger looked back at his file. 'Jacob, I
hate to do this to you, but I need your help. Forget Ibach. You
cannot touch him now and he cannot harm you. A ring of steel
is tightening about us, Jacob. We are what we were in 1948, a tiny
people in a very hostile sea. And the language has remained the
same. Do you remember listening to Azzam Pasha, in that little hot
room in Jerusalem, right after we'd listened to the Proclamation of
Independence? He promised a war of extermination and momentous
massacre. I have here Nasser's words from the speech he made in
Sinai last night. "The battle against Israel will be a general one ...
and our basic objective will be to destroy Israel." Nothing's changed,
Jacob, except the people delivering the message. In Cairo, Damascus,
Baghdad, Amman, the people bay for our blood. You've seen the
mobs on the television. If Nasser and his allies have their way, they
will get to taste it.'

'So what can I do?'

Levinger smiled a weary smile. We need a kind of roving ambassador, to tell our friends in the world what is happening.'

'Will it do any good, will they come to our aid?'

Levinger wasn't quite looking at him.

'The only way we can stave off defeat is if we make a pre-emptive
strike. If we could take out their air forces, for example, then we
might have a chance. That's not for anyone's consumption, by the
way. But we want to be sure our friends would understand, if we
have to take such measures. You're the ideal person to explain
to them. A KZ survivor, a hero of the War of Independence,
Knesset member, someone known for their humanity, your belief

in the possibility of a new and better world ... I can't think of anyone better.'

Jacob folded his arms defensively in front of him.

'Are not both my sons with you? Is it not enough that a man fights himself, and when he is too old he lets his sons take the burden? Saul and David are strong young men, I am old and tired.'

'You're tired because you've been sitting *shiva*. You're strong, you're a brave Israeli. *You* could put our case to the world.'

'It won't look good.'

'It will, if you just make people see it as retaliation. These are the lands of the Old Testament, not the New. We're dealing with people who want kill us. Christianity is the religion that turns the other cheek, not Judaism. We take an eye for an eye, a tooth for a tooth. Two eyes, and two teeth, if necessary.'

Jacob got up.

'Young Avi Cohen, who was with me in Unit 101, before he changed his name to Shahak and became a brigadier-general preferred tenfold, I recall.'

Levinger got up to see him out.

'I'm sorry,' he said. 'About your comrade. About Baruch. But for now we have bigger things on our mind.'

'Yes,' Jacob said bitterly. He stood at the door, stiff with sudden anger.

'It is not right,' he said.


# Central Intelligence Agency, Langley, Virginia, May 1967


The spars of the curious curved roof below dug into the ground like an enormous fork. Cars and trucks trundled around the network of roads that surrounded the vast, slab-sided complex set in the woods. There was no fear here, Jacob felt. Here was power. Here things were organized to be done to others, and not the other way about. He felt a very long way from home.

The door opened, and a smiling man came in. How they smile, he thought. Do not their mouths get tired?

'Mr Ben-Levi, I'm Hank Snow, I'm one of the Middle East analysts here, I used to be in military intelligence, Mr Helms asked me to see you.'

Quick, intelligent eyes gleamed behind the large, oblong-framed glasses. They sat at the wood and glass table, clip-on badges hanging from the breast pockets of their short-sleeved shirts. Jacob's tie made his neck uncomfortable, he was unused to wearing it.

'First I'd like to say how impressed we've all been with your efforts to bring Israel's plight to the attention of her friends in the West. You've done a first-class job, I'd imagine you're destined for higher things than plain Knesset member.'

'My only interest is to serve my country, Mr Snow,' Jacob said simply. 'And we face annihilation.'

'Call me Hank. May I call you Jacob? Jacob, when you saw President Johnson two days back he too was impressed by what you had to say, and he asked us in the intelligence community to check it out. I have to say that the picture you have so ably presented of your country facing imminent extinction by Arab armies does not appear wholly likely to us. That is not say that they wouldn't do it if they could, but that they do not at the moment seem either capable of it or in the posture of sufficient military preparedness to begin such an enterprise even if they were.'

'But Egypt, Syria and Jordan are standing shoulder-to-shoulder,' Jacob protested. 'There is indeed a ring of steel tightening about us. The Straits are closed to our ships, and the Egyptian army is on the border in Sinai.'

'Oh, right,' said Snow. 'It is as you say, but things are not always as they seem, are they? As far as we can reconstruct it, President Nasser has most ably been drawn into a horrible trap by your guys, from which he is desperately thrashing about trying to escape. The moment when your guys' boot thudded into the ball for the kick off appears to be when they began whipping up on the Syrians in the border areas earlier this year. You shot down six Syrian MiGs on 7 April. The Syrians responded with guerrilla raids, which brought some very strong language from the Israeli leadership regarding what they might do next. The intelligence sources of President Nasser reported to him that the Israelis looked like getting ready to go to war with Syria.'

Snow took off his large oblong glasses and polished the lenses with a brightly coloured red and yellow handkerchief.

'Now this he cannot allow,' he continued. 'As he himself has said, "Who starts with Syria will finish with Egypt." It seems to me that your guys are quarterbacking this much better than he is. Their timing is spot on. Nasser is the Arab champion. But he's past it. He's psychologically rattled, too buddy-buddy with the Russians –

who won't help him if things go wrong – on very bad terms with the USA. He cannot control the Syrians, who are reckless and a menace. Jidda radio and the Jordanians have been jeering at him for not helping the Syrians, and for allowing Israeli shipping to pass freely through the Egyptian Straits to Eilat. In these circumstances, he has to enter the fray, or be deposed in a *coup*.

'So what he has done is to try to move the problem from the Syrian border, over which he has no control, to the Egyptian one, over which he believes he does. Hence moving the troops into Sinai. But not, you will notice, closing the Straits, which he knows quite well Israel has made clear would constitute a *casus belli*. Now here is where I think your guys played their cards beautifully, and displayed psychological warfare skill of the highest order. They said nothing. Nobody warned him not to go any further. In so doing they showed that they completely understood their man. Nasser is basically a very cautious politician, very experienced. But he longs to put the clock back to before 1956, when things were golden, before he was whipped by Israel. And he took the bait. He occupied Sharm al-Shaykh and closed the Straits. The wild applause from the Arab world must have seemed like a draught of nectar. And yet the truth is that he stands at the edge of a great pit which he has himself dug, and into which, if I am correct, your guys are about to shove him.'

'But what of the pacts between them? And the Egyptian army in Sinai?'

'The pacts are more of a military liability than anything else. The Arab nations are hopelessly quarrelsome. Far from standing shoulder to shoulder they're all milling about trying to stab each other in the back. As for the Egyptians, one third of their army is in the Yemen, and the lot that's poured into Sinai is in a terrible state.'

Snow shook his head in disbelief. 'The National Security Agency's been monitoring the radio traffic for us. It is total chaos in there. Fuel and water aren't arriving where they're supposed to, none of the units know where they are, let alone which way to face. They have no training in attack or manoeuvre, and precious little in defence. The Syrian army is crippled by politics and purges. Suwaydani, their chief of staff, has promoted officer cadets to command because the real ones have been executed. They too have no notion of what mobile combat is. The Jordanians are the best but have virtually no good equipment, and furthermore, because of the pact, are under the command of a really poor Egyptian general who will see to it that they are massacred. Egypt, Syria and Jordan have no joint operational plans for offence or defence, and furthermore, loathe each other.'

Jacob sat at the table, frowning.

'You're quite sure of all this?'

'Absolutely. You see, Jacob, we *know*. We can actually *see* what's going on – we have the overhead photographs of the situation on the ground within a few hours at most. We can *hear* what they're saying – everyone from Nasser downwards. We can *sense* what frequencies their radars and communications work on.'

'How?'

'The details are what we call "black", Jacob. Ultra secret. But I can say that because of the Cold War we have required to know far more than human spies can tell us. We need not a trickle of information but a torrent. War is becoming electronic, and we have in the computers the kind of electronic capability to manage all this information. *Knowing* means safety. If you *know* how many missiles the Soviets have, and what they can do, you don't get suckered into "missile gaps". You can make better use of your resources. And if it ever comes down to war, which God forbid, you know where the missiles are, you know what radar protects them, and how to defeat it.'

'You have photographs. Overhead, you said. Aircraft?'

'Some, yes. Also satellites. The Apollo programme to the moon gets all the publicity, but between you and me, as intelligence professionals, it's our overhead reconnaissance capability that's Number One in importance.'

'And you can turn this spotlight on events in the Middle East?'

'Sure.'

'So what's going on there?'

Snow gave a deep chuckle. 'Come on, Jacob. I checked up on you. You're ex-Mossad, ex-commando Unit 101, a real sharp operator. You've been sent on your mission by Chief Levinger, who is a man I for one have real respect for. This is the CIA. Ain't none of us virgins here. Levinger and the men who matter, the other generals, have your opponents about where they want them. Now it's ass-kicking time.'

Jacob suddenly remembered Levinger's face, not quite looking at him.

'A pre-emptive strike,' he murmured. 'Called retaliation.'

Snow chuckled again.

'I said you were a sharp operator, Jacob.'

'I see . . .'

Jacob looked at Snow thoughtfully.

'This is fascinating. About your space programme, I mean. As you say, it's the Moon programme that gets all the publicity. Those astronauts of yours are real heroes, aren't they?'

Snow sat back in his chair, allowing himself to relax, taking up the signals that Jacob was making, that he had accepted the American's argument.

'Sure are.'

'And yet the real emphasis is on the satellites. What about the rockets that get everything up there, it must be quite a programme.'

'NASA runs it,' Snow said promptly. 'They got rockets that make the Fourth of July celebrations look like a child's firecracker.'

'I don't suppose you could show me round sometime?'

'Why sure . . .,' Snow looked at him curiously. 'You interested in rockets, Jacob?'

There was an odd expression on Jacob's face. Ibach's green eyes swam before him.


## Egypt, 5 June 1967

The crackle of the Israeli Mirage on full afterburner was lost in the hammering of the array of flak about the airfield. The torch of light from its tail blurred in the smoke and flame and vanished, and in a ragged fashion, the guns fell silent. There was just the sound of the fires, the shouting of the injured and those helping, the sudden bang as ammunition in the burning MiGs cooked off, the cries of horror.

Jawad Saifan was staggering as they hustled him into the hangar, his olive skin paled to khaki with shock. It was eight thirty in the morning; half an hour earlier he had landed after the initial alert of the day, had made a fine landing on the numbers in his MiG-21 fighter, had got into the waiting Jeep and gone to breakfast. The Mirage had come over the perimeter fence as he was raising his coffee cup to his lips. The bombs under its wings had turned the runway into lumps of concrete, the cannon in its nose had torn his shiny fighter and those of his squadron companions into ragged bits of alloy. Now it was gone, and they hustled him into one of the few aircraft still intact.

They did up his straps, pushed his helmet down on his head, and as though dreaming he saw his hands perform the routine tasks that brought the turbine behind him to life. He switched on the radios, selected number one and found it already tuned to ground control.

'This is Jawad,' he said. 'I'm coming out of the hangar. What do you want me to do?'

The formal routines were gone. Acrid smoke was whipping past the cockpit, making his eyes water, and he closed the canopy.

A burst of excited Arabic rattled in his earphones.

'Take off. Take off. Climb to fifteen thousand feet, heading off zero eight zero. Wait for further orders.'

Jawad fed the power to the engine, rolling along the taxiway.

'Hurry. Hurry. *Yahud. Yahud*. More Jews are coming.'

He came out onto the numbers where he had so proudly kissed the tarmac only a short time before. The straight black runway in front of him was a mess of rock and rubble.

'The runway is ruined,' he protested.

'*Use the taxiway!* Quickly, *Yahud!*'

The sun was beating through the canopy, he could feel the sweat streaming off him. Laboriously, he managed to turn the unwieldy fighter around, heavy with fuel and bombs, turbine howling, the tyres leaving curved black stripes over the giant white numbers.

He was on the taxiway, as narrow as the ribbon in a girl's hair, disappearing into the smoke.

'*Take off! Take off!*'

His hands were wet, his gloves soggy with sweat, it was running down into his eyes. He pushed the thottle to the stop, feeling the power kick into his back, his feet shaking on the pedals, desperately trying to keep it straight. The silver fighter screamed down the taxiway, in the smoke men threw themselves into the ditches at the sound of its coming.

Through his blurred canopy Jawad saw the hangar, filling the screen. He hauled back on the stick and with the stall warner howling the fighter sagged into the air. He instinctively held it in ground effect, the tyres thumped as he hit the ground, the impact threw him back up and he was flying.

With the nose down and the gear in he gained proper flying speed, and on the ground they saw his machine gleam gold and silver in the sun as he climbed away towards the east.

'This is Jawad. I'm going through five thousand feet, heading eighty degrees.'

In his earphones a voice crackled, unintelligible.

'Say again,' he commanded nervously. 'This is Jawad.'

A voice came through then, clear and crisp.

'Jawad, Jawad, what are you doing?'

'Climbing out as instructed,' he said. 'What is it you want me to do?'

'Look, old friend, I just think you should save your behind. I'd get well away from here.'

'What do you mean?' Jawad howled into his mask. 'I have taken off as instructed.'

'I *know*,' the voice said soothingly. 'I'm so glad you're safe, Jawad old friend. But honestly, you're going the wrong way. Only lots of nasty Israelis where you're going. Why don't you just fly out over the sea and drop your bombs.'

'Who is this?' Jawad said desperately.

'This is your friend. Your friend who wants to save you. I'd turn away now, Jawad. There are Israeli fighters coming.'

Unwatched, the heading indicator on his panel was wandering. He craned his head frantically, looking out into the bright glare.

'Coming now, old friend.'

The wings lurched first this way, then that, as he searched for the enemy.

'On your tail, Jawad. *Coming to get you.*'

In the sky there was a sudden bright flare of light arcing away from the fighter. The MiG slowly rolled on to its back, heading for the ground, a dying silver fish in a murky pond. Above, a parachute blossomed white as Jawad Saifan floated down.

Sixty miles away, in a Dakota orbiting over the Sinai desert, Saul Ben-Levi grinned happily at his console, headset buried deep in his black curls. Next to him another operator was tuning a dial.

'Here's another,' he said. Saul listened. 'You know him?'

'I know him,' said Saul. 'It's Anwar. Married with a baby daughter. You got him for me?'

He took a sip of water from the glass in its holder beside him.

'Say, Anwar, old friend . . .'

The radio was quiet. The Egyptian Air Force, to all meaningful intents and purposes as a military force, had ceased to exist. The DC3 grumbled in over the perimeter fence and touched down with a double squeak of its fat tyres. The big radial engines gulped to a halt on the hard standing, and the rear door opened. Saul jumped down onto the hot concrete, dressed in his olive flight suit, his white flight helmet in his hand, hoses and connections dangling.

A line of low, V-tailed jets stood in the hard standings, sand and rock coloured, the air was filled with the rising shriek of their

engines. The light was blinding, the heat slammed up at him from
the rock and concrete. He pulled his helmet on as he ran over to
the small fighters with their twin cockpits; he pulled the dark visor
down and there was number 17 on the side, waiting for him.

He scrambled up the ladder on the side and the ground crew
strapped him in. The radio spoke in his ears firmly and clearly, his
map was on his knee, he wrote down his instructions. The turbine
was spooling up with a rising howl. He lit its fire and felt the thud
as the kerosene burned, saw the percentage rise on the gauge.
The Magister jet trainers came waddling out of their hides, one
after the other, he gave his the power, guiding it with his pedals,
the canopy hissing down shut about him. The little fighter was
heavy, he could feel it even on the ground, its wings hung with
rockets.

One after the other, in vics of three the fighters hissed down the
runway, and he was flying. His thumb twitched to and fro on the
trim, the aircraft heavy with fuel and weapons, the wheels came up
and they streaked through the clear air.

He could see it coming, the dense cloud of yellow dust that was
drifting across the whole countryside below. At its cutting edge were
the forces of redemption, the forces of god. As the little fighters
put down their noses, streaking overhead he saw the tanks striking
forward against the Egyptian positions.

The voice, clear and firm, ordering the administration of just
wrath.

'Here they come. All blue and yellow aircraft, pick your targets.'

He could see the Egyptian gun emplacements, shimmering in his
gunsight. The switches were 'on', his forefinger began to tighten on
the trigger, his hand on the stick making tiny, continuous corrections,
the jet as smooth as silk, its outstretched wings, as perfect as an
angel's trembling as they sliced through the air, bumpy and lumpy
as a rock-strewn riverbed.

The gun emplacement filled the sight, with its walls of sandbags,
the long barrel of the gun poking out like the proboscis of some
insect. Men were scurrying frantically about it like verminous bugs.
Saul's lips were drawn back from his teeth, his finger made the
final movement that completed the circuit and four streaks of
flame shot from under his wings, leaving even black lines in
the sky.

It would do them no good to run. Their death was ordained. The
gun site vanished in an immense flash. The air became suddenly
brown and bodies flew like tiny cockroaches, tumbling over and

over. Saul twitched back on the stick, screaming over the billowing smoke, and then back down, skimming over the desert.

A missile site. Huge, bulky, a roman candle pointed at him. Smoke wisped about it as he streaked towards it. Flame. As big as he was, belching fire, weaving in his direction.

Saul laughed in a peal of joy. The efforts of Satan were feeble, his creations but feeble copies. As the monstrous rocket lurched clumsily through the sky he whipped the stick left, and then right, the wings of the fighter vertical, his G-suit squeezing his lower body as he dodged, nimble as a hawk in the air.

Through the canopy he felt the rattling roar of the missile as it bellowed past, its smoke streaking the sky. Then he was in clear air, came back on the throttle, nose down, and with the boxes of the control trucks below him, he fired and as sharp as an arrow's flight the missiles stabbed into their targets.

A tank. A lumbering thing staggering towards the fighting like a beetle. He fired again, and the flame and smoke of his power sliced down. The tank exploded, as he swept over it for a fraction of a second he saw every seam of it illuminated from within, in blinding orange.

All over the sky the deadly, sharp-winged fighters were swooping, like barracudas through muddied water. Smoke was pumping up from the line. Beyond, the yellow dust heralded the inexorable advance of the Israeli tanks.

Saul whipped the stick across and then back, pulling round in a steep flat turn over the desert floor, sharp white trails of condensation suddenly spilling from his wingtips. In the gun emplacement, they were looking the wrong way, lining up on the coming Israelis.

He fell on them like a wolf on sheep. When his rockets were gone, he slaughtered those who ran, who staggered, who crawled from the ruins with his cannon.

When he was low on fuel, as the venomous fighters turned for home, they climbed up into the clear sky. There they were near to God, and in his cockpit, Saul swayed and bobbed briefly in prayer, thanking Him for making him his instrument.

When they landed there were as many of them as had taken off. Their rocket racks were empty, poking forward like fingers, the noses of the fighters were streaked from the firing of the cannon, the very fuselage bodies patched with smut and dark chars from the explosions they had caused.

As Saul climbed out he was overwhelmed by *simcha*, a fierce and burning joy. On the concrete, as the dust whipped about him, blown by the jets thundering and crackling down the runway, he did a somersault, his helmet leaving a white splash of paint on the ground, springing up with his arms outstretched, laughing up at the god who ordained they could do no wrong.

## The Mitla Pass, Sinai

'The fucker's fucked.'

Ben Cohen stood at the side of his British-built Centurion tank and listened to the grinding crunch of his driver attempting to select a gear. Next to him was David Ben-Levi, commander of the neighbouring tank. The two men were sweating in the heat, the dust of the little convoy sticking to their skin.

'You still have power,' said David. 'We can tow you into position, same as Ruven's tank.'

They backed up his Centurion and attached the heavy cable. The two men climbed back into their turrets and with a jerk, David's tank took up the strain, grinding up the rock-sided road. When they cleared the summit they could see the mauve and white of the Sinai *wadis* and sand dunes below them.

David chose the ground, and the two working tanks prepared emplacements with their dozer blades. In the distance, the sky was marked with dust and smoke. They dragged Ben Cohen's tank into position and the crew fell on its rear, hauling off the engine covers to get at the transmission. Cohen remained in the turret, watching down the black road, and David climbed up, standing on the deck.

'I think they're coming,' said Cohen. He was stocky and balding, with the beginnings of a paunch.

'Right,' David said. 'Hell, I wish I was back in the university reading about Arab history, not making it.'

He climbed down, across to his own Centurion, slab-sided, riveted and bolted, and got into the turret.

Ragged, unco-ordinated columns were moving on the plain. Someone down there had seen the Israeli tanks holding the pass and the someone was trying to put together a force. David could see the T-55s coming out of the rabble that swirled about. Fighters were dipping in and out of the smoke, and through the air came the soft crash of their bombs.

The Soviet-built tanks were coming up the slope. There was no cover.

'Go away,' David said softly.

They were still coming. He slipped down into the turret, where he could see them through his commander's periscope.

'Go home.'

The turret moved, the electric motors whining softly.

'Select targets,' he ordered. Through his periscope the olive T-55 filled two bars of the sight.

'Open fire. Fire at will.'

The great crash of the armament going off blew dust all about them. The shell case flew from the breech, the next slammed home. The gun barrel twitched, selecting its target. Down on the slope, a scarlet mouth of fire kissed the T-55 and smoke billowed out from the turret.

There was an enormous clang like a gigantic sledgehammer striking metal. Bits of debris rained in through the open hatch and David poked his head out. Ruven's Centurion was on fire. As he pulled his head back in, the ammunition began to explode.

The Egyptian tanks were burning on the slope. He fired again. Part of the front armour of the T-55 closing in on him flew off and he saw the shell, a misshapen lump of metal, tumbling black up in the air. The tank was close, no more than fifty yards of scrub and rock away. He saw Cohen's turret turning, the over-pressure of the armament going off suddenly obscured it from sight. The T-55 slammed sideways like a child's toy, the whirring sprockets throwing the snaking track high in the air.

A man came out of the wreck, a slithering, sliding, jumping man, shouting as he came. He had a revolver in his hand and was very angry. He fired at David as he ran, his wrecked tank on fire behind him.

David was standing up in the turret and heard the bullets go past like wasps. His hands fumbled with the .303 machine gun on its mounting. The man in his olive coverall was running at him, he hurled his weapon at him and the gun suddenly drummed in his hands. Rock exploded on the ground, fragments screaming in the air, and the man tumbled over and over, until he lay still, clutching his leg.

The revolver hit the armour with a clang, and it was quiet, just the noise of the tanks burning down on the slope and nearby. The man groaned. Dirty, oily smoke drifted about him and David climbed out, dropping down onto the dirt. Down on the plain, the Fougas were dipping in and out of the smoke like piranhas.

The Egyptian tank commander looked up at him, clutching his leg. Blood was pumping through the torn cloth.

'Ai . . .' The breath hissed in his teeth. 'This is horrible.'

'Sorry . . .'

'You speak Arabic . . .' The dark eyes, wide with pain, looked at him in surprise.

'Yes.' David fumbled for his pack of field dressings, placing a pad over the wound. He began to bind it.

'It would have been easier not to have shot me first,' the Egyptian observed. He fumbled in his pocket and took out a packet of cigarettes. 'We are not allowed to smoke in the tank. Would you like one?'

'Yes.'

'I am Fat'hi.'

'David.'

'It is very painful, David.'

David found the syringe of morphia, and injected him. He summoned his driver, and they carried him over to the front of the tank, where there was shade.


The Jeep came bouncing down the road and stopped by his tank. A big, tall officer stood up by the driver, and David recognized Shahak.

'Move out,' Shahak yelled. 'Take your force down off the mountain. They're in retreat. Get in amongst them.'

'To do what, sir?'

Shahak's ruddy face flushed near purple with fury.

'*To kill the bastards.* Get down there.'

'But they're in retreat, brigadier,' David protested. 'They've thrown away their arms, they're just trying to walk out. Let them do it, they're no threat.'

Shahak jumped down, clambering up with thudding boots onto the deck of the tank.

'You stupid little bastard,' he said dangerously. 'Every one of them we let walk out of here will come back, one day, with another gun in his hand, and fifteen of his children behind him, also with guns. So get down there and do it. Either we do it to them or they do it to us.'

'I cannot kill unarmed men,' David said stubbornly.

Shahak looked at the name tape on David's tanker's coverall.

'Ben-Levi,' he said suspiciously. 'No relation?'

'Jacob is my father, yes.'

'He's a gutless bastard who can't kill his enemies,' Shahak said brutally. 'Are you the same?'

David pointed down the smoky slope, at the burning T-55 tanks.

'We did that.'

'Then get down on to the plain and do some more.'

'I'm not a murderer,' David said steadily. 'They are not fighting, down there.'

Shahak kept his gaze on the desert below.

'I'll have you court-martialled, for cowardice,' he said, in a flat, unemotional voice.

'I won't do it.'

'Get out. Get out of the turret.'

David climbed out. As he was getting down the tank moved forward with a jerk, throwing him to the ground. As he got to his feet in the dust he saw the unit moving forward, one by one. Shahak was in his turret, the long barrel of the main armament was elevating.

On the plain a pathetic column of trucks and ragged soldiery was moving in the white and mauve *wadi*. David saw the blast of dust as the Centurion opened fire, heard the flat crump of the gun going off. He saw the flames below, saw some men tumble, saw some men run, but he could not hear their screams.

## Kennedy Space Center, Florida

Half a mile away the tall white tower erupted into smoke and flame, white and orange, and the very window in front of Jacob vibrated. Next to him Snow chuckled, and put his hand out to touch it.

'Feel the power, Jacob,' he said, and through his fingertips Jacob felt the energy of the enormous rocket engine blasting its cargo into the air.

They saw the gantry fall away, and as the rocket lifted from the pad the packed room broke into cheering and applause.

'Riding the fire, Jacob!' Snow said triumphantly. 'Riding the fire.'

The white rocket on its pillar of flame was moving, quicker and quicker now, and they had to crane their necks to keep it in sight. It went through the layer of growing cumulus over the Atlantic, and the television screens in the white room took over.

Among those watching there was a sense of relaxation, while those still concerned sat at the rows of consoles and visual display units, their identity badges tagged to their short-sleeved shirts. Here and there companions of the men riding in the rocket high above were conspicuous in their flight suits, their mark of status. Snow nudged Jacob.

'There's Neil Armstrong,' he murmured. 'They say he may be the one, you know.'

'The one?'

'The first man to actually step on to the moon. Want to meet him?'

'He looks very busy,' Jacob demurred. 'Let's not disturb him right now. But, you know, I would like to meet one of the people who actually designed that rocket.'

'The Saturn? You want to meet one of the engineers?'

'Yes. I think I told you, I have been interested in such rockets since I was young.'

'Why, sure. What about Heinz Ibach? The guy's practically a genius with rockets, they say.'

So it was all for this that Dora did not exist, that there was to be no justice for Jews. For his father, mother, David, Baruch.

'Are you okay, Jacob? You're not looking too good.'

'It is the excitement of the day,' Jacob said. His eyes fixed on the engineer in his short-sleeved shirt and slacks. He had gone a dreadful pale, waxy colour.

'But do take me over,' he urged. He had not been able to murder Ibach but maybe it was not too late to destroy him. 'You see, we have met, some years ago. I should like to renew the acquaintance.'

'Okay,' the CIA man said amiably. 'Then we can go get a bite to eat. Maybe some food will make you feel better.'

'No doubt.'

They went through the clumps of people. Ibach was looking at a screen, checking some figures moving there.

'Heinz, you free for a moment?' asked Snow.

'Yes, I am free.'

The German accent was still there, somewhere underneath the acquired New York American. Jacob found his breath tightening in his chest, his heart pounding so hard he felt it hitting his ribs.

'Heinz, this is Jacob Ben-Levi, emissary of the Israeli government.'

He knew him, this time, the moment he lifted up his eyes and saw him. How could he forget the Jew who had spared him.

Jacob's mouth was dry, the words came out as a croak.

'We have already met, have we not.'

Snow sensed that something was wrong.

'Really?'

'Oh, yes. We are fellow engineers, he and I, we made rockets together, years ago, in a place called Dora.'

He had recovered his composure quickly, the German.

'You cannot try to kill me here,' he said.

'Do you remember Baruch? He died at his own hand, because of what you did. He saw the rockets on his television.'

'One less Jew,' Ibach murmured, so that only he and Jacob could hear.

'You bastard.'

'Insults cannot hurt me.'

On the great television screens the giant Saturn rocket suddenly flared, its enormous booster falling away.

'You know who this is?' Jacob screamed, at anyone who would hear. 'He is a Nazi war criminal! He made rockets for Hitler.'

They were all watching the screens avidly.

'Say, keep it down over there,' someone called, over their shoulder.

Ibach stared contemptuously at him.

'Think I'm the only one?' he sneered. '*They* could not do *that* without *us.*'

'This man hanged my comrades!' Jacob shouted, all control lost. 'He hanged them from a crane, he murdered them slowly, he laughed to see them die!'

Some people had turned to see what the commotion was. Ibach looked across at them, rolled his eyes, tapped his forehead in the universal signal for the insane, the loopy, the one not tightly wrapped, and they nodded in understanding.

'I know this man,' Ibach said to Snow. 'He is a Jew, I believe. He has some fixation about me because I am German, he thinks I am somebody from his past. I have had cause to complain about him.'

Jacob had started to tremble all over, he felt dizzy and weak. Snow took him by the elbow.

'Jacob, come on, I'll get you some water . . .'

Jacob looked up at them.

'You Americans,' he said. 'You do not know what you have done.'

'But they do,' Ibach said triumphantly. 'They do.'

Jacob looked around him and he saw that it was so. He suffered himself to be led away, like the afflicted person they thought him to be.

On the screen, the rocket was a bright yellow dot against the deep blue of the sky.

# PART VII

## Tel Aviv, August, 1967

'YOU all right, now?' asked Levinger.

'I am as well as can be expected,' said Jacob.

The windows of Levinger's office were open, outside in the street they could hear, could sense the pumping triumph that pounded out in every Israeli. *They had won.* In six days! Defeated, totally, absolutely without question, every one of their enemies. *Triumph.*

'You were in the hospital a week. I wanted to be sure you were all right.'

'I was back in Dora,' Jacob corrected him. 'They walked away, every day, you see, the SS and the engineers. We went back to the camp. Until the next day.'

'You collapsed, in the space centre. They took you out on a stretcher. I wanted to be sure you were all right to come back to work.'

'You don't need me any more,' said Jacob. 'Anyway, I am thinking of taking a holiday. I wish to go wine-tasting along the Loire valley.'

'Jacob, Jacob . . .' Levinger said gently, reproachfully. 'You can't leave us just now, not yet, while we have to finish the job. Not if you are fit again. We need you.'

'Is it not done? We have Jerusalem, we have Hebron. The Biblical lands are ours again. As you and your companions planned, all along.'

Levinger spread his hands out, palms up. A cup of brown coffee, the consistency of muddy sludge was cooling there, on his desk.

'You're blaming me, because I didn't tell you all I knew. But you know, in the Bible, it says, with *taboulah*, with stratagems shall ye wage war. You don't think we're going to be able to keep all the land we now have? Jerusalem, Hebron, these cannot be given back, they must be open to all, Jew, Muslim, Christian. But Sinai, the West

Bank, Gaza, these are cards in our hand, to be dealt out for peace. A secure, everlasting peace.'

'So deal,' said Jacob.

'We shall. But we need you. As an ambassador. As one who can talk to the Arabs. You are unique, you they trust.'

'And what am I to be offered, for doing this?'

A watchful expression had come over Levinger's lean face, but he held out his hands in appeal.

'This is Jacob Ben-Levi? Jacob, who never asked for any reward except that of serving his people? What is it you want, Jacob?'

'I want Heinz Ibach brought to trial. He killed my brother,' Jacob said quietly, flatly, his voice almost metallic.

Levinger put his hands flat on the table.

'You don't know that,' he said quickly. 'By your own admission, you escaped, you found your brother after he had been shot. You don't *know* that Ibach did it, that he was there, even.'

'I know. In KZ Dora, Karl Franz, the Butcher's Boy, hanged us from an iron beam in the tunnel outside Ibach's office. He rammed rough pieces of wood into their mouths, to stop them screaming. I was there, because I was made to watch. My comrade Baruch was there, because he was made to watch too. Ibach was there too, at his window. He was not made to watch, he watched because he liked to watch. And when they were dead he came out and went down the row pushing the feet to make them swing, laughing as he did so. My brother died on his knees, his hands were together. He was asking them not to kill him, and both Franz and Ibach enjoyed that. Ibach would not have missed it. Dora did exist.'

'You have no proof,' Levinger said again. 'And the camp Dora does not feature in the literature of the Holocaust. You cannot bring charges against Ibach. He denies ever having been there. He says he was at Peenemünde, with the design staff. He says that you are taking him for someone else.'

'Oh, so I was not really there?' Jacob said bitterly. 'I was not a slave making weapons of mass destruction for the Nazis. What was Dora if not a KZ, and one of the worst? Give me the SS files and I will prove that Ibach was there.'

'Jacob!' Levinger said sharply. 'I was not there. As a fellow Jew it grieves me to talk like this to you. But you know why Dora is not listed. It is because the American Army closed the file. The information is classified. You cannot have the files.'

'Because Ibach and plenty of other German scientists are working for the Americans.'

'Yes. It is not a subject for discussion. Their space programme is too important to them. In the scale of things, Jacob, Heinz Ibach, space engineer, is more important than Jacob Ben-Levi, KZnik. If you start to make trouble, you are making trouble with the American side of the Cold War. They won't let you do it. They can apply pressure on us, Jacob. We exist here, because the Americans want us to exist here. If they wanted to, they could make me do things to you that I wouldn't want to do, but I might have to, for the sake of Israel. And I wouldn't like that. But listen, it isn't going to come to that. I know we can work this out.'

He got up. A small white refrigerator sat in a corner like a squat white toad, grumbling to itself. Levinger opened it and took out two green bottles of cold beer. He levered off the tops, and passed one to Jacob.

'Thank you.'

They sat, sipping from the necks of the bottles.

'How's the family?' Levinger said casually. 'Ruth all right?'

'Not very,' Jacob said honestly. 'Israel is not a very good place for KZniks to live. Some of us adapt better than others ... Ruth is among the others. She doesn't go out much, she is sometimes strange ... It is the *kazett*. It is always with us, those who were in it. It is killing us like it has already killed my comrade, Baruch.'

His eyes flared.

'It kills, and goes free.'

'Let's not start on that again, not for a moment, anyway ... I see your boy had a good war. Saul did a fantastic job under cover in Egypt. When the Air Force took out the Egyptians on the first day, it was down to him, and a few others. I know they think a lot of him, in Amman.'

'And David?' Jacob asked quietly. 'Do they think a lot of him too?'

Levinger allowed a pause to develop before he spoke. Outside, the very cars seemed to be going faster, there seemed to be more horns blowing in triumph.

'You remember when you were going to kill Ibach?' he said finally. 'You couldn't do it, couldn't shoot him and Hamouda ... because you would have become the Butcher's Boy. I understood that. Shahak didn't. You know he lost most of his family when he was a boy, murdered in front of his eyes, most horribly. Shahak hates Arabs. He wants them punished. David was in Sinai, his group had fought hard, fought well. With the Egyptians in full retreat Shahak ordered them forward, to keep killing. David wouldn't do it.'

'He would have become the Butcher's Boy,' Jacob said quietly.

'Yes, I see that,' Levinger agreed. He paused again. 'Others might not . . .'

He tipped back his beer and drew patterns in the condensation on the bottle with his finger.

'Shahak wants David court-martialled,' he said.

Jacob sat silent.

'I've got him to hold off. For the moment. He'd be in the stockade. For years.'

He put the bottle down with a thud and rivulets of water ran down the sides.

'It would kill his mother,' he said.

Jacob opened his mouth to speak, and Levinger held up his hand.

'Heinz Ibach, NASA space engineer, may be more powerful than Jacob Ben-Levi, one-time KZnik. But Special Minister Jacob Ben-Levi would have more power . . . And who knows what might happen in America? Maybe we can get the files reopened . . . But first, you have to take the job . . .'

'Yes,' Jacob said slowly. 'I see that now.'

'What exactly is it that you want? You had the chance to have him dead.'

'Public ruin,' Jacob said flatly. 'I saw him swagger in the space centre. He was not repentant, he did not regret. I told him that Baruch had killed himself and he sneered at me. "One less Jew," he said to me. Very well. Let him pay, I want him to suffer, just one tiny part of what we suffered. Baruch killed himself because he could not stand the pain any more. I would like Ibach to taste just a portion of that pain.'

'So trust me,' said Levinger. 'You know I have ways of making things happen.'


## Jerusalem


Shahak took his son to the Western Wall. They went early, as soon as the sun was up, because later it became too crowded with American Jews in Bermudas and cardboard *kippot* paying homage to God for the victory of Israel in the war of miracles, that had restored Jerusalem to those of the one true faith.

Shahak's son was named Haazev, which meant Wolf. His mother had wanted him called Joseph, after her father, who lived in Brooklyn, but Shahak had ignored her wishes. His judgement as to her true Jewishness had been vindicated by her inability to live either with him or in fact in Israel at all. She had gone back to Brooklyn, wholly saddened by her experience, and without her son. Shahak had retained custody. She had taken refuge from time to time from the bleakness of her existence in smoking marijuana. Shahak knew about it and had seen to it that the judge, whom he also knew, did too, thereby having her branded a drug addict and as such an unfit mother.

Shahak and Haazev stood in front of the wall and prayed. At that hour the great wall of masonry blocks, which held up the sacred Muslim Temple Mount, was peopled fleetingly by young soldiers swaying briskly back and forth, sub-machine guns waving from their straps, and more enduringly by flocks of the Orthodox, assembled like crows, *davening* wildly, *payot* sidelocks swinging like bellropes, *tefillin* boxes containing parchment fragments of the Torah wound about head and arm with straps.

Haazev was five, tall and strong for his age. He prayed as his father instructed him to, and then they went for a walk, leaving the Chasidim swaying, keeping *mitzvot* behind them.

They were demolishing a lot of the old Arab buildings to make a new plaza to accommodate the tourists and hold military ceremonies of the state. Shahak took his son through the *souk*, already crowded with Arabs and Bedouin, crammed with odours and sound; tea vendors and Bedouin women in exotic robes, black-robed Orthodox monks, men carrying trays of eggs on their heads away from the crush, and women rolls of cloth likewise, for the same reason. They went through, dark eyes sliding sideways to look at the conqueror as he went. Shahak and Haazev left behind the lanes of the butchers, the alleys of the cloth merchants, the dealers in gold, the mosaics of spices, the smoke of the schwarma stalls and went past the mosque with its high minaret, on through the dusty streets, past the low, flat-roofed houses where squatting women baked bread in ovens of stone and baked mud. In the courtyards and on the roofs apricots, tomatoes and bunches of brightly coloured peppers were drying in the sun.

It did not take long to get out of the city onto the hill. An Arab shepherd was tending a herd of goats among the wild oats that had blossomed there. The city was built high up, and they looked down through the clear air over the land below. Shahak sat holding

his son between his knees. It was a natural place to sit and look
over the landscape. Once Hadj Hamouda had sat there with his
son, Hasan.

'All the land you see before you is the land of our people, and has
been since a time long forgotten. It is called Israel. It is a beautiful
land, watered by the rains and by the dew. It is the land they say
that flows with milk and honey, here our sun shines on green trees
and flowing wheat, and the very rocks produce sweet water for us
to drink.'

The little boy stared solemnly at the country spread out beneath
them.

'Once evil men came and took our land away from us,' Shahak
continued quietly. 'Because we were weak and they were strong.
Hundreds and hundreds of years ago. We were scattered to the
four corners of the earth. But now we are back. We have had to
fight. The evil ones still seek to scatter us once again, but as we are
as strong and as big as that wall where we prayed, their efforts merely
beat upon us like weak waves of water against such a wall. One day,
there will be one final battle and we shall defeat them all for ever.
Those people we walked through back there, those Arabs, we shall
throw them out, for they do not belong in the land of Israel. Israel
is for Jews.'

'I understand, father,' said the boy.


## New York, January 1970


'Why are you wasting your time going out there and fighting the
*schvartzers?*'

Levinger peered out of the high window, looking out over the
East River. Rabbi Gideon Weiss bridled.

'Hebrew Defence Corps *chayas* on the streets mean more safety
for Jews. Fewer Jews mugged by niggers, fewer Jewish women raped
by niggers.'

'Who cares?' Levinger said coldly.

Weiss came off the sofa, hyper-active, bouncing about the room,
his *kippot* pinned to his hair, his eyes glittering. He was charismatic;
when he stood up to talk people listened. Now Levinger watched
him with cynical eyes.

'*I* fucking care! The HDC is a fast-growing organization. I can hold a fund-raising dinner and come out with cheques for twenty thousand bucks. That's not peanuts. How do you think I got this apartment, the Lincoln downstairs? And what do you mean, who cares?'

'Who cares?' said the Mossad chief. 'These fat Americans that give you money aren't Jews. I couldn't care less if some get mugged by *schvartzers*. The only Jews in the world are those that want to live in Israel. The ones who are there, or the ones who would be there, if they could. The only purpose these fat Americans called Gold and Weinberg and Zimmerman serve is to make money and give it to us, those who protect the Jewish people in Israel. And the Hebrew Defence Corps won't last. Good idea, but too small.'

'You got a better one?' Weiss demanded angrily.

'Yes,' Levinger said quietly, and Weiss stopped moving about the room. He stood in front of the leather-cheeked spymaster like a hunting dog waiting for its command.

'What is it?' he said, and he sounded hungry.

'We want Jews. We need them. Since we took Gaza and the West Bank we got all these Arabs. They breed like . . .'

'Niggers.'

'I was going to say rabbits. But we need more Jews, or one day there'll be more of them than us. So where do we get more Jews?'

Weiss's eyes lit up.

'The Soviet Union,' he crowed.

'You have it. Hundreds and hundreds of thousands of them. If we can just get the Soviet authorities to let them out we can ship them in.'

Weiss's face fell.

'But how the hell do you do that? The Soviets are mean sons of bitches.'

Levinger's eyes gleamed in their folds of skin, leathery, like bat wings.

'Are they as mean as us? Look, Gideon. You impress me. Yes, I mean that. You're a militant Jew. You got a genius for public relations, for promotion. You've got good ideas, you can think of the right slogan.'

Levinger pointed to a bumper sticker slapped to the wall.

'"Each Jew, a .32." Genius. Now all the little old ladies got an automatic. You built up your HDC from nothing.'

'Damn right,' Weiss said with feeling. 'It wasn't easy. I tell you, I was real glad when the niggers started getting out of hand.'

'Well now you got something bigger to get your teeth into. The

Soviets are godless. Just like Hitler. They're going to liquidate our people. Just like Hitler. Unless we can get them out.'

Levinger pointed to another fluorescent sticker on which a clenched-fist black marched next to a Nazi.

'*Never Again*,' he read. 'You got it, you got your market. Tens of thousands of worried American Jews. You just need a bigger enemy. Not the *schvartzers*. Nixon'll see to them. The Soviets.'

'But how?'

'What do they want, right now? They want *détente*. If we can put the US–Soviet relationship under enough strain the Soviets will have to let the refuseniks go, rather than risk losing out.'

'How do you suggest we do that?'

'Oh, I'm sure you'll think of something,' Levinger said casually. 'I'm sure you read history. And look, you'll have us if things get . . . a little out of hand. You'll have friends. Listen, I have to go. I'll send someone round with some money. You get results, there'll be some more.'

'You can count on me,' Weiss said by the door.

'I know I can,' said Levinger.

The man was short and bald, with deft, tobacco-stained fingers. He handed Weiss a shabby black briefcase; he opened it and saw it was tidily packed with notes.

'I'm Lewin,' he said. 'You're supposed to count it.'

It took Weiss some time, and when he had finished Lewin was still there.

'I come with the money,' he said.

'What do you do?'

'I was with the Irgun.'

'So was I.'

'I left. They were too soft. I joined the Stern Gang. I'll show you how to make bombs.'

He was a sleazy man, he came out of the bar with rock music still in his ears, a pitcher of Bud in his belly and young tits shaking in front of his eyes. It had been a long time since any young girl had voluntarily let him get his hands on her breasts or any other part of her anatomy but he had a roll of greasy notes in his pocket and he headed for the payphone.

He got a quarter in his hand and ran his eyes over the selection of stickers on show. There was plenty to choose from. He avoided Miss Lash's Academy, *Strictly* for Naughty Boys, and also Rubber

Rhona, *Gay* Gordon and Corrective Cora. A new one caught his eye. *Come* with me, a sultry blonde purred. *Really* get your rocks off with Rose.

He slid the coin into the slot and dialled the number.

'Yes?' said an icy, foreign voice.

He frowned.

'Hey,' he said hoarsely. 'I want to get it on with Rose.'

'*Get off the phone, you filthy pervert!*' the woman screamed. 'This is the Soviet Embassy!'

The man in front of the Steinway stretched out his hands and snow-white cuffs protruded from his black coat of tails. The audience in their finery was very quiet, rapt. Up on the wide stage he began to play and Bach filled the air in a stream of liquid gold. The orchestra bent ready, bows cocked, fingers pressed into the silver and gold of their instruments, ready to pluck and drum, to blow, to create magic, their eyes on the conductor. He raised his baton to bring them into the symphony, and in the audience, a woman shrieked. First one, then another, people rising up, shouting, brushing at their clothes.

The frogs hopped everywhere, the mice ran squeaking. From the back a voice bellowed through a bullhorn.

'*Am Yisrael chai!* The Jewish nation lives! Let the Soviet Jews go!'

The stewardess closed the door of the *Aeroflot* Tupolev jet airliner. In the cockpit the crew continued to go through their pre-flight routines. With the doors closed the internal air conditioning system came on to keep the passengers cool from the heat of Kennedy International Airport outside, and the cabin staff began to go through their own safety routines and exhibitions.

Suddenly voices began to shout in disgust from the front cabin, and people appeared, holding handkerchiefs over their faces. The air conditioning swiftly spread the stench of rotten eggs throughout the fuselage, and the entire complement, passengers, cabin staff and aircrew were soon stumbling out into the fresh air of the departure hall.

When they got back in the aircraft the cabin walls and cockpit windows had been spray-painted in scarlet Hebrew letters. *Am Yisrael chai!* Let the Soviet Jews go!

'They're upset about culture,' said Weiss, and the cameras whirred outside the Amtorg Soviet trade centre. 'Suddenly, they're all shouting, because they can't get to hear Russian musicians, see Russian dancers.

Did they shout when they heard that Hitler was packing their European relatives into rail cars, into cattle trucks, and sending them to the gas chambers?'

He looked left and right, demanding that the black eyes of the cameras answer him.

'No. While millions of Jews were dying they held rallies and whined that the government did something. *It didn't!* The Jews – our Jews – died. The Soviet government is slaughtering Jews in Russia, and what do they do? They whine because we, the Hebrew Defence Corps, is doing something for them!'

Behind the cameras the cars rolled along Lexington Avenue, and Weiss kept up his voice to compete, beginning to pace, the *kippot* bouncing on his head.

'*We* care. So okay, we aren't respectable, we do some bad things. What bad things? We aren't going to let it happen again. Never again! We will do what has to be done. We'll shake the world and spotlight what the Soviets are doing to the Jews so that this time, the US government can't not do something, so that it is forced to demand justice for Jews if the Soviets want the West's friendship.

'We don't take it any more, we dish it out. Tiny Israel just whipped six Arab armies. Six! These are days to be proud to be Jewish. The Russian Jews are proud. We don't crawl any more. We demand. We demand justice. We're proud. We'll whip anyone who doesn't give us respect. If the PLO attacks schoolchildren in Israel, we'll attack them. We just did. The PLO won't be using its Manhattan office for a while.'

Weiss glared into the camera, wiping his mouth with the back of his hand.

'One day, your children or your grandchildren will ask you: "What did you do for Soviet Jews?" If you say to them: "I sold leather handbags in Manhattan," if you say: "I baked bagels in Brooklyn," you know what? They're going to spit right in your face.'

Weiss pulled his olive combat jacket up around his shoulders.

'Me, I know what I'm going to do. I'm a fighter. I've been fighting for Jews all my life. I know what the Hebrew Defence Corps is going to do. We're all fighters. Fighters for Jews. Don't you forget it.'

Turning his back on the reporters he shouldered his way through the crowd, and the cameras followed his back as he went down the avenue.

From above them there was a sudden bang. People ran for it screaming as glass rained down from the eighteenth floor of the

Soviet building. Smoke gushed out from the shattered windows, but Weiss didn't look back.

You could have thought you were in some strange Russian store, Brenda Deutsch often felt. In the week the offices buzzed with activity, there would always be one or two of the performers coming by to talk to Solly, fresh off the aeroplane, and they'd bring him something from home. That's why it looked like a strange Russian store, with everything from *babushkas* to *karakul* hats, real icons and pots of caviar. Solly Eisenberg brought all the great Russian artists and performers over, and they only occasionally defected.

It was Sunday, the offices were quiet and her daughter Clara ran down the corridor in delight. She knew the room she wanted, filled with toys the performers had brought.

'Be careful, now, darling,' her mother said, and the five-year-old called back,

'I will, mummy.'

There was a *babushka* there that was her great favourite. No fewer than twelve of the dolls fitted inside each other until you got to the one that didn't come into two halves – it was no bigger than one of the child's fingers.

The executive fetched the files from the cabinet and sat down at her desk. She shouldn't be doing this on a Sunday, but it was the busy time. Just an hour to get caught up, she thought, and then she'd take Clara out for a pizza and on to the park to play.

The explosion was shockingly loud in the silent offices. She flinched, papers crumpling in her hand, then ran for the door.

'Clara! *Clara!*'

She hauled the door open and smoke billowed about her. The door to Solly's office had been completely blown out, and flames were roaring out of the gutted room. Blazing paper spewed out in sheafs, gushing down the corridor.

'Mummy! *Mummy!*'

She ran through the flames. Her hair caught fire, and she screamed as she beat at the flames. Clara was in the room, crouched by a huge teddy bear, halves of the doll scattered on the carpet, her face pinched with fear. Brenda ran in and the smoke followed her.

She scooped up her child. The smoke was filling the room, she could only see the door by the red light of the blaze outside. She was gasping for breath, the smoke tearing at her lungs as she tried to cough it out.

For a moment, she went to the window, but they were on the

twenty-third floor, and the windows didn't open. She clutched her daughter, and ran forward into the smoke.

She was feeling dizzy. The fire was filling the corridor, the flames licked at them and the little girl howled in terror. Her mother backed into the washroom, where she turned on the tap, splashing them and their clothes with water. Smoke began to seep in around the edges of the door, the paint started to burn.

# Part VIII

## Tel Aviv, 6 October 1973

DAVID turned into Rehov Beeri. The American ambassador lived at one end of the long street, but at this end the houses were concrete apartment blocks on stilts. He parked his old Fiat between the stilts and got out, drab in his olive fatigues, the only splash of colour his arm band with its red cross. His curly hair was long, held back by a red and yellow tie-dyed scarf which bobbed over his shoulders, and he looked out at the world through sunglasses with small purple oblong lenses.

In the dusty lobby he climbed into the little doorless Schindler lift, pressed the button, and it whined him up three floors, the dirty concrete passing in front of his nose. The door of the apartment was decorated with little metal cylinders, *mezuzahs* that held fragments of the Torah. He glanced at them expressionlessly.

The door was just ajar, so he gave it a push and went in. In the living room his brother was swaying and muttering in prayer, a fringed *tzizes* bizarre over his olive flameproof flight suit with its many zips and pockets. The menorah was lit, the accoutrements of Yom Kippur were laid in the room.

Saul looked across at him, and paused.

'Have you come to pray?' he asked.

'No. I thought I'd give you a lift to the air base. I'm going up to the Golan. You can leave the car for Deborah.'

Saul nodded.

'She's taken the kids to the nursery.'

Without further comment he resumed his praying. The sight of him irritated David.

'They have God on their side too,' he said, cutting in.

'Who?'

'The Arabs. The ones who're coming over the frontier any moment.'

Saul flushed with anger.

'They have Satan,' he retorted. 'Only the Devil would declare war on the Day of Atonement.'

'Any competent general would. They have us with our pants down.'

'They'll be sorry,' Saul promised viciously and stared at David.

'Are you going to keep interrupting me?' he demanded.

'Probably. What on earth are you doing? We aren't religious. Did you ever see Dad down at the synagogue?'

'God touched my soul,' Saul said sincerely. 'He showed me how wrong I had been to ignore him. Now I follow his will, and he makes me prosper. Come on, let's go.'

They went out and down the stairway. Saul looked at his brother in irritation. A Grateful Dead T-shirt was under his fatigues and he smelled vaguely of some scented incense.

'You look like shit,' he said. 'Like some filthy hippie, not a soldier.'

'I'm a medic,' David said pleasantly. 'The wounded don't care what I look like, just so long as I come for them.'

They emerged into the air and climbed into the old Fiat. Saul looked about him with contempt.

'If you believed in God you too would prosper.'

David engaged the gears with a rattling crunch.

'Journalists don't earn much,' he said cheerfully. 'But they have a good life.'

He sent them into the thickening traffic, full of reservists hurrying towards the coming war.

'Seriously,' he said. 'When did God pick you out?'

'Laugh. Go ahead. See who laughs last. I realized that I did the will of God in *milchemet shel mitzvah.*'

'The Holy War?' David asked incredulously. 'I thought the Maccabees had the last one.'

'The Six-Day War,' Saul said icily. 'Organized for us by God.'

'I thought Moshe Dayan and Ezer Weizmann had rather more to do with it.'

'Only instruments of His will,' Saul said assuredly. 'Like me.'

David pulled in at the gate of the air base, hot, dusty and bleak, where the air was filled with the shriek and howl of the turbine engines. Saul got out, carrying his white helmet. It still bore the imprint of the concrete on its surface. In the mirror, as he headed up towards the heights of the Golan, David watched him stride in without a backwards glance, tall and handsome, powerful and certain.

*     *     *

At 14,000 feet the flight of four Skyhawks seemed to hang almost motionless in the air. The sun filtering through the high cumulus gleamed on their outstretched wings, glinted from their hunched backs and on the mass of ordnance poking out from beneath them.

Below was Sinai. Its air was streaked with little lines of greasy smoke, and Saul grinned savagely. The first casualties of combat, burning enemy tanks. The Skyhawks put their noses down. Inside the cockpits the armament lights shone red, the barber's poles of their machmeters began to wind around the dials as the fighter-bombers accelerated down through the air like toboggans down a run of ice.

The surface of the desert looked blackened with bugs. It crawled with Egyptian armour.

'There they are, boys!' Saul yelled. 'There's plenty for all, let's help ourselves.'

They were almost in line. His gunsight shone, through it the bugs flashed and glowed. The surface of the desert lit up with twinkling light. White and black puffs of smoke erupted in front of Saul.

*Where was it all coming from?*

They were diving into smoke. A terrific bang, the Skyhawk shuddering with impact, explosions, balls of luminous fire whipping past the cockpit. To the right, at two o'clock from the ground a ripple of flame and something lancing towards him with terrifying speed.

Saul was suddenly terrified, his hands slippery inside his gloves, his toes clenched in his boots, the controls seemed stuck in glue.

The missile weaved like a ballet dancer, to the right a Skyhawk lurched as clumsily as a pack-laden soldier with a bayonet. The explosion almost blinded Saul. He saw flaming pieces of aircraft tumbling past him, then he found himself in the smoke, where balls of orange fire pursued him.

The desert! Bangs about his wings and dreadful flashes of light, guns, armour, tanks.

They were at about a hundred and fifty feet.

'Lower!' he screamed. The array of battle tilted in front of his eyes, tanks and missiles, the switches were on and he squeezed the button. The jet lurched as the bombs dropped away. He fired, firing frantically, his finger clamped over the trigger, the shells forming a ribbon of white explosions worming through the armour, striking fire from them like phosphorus. A bowser exploded beneath him, tossing the fighter-bomber high up in the air with its burning gust. Desperately in a maelstrom of slashing

tracer he forced the stick forward, looking for the safety of the
ground.

'Look out!'

A Skyhawk was coming straight at him at enormous speed. Its
canopy was blown off. It hit a radar truck, pieces and men flying
in the air, the dish tumbling over and over, miraculously intact. The
Skyhawk furrowed through a line of lorries and vanished in a blinding
flash of light. Saul shot through a whirlwind of flames and fragments
with his controls locked.

He pulled back on the stick, shooting almost vertically up, the
breath grunting out of him. Flashes of light pursued him, something
burst so close it blinded him and he never felt the explosion. His
panel was alight with blazing red, squinting behind he saw his
tailplane ragged with torn metal. Columns of greasy smoke stained
the surface of the desert and it sparkled in a firework display of
blazing magnesium.

A torch blazed in pursuit. In terror he slammed the stick forward,
reaching for the safety of the ground. Something massive slapped
at the Skyhawk, blowing it across the sky. He levelled out over the
desert and grit coated his teeth. The jet was barely flying, it staggered
through the air, one wing low.

'Formate on me. All red aircraft formate on me,' he croaked.

He set course for base.

'Formate on me,' he ordered again, but the radio was silent. From
somewhere on the half-wrecked aircraft something was banging. A
stream of fuel was spraying from punctured wing tanks.

A column of smoke rose ahead and as he passed he saw it was
a lone tank, its tracks blown off, pointing towards Egypt.

The dull glow of the buildings and vehicles, burned to embers, and
skeletons of charred metal were fading as the dawn brightened the
sky. The stench was still in the air, wafts of propellant, diesel, blood,
and incinerated property, equipment and people, blew on the breeze.
The half-track with its huge red crosses ground over the rocky terrain
and arrived on the pocked road with a thump that set someone inside
moaning in the pain of shattered bones.

In the half-light David jumped down from the cab clutching a
sheaf of bamboo poles, all with fluorescent flags on. He had a pack
of equipment slung over his shoulder.

'I'll start the search here,' he called up to the driver. 'I'll mark
it. I'm going over that way, where the fighting was last night. You
come back for me when you've put them into the field hospital.'

'Okay.' The driver was chewing gum to alleviate the taste of the air, which caught in the back of the throat. He looked tired, as they had been scavenging the battlefield for its wounded since the previous afternoon.

'I'll bring some coffee.'

He engaged the gears with a crunch and the vehicle jerked away with a whirring of its tracks. Where it had been standing lay a pool of blood that had dripped through the floorboards. David went to the side of the road and plunged one of his markers into the ground.

In the distance he could hear the irregular crump and rattle of fighting from somewhere around the Yaakov bridge. The sun creeping over the horizon caught on the shattered glory of the Crusader ruins. Smoke was drifting from the abandoned *kibbutz*. He could see tanks scattered amongst the apple trees like broken toys, and he headed towards them.

He was following the line of an advance. Blackened and twisted pieces of weaponry and chassis were scattered about, lying on the dirt like dead cockroaches. A lifeless Syrian hung out of a destroyed wheeled personnel carrier, his head resting in a pool of his own congealed fat. Flies buzzed angrily as David passed by.

Against the pale, powder-blue sky birds were flying, dark shapes, wings outspread as they glided through the morning air. Kites and crows, without whose presence no scene of battle was complete. As he watched he saw a small group losing height, whirling gracefully down, landing on the ground in a flare of wings, hopping through the scrub. The silent carcasses of tanks poked up from the scrub. He changed his direction, heading towards them. What carrion birds ate was not always dead.

They were displeased to see him, rising in spread black feathers to land a short distance away, staring at him with cold yellow eyes as they strutted to and fro.

Some vile struggle had taken place. Plants were crushed, the ground scuffed and scarred with the impact of boots and buckles, fists and knives. Black blood was spattered everywhere.

Dead men lay scattered about among the tanks, an Israeli Centurion and a Syrian T-55 were locked together, jammed in a mutual rape of armour plate. Amongst the ghastly debris of the fighting were knives and pistols, spades, hammers and axes from the toolkits of the tanks. At David's feet lay a man who had lost, his teeth bared in a rictus of agony, his clothes in a bloody tatter. His knees were raised, his arm outstretched, with a piece of cloth jammed between the clenched fingers.

He lay like the carcass of a hog, most fearfully butchered.

David stood in the trampled glade, staring down at the man. What he had left about him indicated that he was an Israeli tanker. David felt a sense of sickness in his stomach, that became revulsion. Horrible things he had seen on the battlefield. The fearful injuries inflicted upon flesh and bone by the impact of modern weaponry. But it was, somehow, impersonal, death and mutilation inflicted from a distance, by a cruel but indifferent god.

What he saw now on the ground came from a much earlier age. One man had murdered another, had hacked him to death with hatred in his soul.

He bent over him, looking for identification.

'He's dead,' a voice called out, in English.

There was a sudden outraged cawing, a flutter of wings. He looked up. A soldier was lying in the shade of the T-55, propped up against a steel wheel, the sun at his back. Smoke from the burned-out building nearby was drifting across.

He stood up, his red arm band clearly visible, and went over to the soldier. A dead kite lay a few feet away from him in a spray of black feathers and gore. The soldier held a pistol in his hand.

'I'm damned if I'll let a god-damned bird eat me,' the man said. He had an American accent, but wore the uniform of a Syrian tanker. On the name strip across his breast he had a title, Hamouda. Captain Hasan Hamouda. He seemed to be a little older than David, handsome, with very white teeth in his olive face, curly black hair now matted with blood and dirt.

'It was hand to hand,' he explained. He had bound up his thigh as best he could. David bent over him and took the field dressing off.

'I'm waiting for our boys to come through,' said Hamouda. He had been knifed through his thigh muscle. 'I'll hitch a ride to Jerusalem with them.'

'You'll wait a long time,' said David.

'You've held us?' Hamouda's face tightened in anger.

'Yes.'

Hamouda reached inside his overall, and took out a cigarette. He lit it, inhaling sharply as David bound the wound. He looked about the battlefield.

'We nearly did it.'

'Nearly's not good enough.'

'No,' Hamouda said thoughtfully. 'It isn't, is it.'

'The *ta'gad*, the medevac will be back soon. We'll get you to a hospital.'

'An *Israeli* hospital? Never!' Hamouda said certainly. 'Give me one of those sticks and I'll walk out.'

'Suit yourself,' David said. There were hundreds of smashed Israeli and Syrian tanks scattered over the battlefield. The tank corps had never known such combat, had never believed the Syrians could fight so well. He had work to do, looking for survivors.

Hamouda heaved himself up, supporting his weak leg with his stick.

'It's that way,' said David.

'I know,' Hamouda said. 'I came up it.'

He began to limp away, and David resumed his search.

'Hey!'

He looked up, and Hamouda had paused. His eyes gleamed with a hostile certainty.

'*Jerusalem next time!*'


## Damascus, January 1975

The officers in their olive uniforms stood to attention as the president came into their brand-new lecture hall. He was dressed as they were, as President Asad had been a career soldier, a pilot, before the *coup*. He had come to power with five other colleagues, but only he was left.

'Please sit down.'

Asad had come in bearing two plaques, framed and glassed, ready for hanging, which he placed on the table in front of him. Outside the chill winter wind was blowing over the villas of the Malki quarter. The men in the hall lived there. Hasan Hamouda, with bright decorations from the battles in the Valley of Tears, lived there. Like many, he wore a black arm band, in memory of his own loss. They were a new elite, their president had come to command them.

'We have been betrayed,' Asad said quietly. 'Kissinger said to me, "I will not promise what I cannot deliver, but I will deliver all that I promise." I did not realize that the promises were being made to someone else. To Israel. For Henry Kissinger is a Jew. Very shortly now, under his auspices, Sadat will sign the second disengagement agreement with the Jews. He will have split us Arabs, which was, I now see, his intention all along. Our solidarity has been destroyed and now Syria is isolated. As for the Palestinians they are even worse off than before. So we have fought our war all for this, for nothing. *Al-Nakba.* Disaster.'

He let the words hang in the air, so that they could all feel their defeat.

'You are the best,' he said. 'The most able, experienced and intelligent of my officers. I have chosen you personally. Why? For intelligence. Intelligence in our Arab countries nearly always means internal intelligence – what are those who would unseat me doing, and who are they? I have my internal intelligence.'

His eyes swept over them and he smiled his sad, knowledgeable smile. He knew those who hated him, knew what had to be done.

'That is my affair. To keep myself as president, to defeat the Israelis, to expel them from the Middle East, where they do not belong.'

The men in the room had recently fought a devastating war, in which early victory had turned to the ashes of defeat and left their enemy stronger than ever before. They listened impassively, Hasan Hamouda among them.

'You are going to help me do that. You are the men of my new intelligence. Not inside Syria, but outside. The intelligence you will give me is called "real-world intelligence". An American expression. Kissinger would understand it. The world is becoming more difficult to handle all the time; the pace of change is enormously fast. It is an information-driven world. To succeed you have to know as much as you can about what is happening – and what is likely to happen – throughout the whole environment in which you and your enemy are operating, like two rival fish, in water. That water is dark, and in it are powerful currents: Science, technology, politics, economics are the swirling forces in the water. Knowing where they are, and where they are going, you can manage to be in control. Swim blindly about and one or more of them will sweep you to your doom.

'This is dark and dangerous water into which Henry Kissinger has tipped us. A tidal wave of disturbance is about to wash over the whole of the Middle East. With Egypt gone, who will restrain Israel from expansion, from striking at will? Where will the Palestinians go? I fear they will go into Lebanon, and civil war will result. And what of the Iraqis, who hate us?

'I have to know. I have to have "real-world intelligence". The organization I have formed with you resembles the on-board navigation system of a jet aircraft. The policymakers take the decision as to where the enterprise is headed, those in intelligence keep them informed as to where they are, whatever the conditions, and furthermore, what dangers and opportunities lie ahead, so that the policymakers can make their appropriate plans in good time. So, I will tell you the destination, you wil provide me with the information I require to get there. The destination is very simple. It is the removal of the Jews from the Middle East, and the consequent restoration of Syria to her rightful ownership of *bilad al-Sham*, the lands of Damascus. As symbols of your task I have brought you two gifts.'

Asad took a small hammer and a packet of picture hooks from the table and went to one wall.

'Gather round, gentlemen,' he said, and they came down from their seats as he carefully knocked the hook into the wall.

'Major Hamouda,' he said, bestowing recognition. 'Pass me the smaller of the two plaques, please.'

Hamouda took it carefully from the table and gave it to Asad, who hung it level from the hook. It was a very old tablet, inscribed in a strange tongue.

'As you all know, gentlemen, I study history. A study of history enables one to distinguish between truth and lies. The two often cohabit. As Winston Churchill once said, in wartime truth is so precious she must be surrounded by a bodyguard of lies. That is what the Jews have done. There are two truths about their return to the Middle East which they have surrounded with lies. They claim that history justifies it and that the land they call Israel, which the Palestinians call Palestine, is theirs by historical, if not God-given, right. These are the lies. And what is the truth?'

Asad tapped the glass covering the ancient tablet.

'This is four and half thousand years old. It is written in an ancient Semitic tongue. It is one of fifteen thousand such tablets found at the archaeological site of Ebla, south of Aleppo. The tablets locate the origins of the Arabic language and monotheism itself within Syria. They describe a world of high civilization equal to that of Egypt or Mesopotamia one thousand years before Abraham. The Israelis quote the Old Testament to justify what they have done. The Ebla archives prove that we Syrians were great when the Israelites were a mere bunch of poor, root-chewing nomadic savages.'

Asad turned to face the officers clustering about him.

'We shall be great again. That tablet proves that we have more right to Palestine than they, whom Vespasian expelled two thousand years ago. And if occupancy in the past provides any right to a lease, what of the Hittites or Sumerians, the ancestors of the Palestinians, whom the Jews have expelled, as latter-day Romans?'

Asad walked across the floor to the opposite wall and once again carefully knocked in a picture hook.

'The other argument used by the Israelis to justify the theft of the land they occupy is that they require a national home to keep them safe. They point to the Holocaust, the six million dead. They have a great memorial to it, Vad Yashem.'

Once again, Asad turned to face his officers.

'Well, yes,' he nodded. 'Yes, it happened. Hitler's Nazis slaughtered millions. Gypsies, communists, homosexuals, Russians, Poles, Czechs. Oh, yes, and Jews. Is Vad Yashem a memorial to all oppressed peoples of the world? No. Just the Jews. And yet while gypsies and communists and homosexuals and refugee Poles and Russians and Czechs make their home where they live, only the Israeli Jews claim to require a homeland. In a place which is very dangerous to them. For they should not be here. Major Hamouda, the other frame, if you please.'

Hamouda did as he was bid, and gave it to Asad. It was a richly-decorated scroll, written in flowing black Arabic.

'What is Israel?' Asad asked rhetorically. 'Is it this precious homeland for the oppressed? No. But for oppressors, yes. For what is Israel, how was it born? It was born at the end of imperialism. It was born as an imperialist state. The Jews are a minority, who oppress the rightful owners. The Israelis ally themselves to the few who dominate the many. They ally themselves with the Rhodesian whites, with the South African Afrikaaners. But history is now flowing against imperialism. We have ourselves thrown off the imperial yoke. Very soon in the entire continent of Africa, from the Middle East in the north to the Afrikaaner state in the south, there will be but two colonial regimes – South Africa, and Israel.'

Once again, Asad tapped the glass over the framed scroll.

'These are the words of Imad ad-Din al-Isfahani, secretary to the great Salah el-Din, whom his enemies called Saladin, King of Syria and the whole Levant. Imad describes the events of the fourth of July, 1187 AD.

> They retreated to Mount Hattin to escape the storm of destruction; but on Hattin itself they found themselves encompassed by fatal thunderbolts. Arrowheads transfixed them; the peaks laid them low; bows pinned them down; fate tore at them; calamity chewed them up; and disaster tainted them.

'Many centuries ago the Christian Crusaders came and occupied the land the Jews now call Israel. Mightily armoured, militarily strong, they built vast castles from which they dominated the land. But the day came when our ancestor, Salah el-Din defeated them in combat at the great Battle of Hattin, and now all that remains of their presence are the castles they built.

'The Jews too are mightily armoured, and militarily strong. They have made of their country a castle, but the day will come when they will be defeated, and then all that will remain will be their memory.'

Asad looked about at his men, the best he had.

'That is your task. To bring me the Battle of Hattin.'


## Transkei, South Africa, May 1975


'There he is!' Ruth cried happily, and Jacob slowed the Hertz South-African-built Mercedes even further, pulling over to the side of the road. In the open-air cafe under the leafy trees in the square a dark-haired handsome man waved cheerfully, rising from the round table where he had been waiting. Ruth and Jacob got out of the car and he came running over, wrapping his arms about his mother, holding her thin frame carefully, as though she might break, stroking her greying hair and then embracing his father.

'Come on. Let me get you coffee, yes?'

'Here I drink coffee,' Jacob agreed.

'But not at home,' Saul grinned.

'It is sludge. Why after all these years you cannot have a cup of good coffee in the State of Israel I do not know.'

'Oooh, hush,' Ruth said reprovingly. 'You see Saul for the first time in a year and you complain about coffee. Saul, darling, it was wonderful to get your call last night. Deborah and the children, they are at home? They are well?'

'Of course! Very well indeed. I am here on business.'

'Ahh . . .'

'I have a client at my law practice. He asked me to come down.'

'A client like that already!' Ruth beamed, her face lighting up suddenly with its old beauty. As the coffee came Jacob eyed his son warily.

'Aren't you pleased, Dad?' Saul asked.

'Of course, of course. He pays your expenses, I hope.'

'More than that! He wants me to join his partnership. He needs a smart lawyer.'

'Back where I came from the only people who needed a smart lawyer were the crooks,' his father muttered.

'*Jacob*,' Ruth snapped.

'Just an observation.'

Saul beamed at his father, refusing to be put off.

'So what are *you* doing here? I called your office.'

'Oh, government business,' Jacob said vaguely.

'Sure, but where South Africa's concerned, there's much more hidden than what is known,' Saul said, eyeing him carefully. 'Isn't that right?'

'If you say so.'

'Down for the plutonium shipment?' Saul asked softly.

'*Saul*,' Ruth hissed, looking about her.

Saul grinned.

'You get to hear all kinds of stuff, as a lawyer.'

'I think it is reasonably common knowledge among those who have any interest in the subject that the State of Israel will acquire whatever defences it considers necessary to prevent its destruction by its enemies,' Jacob said carefully. 'Whether that might include nuclear weapons of whatever description I am not prepared to say. Nor do I wish to discuss the matter further here or anywhere else.'

'Okay, Dad,' Saul grinned. 'Just testing. But say, now, what do you think of this place?'

'The cafe? Very nice. I wish they would come and make coffee in the Knesset. The stuff there is terrible.'

'No, no. *Here*. Transkei.'

'The climate is pleasant. The people seem friendly.'

Saul glanced around at the Africans wandering through the square, white teeth flashing as they paused to talk to friends and acquaintances.

'It's more than that,' said Saul. He had a small blue skullcap resting on his hair, he reached up to adjust it out of habit.

'It's a new independent nation,' he said.

'It's a Bantu homeland, isn't that right?' Ruth chimed in.

'That's it, Mama. The first of several.'

Saul turned to Jacob.

'You must know about this, Dad.'

Jacob nodded.

'The first of the Bantustans. Independent homelands for South Africa's blacks within South Africa itself. They plan for some ten, I believe. Transkei, Bophuthatswana, Ciskei, Kwazulu . . .'

'You know, it's a good idea, Dad, isn't it?' Saul enthused, leaning forward over the round table. 'Maybe we ought to do the same with the Palestinians. Give them Gaza.'

'My son, the left-wing radical,' Jacob said, smiling. 'Myself, I think the Palestinians are Arabs, and should be absorbed by their Arab friends in the countries that surround us. Perhaps we can do a deal, trade Sinai and the West Bank in return for Egypt, Jordan, Syria and the others taking in the Palestinians as their citizens. It should not be beyond the capabilities of diplomats. Countries have taken in refugees from elsewhere since time immemorial, and nearly always to their benefit. That is what I think we must do.'

'Wouldn't a Palestinian Gaza be a good idea?' Saul persisted.

'Why?'

'The same as here. A docile workforce. A good place for investment.'

'Ah,' Jacob said bleakly, putting down his coffee. 'Not my son the left-wing radical, but my son the money-maker.'

'What is wrong with making money?' Saul protested. 'Have we Jews not made money since the world began? We are better at it than the goys.'

'I do not object to making money . . .'

'We do not!' Ruth laughed.

'It is *how* the money is made that is important,' Jacob finished.

'Of course,' Saul said, wide-eyed. 'I'm not a crook, you know.'

'I did not say you were. Though you should be careful when dealing with some of your clients, who will be.'

Saul laughed.

'Don't worry, I can spot a crooked client before he gets through my new plate glass door into the air conditioning.'

'And this client who has paid for you to come down here, he is not a crook.'

'Meyer? No, no. A fine businessman.'

'The jails are full of people who were once described as fine businessmen,' Jacob said obstinately.

'*Jacob Ben-Levi!*' Ruth snarled. 'I despair of you! Our son is making a fine career and all you can do is criticize him. Apologize, go on, I insist.'

'I am warning him that not everyone is what they may seem,' Jacob said mildly. 'Although I suspect he does not need my advice.'

'There you are again . . .'

'Mama!' Saul held up a hand, smiling pleasantly. 'You know how Dad and I spar with each other. But see, now, I have not come to argue, but to offer you both an opportunity. There's going to be a lot of involvement for us Israelis in the Bantu countries. Good, liberal people like yourself, Dad, are coming here, helping the Africans revive their own authentic tribal structure, offering help with government initiatives, providing business opportunities, sport, security, tourism, you name it. Isn't that right?'

Jacob nodded.

'That's so. Which one of these things is your client interested in?'

'Meyer considers Transkei to provide a very good business climate,' Saul said smoothly. 'I agree with him.'

'I know little about climates other than the weather,' Jacob said obtusely. 'Why is it so good for your client here?'

'One, a good workforce.'

'They are docile, they will not strike.'

'I don't think they're allowed to.'

'What else?'

'If you set up a corporation here most of your initial capital will be provided by the South African government.'

'I see. They will then require a return on their investment.'

'Profits will be largely tax free.'

'It sounds wonderful!' Ruth said brightly. 'Doesn't it, darling?'

Jacob grunted, and Ruth kicked him under the table.

'What artefacts of local authentic African culture will Meyer be producing?' he asked.

'Ah . . . you have to remember, we shall be bringing much-needed jobs to this poor country.'

'Yes, yes. Save me the soap. What will you be making?'

'Cars.'

'Cars? The world needs more cars?'

Saul smiled.

'Not ordinary cars. Replicas! You have no idea how people like replicas of classic cars of yesteryear. Glass-fibre body parts on a chassis, off the shelf working parts. It's a profitable thing to get into, let me tell you. We plan to make British MG sportsters of the 1930s, and Porsches of the 1950s.'

'As I understand it, it is profitable if you can keep the costs down.'

Saul nodded vigorously.

'That's right. But as I've said, this is a wonderful business climate.'

'You won't pay the African workers much.'

Saul threw his hands up.

'Dad, these people have very low expectations. That's the beauty of the place. If they can go home at the end of the week with enough for a chicken and a bottle of liquor they're happy.'

'Good working conditions?'

'Sure,' Saul laughed. 'You know how the Afs are. Loose shoes and a warm place to go take a crap and they're happy.'

'Let me wish you the very best of luck in your venture, then.'

'Dad, Dad. I don't want to take all the profit for myself. I want you and Mama to benefit too.'

Jacob spread his hands wide.

'But this is too generous.'

'Seriously. I have Meyer's permission to offer you a seat on the board. Share options. A company villa right here for your own use whenever you like. Swimming pool, barbecue, servants, the lot.'

'It is true that I once assembled rockets, but that was a long time ago. I know little about putting cars together.'

'Jacob, don't be difficult,' Ruth said, sensing trouble and trying to be playful. 'You know Saul doesn't want you to *make* the cars.'

'We have a great guy from Detroit who knows all about assembly lines,' Saul reassured them. 'No, Dad could help in other ways. With contacts. You know all the right people down here.'

He looked his father in the eye.

'I heard they offered you a post in the government itself.'

'You didn't tell me that!' Ruth said indignantly.

Jacob drank some coffee.

'I turned it down,' he said, in a muffled fashion.

'*Why?*' they demanded, in unison.

Jacob put down his coffee cup.

'You must understand I wish you well with your business dealings. It is right that a man should support his family, and you have Deborah to look after, and also the children. But I have to say I do not wish to join your company. I understand the motives of the South Africans in promoting these Bantustans, it is all a part of their grand apartheid policy which will make the Africans of South Africa into foreigners by creating these artificial homelands. Thus they will have no reason to grant them rights within South Africa itself.'

'So what?' Saul asked coldly.

'So everything! To invest in these places is to legitimize the apartheid regime of South Africa.'

'Again, I say, so what? Is not South Africa one of our best allies?'

'We share some common interests, yes.'

'Survival! We are both threatened by people who hate us.'

'It is true,' Jacob admitted. 'But I, Jacob Ben-Levi, whatever I may have to do for my government, I do not have to do some things as a private man. I do not have to invest in apartheid.'

'What exactly is your objection?' asked Saul, puzzled.

'Objection?' Jacob cried. 'You ask me that, who was once a slave? I know how slave systems work. And what is more, I know how these places, these Bantustans will end up – as mere cruel and bloody tyrannies. I wish, as ordinary Jacob Ben-Levi, to have nothing to do with it. And I wish that all Israelis felt the same way.'

'Why? The richer we are, the stronger we are.'

'What is Israel?' Jacob asked passionately. 'We are nothing if we are not a moral country. We *founded* ourselves as a refuge against hatred, against slavery, against genocide. How can we then associate ourselves with those in the world who do thus to others, as was once done to us?'

'Morals, shmorals!' Saul yelled suddenly, finally losing his temper. 'All our old relatives had morals, their morals took them all the way to the ovens and the gas chambers. You want to know what keeps Jews safe today?'

He stared furiously at his father, his eyes bulging, and Jacob stared back.

'You want to know?' he demanded. 'Being strong. That's what. Being rich and powerful. Being able to whip our enemies. And having *this*.'

He whipped the blue *kippot* off his head and thrust it under Jacob's nose.

'You are not a Jew if you are not strong in our faith,' he stated flatly. 'You must believe totally, and then God will protect.'

'There is no God,' Jacob said wearily. 'I saw thousands like you calling to him, and little good did it do them. "God is on leave," we would say. *I* survived, and I did not believe in your god or anyone else's.'

'There *is* no other god,' Saul said viciously. He replaced his small skullcap, adjusting it on his head.

'Well, I must be getting on . . .'

'Saul, Saul, darling,' his mother said frantically. 'Don't go so soon, we hardly see you . . .'

'I have business to attend to,' Saul said, with a certain and new measure of satisfaction in his voice. He eyed his father in anticipation.

'I have a new client.'

'That's wonderful . . .' Ruth said.

'Rabbi Gideon Weiss,' Saul said succinctly, and Jacob sat up with the jerk of a stung man.

'What do you want with that bastard?' he demanded.

'He is a Jew, he wishes to come home,' Saul said softly. 'He wants to become an Israeli citizen. He's in a hotel in Haifa right now, in fact.'

'He is a murderer and the FBI want him in America!' Jacob shouted angrily. The African bar-keeper looked up from his glass-polishing in alarm.

'Not so,' Saul said smoothly. 'He is the victim of a vicious anti-Semitic campaign as a result of his campaign to protect Jewish people in America. If he returns to America he will not receive a fair trial. He is a Jew, the son of Jews, and as such he cannot be denied citizenship. "This right is inherent in every Jew by virtue of his being a Jew, if it but be his will to take part in settling the land." That is what David Ben-Gurion said. It's there in the Declaration of Independence. The Law of Return. Enshrined.'

'Section 2(b)(3),' Jacob snapped. 'Which denies citizenship to a Jew with a criminal past, likely to endanger the public welfare. Weiss *is* a criminal, and what he stands for, which is rabid, racialist nationalism at its worst most certainly constitutes an endangerment of the public welfare.'

'He has never been convicted of anything,' Saul said calmly. 'He is a war hero . . .'

'A murderer.'

'War hero who fights to keep Jews safe, wherever they are. And let me tell you, there are plenty in the Likud Party who think that he's just the sort of Israeli we need.'

'The Likud! The Likud should be banned. Who leads it? Begin. I know Begin too, he led the Irgun, which *was* banned. Murdering bastards all of them.'

'Dad, Dad,' Saul said quietly. 'These are not the old days. Holding these old-fashioned liberal views is like being a little fleecy lamb alone in the woods with wolves about. We need men of conviction, men of courage. Menachem Begin and Rabbi Weiss are strong men, they are patriots.'

'So was Adolf Hitler.'

Saul took control of himself, and sat looking at his father in frustration.

'Don't be difficult, Dad.'

'Try telling him not to breathe!' Ruth shouted furiously.

Saul got up, pushing his chair back. He put a note down on the table, anchoring it under his cup.

'I have to go make arrangements for Meyer's company,' he said.

'We'll wait for you, darling . . .,' Ruth said entreatingly. 'Let us have lunch . . .'

'I have to be back later for the plane, Mama.'

'We are on our way to Rhodesia,' Jacob said gruffly.

'You're staying with Seamus Flynn?' Saul asked politely, and Jacob nodded.

Saul bent and kissed his mother. He and Jacob embraced stiffly, then he walked across the road to his car.

Ruth put her face into her hands.

'Can you not, just once, try to understand him?' she cried. 'Must you always create these arguments?'

'I did not . . .,' Jacob protested.

'You did,' she said flatly. 'You always do. So I have one son who lives abroad and does not come to see us because he does not like Israel and I have one son who lives in Israel and does not come to see us because he does not like his father. For this I am a mother?'

'Saul is a Crusader! He is just the same as a Knight Templar. They combined a fanatical devotion to God and Mammon with a hatred of everyone else, whom they were ready to slaughter at a moment's notice. Saul could have joined them.'

'He could not! He is a Jew.'

'So he is a Jewish knight.'

'He is a patriot, a war hero.'

'So were members of the *Waffen SS*. It is not relevant.'

'It is relevant to me,' she said quietly. She was very pale, her skin had taken on a waxy appearance. 'When I . . . when they . . . in the camp. When we were without power, when they . . . and did . . .'

She looked up at Jacob, tiny beads of sweat lining her upper lip.

'I *prayed* for a Jewish warrior to come, to kill them,' she whispered. 'I found you, I was so proud of you as you fought in the war, fighting against our enemies. I don't know what has happened to you.'

'We cannot fight forever. We must win, every time. What happens if one day we lose?'

'Then let us have this bomb. The South Africans give us the uranium, we make the bombs. Nobody will attack us if we can annihilate them.'

She pushed herself to her feet like an old woman.

'Come. Let us catch this plane to see your comrade Flynn.'

She looked up at him viciously.

'Are you sure you want to? Flynn hasn't lost his balls. *He* still fights for his country, he isn't afraid.'

'I am not frightened,' Jacob protested. 'I have fought in many battles.'

She turned her back on him, walking to the car.

'At least I have one man in my life who isn't a coward,' she said.

# PART IX

## Salisbury, Rhodesia, 1975

FLYNN's dyed his hair, Jacob thought in disbelief. He and Ruth came through the customs gate into a scrum of people embracing each other and swapping suitcases, and Seamus Flynn, having seen them first, was pushing through the crowd in his summer-issue army uniform, complete with baggy shorts and colonel's crowns on his shoulders. Jacob was caught by surprise, the youth he remembered had grown into a broad-shouldered, powerfully built man. He will think I have aged, have become old, he thought. The thick band of freckles aross his nose contrasted strangely with his curly black hair. Jacob decided to say nothing. Vanity was a strange thing.

'Welcome to Rhodesia!' he called cheerfully. It seemed to be a popular thing to say, a smartly-dressed young woman in a tailored skirt had just said it to a happily smiling, pale-faced family off the plane, who had transferred from a London flight in Johannesburg. All around was bustle and purpose. It rather reminded him of being in Israel.

'Is this the new slogan?' he enquired, shaking Flynn's hand.

'New immigrants,' the Irishman said proudly. 'Pouring in every day. Everyone wants to live in Rhodesia. Grand to see you again, Ruth.'

'I thought there was rationing,' said Ruth, as Flynn headed them outside. It was almost the first thing she had said since she and Jacob had left Transkei, and Saul.

'You can't get Johnny Walker Scotch, that's true,' Flynn said breezily. 'But then we make our own. UDI Special, not a drop sold until it's three months old. And if you don't like it, you can fill up your car with it.'

Jacob laughed.

'Petrol's still rationed?' he asked, as they got into a pale blue Morris saloon.

'Flowing like the Niagara,' Flynn said expansively, his Irish accent now overlain by the Rhodesian twang. 'We're simply running rings round the Brit sanctions. Petrol came off the ration three years ago. I tell you, man, declaring independence was the best thing we ever did.'

Flynn drove them through the broad, colonial, leafy streets of the capital.

'Things seem prosperous enough,' Jacob admitted. 'You get a different story though in the British press.'

'Smithy just raises the ante every time he negotiates with the Brits. We'll have an agreement any day that's give us all we want. The Brits want shot of it all, they've lost their taste for empire.'

Seamus Flynn grinned broadly, unapologetically.

'But we haven't!'

He pulled off the road through a pair of gates and drew up outside the handsome pillared porch of the hotel. Large trees were planted in the grounds, casting a dappled shade. Brightly-coloured birds hopped about on the branches, flowers were in profusion in beds along the walls. A smiling African man in a porter's uniform hurried forward to take their bags.

'They'll show you to your room,' said Flynn, in the airy lobby. 'I'll wait for you here.'

In the room with its colonial fittings Ruth sat wearily on the bed, folding her thin limbs up like a stick insect.

'I do not feel well,' she said flatly. 'I shall bathe, and rest. You go with your friend Flynn.'

'Wouldn't you rather I stayed?' Jacob asked anxiously.

'You could not help me this morning,' she said bitterly. 'Why should you help me now? Leave me, and I shall be better later.'

Out in the lobby, Jacob found Flynn waiting.

'The Missus all right?' he enquired.

Jacob shrugged.

'I had an argument this morning with Saul. Now she's cross with me.'

'Ah, to be sure, the ladies are always becoming cross with us,' Flynn said cheerfully. 'Never marry an Irishman, that's what my wife is always saying. What about a Tiger beer?'

'Tiger beer? Any wine?' Jacob asked.

'To be sure. The best our South African friends can offer. Let's go to the bar.'

Flynn sat Jacob down at a small low table with two wicker chairs, and fetched the drinks himself. As he put a glass, frosted with condensation down in front of him he spoke without looking.

'The Missus well, then, is she?' he asked casually.

'We are none of us as well as we should have been, we who were in the KZ, in the camps,' Jacob said directly.

'Do you mind me asking, or should we talk about something else? She seems . . . ill? I remember her differently.'

Flynn sat down, and reached for his tall glass of light beer. Jacob raised his own glass to him.

'It is good to see you again,' he said. 'Me, I do not mind talking. For some it is difficult. It is difficult for Ruth.'

'She was not where you were, was she?'

'No, I was in Dora. But people do not hear of Dora, because it was where they made the V2 rockets. The Russians and the Americans, between them, have all the German scientists. Ruth was not there, she was in a place called Radom, in the weapons factory.'

'Nasty place, I take it,' said Flynn, sipping his beer.

'They were all nasty,' Jacob said frankly. 'Very nasty indeed. But some were nastier than others. Radom was vile. Because Ruth cannot talk about it I cannot know the full details, but I do know that after the war they hanged the commandant. He had a peculiarly horrible way of relaxing after work. He liked to pick a girl from the slaves – the prettiest he could find, always – and have them brought to his room. There he would tie up the girl and proceed to whip her savagely, so that she bled from innumerable wounds. When she resembled nothing so much as a piece of bloody meat he would rape her.'

The Irishman's face wrinkled in disgust.

'I believe that this is what happened to Ruth. She bears the marks of the whip to this day. However,' Jacob continued steadily, 'he progressed to something more awful. The day came when mere mutilation was insufficient to excite him. He hacked open the victim with a knife, and would consume parts of her still-living body as she died. As some kind of refinement he had other pretty girls in and tied up to watch.'

Jacob reached over to his glass and drained it.

'This I too believe happened to Ruth. So when from time to time she is cross with me I do not bear a grudge.'

Flynn sat silent, trying to absorb what he had heard.

'Equally, what happened to me has made me what I am too,' Jacob said levelly. 'I, too, cannot change, and there are things I cannot do. Although there are some I can. There is a man called Ibach, who killed my brother David. It is a long story, and I, too, had the opportunity to kill him, but I did not, because of what happened to me in the camp. I have not finished with this man, however, who walks in the open without shame. One day I shall settle with him, for my brother's sake. But Ruth and I, we understand one another. It will all be well in the morning.'

'These memories, they must be with you always.'

'Always,' Jacob agreed. 'That is what one fears, that the nightmares become the day.'

'That's a foul business, that,' Flynn said shaking his head. 'I hope he suffered, that man, when they hanged him. The terrorists we're fighting here – they did something like that to a man and his wife. Two Africans. They cut off his ears and made the wife fry them. Then she had to eat them. Now he goes about without ears and all his village knows what happens to those who go along with us. It's something we have to counter.'

'How goes the war?'

'It's not like when you and I were fighting all those years ago. Not a full stand-up battle. The guerrillas infiltrate through the Tete province of Mozambique where they have support from amongst the Frelimo terrorists.'

'They're fighting the Portuguese in Mozambique.'

'That's them. Our lot, Zapu and Zanu, share their use of bases and supply routes. They come across from there, which is better for them than having to cross the Zambesi from Zambia.'

'They're giving you trouble?'

'We've called up white reservists, recruited more Afs into the army and police; the farmers are tough and we have highly mobile forces to counter them. Helicopter-borne commandos and paratroops in DC3s. The intelligence is flowing. Yes, we'll win.'

'Expensive, all of that,' Jacob observed.

'Yes,' Flynn agreed. 'Look at Israel. Where would you be without the Americans pouring in all the aid? I wish we had a bit of it. I can see how expensive it is, having your kind of militia army. But the sooner we win the sooner we can get back to normal.'

'What about support for the guerrillas amongst the local population?'

'Among the Afs, you mean?'

'Yes.'

Flynn shrugged, his face unsmiling.

'Smithy's party line is that the Afs have always lived under the system of white rule, and that it has brought them material benefits – which it has – and that they are satisfied with it. But I read the intelligence reports. I know there is a lot of deep resentment, fear and hatred of us out there, which the war is making worse. But this is empire, man. Are your Arabs happy in Israel? No, they're not. And our Afs had better ask themselves what would happen if we ever went. Would the Bantu sit down with the Ndebele and the Kalanga? Like hell, man. They all hate each other. But we'll give them someone of their own, a figurehead. Smithy'll make some deal with one of the leaders to bring him into the government. Someone like Muzorewa. Muzorewa's good, he's a Bishop. The Afs like men of God.'

'Muzorewa has no troops on the ground,' Jacob pointed out. 'What was it Stalin said? "How many divisions has the Pope?" Wouldn't it be better to deal with Nkomo or Mugabe?'

'What are you trying to do, Jacob?' Flynn asked jokingly. 'Hand over power? Nkomo and Mugabe are the ones running this war. They *have* troops on the ground. Anyhow, we can always point to what's happened in all the other African countries if the Afs here get too ambitious. Look at bloody Idi Amin, if you want to know what happens when the Afs take over. No, Jacob, man, we'll win.'

He leaned forward and made a pattern of coasters on the table.

'See how it is strategically. We're like a tank. We're armoured to the left with the Portuguese in Angola, to our right with the Portuguese in Mozambique. Behind us we have South Africa. Man, all we have to do is shoot straight ahead!'

Jacob nodded.

'I wish we only had a one-front war each time we have to fight.'

'You whip them each time.'

'It's getting more difficult,' Jacob commented. 'They don't *run* any more. Dayan noticed that. Hit them hard enough and they go back, but they *retreat*. Not break and run. And they're very good if you allow them to fight the kind of fight of their own choosing. But so far, we've stopped them from doing that for long enough.'

'I remember our war,' said Flynn. 'They fought well when they had a good leader.'

'Yes. And the technology makes such a difference, now.'

Flynn raised his eyebrows.

'Capitalist weapons are smarter than communist ones,' Jacob observed cynically. 'We get ours from the West. They get theirs from Russia. I'm just glad it's not the other way about.'

Flynn drained his glass.

'Jacob, I'm sorry to leave you so quickly. I have to lead a mission tonight. We have word that Zapu are bringing arms into one of the villages. We're going to be there too. I have to get out of this gear, get cammed-up and into the bush.'

He rubbed his dyed black hair.

'It's a rinse,' he said. 'In case you thought I'd gone mad.'

'Colonels lead ambushes?'

The Irishman smiled.

'I'm one of the Fighting Flynns, did I ever tell you that? And you taught me something all that time ago. *Acherei*.'

'*Acherei*,' Jacob repeated. 'After me. Yes.'

'You were a great infantry leader,' said Flynn. 'Say, do you want to come, see how we do it out here in the bush?'

It had stung, being called a coward. Jacob got up.

'I'll leave a note for Ruth,' he said.

It was very dark. The only light there was came from a quarter moon, carved as sharp as a shining ear-ring in the sky, and the glittering stars. It was cold. Jacob wriggled his toes in his Nike training shoes. The ters, terrorists Flynn had explained, used them in preference to boots out in the veldt, and the elite scout troops did too.

The mud huts of the village lay all about them. Jacob could smell the foliage of the roof above him. From the veldt came the steady high-pitched creaking of the crickets, nearby the stream that ran through the village gurgled over the rocks. In the early light of the morning the women would be there washing their pans, filling up the water jugs, the children would be fishing.

In the black night, the men were waiting for arms.

Flynn squatted by the wall of the hut, scanning the village ahead with a pair of image-intensifying binoculars. They had walked in with the troops in the night. Some miles upwind, two Alouette helicopters waited on the ground, ready to pursue any guerrillas that might escape the net.

'They're gathering in the square,' Flynn whispered. Jacob peered into the darkness, vaguely able to make out the centre of the village with its area of beaten earth. The radio transmitter in Flynn's ear squawked softly.

'The picket thinks a column's coming down the dry creek.'

Flynn issued orders, speaking softly and quickly into his microphone.

Something moved in the periphery of Jacob's vision, he saw something pale.

'There's somebody here,' he hissed urgently. Flynn stuffed the night-vision binoculars down by the bottom of the hut, and switched off his radio.

Jacob could smell tobacco smoke. There was a faint glow at hand height. A big, moon-faced Ndebele was suddenly, silently next to him.

'Anybody heah?' he asked quietly, in English.

He thinks I'm a guard, thought Jacob.

'Uh-huh,' Jacob grunted, thinking quickly and unwilling to trust himself speaking with a tribal accent.

The African man put his cigarette to his mouth, standing close to Jacob. He inhaled deeply and the tip was suddenly incandescent. In its light Jacob saw a pair of deep brown eyes staring searchingly into his.

'Well, that good,' the man said. Jacob saw that he carried a Russian Kalashnikov assault rifle in one huge paw, as easily as a limb of bamboo. He turned away from Jacob, and he realized that he had seen Flynn, by the wall. He squatted down next to him.

'What about you, ma friend?' he enquired.

'Nobody heah but us,' Flynn answered comfortably, sounding just the same.

There was the sudden red glow of the cigarette once again, and Jacob saw the two faces staring impassively at one another, Flynn's blackly camouflaged one and the African one.

The Ndbele got up easily, his rifle swinging his paw.

'They be heah soon,' he said casually. He walked forward back into the night, and Flynn squatted, watching him.

'Fee,' the African said, as he left.

'Fee?' Flynn repeated.

'Fee-Fie-Fo-Fum!'

The Ndebele whirled in the dark, his cigarette flying in a glowing arc.

The night was ripped apart by the blazing blows of light and noise as the Kalashnikov went off.

Jacob leaped for the cover of the hut. As he lay there the wall exploded all about him, showering him with mud and branches. The firing stopped as suddenly as it had started. His ears sang in the silence, and from somewhere he heard the voice again.

'I smell the blood of an Englishman . . .,' it called mockingly.

From the night behind him automatic weapons opened up. Bullets cracked over his head like whips. Down in the village there was a sudden yelling of alarm. Firing started on the other side. From behind he heard shouted Rhodesian orders. Men were moving, he heard the short stabbing rip of Israeli-supplied Ruzis, and from the sky, the slapping clatter and whine of the helicopters hurrying. The firing was moving into the village, and as he peered up he could see the yellow gunflashes. Patches of orange light flickered as thatch began to burn.

Jacob crawled forward in the dirt, his breath panting, his teeth full of grit. There was something there in the half-light, lying like a crumpled sack of old clothes.

Flynn was still breathing, a harsh liquid gargling that rattled in his chest and sent dark blood up his throat to spill from his mouth.

'Lie still. It's me, Jacob.'

Jacob went to undo the shirt to assess the wounds and his hands dipped into hot spouting blood and ripped flesh.

'Don't bother . . .' Flynn rasped, and fresh gore spilled from his mouth.

'Cheeky bastard . . .'

The air above was filled with the thudding of helicopter blades. A sudden savage blast of pure white light lanced down from the hovering craft, and began to move about, searching.

Jacob went to get up, to wave, and Flynn gripped him with tremendous strength.

'You'll get shot,' he gasped. 'They'll think you're a ter.'

The light swept past a hut. As it left Jacob saw a huge figure step out, swinging his rifle up to his shoulder. The African leader fired in three short bursts, at short range.

There was a scream of anguished metal from above them. The light wobbled, something huge fell in a blaze of burning fuel. There was a mighty crump as it went in, and the night sky was orange.

In its light Jacob ripped off his shirt, attempting to stuff Flynn's terrible wounds.

'Cheeky bloody bastard . . .' Flynn whispered. 'To call me an Englishman . . .'

A light and a heat assailed Jacob; he looked up and saw the stream next to him was on fire. He turned back to Flynn, who now lay still, his chest having ceased its heaving. Green Irish eyes looked up into the burning African sky, and Jacob closed them.

He was still in his green camouflage trousers and Nike trainers when he walked into the hotel. They had given him a clean shirt, and the only traces left of the black camouflage made him look like a sweep, running in the seams and wrinkles of his face. The army car crunched into gear and went off down the driveway into the dawn.

The female African clerk gave him his key quietly and impassively. As he reached out his hand for it he saw dried clots of blood around his nails and he knew that she had seen them. He knew he wore the smell of a battle, that there had been death. She passed him the key, and he saw in her poker face the knowledge of a defeat.

He turned, walking down the corridor to his room.

He put the key into the door quietly, turning it carefully, so as not to waken Ruth.

The room was dark, a little light seeping in from the dawn through the window.

A switch clicked softly, a lamp glowed. Ruth stared at him from a chair with bulging, terrified eyes.

She was bound to it with white tape, she was gagged. The two men that had been sitting with her stood up. They wore black masks that covered their faces, showing only eye and mouth slits, they carried silenced pistols in their hands. One spoke.

'Well, now, isn't it the longest time we've been waiting for you, Jacob. But we're glad you're here at last. Shall we be off, then?'


Ruth stared at Shahak in disbelief.

'What are you doing here?' she asked, bewildered. 'And where is this?'

Shahak held out a chair for her, and she sat down in it with a thud, her legs still shaky. From outside there came the changing hum of Salisbury traffic, of people going about their day. In the office with its desk and grey electronic equipment a vase of bright lilies glowed yellow and orange. Shahak cannot have put it there, a small part of her brain thought.

Shahak was busying himself with a kettle making coffee.

'This is our mission here. We're advising the Rhodesians with their war. We know about guerrillas. Me? I'm defence attaché in Pretoria. I happened to be up here when I heard about Jacob. There's been a *coup* in Portugal. It may affect their empire in Angola and Mozambique, which will mean a whole different war for the Rhodies. But that's another thing. I'm going to try to get Jacob back.'

'But you don't like Jacob . . .'

'Jacob is an Israeli!' Shahak said savagely. He gave her a mug of coffee. 'I will do anything to save any Israeli.'

He sat down opposite her, big, burly, intense.

'The Rhodies say it's okay for you to stay here. I'm going to help them in the hunt for Jacob's kidnappers.'

'What can you do?'

'I have contacts they don't. With the Americans.'

'The Americans are the other side of the world!' she wailed. 'Jacob is *here*. The people who want to kill him are *here*.'

'The Americans are everywhere,' Shahak said enigmatically. 'And anywhere they want to be. Jacob . . . must be not far. In the country. We have received a demand from the Palestinians.'

'What do they want? Can we give them what they want?' Shahak smiled grimly.

'We can never give them what they *want*,' he said. 'They *want* Israel. But . . . they have made demands. They want Gaza, for example. All out of the question.'

'But they will kill Jacob!'

'Not yet,' he said with certainty. 'What they *really* want from all this – they know that one Knesset member does not equate into Gaza – is publicity. Well, okay. We can give them that if it keeps Jacob alive, and while we look for them. I feel we can find a bunch of Palestinians in a place as race-conscious as Rhodesia.'

'The ones that took Jacob . . .,' she said slowly, 'they were not Palestinian.'

'*What?*'

Shahak stared at her intently.

'How do you know that?' he demanded. 'You said they were masked.'

'You must understand . . . Jacob and I speak many languages. When we were sent to Damascus by Levinger, it was in part because we could pass for Syrians. We have an ear . . .'

'Yes . . . so who are they?'

'They sounded like Flynn.'

'They were Rhodies?' Shahak said, puzzled.

'No, they sounded like *Flynn*.'

'They are *Irish* . . .,' Shahak breathed, in sudden understanding. 'Flynn's dead . . . did you know?'

She put her head in her hands.

'No . . . how did he die?'

'Some skirmish out in the bush. Jacob was there, that was why he was so late back.'

'They were worried,' she said, her voice muffled. 'I could tell.'

She lifted her head up.

'Why Irish?'

'Terrorists are getting together to help each other. Places the PLO train – the camps they have in Syria and Libya – they get people like the IRA, the German Red Army, ETA and all these other bastards . . .'

He looked at her with a strange expression of awakening hope
on his face. It was slightly frightening.

'I wonder . . .' he whispered to himself.

'You wonder what?'

'I wonder if I know who's behind this . . . I've waited a long
time . . .'

He ran his tongue over his lips unconsciously, thinking of
something she did not know.

'The Americans,' she said harshly, breaking in on him. 'Why the
Americans?'

'TECHINT,' he said succinctly.

'Who is Tekint?'

'TECHINT is information. From spies. Not live ones like you
and Jacob were. That's HUMINT, human intelligence. The problem
with human beings is that they suffer from emotions, they drink, get
jealous, can be fooled, tell lies and so faith. So the Yanks have gone
for technology, TECHINT. They've been spending a fortune on it
ever since the Second World War. Computers, gathering and listening
systems. U2 aircraft, EC-130s, satellites with cameras on board. We
have a computer at our headquarters, an IBM. We're very proud of
it. The National Security Agency have computers you can't buy, and
they have about five *acres* of them.'

'To do what?'

'They eavesdrop. They listen to electronic emissions. SIGINT,
mainly. Signals intelligence. Communications. People talking on the
telephone. The Americans can listen to the Russians talking to each
other in Moscow. I know a guy in the CIA, I deal with him. Jacob
knows him too. Man by the name of Hank Snow.'

He jumped up.

'I'll get in touch now,' he said.

Ruth reached for her cooling coffee.

'Ask Captain Snow if he knows where Dora is,' she said.


'Hank? It's Shelesh Shahak. You've heard about Jacob?'

Hank Snow's voice came through, via scrambling system, micro-
wave transmitter and satellite as clear as if he were in the next
room.

'I heard,' he said. 'What can I do to help?'

'Some information for you. The men who conducted the kidnap
aren't Palestinians. They appear to be Irish. You're looking at
members of the IRA, at a guess.'

'*Provos* . . .,' Snow breathed. 'Now there's a twist.'

'It's smart,' Shahak agreed. 'The Rhodies are enjoying a tourist boom. *White* guys fit in, no trouble. I'm going to set them to combing through the travel agents. See if we aren't looking at a holiday let on a villa somewhere.'

'Good thinking. And you'd like me to get something going with the National Security Agency. See if we can get some voice matching on any telephone calls. I'll have them go back a week or two.'

'Good. And there's something else.'

There was a strange frisson in Shahak's usually brutally unemotional voice, that somehow set Snow's teeth on edge.

'What?'

'It was the thought of the training camps that did it for me,' Shahak explained. 'That's where these terrorists all get together. And it's a smart plan. Have the IRA do the snatch. In exchange for what? Arms maybe?'

'Sure. The Provos always want plastic explosive. They'd *love* a shoulder-launched ground-to-air missile or two, to use against the Brit helicopters in Ulster.'

'The Palestinians are claiming responsibility, so we can assume they're the ones arranging payment.'

'Abu who?' Snow asked. 'Lots of rag-head weirdos amongst the camel-jockeys.'

'This one has done a pretty good job,' Shahak pointed out. 'Whichever Abu it is, he's able to pay in hardware, up front. The IRA aren't into credit. I was wondering if we might not be dealing with Abu Hataf here.'

'Hataf? That's Hamouda, isn't it?'

'That's right,' Shahak said softly. 'Hadj Hamouda himself . . .'


The man who had spoken to Jacob stood by the window, then spoke into a military radio he took from his bag.

'We're coming out,' he said briefly, and there was a short, answering squawk from inside the olive-coloured set. Then he turned to Jacob, who stood under the pistol of the second man.

'Now, Jacob,' he said, pleasantly enough. 'We know that you're a tough kind of a fella. A commando, you was. So if you look like making trouble for me I'll just shoot yez and worry about it afterwards. And my companion here is going to wait with your wife. Only when I call him will he leave. So I wants you to do just as I say and come with me.'

'I won't make trouble. Don't harm my wife.'

'That's good, then.'

He led Jacob to the door, and just before they went out he pulled
off his mask, stuffing it into his pocket. The corridor was deserted,
they went quickly along it, away from the reception area and through
the back of the hotel. They emerged where large rubbish bins stood
on wheels. A van was waiting there with its engine ticking over, and
Jacob was put inside.

The sun was up. It gleamed on the wire mesh of the cage, and on
the white teeth of the red-haired dog inside. It stared patiently and
unforgivingly at Jacob.

'There's a boy, Lion!' the man said, coming up beside him. It
wagged its tail briefly, and continued to stare at Jacob.

The man handed Jacob a length of chain.

'Jest whack the cage about with it for me, Jacob,' he said amiably.
'Before I make me call.'

Reluctantly, Jacob lashed out, and inside, the dog launched itself
at the wire in a frenzy of hate. After two minutes Jacob was drenched
in sweat and the dog foamed at the mouth with rage.

'There,' said the man approvingly. 'He knows yez now, Jacob. Let
me show you to your room.'

They were out in the countryside. Jacob could see the red dirt road
they had come down through the leafy trees. A long white-painted
colonial bungalow stood sheltered by them and nearby there was a
small guest house, almost like a summer house. The man led Jacob
there and showed him in. It was a simple, airy room equipped with
bed and chair, with a small bathroom off it.

'I hopes you'll be comfortable here. I'll bring you something to
eat in a minute.'

Jacob sat down on the edge of the bed.

'Are you all right, now, Jacob?'

'Yes. I suppose so. Last night, a friend of mine died. He
was killed in a battle. He was a comrade from the war. I miss
him. I had only just got to know him again, and now he is
gone.'

'These are hard times we live in,' the man said, not unsympathetically.

'How long will I be here?' Jacob asked.

'As long as it takes for your government to give us what we
demand.'

'What can the government of Israel give an Irishman? What is it
you want from us?'

The man smiled broadly.

'Now there I was thinking I sounded just like one of these Rhodesian Brits. You're one with an ear, Jacob.'

'What shall I call you?'

'Call me Paddy. That's what the Brits call us.'

'Well, Paddy, Israel's a long way from Ireland.'

'So it is to be sure,' Paddy said pleasantly. 'And then again, it's just next door.'

'It is?'

'To my way of thinking. You see, if you were lying in bed one morning and some people came along and tipped you out of it on the floor, you'd be a bit cross. And if they chased you out of your house and lived there themselves you'd get crosser still. Wouldn't you be cross, Jacob?'

'I would,' Jacob said quietly. 'In fact, it happened to me. The Germans came and drove me and my family from our house. They did more than drive us from our house, they killed us all.'

He reached up into his hair and felt the ridge of the old scar.

'They almost killed me too.'

'That was a terrible thing that happened,' Paddy said. 'It happened to me and my family too.'

'It did?' Jacob asked, surprised for a second.

'To be sure. Cromwell came with his bands of murderers and killed us, and took our homes and land.'

'Wasn't that a long time ago?'

'When was it that the Romans drove the Jews from Israel?' Paddy countered.

'A long time ago. But we are home now.'

'The Romans aren't there now, I suppose.'

'No.'

'Did God just leave the land waiting for you to come back, then?'

'Something like that,' Jacob said levelly.

'But you were a soldier, Jacob, they told me so. You fought a war to get your land.'

'Against the Arab armies,' he explained.

Paddy furrowed his brow.

'And the Palestinians?' he asked. 'Who are they?'

'Refugees from all the turmoil in the Middle East since the Second World War. There has been a great movement of people, what with fighting, decolonisation, the fall of the *ancien régime* . . .'

'*Ancien régime* . . .,' Paddy breathed. 'It's a joy to talk to a man with such schooling. The only problem is when I talk to these Palestinians they say they want to go home.'

'They can. All that is required to solve the so-called Palestinian problem is for the Arab countries to stop keeping the refugees in camps, and to give them citizenship.'

'Like the Jews in America, or England, or other countries.'

'That's exactly it.'

'But they say they want to go home,' Paddy said quietly. 'They say they want to go back to Palestine. What is it they call it? *Filastin*. That's it. They say the Jews in Israel should go and live in America and England and places like that, and give them back Filastin.'

'Can the Red Indians have back America? There are things that are not possible.'

'The Red Indians now ... I've often thought I'd like to go talk to them about Cromwell, and they could talk to me about the US Cavalry. But aren't you changing your line of argument here, Jacob? That's Cromwell's argument. Might is right.'

'The Jews have come home!' Jacob shouted. 'Don't you know that we must have our own nation, for when we lived with others, they tried to kill us all? We had to be safe.'

'You would have been safe if you'd lived in America,' Paddy pointed out cruelly. 'You have done nothing but put your life at risk since you came to Israel. Your life is at risk now, is it not?'

'If you say so.'

Paddy laughed.

'Here I am, talking away. I'll get you something to eat. But what was it you asked? What an Irishman was doing with an Israeli? Cromwell threw me out of bed, out of my house. When I walked along the road in the rain, with Cromwell sitting by my fire, eating my food and drinking my stout, I met a man coming the other way. He said he came from a land called *Filastin* and that people had thrown him out of his house and were busy enjoying his food and drink by the fire. So I said to him, you help me get rid of the people in my house, and I'll help you get rid of yours.'

'Here?' said Jacob. 'Here in the middle of Africa?'

Paddy paused at the door and beamed.

'To be sure. Didn't Cromwell come here too?'

'Paddy?'

'Yes?'

'You aren't worried I may escape?'

Paddy motioned to Jacob to come to the glass-topped door. He peered through and the baleful yellow gaze of the dog met him from the little verandah.

'Lion hopes you'll try,' Paddy explained.

* * *

Ruth did not know where she was.

They had wanted to move her from the office, but she was afraid, and cried out. Shahak had told them to leave her, there was a sofa along one wall and she sat on it hour after hour, staring at nothing. From time to time an Israeli girl came and brought her coffee and things to eat. Later she would take away the half-cup of cold coffee and untouched food.

Shahak answered the telephone from time to time, and this brought her back to the present. Sometimes he went away, and with him went the present too. Then the past swirled about her like a dark and chill fog. Hiding in it were terrible creatures and things she did not want to see. Then she tried to shore up the crumbling walls of her mind, tried to lock the rotting shutters against the invaders. She thought of her sons, and of Jacob, and feeble rays of sunshine penetrated her miasma. With them she held on to her sanity. *Never leave me Jacob.*

'Ruth. *Ruth.*'

A face was staring at her. Shahak.

'Do you hear me, Ruth?'

He knows I am mad, she thought.

'Yes, I hear you.'

'They think they have found where they're keeping Jacob. An old colonial farmhouse about 30 miles from here. The Rhodies are going to surround the place.'

'Good. That's . . . very good.'

Shahak went and sat at his desk.

'Snow's calling me,' he said, almost to himself. 'They've been communicating with somebody else, right here in Salisbury.'

'Who?'

'Ahh . . .,' Shahak whispered.

She wished that Jacob was with her. He knew, when the air hissed as the whip sliced it open, he knew when they took her down the corridor in the dark, when the shrieks grew louder in her mind, knew as she struggled not to go. Jacob knew, because he too was of the *kazett*, he would pull her back.

Her skin had acquired the texture of wax, pale, clear and shiny.

'*Wstawach* . . .,' she whispered.

Shahak did not hear her, he stared at his telephone with a terrible controlled impatience.

It rang.

'Shahak. You got it. Yes, give it to me.'

His voice penetrated the fog in her mind, she focused on him, saw him scoring his writing pad with brutal strokes of his pen, writing down what he was told.

'I have it,' he said. He stared at what he had written with burning eyes.

'Nobody else,' he ordered. 'Don't call anyone else, I'm dealing with it.'

The telephone clattered down into its rest. Now moving quickly and expertly, he went to a cupboard by the wall. He shook off his shoes, and pulled on calf-high paratrooper's boots, lacing them tight. He shrugged on a flak jacket and then secured about him a webbing harness that carried a short-handled axe, a fighting knife and a pistol.

He ripped what he had written from his pad, and was gone.

In the empty room, Ruth stood up slowly. She went over to the desk. A memory, a useful one, surfaced in her mind. Training. A man showing her how writing on a pad made an impression underneath. She took a pencil, and as though it were yesterday, brushed the lead gently back and forth across the paper.

A pale address appeared in Shahak's savage handwriting. Like him, she pulled the piece of paper away from its pad. She had her bag with her, on the sofa. She picked it up, and went out down onto the street.

'Yez see, Jacob,' said Paddy, 'it's a smart way around it. The authorities, they'll be looking for a whole bunch of rollin' eyed rag-headed fanatics, waving AK47s. Instead, what have they got? One Irish lad thinking about emigrating from the Emerald Isle to take up farming.'

'And a dog.'

Paddy levered the top off a couple of bottles of cold beer.

'Here, it's not stout, but it keeps ye from the thirst.'

'What about the others?' Jacob asked.

'Gone away,' the Irishman assured him. 'Back in County Down, by now.'

Jacob drank some of the cold Tiger beer.

'Have you killed anyone?' he asked.

'In the war, you mean?'

'Which war?'

'The war against the Brits. Yes, I have,' he said soberly. 'Two soldiers. I blew up a monument on the mainland too, but nobody got hurt.'

Out on the verandah, he heard the dog get up and begin to walk about, its claws clicking on the boards.

'Do you feel that's right?'

'I don't go about boasting. I'm not one of those. But it's right. Anything that gets the Brits out of Ireland is right.'

'But where do you draw the line? Should the Welsh become a nation again, and rule themselves, and the Scots too?'

'Why not?' Paddy grinned. 'The English prime minister, Harold Macmillan, he made that speech did he not now, he talked about this "wind of change" sweeping through Africa. I say the wind is blowing towards Britain too. What is different about giving back power to these African fellas and giving back power to us Irish?'

'You think they'll talk to people who use terror?'

'Why not? Isn't the big fella Kenyatta President of Kenya? And wasn't he leader of the Mau Mau? What about your own man, Jacob? Menachem Begin. Wasn't he a man of terror?'

'The Irgun,' Jacob said sombrely. 'You see, Paddy, I have never believed in terror.'

'You have to do what you can.'

'And what of the people in Northern Ireland, the part that you want. What will happen to them if your wind of change blows through there?'

'You know what I think will happen?' Paddy said sincerely, still holding his bottle by its neck. 'I think we'll all stop hating each other. I think that as the years pass some of the Prots will go and live down in the south. I think some of us will go and live up there. I think that our grandchildren might even get married to each other. But it won't happen while the Brits are there.'

Suddenly, from the verandah, there came a fearsome, low growl. It was the dog. In a second, there was a pistol in the Irishman's hand.

'*Paddy* . . .,' Jacob said urgently. He gripped the other by the arm.

'If they've found us there's no point in fighting.'

Sudden, pure white light blazed in at the windows. A clipped, stentorian voice bellowed at them from the night.

'*We have you surrounded by armed troops. Come out unarmed and with your hands up.*'

'Put the pistol down,' Jacob urged. He reached out, and took it from the Irishman, dropping it on the floor.

'Come on. I'll take you out.'

They stood in the terrific glare of the floodlights, and the dog, Lion, snarled at his master's side.

They were suddenly surrounded by men, and Jacob reached down to the collar of the dog, holding him. For a second, the jaws opened, and then he sat down by Jacob's feet, glaring out at the people around them.

Shahak parked his car at the top of the street, and slipped through the shadows. He had a light jacket on over his webbing, so that people might not see his weapons, but there was nobody about. It was a very quiet part of town, with the houses standing in their own grounds, set back from the road, shielded and calm behind soft walls of vegetation.

Here it was. The Rhodesians were still secure in their rule in their capital, there were no high wire fences, simply a white-painted English gate, which he vaulted with ease, padding forward towards the house in the darkness. He shed his jacket, and took his long fighting knife in his fist.

A back door was open. Peeping through, he saw a man seated with his back to him at a kitchen table, reading a paper. A black-haired man. An Arab. Shahak slipped inside, quiet as a cat in his rubber-soled boots, he was behind him, he wrapped his hand about his mouth as he plunged the blade up through the mid ribs of his back. He slumped forward, and as Shahak went forward into the house a man came the other way, carrying an empty coffee cup.

It was Hamouda.

Shahak was the younger, the quicker, his beret was in his hand, he threw it in Hamouda's face, blinding him, and launched his boot in a terrible kick to the pit of his enemy's stomach. Hamouda snapped over, buckled up, clutching himself, and Shahak reached down for him. He gripped him with powerful hands. He stuffed a rag into his mouth as Hamouda fought for air.

'It's me,' he whispered, pulling him up so that he could see into his eyes. 'I've come for you,' he said joyfully, and threw him over his shoulder like a sack. It was important that it be outside. Shahak did not know why, but it was imperative.

Outside it was dark. Scrub whipped at his legs as he ran with his captive. Away through the bushes and trees he threw Hamouda down. Before he could rise he slammed a boot into his back, and slashed through the tendons of his legs. Hamouda screamed through the rag in his mouth, flapping like a landed fish.

Shahak turned him over with a powerful arm. He slashed with the knife again, hacking at Hamouda's groin and the Arab thrashed in agony. The breath rasped in his throat and his arms were wet, sticky. He reached down, ripping through the bloody tatters of the uniform, and seized Hamouda's torn genitals. He sawed through with the knife, and howled like an animal as he held them up in the air. Then he bent again. Hamouda's mouth was open in a silent scream, the lips back in rictus. He plucked out the rag, and stuffed the bloody offal in.

'It isn't over,' he yelled. 'Was it over on the hillside? Was it over until it was done?'

He could see Hamouda's eyes looking at him. The arms flapped feebly in protest. He rammed the knife into the chest and heaved upwards, opening out a terrible wound. He plunged his hand inside, and felt the frantically beating heart, thrashing like an animal as he grasped it.

He tore Hamouda's pumping heart from his body, he held it up to the sky, throwing his head back in a long, gargling howl of triumph.

He thrust the still twitching organ to his mouth, and tasted his enemy's blood.

Ruth got out of the taxi. She paid the driver and heard the car going away down the hill.

It was the right road, the sign said so. She walked along in the dark, stopping and peering at the small signs on the gates.

Here it was. Here was the name Shahak had written. This must be where Jacob was. She reached out and opened the gate. It swung smoothly on oiled hinges.

Somewhere in the darkness, something howled like a wolf.

# PART X

## The Knesset, Jerusalem, July 1975

'WELCOME to Israel,' Shahak smiled. He came round his desk and took the hand of Gideon Weiss in a powerful grip.

'You took so long to come back!' he said. He paused. 'Any problems with immigration?'

Weiss looked into Shahak's eyes with an unblinking, intense gaze. In the lean face in which belief had rendered away all fat Shahak saw the youth, Sten gun in hand.

'No,' he said. 'I've sent in my application. I'll be an Israeli now.'

'I fixed it,' Shahak said.

'I know,' Weiss said absently. 'I've come home. God had to show me the way. When I lost my elections in America, I wondered what I had done wrong. I went to the Talmud, I prayed to him for guidance. He told me what he wanted. He told me to come back home, that his people needed me here.'

Shahak eyed the rabbi shrewdly.

'What about people wanting you *there?*' he asked. 'What about the FBI? That's all been sorted out?'

'Charges have been dropped,' Weiss affirmed very quickly. 'Lack of evidence.'

Shahak grunted in approval.

'That's what I was told. I put in the word for you with the right people. Ben-Levi's boy came to me.'

'He did a good job. He works for God.'

'Yeah ... You wouldn't believe man and son were the same. Jacob's a real old-fashioned liberal.'

'How come he's still in politics?' Weiss asked angrily. 'A man like that pollutes the very spirit and essence of Judaism. *How will the redemption come when we keep people like that within us?*'

'Jacob's useful,' Shahak said pragmatically. 'We can show him off to the foreigners and they think maybe Israel's like that.'

He eyed the rabbi, fidgeting with excess energy and thought on the other side of the pine desk.

'They don't understand how you need to be with the Arabs here,' he commented. 'I'm seeing him soon, funnily enough. He asked to see me. Anyway, never mind Jacob Ben-Levi. When he dies we'll stuff him and put him in Vad Yashem as an example of the kind of Jew we once were and never will be again. Let's talk about you. There's quite a few people here like what you did against the Soviets in America.'

'I know,' Weiss said quietly, and confidently. 'The real terror belongs to the Soviet authorities who are applying it to the citizens of God in Russia. Any actions I have taken against the Soviets is the direct manifestation of His will.'

Shahak was assessing Weiss, whom he had not seen for some time.

'There's some over here who say that as long as the Arabs endorse terrorism we have to counter them. We can't always be good boys. If the Syrians act like madmen, then shouldn't we have our own madmen too. What do you think?'

'The irrational Jew is the rational one,' Weiss said coolly. 'Democracy, Western humanistic values are foreign concepts which the organic body of Judaism will reject like an unwanted implant. Did we survive for two thousand years by being rational? No we did not. Had we been rational we should be at one with the Spartans. We survive because we have a covenant with God. So long as we fulfil our covenant with God our destiny is assured.'

Shahak made his decision. It was what they'd thought. This man could be useful. He could bring in a big slice of those on the far, far fringes, where normal politicians did not go. It would be worth the favours he demanded.

'I didn't clear the way for you just out of goodwill and old memories, you know,' he said.

'No?' Weiss said equably.

'I'm standing for the Likud in the next elections. We're going to win. Begin will be the next prime minister. I'm authorized to offer you a place. Do you want to come aboard?'

'You want *me* to join *you*?' Weiss said, sounding slightly amazed.

'We can get you on the team. Work your way up.'

Weiss laughed.

'Team . . .' he said derisively.

He looked up at Shahak.

'Are you married?' he asked. Shahak shook his head.

'I was. An American Jew, but she did not understand Israel . . . I have my son, though.'

Weiss continued abruptly, 'She was not a Jew. How can she be a Jew and not live in the country God has provided for us? American Jews in the *galut*, in their exile but follow ritual. Only those who follow the hardest *mitzvah*, the real commandment to settle the land, are Jews.'

Shahak nodded. There had to be some way he could harness this attractive theology to the cause.

'You married either?' he enquired.

'Women are treacherous,' Weiss said darkly. 'Satan resides in their souls.'

A sudden image came into Shahak's mind, a dim room smelling of blood and fear, tainted by shrieks from outside. Weiss grinning as he stood over the naked body of the girl. Bloody punctures in her back. Weiss casually doing up his trousers. 'Not me, Avraham! *Them.*'

Weiss leaned forward, his dark eyes flashing.

'Why else do Arab men hunger to penetrate Jewish women? All around us, Arabs seethe, longing for the day they can violate Jewish women. It is because in all women Satan lurks. There the Arabs wish to find their destiny, their master.'

He paused for a moment to wipe a fleck of spittle from his mouth.

'When God created the world, he made a spark, a divine spark that he named Israel. As he created it, it fractured into one million fragments.'

Weiss thumped his chest.

'I am a bearer of that divine spark. God has told me what to do. He has made me fail in America, He has given me the vision to see what is in women's hearts, He has brought me home for His own divine purpose. It is my task to gather up all the other sparks, to reform the act of Creation, to make the world whole again.'

He stood up, staring eagerly out of the narrow, arrow-slit window at Jerusalem beyond.

'They are there,' he crooned. 'They are waiting for me . . .'

'Look,' Shahak said abruptly. 'I didn't do favours for you for nothing. What the hell have you to offer me, if you don't want to play ball?'

'But I do,' Weiss assured him, with his unblinking stare. 'I didn't come here to see you to share old memories either.'

'So?'

'I want *you* to join *me*,' Weiss said confidently. 'I could use someone like you, an organizer, a general.'

The proposal took Shahak's breath away. It was a reversal of roles. Weiss, usually so impatient, for once sat quietly, waiting for him to reply.

'Take your time,' he said generously.

Shahak stared across the desk at the religious leader. He knew his country, knew his countrymen, he *knew* that Weiss was on to something really powerful, the rejection of all notions of democracy, the putting in place of one overriding theology of God's own people.

Images flickered in his mind. Dead Arabs bloody in a ditch. A dead girl on the ground. A child burning to death in an inferno. And what was it, the FBI man had said?

'Somebody told me . . .,' he said hoarsely. 'Before the war . . . the first one . . . you were on a rape charge. What happened to that?'

'Never came to anything,' Weiss said casually. 'The girl was unbalanced. She . . . hanged herself not long after I came home.'

Shahak teetered on the edge.

'Forget all this party shit. The Likud this and the Labour that. When *we* take power for God we shall reshape Israel in our own image.'

'You'll have to get into power first,' Shahak warned.

'Of course. Which is why I want you, an experienced politician. Once we have power, we have a mandate from God to do what He asks us to.'

Shahak's palms were slippery with sweat.

'Look. Let's keep a line of communication open between us,' he suggested. 'What you say is attractive, but I want to see it work.'

'You will,' Weiss assured him. 'You will.'

'Weiss is in town,' Shahak said offensively. 'Your boy got him his citizenship.'

'A boy becomes a man, his father does not have responsibility for him,' Jacob said equably. 'And I heard that some politicians helped him in.'

'Weiss thinks he's a prophet.'

'Weiss is a murderous psychopath,' said Jacob. 'I am surprised you have not asked him to join you and your kind.'

'All right, Jacob,' Shahak said roughly. 'Enough of the pleasantries. What do you want?'

'Justice.'

Shahak looked out of the same small window as had Weiss.

'Then you need a lawyer. Go ask your boy to help you.'

'No. I'm going to ask you.'

'Me?' Shahak asked in surprise. 'Why me?'

'Because you have darkness in your soul. You know the people upon whom to call. I do not. I have to ask you to do what I cannot.'

'Do what?'

'I want a man ruined.'

'This is rather unlike you, Jacob.'

'I said I wanted justice. A long time ago a man was involved when my brother David died. His name was Ibach, he was an engineer in the V2 rocket factory of Dora where my brother and I were slaves.'

'I recall all this,' Shahak said shortly. 'You had the chance to shoot him and did not take it.'

'That is right. I will not kill like that. I am not even sure I could fight as a soldier again. But that is beside the point. I know where this man is, he still works on the American space programme. It was explained to me that I may not have him arrested, any more than any other of us *kazettniks* may get at any of the other German scientists who work there. Levinger told me this, when he was with Mossad. This has not changed. We require American aid so much that we dare not upset them. Very well. I accept that I cannot have Ibach on trial. I have bided my time but still I want him ruined, his past brought out into the open somehow where he lives in America. And I want you to do it.'

'Me?' Shahak said, feigning incomprehension. 'I am a general on the reserve, a politician. And anyway, Jacob, why bring this all up again, why ask me now, all this time later?'

'Because of my wife. In my wife's mind my failure to kill Ibach means that she will always be in danger even though he was not the man that tortured *her*. And then, there is something else . . . But I must take some blame. I have one son, David, who is understanding about my not killing Ibach, but I have another, Saul, who is not. For all their sakes, and indeed for my own, I must take action against Ibach.'

'We all have our problems,' Shahak said indifferently. 'Why should I do it, even if I could?'

'You can and you will,' Jacob said, with steel in his voice. 'You know that I was kidnapped in Rhodesia. You were there.'

'Yes.'

'I was found, the Rhodesian authorities released me. An IRA man who held me is in jail there.'

'Yes.'

'The IRA didn't plan it, they lent some of their members in some kind of exchange with the Palestinians. We think Abu Hataf did it.'

Shahak shrugged.

'A fearfully-mutilated body was found in a Salisbury garden. A Syrian citizen, apparently. The Syrians asked for it, anyway, they had it flown home.'

'So?'

'My wife Ruth was found wandering in the city that night I was freed. She is in a hospital here in Israel now. She may never leave. Her mind is in the past, in the *kazett*.'

Shahak's palms were suddenly running with sweat, under the desk he wiped them on his trousers. The horror filled, staring face of the woman in the dark, the corpse at his feet, the blood running hot in his throat.

Jacob's eyes were locked on to Shahak's face, suddenly slick.

'Yes . . .,' he said. 'You know. My wife has finally fallen into the abyss of madness, and it is you who has put her there. When you tasted your enemy's blood, Ruth thought she was being made to watch again as one was in the camp. She thinks they are coming for *her*. I am going back to that country, the South African government wish me to perform some diplomatic duties for them. If I so choose when I am there I could, I am sure, find out the identity of this Syrian, could ascertain what your role was there. What I would find would finish you here, I am certain of it.'

He stood up, his baggy jacket over his arm.

'Equally, I am a long way from America, I can obviously have nothing to do with the events that will ruin Engineer Ibach there. If I see him destroyed, I will have no reason to make these enquiries. I must try everything I can to bring my wife Ruth back to me, I too have relatives who must be avenged.'

'I'll do what you want,' Shahak promised.

'I knew you would.'

'What do they want you to do, in Rhodesia?'

'Talk to the terrorists, or the freedom fighters. It depends on your point of view.'

'Why?'

'Portugal's gone. Macmillan's "wind of change" has blown them away. With Angola and Mozambique gone, Rhodesia's next. Kissinger and the South Africans know it. I'm a neutral, I can go and talk to anyone for them. So off I go.'

'Watch the papers,' Shahak said hoarsely.

'I plan to,' Jacob promised.

He got up.

'How strange,' he mused. 'That I have to use evil to fight evil.'

'I am not evil.'

'Evil creeps up on a man unawares. You consort with Weiss, you eased his passage here, you have protected him. You are, I suspect, thinking of making an alliance with him. You should bear in mind the old saying about supping with the Devil.'

He went to the door.

'I'll read the papers,' he said.


## Damascus


Asad himself was waiting for Hamouda outside the morgue. Hamouda had come as soon as the summons had been delivered. He had not expected to see the president, but he was there standing patiently in a dark blue striped suit, only a pair of bodyguards, as alert as Alsatians, betraying his rank. Asad embraced the younger man, formally.

'I have had your father brought home to you,' he said. 'He was a warrior, a patriot, an Arab. I shall accord him full honour.'

'Thank you,' Hamouda said quietly.

'Go see him now, pay your respects. I shall wait for you.'

It was cold in the morgue. Hamouda shivered in his summer uniform.

It was an old building that the French had made, with marble tiles on the floor and glass lights in the roof. It smelled of generations of embalming fluid and dead men. It was musty with the processes of death. The pathologist was waiting by a sheet-covered iron trolley in his heavy rubber gown and gloves. When Hamouda went over to him, he felt suddenly reluctant.

'I am Hasan Hamouda,' he said.

'Then you are this man's son,' said the doctor. 'Will you see him?'

'Yes,' Hamouda said steadily.

The man carefully pulled back the sheet to expose his father's head. Tears suddenly sprang into Hamouda's eyes. The skin was tight on the skull, the lips pulled back from the teeth in agony.

'He suffered,' he said thickly.

'To be certain,' the pathologist agreed.

'You would like me to make the arrangements to have him taken from here?' he asked.

'I can arrange for you to see the mullah, should you wish,' said the man. 'But that is not it.'

'We are Christians,' said Hamouda. 'I will arrange for a priest. What is it that you want with me?'

'I am ordered that you should see him before he is buried.'

Hamouda frowned.

'He has been identified. Here I am, I say it is my father. You are in no doubt that it is my father?'

'No, it is not that.'

The pathologist spread his hands expressively, unhappily.

'It is his injuries . . . how he died. They are not what one is used to seeing . . . even on a battlefield.'

The pathologist looked up at Hamouda.

'I am not explaining this very well.'

'Perhaps you should show me his body.'

'Yes. That is best.'

'Here,' he said, his eloquence returning with contact with his profession. 'Some of these wounds are unusual . . . you do not see them even in war.'

Hamouda's face was the same colour as his father's, a waxy yellow. The skin, too, was drawn tight, showing the skull.

The pathologist had picked up his large knife, from habit, was using it as a pointer. He moved its tip up the body.

'But here,' he said. 'Just look at the upper thighs. Almost forty individual slash marks.'

The groin gaped, ragged flesh showing through the hair.

'The genitals have been hacked away, torn out.'

The pathologist turned to look at Hamouda, silent beside him.

'This is not a normal battlefield injury. This is the attack of a frenzied man with a knife in his hand. This is murder.'

He reached in his pocket, taking out a scrap of olive fabric.

'He was gripping this. An Israeli epaulette.'

Hamouda stared at the massacred corpse of his father.

'The chest,' he whispered. 'What has happened to his chest?'

'Yes. That is the strangest part. The wound, you can see, has been made by the same knife. Tremendous strength must have been used. The strength of a madman.'

The pathologist took two retractors, putting them into the shattered rib cage. He pulled to open out the wound and air hissed within the chest.

'Look,' he said, and Hamouda bent to see into the cavity.

'I do not know what I am to look for,' he said hoarsely. 'It is what the butcher throws away.'

'The heart,' said the pathologist quietly. 'The heart has been torn out. Your father was murdered. By a madman.'

He relaxed his grip on the retractors, and the dead man groaned as the air left the lungs.

'I know who the madman is,' said Hamouda.

He went out, and Asad was still waiting patiently. He held him at arm's length, looking deeply into his eyes.

'You have seen?' he demanded.

'Yes.'

'Your father died because he could not see into the darkness ahead of him. He did not realize the technical capabilities of his enemy. When our day comes, when we fall upon him, when we do to the Israelis what has been done to your father, we must know. We must know that our technical capability is greater than his. Remember your father as he is, as he lies there. Keep him in your heart. One day, you will be able to do to them what they did to him.'

'I will,' Hamouda promised.


## Beersheva, Israel


'Don't leave,' said Jacob. 'Don't leave me.'

He stood beside Ruth as she stared out of the window. In the distance the slate sky was raining sand onto the desert dunes, obscuring them in a white haze.

Behind them the nurses were stripping a bed. They had taken the man away, on the flat bare trolley, with the sheet over him, from his toes to his head.

'They did everything they could,' he said. 'If they could have saved him they would have.'

'You do not come to the *revier* to get better,' Ruth said flatly. 'The SS, they bring them here to die.'

'We are not in the KZ!' he said desperately. 'This is not Radom. We are here in Israel, in the hospital.'

'They call it a hospital,' she said cunningly. 'That is to get people to come here when they are sick. Then they kill them.'

She turned, and pointed at the empty bed.

'See. A fine young man they had in there.'

She looked about her, and saw the nurses. She lowered her voice, whispering. Strands of long white hair fell about her once beautiful face.

'They killed him, you know. I saw them do it. One of them injected him.'

Jacob took her thin shoulders in his hands, shaking her in his desperation. She did not protest, but looked at him as a stranger, without recognition.

'That was a man who was ill, he had a fatal illness. These are our nurses. Our sons, David and Saul, they are alive, they want to see you. Won't you come and see them?'

'No, I have no sons. They took me before I could get married.'

Outside, on the street he could see the stalls of the Bedouin bazaar, the splash of colour of cloth, peppers, pizza and rugs.

'Let's go out,' he said. 'Let's walk around in the air a little.'

'It's not safe,' she said knowledgeably. She tapped her nose. 'They make the *selections* at this time. Don't go out. You could get caught up in it.'

'Ruth! Come back to me!' he cried out. 'Ruth, we are in Israel . . .'

'Israel . . .,' she said. 'I will never see Israel now . . .'

She glanced across at him, and reached out with her hand, brushing his face.

'You must not cry,' she said quietly. 'It is not safe. They take you away, if you cry, in the *kazett*.'

'All right,' he whispered. He wiped his face with his hands. 'I will not cry. If we are in the *kazett*.'

She turned again, looking out of the window.

'There they go,' she said sadly. 'See, I told you they made the *selection* at this time. See the chimneys, how they burn!'

Jacob looked behind them, into the room.

'Nurse,' he called. 'Nurse, could you come here, please?'


## Vero Beach, Florida


'*Who the fuck're you?*'

The German accent was overlain with acquired American, but

it was still there, more pronounced than usual as the speaker was anxious. Hasan Hamouda held up appeasing hands as he entered the kitchen, smiling reassuringly at the seemingly half-demented old man crouching behind the near-closed venetian blind. Through the slits he could see the parading Jews, the signs, the photographs of the dead. He could hear the steady chanting, he had passed the buses parked along the road. The local police were doing nothing to stop them.

'My name is Hamouda, Mr Ibach,' he said soothingly trying not to shout above the din outside. 'I came in the back way.'

'You get out with your fellow kikes! Fucking Jewish swine!'

'I'm not a Jew,' Hamouda said solidly, clearly. 'I hate the bastards as much as you.'

The German stared at the Arab. Silvery stubble lined his jaw.

'Who are you then? What do you want?'

'Me? I am a Christian, in fact, the same as yourself, no doubt. I represent the Syrian government.'

'Yes? You do?' Ibach said distractedly. Outside a fresh contingent of concentration-camp survivors had turned up with new banners. One of them was climbing up onto a platform. A television crewman was setting up his equipment.

'Pay no attention to those outside,' Hamouda suggested. 'They have what they want.'

'They have what?'

'They have your head, Mr Ibach. Don't they? You'll not be going back to NASA, will you?'

'How did this happen?' Ibach howled. 'We were told there'd be immunity from all this kind of harassment. Have you seen what they've done to me? Radio, television, the newspapers. These fucking kike bastards outside my home every day . . . Nobody wants to know me. I can't get through to anyone on the phone, they don't return my calls.'

He wiped his palm across his eyes. They were red and deeply shadowed.

'I could kill them!' he screeched. 'Who's done this to me?'

'The Jews,' Hamouda assured him. 'The Israelis, to be more precise.'

'We were assured . . .' Ibach muttered again.

Hamouda pulled up a kitchen chair without being asked, and sat down.

'No point in crying over spilt milk,' he said in a matter-of-fact voice. 'You're finished here, that's plain to see. The Yanks will use

you as a scapegoat, now it's all come out. Heap all the blame on to
you and just keep on employing the others. Here, put the kettle on,
let's have a coffee. I haven't come all this way to watch a bunch of
Jewish activists; I've come to talk to *you*.'

As though grateful for the direction, Ibach went to the sink and
ran water, hunching over the plastic kettle.

'You like milk or sugar?' he said, bringing out a couple of mugs
and a jar of Maxwell House.

'Both,' Hamouda assured him.

'So what do you want?'

'I work for the Syrian government. I am a part of a new sort of
unit. As an expert in guidance, you will probably understand what it
does. We, my colleagues and I, we are part soothsayers, part scientists,
part weather forecasters, part intelligence experts. What we try to do is
provide the government, and most specifically, President Asad, with
some idea of what is ahead of him. If the president can be likened
to the pilot of the aircraft of the state, which is flying fast through
dark and without doubt dangerous skies, we attempt to provide him
with as accurate as possible a forecast of what weather conditions lie
ahead for the aircraft.'

Ibach nodded, and poured boiling water over the coffee. A pleasant
aroma filled the air.

'I know what you do.'

'It is an arcane science,' Hamouda admitted, 'but most necessary.'

'Most.' Ibach essayed a small smile. 'I wish I had had your services
to predict the arrival of these godforsaken Jews.'

'As a part of what I do I should like to ask you something.'

Ibach sat down at the table.

'Go ahead,' he said. 'I'm not going to work today.'

'Tomorrow neither,' Hamouda observed. 'At least, not here.'

'What do you want to know?'

'When we fight the Israelis, we lose. We never win.'

Ibach nodded.

'Why?' Hamouda demanded. 'We are as brave as they are. We are
not cowards.'

Ibach nodded again then began to speak.

'You are missing the point. The soldiers of the Mahdi who encoun-
tered the soldiers of Lord Kitchener at the Battle of Omdurman
in 1898 were certainly no less brave than their British opponents.
However, the British massacred them in their thousands because
of their possession of technological and tactical superiority. The

British deployed superior fire power in the nature of the Snider breech-loading rifle, volley firing and the Maxim machine gun. Their tactics, notably steadiness in squares and the well-chosen use of cavalry, made the best use of their technological advantage, which, of course, included considerable communications advantages on a local and strategic level, and better health and logistics. At Omdurman the British lost forty-eight dead as against ten thousand Dervishes – those were the Mahdi's men.'

Hamouda listened, noticing the lines of stress in Ibach's face smoothing away as he discussed his subject.

'You certainly know a lot about it,' he said flatteringly.

'I should,' Ibach retorted. 'That's what I do. If you can guide an Apollo rocket to a small place on the moon and back again you can certainly place an ICBM's warhead in Red Square from its starting point in a submarine somewhere under the surface of the Atlantic. Don't think the Russians don't know that.'

'Technological advantage is sufficient to win a battle, or a war?'

'Of course not. As I said, the tactics appropriate for its use have to be brought into play to maximize its effect. The French had a form of machine gun in 1870 called a *mitrailleuse*, only they thought it was an artillery piece. Instead of cutting down the Prussian infantry with it they kept it back where the Prussians blew it and them to bits with their Krupp steel field guns. The French lost the war. Also, the political will and skill must be present to take advantage of the technological and tactical superiority. The British, for example, again, proved expert at this, and ruled their vast inter-war empire through displays of devastating military or naval superiority. They ruled Iraq, let me point out, through their civil service, which was able to draw upon just two battalions of troops and six RAF bomber and fighter squadrons. It was quite enough.'

Ibach drank some coffee.

'It is proper to point out that military control does not necessarily equate with political victory,' he went on. 'A factor realised by General de Gaulle in Algeria but not by the generals who attempted a *coup* to prevent him pulling them out.

'Technological superiority must also be deployed with sufficient force to make it work. I myself began my career as an engineer on the A4 rocket, more popularly known as the V2, against which at the time there was *no defence at all*. This made it analagous to the modern predicted phenomenon, the airplane which is invisible to radar. Such a bomber can go out, bomb its opponent and return again and again, its only limit the arsenals of its home country. Like the Messerschmitt 262 jet fighter the A4 was a war-winning weapon, but as in so much of the German war effort political incompetence prevented effective use.'

Ibach's face twisted briefly.

'So. You see. Trying to predict the weather ahead of your President Asad's aircraft of state is a complicated matter, as I am sure you have already realized.'

'Oh, we have,' Hamouda assured him. 'But to return to the Israelis . . .'

'The Israelis who win. They do, you are right. Yet they need not always. They too have their weaknesses, some of which are known to you. They cannot fight wars of any endurance, they must always win quickly. They are dependent upon American aid, for which they perform surrogate military duty. Their professional forces are dependent upon their large civilian militia in reserve.'

'The *miluimniks*, yes.'

'Were it possible to make the Israelis fight a protracted war in which their reservists had to be called up for a long period then the political and economic consequences would be so grave – as per the Rhodesian model – as to increase net emigration and perhaps force some kind of peace settlement agreeable to the Arabs.'

'What of a clear-cut military victory? The kind that they do to us.'

'Yes, your original question.'

Through the venetian blind the television cameraman was photographing a survivor of the death camps, in front of a poster of a dying *mussulman*. Ibach was now oblivious to what was going on outside. He picked up a pencil from the table and drew a piece of paper towards him. He smiled at Hamouda.

'Any good at maths?' he asked. 'Know what a payload index is?'

'How many bombs you can carry?' Hamouda hazarded.

'Very good,' said Ibach, writing down some figures. 'And what about CEP, or circular error probability?'

'No.'

'Basically means how close you can get your load of bombs to whatever you wish to destroy. But for our purposes we want CEP-squared . . . and surge sorties per day . . .'

He tapped his formulae and rows of figures.

'In essence, that is the technological summary of why the Israelis win when you do not.'

'I would like you to explain it to me in more detail. In Damascus, perhaps.'

Ibach looked warily at him.

'Well, you don't want to stay here, surely?' Hamouda asked reasonably. 'I am empowered to offer you a job. The job is in Syria. We would like to show you around before you decide whether to accept.'

'A job doing what?'

'As we have agreed, the Israelis always win. At least so far. As you say, they must *always* win. Quickly. We believe them to be modern-day Crusaders, in possession of technological military superiority. For the Crusaders the Battle of Hattin came when they were tactically and politically outmanoeuvered, their technological advantage no longer active. We believe that one day we can manoeuvre the Israelis into a similar position. We do not as yet know how to do it. We would like your help in finding out. For, you see, the converse of the Israeli position is also true. They must *always* win. *We* only have to win once!'

# PART XI

## Tel Aviv, September 1980

THE playground was nearly empty. The sons of Saul Ben-Levi were waiting for him to come and pick them up, but he was late. He was often late, they were used to it. They were assembling a game. The only other person in the playground was an older boy, Haazev, the Wolf, Shahak's son. He was playing some kind of game on his own that involved him running in and out of a crooked line of plastic cones he had arranged on the ground, and over the climbing frame and net to leap silently and savagely from a wooden platform onto an imaginary enemy.

They were all, in their own fashion, playing at being Arabs and Israelis, only nobody wanted to be the Arabs, so they had to invent them. The Ben-Levi boys had assembled a force of pedal cars, trucks and tricycles on one side of the climbing frame that were the Arab invaders, and were debating how best to massacre them on the other.

Shemaah was the eldest, with an oversized *kippa* clipped with a plastic star of David to his hair. He had a large pedal car into which he could squeeze himself and had attached a plastic tube to it through the windscreen. A tank.

'I'll go round the west side of the mountain,' he announced.

The next in line, one year younger was Eli. He stood high up on the climbing frame, and seeing that the game was to start began to whirl a length of girl's skipping rope around his head.

'*Whupwhupwhup* . . .'

Cobra attack helicopters had arrived from the USA, mean and menacing, their mouths full of cannon, racks of rockets at their sides.

'What are you going to be?' Shemaah asked the youngest, Yitzhak, who was squatting under the frame. He grinned.

'I'll be the scout who tells you where to go,' he said.

Agile and quick as a ferret, he ran through the pillars, two fluorescent plastic balls in his hands. Shemaah pedalled madly, and the tank came rattling around the climbing frame. Yitzhak lobbed the two bright balls into the middle of the attacking Arab army. Eli jumped down with his rope swinging.

'*Whup-whup-whup* . . .'

'*Booom* . . .'

'*Crash!*'

The Israeli forces piled into the passively waiting Arab army and scattered it all over the playground. It was a great game. When they had had enough they extricated themselves from the wreckage. Haazev, the Wolf, was standing watching them, his chest heaving from a number of runs through his particular combat course.

'How do you smash the Arabs, Haazev?' Shemaah called.

Haazev grinned, not unlike his namesake.

'Arabs always run away,' he said. He sprinted in a zigzag around the destroyed army. There was a mop on a pole which was normally designated the leader. The mop was old and straggly, they called it Arafat.

'So I run them down,' said Haazev. He held out his hands, large for his age, as he was.

'And squeeze them to death.'

He grabbed a hold of the mop very deliberately. A rubbish bin was nearby and with an expert jerk he threw it head first inside. They all laughed, like anything.

'Boys!'

They looked up and their father, Saul was at the gate. He was wearing an olive flight suit. He appeared to be holding ice lollipops, so they forgot about the Arabs and rushed over.

'You too, Haazev,' Saul called. 'Your father asked me to pick you up.'

Haazev strolled over with the languid ease of the athlete, of any age. He accepted an orange lolly.

'Thanks.'

They all climbed into the Volvo.

'Want to go to South Africa this holiday?' Saul asked.

'Yaaay . . .'

'We can have the company villa for two weeks. You may be coming, Haazev. Your daddy's joining the board.'

Haazev nodded.

'He told me.'

'Have you been flying, Daddy?'

'Yes, that's why I'm late. We reservists have to keep current, you know.'

'Have the F-16s come yet?'

'Not yet.' Saul smiled. 'Not that I'll get one of those, anyway. Old Phantoms for me.'

'Even Phantoms are better than what the Arabs have. Rotten old MiGs.'

'We always have better aircraft than they do,' Saul assured them. 'And we fly better than they do. And . . .'

'God is with us!' each and every one of them shouted.


# The Bekaa Valley, June 1982


'It is not the Battle of Hattin,' Asad said bleakly.

They stood on the high ground, looking south. Smoke was still drifting from the piles of wreckage, as far as the eye could see. Somewhere down there in the dirty haze Ariel Sharon and the Israeli army were pounding their way into Beirut.

'It was not even a proper war. The Israelis are off to murder the Palestinians and they stopped by to give us a bloody nose on the way.'

'We did much better than before, sir,' said Hamouda.

'I do not call seven entire missile batteries, and ninety fighter aircraft destroyed – all ours – for no Israeli loss doing better,' Asad said coldly.

The president and his small team of aides began to walk. Nearby a graves unit was completing its work in the hulk of a burned-out T-72 tank.

'I was thinking more of our ground forces, who conducted an excellent fighting withdrawal against a stronger enemy,' said Hamouda smoothly. 'Although no one can suggest that our pilots lack courage – yes, and skill.'

An entire wing, shiny and polished except for the torn, ragged alloy where it had been ripped from the fuselage, lay in the olive grove through which they were walking. It bore Syrian markings. Asad pointed to it.

'We Syrians, plus the two others on the Israeli Eastern front – Jordan and Iraq – now have more fighter/attack aircraft and more main battle tanks and associated armoured fighting vehicles than Israel.

We have, as we have always had, more men. All this appears to be good
for is providing the armed forces of Israel with practice for using live
ammunition.'

He turned on Hamouda, angry.

'As one of my senior intelligence officers, would you care to tell
me why?'

'Certainly, sir,' Hamouda said, unruffled. He fished in his uniform
pocket for a black wax pencil, and went over to the aircraft wing,
standing up on its edge.

'Tactical air power and armour are the two keys to war in the Middle
East. Infantry *per se* – as foot soldiers – do not count. Let's take the air
forces to begin with.' Hamouda put figures into rival columns with his
black pencil. 'Tactical aircraft. Israel can field some 50 F-15s of various
marks, plus nearly 150 F-16s. Then there are the *Kfirs*, Skyhawks and
Phantoms. About 700 aircraft all told.'

'We have aircraft ourselves that are equivalent.'

'As *platforms*, sir. It's very important to distinguish between platforms
and the systems the platforms carry. Now, let's gather us all together.
In terms of inventory, the ratio of Israeli to Arab front-line aircraft –
I'm taking best case, assuming Egypt is back in the fold – is nought
point three two to one. Very favourable odds indeed. We outnumber
them three to one.'

In the valley a heavy engine started up, dragging a trackless tank
onto a transporter. Hamouda raised his voice slightly.

'However, it isn't what you have, it's what you can do with it that
counts. They have more pilots per aircraft than we do, so the surge
sorties per day for them is four point five a day. The Jordanians can
manage three, and the rest of us two. In terms of sustained sorties
per day, two and a half for them, one and half for the Jordanians,
and one for the rest of us.

'Now let's move on to the payload index, that is, how much
ordnance can you carry to drop on someone? Here the Israelis can
haul over twice as much as us. This isn't good, but they look much
worse when we move on to the next column, the CEP index. CEP
stands for circular error probability, and is an index of air-to-ground
accuracy. That is, how close can you get your bomb or rocket to the
tank, fighter or bunch of soldiers you're attacking? Our baseline is that
of the MiG-21C, which has an accuracy of 40 miles. The Jordanians
again are the best of us, at one point six, the others at one. The
Israelis, by contrast, are five times as good. This is not because
their aircraft are flown by gods, although their pilots are excellent,
but because of the superiority of their avionics and precision guided

weapons delivery systems. Using iron bombs the lethality of aircraft against ground targets is considered to be the square of the bombing accuracy – CEP-squared – but in real terms the Israeli advantage is even greater than I have said, since Israel possesses thousands of PGM precision guided munitions – *Walleyes*, GBU-15s, *Mavericks, Shrikes* and what have you, whereas we do not.'

Hamouda drew a line under the columns of figures.

'So let's go to what actually matters. Not the numbers of platforms, but what they can do with their systems. This we term the index of attack capability, and is calculated by multiplying the operational aircraft at t plus ten by their readiness, times sorties per day, times payload index, times CEP index, times per cent of attack sorties.'

He wrote the figures on the wing and displayed his mental capacity by multiplying them in his head.

'That is, the Israelis have fourteen point seven six times the capacity to do horrible things to us than we have to them. That approaches the capacity of a lamb to do harm to the butcher walking up to it, halal knife in hand. If we move over to ground forces it is a similar story. Israeli inferiority in numbers is more than compensated for by superiority in armoured and mechanized divisions as well as in better fittings and weaponry for its AFVs. When we work out comparisons on the ground, the figures are not as appalling, but a combat effectiveness ratio of at least two to one in their favour has to be considered very reasonable.'

Hamouda put the cap on his pencil, and returned it to his pocket.

'As I said,' Asad commented wearily. 'Target practice for the IDF.'

'Only,' said Hamouda carefully, 'if we choose to fight their war.'

Asad was looking down the smokey valley, his aides quiet at his back. Defeat was a bad place to be. He swung his head back, testing Hamouda with his eyes.

'Explain yourself,' he said.

'Israel is a colonial regime. Such regimes involve the control of the many – the indigenous natives – by the few, the foreigners. The few defeat and control the many through superior technology. It was not their white skins that enabled a relatively small number of Britons to dominate perhaps a quarter of the globe but their possession of vastly superior medicines, communications, transport systems and fire power, all backed by a sophisticated financial and industrial base – with, let it be said, a powerful and coherent ideology to cement all together. All of this may be said of the Israelis today. But the

British Empire is no more – that which seemed unassailable – and it can happen to the Israelis too. The British have gone home, the Israelis can disappear once again into the diaspora.'

'Talking here one would not imagine we are the defeated occupants of this battlefield,' Asad said jocularly. 'Tell us how to make the Israelis disappear.'

'Don't fight their war. Fight *our* war. The small brown men in Vietnam did not defeat the most powerful nation in the world by fighting the Americans' war. In our case we could, for example, use the following scenario. As in the '73 war, we and this time the Jordanians achieve strategic surprise. Our six to eight armoured/mechanized divisions can achieve local superiorities of eight to ten to one along the Golan and Jordan Valley frontiers. Given good planning we should be able to re-occupy most of the Golan and the West Bank within the first forty-eight hours of combat. Now the Israelis have mobilized their reserves and are preparing to counter-attack. Before they can do so, we immediately acquiesce to a United Nations peace initiative. Provided we have made our political arrangements in advance, and Israel can be forced to accept the truce, we will regain at least part of the Occupied Territories.

'We now move on. Once we have resupplied our forces and trained up the men to replace those we lost, we have the ability to bring all six major Israeli air bases under intense long-range artillery fire. Without the IAF, Israeli superiority of two to one on the ground can be compensated for by superiority of Arab numbers.

'But we must make all our arrangements beforehand. Win beforehand. What, for example, do we do about the influence of the American Zionists? Theirs is a success story indeed. In proportion to its population Israel has received more US foreign aid than any foreign state in history. Roughly speaking, each citizen is subsidized by the Americans to the tune of about 1,500 dollars a year, and each soldier nearly 10,000 dollars. The image of the Israelis in American eyes is that of plucky, gallant, good-humoured White settlers hewing civilization out of the wilderness, constantly threatened by mad Marxist or Islamic zealots who seek to drive them into the sea. In direct contrast, Arabs in general come across as rag-heads in nightgowns, and Palestinians are personified by Yasser Arafat – scruffy, speaking bad English, shifty and boastful by turns, and in command of a shadowy horde of terrorists menacing the Western world. The result of the Zionist lobby's activities within the American establishment has been almost unswerving US political support for Israel. This support has become necessary for the very functioning of the Jewish state. Attack *that*, make people aware that Israel only exists through an original sin every part as bad as that of Cain, and then you begin to win beforehand.'

'At the end of the day, the enemy has to be defeated by force of arms.'

'Yes ... something strange is happening, the world is changing. Arms are changing, and the tactics for their use. The Americans call it ET, the emerging technology. It will make current warfare obsolete. It will be an era of technological surprise and overwhelming advantage for he who can master it.'

Hamouda looked down the battlefield.

'It will be us,' he said.

'Thank you,' said Asad. 'A good presentation.'

The president appreciated a competent exposition. He was no mean lecturer himself, one of the few men ever to talk Henry Kissinger to an exhausted draw.

'I take it you have been talking to the German, Ibach. An interesting man.'

'He's doing a good job for us,' Hamouda agreed.

'So while you have my attention, is there anything you would like to bring to it?'

'Yes,' said Hamouda. He brought out a sheet of newsprint from his inside pocket and unfolded it.

'There's a renegade Israeli journalist working in Beirut. He's writing some very tough articles about what his countrymen are doing there for *The Post* in America. Kind of anti-Vietnam War stuff. Name of David Ben-Levi. I think he might be useful to us.'

Asad nodded.

'May I?'

Hamouda passed it over, and the president began to read.

### The Trouble with Being Ugly

You know what the trouble with being ugly is? It makes you a sucker for any pretty girl who smiles at you. All those years of nobody wanting to go out with you, and then POW, there she is, the one with the hips and the lips and the big smile and she's actually hanging on your arm and whispering in your ear all those good things she'll do to you when she gets you home, well, man, it makes you go weak at the knees.

Weak in the head, too. You're so dizzy with delight you don't actually ask yourself why in hell she wants you in the first place, nor what sort of a girl she is. Take, for example, the Maronite Christians in Beirut. The Phalangists led by Bashir Gemayel. The poor, persecuted

Christians. This particular pretty girl told us she was being raped by the horrible Muslims – who include the PLO, whom we hate more than anybody – and we have galloped to her aid. To be sure, she has promised us her favours once we do in the Muslims, which we want to anyway.

But who, beneath the make-up and our own wobbly vision, are the Christians in Lebanon? Let me tell you, they aren't monks or nuns. They drive about in very heavy Mercedes cars – it's the armour plating – they like to drench themselves in Italian cologne and weigh themselves down with gold chains. And when they get killed it isn't usually the Muslims who do it, it's their fellow Christians. You see, religious belief or dogma has nothing to do with it, it's all about turf and greed, and who gets to control the illegal ports and the patronage, the insurance rackets, the drugs and the prostitutes.

I was about, in fact, when Bashir Gemayel – remember him? he's the pretty girl currently humping the socks off us Israelis in Beirut. We're so delighted to have it happen to us at all we haven't quite noticed what sort of a girl he is – when old Bashir decided he wanted what his old mate turned rival Danny Chamoun had. Remember the score-settling sequence in *The Godfather?* Old Bashir's lot got Chamoun's crew relaxing at the Safra Beach Club. They were having a grand time by the pool and in the hotel rooms with the pretty girls, until Bashir's men turned up. They sat on them as they lay sunbathing, they shot them in the head, they machine-gunned them in the pool, along with the unfortunate keep-fitters swimming that morning, they threw them out of the bedroom windows screaming, and gunned them down as they toppled like ducks in a penny arcade. Man, what a good time they had. Then they got back in their heavy Mercedes Benz cars and went off to enjoy the spoils, leaving a very messy pool behind them.

One should point out that Bashir has had practice at this kind of house-cleaning before, he did in his other main rival Tony Franjieh – son of the former President – a couple of years before. The hit team burst in about 4 a.m. and ventilated not only him but his wife, three-month-old baby, maid, chauffeur and family hound.

And this is the pretty girl we are currently canoodling with. What can it be, since we are so demonstrably ugly, that he sees in us? Well, for a start, you have to remember that gunning down sleeping baby children and people splashing about in swimming pools is the top end of macho behaviour for these soldiers. I saw a parade of Gemayel's troops the other day, and it was a fashion parade. They're very sartorial. They swish about in pressed fatigues and pose like a load of nancy boys with their latest AKs. You see, for *real* fighting they need the ugly crew, they need us.

That's why they talk in such blood-curdling language about the PLO whenever they are near an Israeli, and since we hate the PLO we think they do too. But they don't tell us they hate the Druse and the Shi'ites and the Sunnis just as much. What Gemayel wants is *all* of it, to win the civil war. He doesn't care that much about Arafat and his band of pot-bellied, table-tennis-playing ex-terrorists, but he knows that General Shahak is rabid about him, and that's why he gives him as much intelligence as he can as to his whereabouts.

General Shahak has a new electronic game, complete with POW and WHAM and ZAPP. An electric Arafat runs about a place called Beirut and hides. Shahak has to guess where he is. When he's guessed he presses a button and a Phantom jet appears overhead and bombs him. Shahak hasn't hit him yet, but he figures that all he has to do is obliterate enough of Beirut and its inhabitants to get him in the end. The game has an electronic scoreboard up there in lights and let me tell you, there's no pinball wizard like the Shahak pinball wizard, his score of men, women, children and dogs just keeps on rising, and he just knows he'll hit the jackpot soon. Arafat will just be so much strawberry jam over some bit of bomb rubble and he can go home and we'll make him Prime Minister.

But, you know, whatever you may think about General Shahak, and I personally want to leave the room whenever he comes in, one of the things you cannot say about him is that he is stupid. He *does* understand what he is doing. So if he and Gemayel are in bed humping each other there clearly must be something in it for both of them. What can it be?

Can it possibly be the same thing? What is the greatest myth that the state of Israel is founded on? It is that there is no such thing as a Palestinian people, that the land called Palestine never had any people in it with any particular cultural, historical or ethnic identity attaching them to that piece of land which the people of Zion called Israel. There are, in fact, no Palestinians at all, those calling themselves Palestinian are just maverick members of some great undifferentiated Arab mass stretching from Morocco to Iraq, who for their own perverse reasons refuse to stay at home.

One understands why it was necessary as a Zionist to create this myth – David Ben-Gurion did an excellent job of it – if you want people – Jews – living in Montreal and London and New York and places like this to come and set up a new state with you called Israel then the one thing you can't say to them is 'there is another lot of people already there, they are legitimately there, and will fight like hell to keep it, only we'll kick them out by superior firepower. Of course a few of you may get killed too while we do it. I mean, most of them won't come. No, what you *do* is dream up a nifty slogan – these days it would be a bumper sticker – let's say, how about 'The Zionists are a people without a land, coming to a land without a people' and get them all over. When they come you say the Palestinians are just a bunch of trespassers and when you're ready, you boot them out. It's intrinsically the same argument as you'll find in South Africa if you talk to an Afrikaaner, though not if you talk to a Zulu.

Now, who is it these days who is most responsible for objecting – in word and deed, pamphlet and bomb – to the God-given right of the Jews to Palestine? It's the PLO, and Arafat. So if you can get lucky and turn Arafat into strawberry jam and scatter the rest of his rag-bag followers back into the Arab diaspora, then the problem will go away, and the Israelis can rule Palestine without interference, as God intended. And Bashir Gemayel and his Maronite Christians can rule all the Lebanon, without having to share any of it with the Muslims, of whatever hue.

By the way, if you have a really good time in bed both of you get to have an orgasm. General Shahak is seeing to it that Bashir Gemayel is made President of the Republic of Lebanon not long from now. You'll be able to hear the squeals of joy in Damascus. Or Tel Aviv, come to that.

Asad smiled his thin, sad, wintry smile, and handed the article back to Hamouda.

'What an interesting man,' he said. 'Do you know him?'

'I met him once. On the battlefield. The Golan. He was a medic.'

'Ahhh . . . He doesn't approve of fighting. Why don't you go and make friends with him. Journalists like him, they always need influential sources of information. He'll like you.'

'He's Jacob Ben-Levi's boy. You know, the Polish guy they send out when they want Israel to look human.'

'Ah, yes. Ben-Levi. I have always thought he could be useful not only to them.'

Asad stared over the valley.

'Shahak and Gemayel are making love in a minefield,' he commented. 'If when they roll over one of the mines goes off they may, very briefly, feel themselves endowed with great potency. They will be, however, mistaken.'


# Beirut, 14 September 1982


The telephone rang as David was on his way to the door. The slim cable snaked through a gap in his apartment wall that showed bright as a sliver of glass the outside world. He had reconnected himself the day after an Israeli bomb had ventilated his room.

He hesitated, glancing at his watch, but you never knew. As a journalist it always paid to talk.

'Hullo?'

'David, it's Hasan.'

'Hasan!'

He was pleased to hear from his new and useful friend.

'Fancy a drink?'

'Sure. This evening? I'm got an appointment I can't miss.'

'A hot one? What is it?'

'I'm interviewing the new president.'

There was silence at the other end of the phone.

'Look, Hasan, I have to . . .'

'Bashir? You're interviewing Bashir?'

Hamouda sounded alarmed.

'Yes, he's giving me an exclusive. I've been so critical of him and Shahak, he wants to put the record straight.'

'*Where are you meeting him?*' Hamouda asked urgently.

'Over at Ashrafiye. East Beirut. Look, Hasan, I can't hang about. I'll see you at the bar later.'

He put the receiver down with Hamouda still talking, and went out, hurrying down the blast-dusted stairs, his shoes crunching on the rubble. Arafat and the PLO were gone, the Syrians were gone. The Israelis were over in East Beirut, and if their F-15s and Phantoms still crackled overhead, they did not drop bombs.

David found his battered Peugeot and got in, heading for the eastern part of the city. It was the middle of the afternoon and the sun was beginning to sink behind the ruined buildings.

It was approaching four o'clock when he found the road in Ashrafiye with the three-storey apartment building where the Phalangists had their party branch. Cars crowded the street, he had to park some way off. He walked back down the road, his recorder bumping against his hip in his baggy pocket. A car door suddenly opened in front of him, a man stepped out, blocking his way, smiling. It was Hamouda.

'Hasan? What are you doing here?'

'I felt our drink couldn't wait,' Hamouda said pleasantly. 'Hop in the car.'

'Hasan, I have my appointment . . .'

'*Just get in.* I want to talk to you.'

Puzzled, David climbed into the Fiat. Down the hill, some militiamen stood outside the apartment block.

'What can't wait?'

'Talking to Bashir can wait,' Hamouda said casually. 'How long do you think you'll be here?'

'I don't know. I don't think there'll be much point in staying, frankly.'

'Why?'

'The Israelis have won. Begin, Shahak and the rest have what they want. Asad and the Syrians have lost the lot. Bashir, their man is president. They have Asad whipped in the Bekaa, now they have a client president of Lebanon. It's only a matter of time before Bashir puts pressure on Asad to withdraw. I would say that the whole historic regional position of Syria is at risk. Which means Asad's own domestic position will be too.'

'Yes, yes.' Hamouda murmured. 'That's very true. What do you think of Bashir, now he's president?'

'That's a funny thing,' David said thoughtfully. 'His history is as a bully-boy and gangster, but he might make a better president than these beginnings suggest.'

'Begin's history was as a bully-boy and gangster. He has done well as prime minister of Israel, in some people's eyes.'

'Bashir is showing some backbone of his own, too. He isn't simply a puppet of the Israelis. Although the PLO are gone he's let the Palestinians here stay in West Beirut. There's plenty in Sabra and Shatilla. Begin, Shahak, they wanted them cleaned out. But ... at the end of the day, Bashir will do pretty much what they want.'

David looked down the street.

'He can start by cleaning the place up,' he joked. 'Look, Hasan, I must ...'

Hamouda glanced at his watch.

'In a moment,' he murmured. 'Say, how's your father?'

'Dad? I think he's in Zaire. They send him places when they want things done nicely. He's such a ... good person. You meet him and you just know it. He spends a lot of time abroad. There's not much to come back for. Our mother is still in the hospital.'

'I'm sorry.'

'He comes back to be an archaeologist.'

'Like General Dayan and the others.'

'Dad's interested in something specific. Cousin Avraham.'

'Cousin Avraham?'

'Yes, an ancient ancestor. A jewel-maker. He went out at the time of the Crusades, he was actually at the Battle of Hattin. He seems to have survived, but Dad can't find out what happened then. He's found traces of him in Krak des Chevaliers, and also in Jerusalem.

He's even got a gold ring with his mark. A *menorah* with a letter A for its stem.'

'How fascinating . . .'

Hamouda stared down the hill, and his dark eyes glittered. He slid down in his seat.

'Get down,' he suggested. David looked from the building to his friend and suddenly realized. As he folded into the well of the car he saw the walls of the apartment building blow out, the very roof rise, breeze blocks flying against the yellowing sky, and the roar of the blast was all about them, shaking the car in a giant fist.

The dust rolled in a mighty, filthy cloud and when it settled it coated everything, through it there, was now just a vast heap of rubble.


David shone his flashlight about in the empty rooms. Over a half-moon library centre the words PLO Research Centre were written in Arabic. Somebody had fired rounds from an automatic weapon into them. Somebody, possibly the same person, had defecated on the counter where the books were passed to be checked.

The shelves were empty, the drawers of the filing cabinets hung drunkenly on their hinges.

'What is this place?' asked Hamouda.

'This is the heart of Palestine,' David said. 'The Israelis promised to stay out of West Beirut if the PLO left; they thought it was safe to keep everything here. They were wrong.'

'It's a library?' Hamouda said, looking around the shell. On the walls the Israeli soldiers had left their graffiti. *Palestinians, fuck you. Arafat, I will fuck your mother.*

'More valuable than guns. Shahak knew that, that's why he's broken his word and stolen everything. It's everything he hates. Books about Palestine. Records and land deeds from the days when the Palestinians ruled Palestine. Historical archives of the Palestinians, photographs of families, maps. Maps of Palestine pre-1948 that show every Arab village in Palestine, before we created the State of Israel, and erased them all. This is the ark, the heart of the Palestine people. Shahak wanted it, now he's got it.'

An eerie white light flickered through the window.

'What's that?' Hamouda asked, peering out. 'It's a flare. Flares. The Israelis are firing flares.'

The two men looked out into the darkness of the ruined city. In the distance, parachute flares were slowly descending, illuminating the land below.

'What's over there?'

'Sabra and Shatilla?' David said, questioningly.

'Yes,' Hamouda agreed. 'That's about it.'

'Let's get over there.'

David illuminated their path out with his powerful flashlight. On the wall by the door there was a last, derisive scrawl in white spray paint.

*Palestinian? What's that?*

The street was deserted in the dawn light. The day before and the day before that the roads round Shatilla had been sealed off by Phalangist militiamen and Israeli soldiers. David and Hamouda had tried to get through, but the cordon was strictly enforced. Nobody could get in – or out. From the camps inside came what had seemed to be sounds of fighting, of gunfire and explosions, but the militiamen and the soldiers had seemed unconcerned. Each night as darkness fell Israeli artillery fired slow-falling flares on parachutes, and the noises continued.

Now the street was empty. Where the tank had sat, with its crew lounging on it reading magazines and listening to American pop music on a huge black ghetto blaster, there were just the marks of its tracks heading away. The Phalangists with their mirror-shade sunglasses and automatic weapons had gone.

David and Hamouda walked cautiously forward into the camp. An old man was sitting on the ground, with his back to a shanty wall. He had a wooden cane in his hand, he wore a neatly trimmed white beard. His eyes were open, he seemed to be looking at them.

David stepped towards him, opening his mouth to talk, and stopped.

The old man's eyes did not move, a tiny trickle of blood ran down from a small hole in his right temple.

The alleyways smelled, they smelled of dead people. A shallow grave of red dirt, a hand protruding from it, a scraping in the ground of a will to live. A young woman with her breasts sliced off, her life blood pooled about her, cockroaches feeding on it. A dead donkey, its belly ripped apart by machine-gun fire. A row of young men against a wall, their ankles and wrists tied together with wire, all shot in the back. More men, all machine-gunned in rows.

An old woman, insane, demented, cradling a little girl who was dead.

'Yi, yi, yi . . . Y'Allah . . . Oh God, Oh God.'

David came out of the dark as Shahak walked swiftly to his waiting car.

*'How could you do it? You bastard, how could you do it?'*

The bodyguards hit him from both sides, they slammed his head into the roof of the car, they had his arms up high behind his back.

'Let him up,' said Shahak. His words were like lumps of lead in the dark.

'He's a reporter,' he said contemptuously. 'He couldn't fight for his country, so he just says bad things about us.'

Blood ran inside David's mouth, he wiped it with the back of his hand.

'Why did you do it?' he said thickly, through swelling lips. 'Why did you kill them all?'

*'I?'* Shahak asked mockingly. 'Who have *I* killed?'

'The people in the camps. *You* did it.'

Shahak spread his hands wide at his two bodyguards.

*'Goyim* kill *goyim* and this so-called Jew comes for Jews.'

He turned back to his car and got in, the bodyguards piling in as well.

*'We are Jews!'* David screamed. As the car went forward he ran at it, beating on the roof with his fists. 'We are Jews, we don't commit murder!'

The car shot away, throwing him into the road. He knelt in the dirt with tears streaming down his face.

'You cannot do this to me,' he whispered.


## Hama, Syria, October 1982


An old man was shuffling along the road that followed the steadily rushing Orontes River, green-banked, snaking through the ravaged landscape. He wore a *gandura* robe and chequered head-dress, a Muslim. Hamouda drove on past him till he came to a yellowish slope by the roadside. He drove up it, over the lumpily smooth surface which was like badly laid tarmac.

The yellow plain stretched around them in all directions for hundreds of yards, edged by what appeared to be some kind of shanty town. Hamouda stopped somewhere out in the middle of it and turned to David.

'Well, here we are,' he said blandly. 'Want to look around?'

'Here we are where?' David expostulated. 'Where is this?'

'Hama,' said Hamouda, his face still expressionless. 'Ancient and beautiful. This is the Barudi district, where time has stood still. As in days of yore the people live in their narrow alleyways and haunting, arch-covered roads. Pause for a moment as you sip a tiny cup of sweet coffee and you will hear the noise of water wheels from the beautiful Orontes, or the cry of the Muezzin calling the faithful to prayer. Travel, perhaps to the *souk* nearby, where you will find traditional . . .'

'*Don't!*' David said, looking about him. 'I can see perfectly well there is nothing here.'

'Have a look around,' Hamouda said again. He took out a thin cigar from his inside pocket and lit it.

David got out. He walked on the flat surface of the plain, which was marked by overlapping straight creases – and he realized that it had been steamrollered. He poked its surface with his shoe, its yellow surface was crushed concrete. He kicked at it with his heel, bringing things to light – a torn book, fragments of painted wood, a ripped and stained shoe. An unidentifiable piece of bone fringed with sticky yellow skin. A piece of a fingernail.

He looked up. The old man, stoop-shouldered and shuffling, was travelling along what he recognized to be a path over the plain.

'Where . . .?'

The old man looked up at him, not slowing any further. He was carrying a kind of dirty flat loaf in a bag.

'Where are the houses?' David asked, speaking Arabic.

'You are standing on them,' he mumbled, toothlessly.

'So where are the people who lived here?'

'You are standing on them too.'

David watched him heading towards the shanty town, made from the debris of what had stood before, and then got back in the car.

'What happened here?' he asked.

'What *happened* is that the Muslim Brotherhood did not like President Asad.'

'I do not like Prime Minister Begin, but he does not bury me in my home.'

'Do you represent a threat to Mr Begin? The Muslim Brotherhood did not like President Asad ruling the country; they felt they could do a better job. They called upon him to call free elections.'

'They also, if I recall, assassinated government officials, kidnapped people, and conducted a campaign of bombing.'

Hamouda beamed. He drew on his cigar, tasting the smoke with relish.

'That's right. That's politics, Syrian-style.'

David waved his hand at the desolation about them.

'Then what is this?'

'This,' Hamouda said grinning, 'is what happens after a general election.'

'How many died?'

'Who knows?' Hamouda shrugged. 'Who can tell? They used tanks, street by street. They used attack helicopters, they used artillery and mortars. They brought the houses down about their inhabitants heads and bulldozed what was left flat. The survivors were taken outside the city and machine-gunned into mass graves. Those who fled to other parts of the city were tracked down. They sealed the doors of the houses and connected up cylinders of cyanide gas, which they turned on. They accounted for the entire leadership of the Muslim Brotherhood and the entire religious leadership, sheiks, teachers, caretakers of mosques. You may look for them where you will, and not find them.'

'But why? Why go *so far?* It's just not necessary.'

Hamouda shook his head vehemently, sincerely, wagging his cigar stem at him.

'No, no. It was not merely necessary, it was *essential.*'

'Why?' David demanded. 'Couldn't Asad cut a deal with the Muslims? If this was their city, why not let them have it?'

Hamouda grinned mockingly at David.

'President Asad is in charge. He is an Alawi. The Alawis are . . .'

'I know who the Alawis are. They are a minority tribe of great internal loyalties, and they have used it to gain great power.'

'Very good,' Hamouda said approvingly. 'The Sunni Muslims are, if you like, another opposing tribe who would like to have what the Alawites have. They tried to get it. All the other enemies of Asad and the Alawites were watching. If he had let the Muslims have *just one district* of Hama then the blood of the Alawites would have been in the water, their enemies would have smelled it, and in a frenzy would have rushed in to eat them.'

Hamouda gestured about him.

'It did not happen. *Every Syrian* now knows what happened. Tell me, if you were a Syrian, would *you* now take on President Asad?'

'No,' David said in sincere agreement. 'I would not. Look, I know my history, I understand what traditions President Asad works within. He is without doubt a descendant of Abul-Abbas al-Saffah.'

'Abul-Abbas the Bloodletter . . .,' Hamouda murmured almost approvingly. 'Yes, now there was a man.'

'Abul-Abbas awarded *himself* the title,' said David. 'He ruled Baghdad, he knew the Arab tribes hated him, he kept them down by the use of fear. The executioner was resident in his court. *My* point

is that Asad is a throwback. We live in a modern age. We in Israel are
a democracy. There is nothing to stop Syria becoming a democracy
too, and Asad al-Saffah will become at one with Abul-Abbas.'

'Yes, yes. We have modern, European-style nation states now, do
we not? Bequeathed to us by those European, imperial states. Britain
and France, in these parts. Which is another reason for Asad to have
crushed the Muslims with the utmost severity. Has not President
Asad done well for his new state? Has he not brought it into the
modern world? Has he not built highways and cheap houses, has
he not brought free education and medical facilities to people who
had never known them? And was not all that threatened by these
retrogressive, Islamic fundamentalist, antiquated bigots?'

Hamouda flicked the stub of his cigar out of the window on to
the mass grave where they were parked.

'To the dustbin of history with them,' he said. 'And you know
what? The people approve. Better this than what has happened in
Beirut, they say. When will *that* end? Now that everyone has had
a chance to see what happens, President Asad will rebuild Hama.
Come here in a couple of years, you will see simply a modern city.'

'So why did you bring me here to see it like this?'

Hamouda eyed David maliciously.

'Ah, it was such a shame. There you were with tears in your eyes,
a real bleeding-heart liberal. You had your monster in front of you,
the terrible General Shahak who'd let the Phalangists murder a few
Palestinians and Shilites.'

'A *few?*' David shouted angrily. 'There were hundreds of them, men,
women, children.'

'We are sitting on top of *thousands*,' Hamouda said indifferently.
'Men, women, children and most probably dogs as well. But there
you were, wailing and tearing at your hair. "Aiii . . . aiii . . . how could
you do this," you cried. "How could you do this to me? I am a Jew,"
you sobbed. "We do not do this."'

'Shahak is a psychopath,' David snarled.

'On the contrary,' said Hamouda. 'Shahak is a man who understands
the rules in these parts. *I* believe that your people understand that too.
They do not disapprove of General Shahak, do they? Is the general
not still holding his job as government minister? But tell me, if Shahak
is a psychopath, what is Asad, whose far-mightier works of death we
have parked our car upon? Why is it that I do not detect the same
burning indignation within you as you sit here?'

Hamouda looked intently into David's face.

'But of course . . . *You expect nothing better of us*. We are Arabs, and

Arabs, it is known, are callous and brutal, a cruel people. You, now, are the Jews. And the Jews are not like that.'

'No . . . I believe to the bottom of my soul that we are not,' David said painfully. 'Sabra and Shatilla aside, the whole invasion of Lebanon aside . . . Why do you think I wrote all my articles. All those Postcards from Beirut. It made me very unpopular at home. My brother Saul who is an ardent Zionist and religious nut now does not talk to me. If I walked down the street people would probably spit on me. Why did I do it? Because I am a Jew. In a different way, I too, like Saul believe that the Jews are special, if I believed in a god I would say that the Jews are chosen by god. I believe we have a duty to be better than others because of our own history, of our diaspora, because of those who have persecuted us, because of the Holocaust itself. Because of these things we do not behave as others do. We should never have gone into the Lebanon. Postcards from Beirut held up a mirror to all Israelis, that's what it was intended to do. If you don't like what you see, you can change it. Why was I so upset about the Sabra and Shatilla massacres, about Shahak? Because we Jews connived at a Holocaust. It must never happen again.'

'But you Jews live here, where we Arabs live. You have become like us. General Shahak understands that.'

'No, we are the Jews who have come back home. We are a new force, because of us, we shall change the region. Instead of us becoming like you, you will become like us.'

'But I say you are an old force, that has come back. I say you are the Crusaders, wearing new clothes. And this region proved inhospitable, to Crusaders.'

Hamouda started up the car.

'Come on,' he said. 'Let's get back to Damascus. We can have dinner before your flight.'

'Do you mind if I write a Postcard from Hama?'

Hamouda wheeled the car in a thin haze of yellow dust.

'Of course not. Why do you think I brought you here? Abul-Abbas never minds people being reminded of the cost of opposing him.'

They rolled down the slope and back onto the road that ran beside the steadily rushing Orontes.

'One day, I'm going to do the whole thing,' David said thoughtfully. 'It's been such a dirty business. Israel is in bed with all kinds of nasty people, all over the world. It has to be exposed. That's what being a journalist is all about. You drag it all out into the open and people just recoil in disgust. Look at what Woodward and Bernstein did to Nixon. People looked at all the filth and they said we don't want to have anything to do with that. That's what I want to do. Israel was founded on the notion of purity. We were a light unto the nations. We have to get back to it. It must be that way once again.'

'Anything I can do to help, just let me know,' Hamouda said blandly.


## Saudi Arabia, 1991


'Hey, Hasan, the pictures from the RPV're coming through. You want to watch?'

Hamouda put his mug of government-issue coffee down and hurried over to the bank of screens in the Desert Storm command post.

'Very much,' he said, and sat down by the American lieutenant colonel.

'Republican Guard positions,' Cy Smith said, indicating on one of the screens. 'And over here, their air defence radars. "Spoon rest" mobile early warning, "Flat face" early warning and target acquisition, "Squat eye" search and target acquisition. Okay, let's wait and see.'

Saddam Hussein's Iraq had occupied Kuwait as a stepping stone on its way to Riyadh. The president of Syria had never wavered from his view that the Iraqis were merely descendants of a few root-grubbing tribes splashing about on the edge of the Euphrates. The idea of having one as the premier leader in all Arabia was repellent, and he had supported the Allied offensive to return them from whence they had come with a will. As part of his reward he was allowed to send trusted officers to see how it was to be done. Chief of these was Hasan Hamouda, head of his external intelligence service.

'Watch the right-hand screen,' said Smith.

The still picture of the radar screens and vans silently erupted, component parts flying centripetally over the sandy desert ground.

'Well *all right*,' Smith said in approval. 'AGM-88 high speed anti-radar missile one, Iraqi clods nil. Okay Hasan, the B-52s now have an unmonitored strike path. Always makes sense to shoot the radar in the face on the way in, that way it can't bother you on the way out. Further to knocking out the radar they have Phase IV ECM, specifically ALQ-172 Pave Mint for their protection. Now what you're going to see isn't that Linebacker II crap, waves of "big belly" 52Ds attacking in waves, we don't do dumb things like that any more. We exploit the B-52s range, capability for precision low-level navigation and autonomous defensive systems. There are six out there, they are all flying different routes. With the MIL-1760 interface they can carry anything from 51 Mk 82s to eight AGM-142A "Have Nap" stand off missiles.'

Acronyms and mark numbers spattered from his mouth with machine-gun certainty.

'Anyhow, each of our boys are carrying eighteen Mk 84 2000-pounders. More ordnance than an entire battleship salvo. For one. Those poor bastards got six on the way. They put weapons on target at a higher rate than any other delivery system. Okay, here we go.'

Huge grey shapes flashed over the target, all from different directions. Within fifteen seconds they were gone, and on the screen there were just the drifting puffs of dust kicked up by the impact of the bombs.

Then the entire target vanished with one long, rippling explosion of pulverized rock and flying metal. They watched for several minutes, as it slowly began to clear, only to be replaced by the dark seaweed of burning fires.

Another aircraft went through the screen, emitting a spreading white trail.

'What's that?' said Hamouda.

'Leaflet raid.'

'Leaflets?'

'Yeah. The ground forces're going in soon. We'd prefer it if the Iraqis quit once they see the tanks coming, basically. So we're taking away their will to fight. Here, I got one.'

He passed over a white printed oblong of paper. It was written in Arabic.

'Greetings!' Hamouda read out loud. 'You have just been visited by the B-52s. Have a nice day!

'PS We're coming back. Three o'clock this afternoon. See you then.'

Smith cracked a slow, mean smile.

'They shouldn't be there. We know that, and they know that. So we're giving them a choice. Quit fighting, or be ground to powder.'

'And are they coming back?'

'Uhuh. Three o'clock on the dot. And then, two in the morning. If you're some poor damn conscript sitting there waiting for it to happen you start to feel the way a fly must when it hears the swatter.'

He got up. 'More coffee?'

# PART XII

## The Knesset, Jerusalem

THE hook behind Levinger's head supported a different portrait every time the chair below changed occupants. Menachem Begin had displayed Jabotinsky, his mentor. Levinger was a traditionalist, a young, shock-headed Ben-Gurion looked down upon them.

The arrow-slit window vibrated under the beating of a sonic boom from the sky above. Levinger rose from his chair, smiling out of the creases of his face. Like Jacob, his hair was passing from grey to silver.

'Jacob. It's been a long time.'

'A long time,' Jacob agreed. 'I am abroad so much.'

'Mr Israel!' Levinger said flatteringly. 'You represent us so well.'

'You are kind to say so.'

'No, no ... I mean it. Sit down, sit down ... You represent all that is best about our nation, Jacob.'

'I have certainly had a number of occupations and professions,' Jacob admitted, taking the proffered chair.

'You survived! You are a foundation stone of our land!'

'Well, maybe. I have been a gun-runner, a commando, a spy and a failed assassin as well.'

'Honourable causes! An ambassador and a politician too. A diplomat ...'

Levinger looked amiably, calculatingly at Jacob.

'Say ... whatever happened to that history of our land you were going to write?'

'I am still working on it. I polish a chapter, when I have a free moment.'

Levinger threw himself back in his chair. He has not changed much, thought Jacob, still the same Captain Zvi with more creases, more lines. Not like some of us.

'How far have you got?' Zvi Levinger asked encouragingly.

'Where do you start? I forget. With the War of Independence? Or before that?'

'Oh, before that. I begin with the Bible.'

Levinger smiled, slightly maliciously.

'Rabbi Weiss will approve.'

'He will not!' Jacob cried hotly. 'That I assure you. But I do begin with the Bible. Were I writing a history of Britain, say, I suppose I should have to begin with the Celtic tribes, and then include all the others who invaded, and left their mark, the Romans and the Angles and the Jutes and the Saxons. Not forgetting the Normans, of course. This country where we live is an even greater mosaic of Canaanites and Israelites, Romans and Jews, Crusaders and Muslims, Mamelukes and Ottomans. If I am to write the book properly I must include Cyrus and Alexander the Great as well as the Kings of Canaan, the Hasmoneans and Vespasian as well as the Judges of Israel. Saladin and Richard the Lionheart must take their place alongside Moses and King David. Yasser Arafat will have to rub shoulders with David Ben-Gurion.'

'An interesting idea,' Levinger murmured. Jacob suddenly thought that he was, if not sympathetic to the concept, not as violently opposed as he might have been.

'You were head of Mossad,' Jacob said curiously. 'You tried to have him killed, on occasion.'

Levinger shrugged.

'This is a history book. Let us let Chairman Arafat in somewhere. Perhaps he can be a footnote. But you began with the Bible.'

'Yes. Thousands of years ago in the land of Canaan, the inhabitants formed a Semitic culture not unlike that of their neighbours. Other Semitic tribes, later known as the Sons of Israel, infiltrated this land, but were not strong enough to reduce the fortified Canaanite towns, and so settled the hills. In the course of time, they merged with the Canaanites to form the kingdoms of Israel and Judea.

'Many misfortunes befell these kingdoms. While at different times the upper classes of the two were exiled, and while the second Jewish commonwealth was destroyed by the Romans, and many of its people scattered, the simple people, the peasants and the shepherds never left the country. A few remained Jewish. Some adopted the Jewish heresy, Christianity. When the land was conquered by the followers of another Semitic religion, Islam, many gradually adopted it as their faith, and its language, Arabic, as their own. They became the Palestinians, and the ones who were scattered, the Jews. Two halves of the same people.

'We, the Jews, came back. And drove our brothers out. Now we are here, and they are there. Soon, before it becomes too late, we must resolve this terrible situation. There are only five solutions. One side annihilates the other. Not, given the extremists on both sides, beyond possibility. Two, one side subjugates the other. This is happening. We hold the Palestinians in total subjugation, and deny them all national and human rights. Is this what we founded the State of Israel for, to become slavemasters? Three, one side drives the other out. They push us into the sea, we push them into the desert. This one is advocated by a number of politicians I know personally, General Shahak being one of them, and will lead only to eternal warfare between Israel and the Arabs, most likely leading ultimately to option one. Four, both sides live together in the same land. Not, as has been proven, a practical option. The South Africans have tried it and called it Apartheid. We have tried it, calling it nothing. It is the same system. Like the South Africans we have ended up with enemies as neighbours, both unable to enjoy peace in our own land. Both Israelis and Palestinians are fiercely nationalistic, both traumatized by their experiences, we by the Holocaust and our national history of persecution, they by the humiliation of colonialism and by the dispossession of their homeland, plus what we have done to them since.

'This brings us to my final option. It is, of course, partition. We are back in 1947. We have our part, and they're to have theirs. We give them the West Bank and Gaza – as we should have done, after the Six-Day War, when we took them – and they give us peace. In the fullness of time – a long time, yes – the border will become merely a line on a map, as with fresh generations the bitter memories of the past fade, and the two halves of an old nation come back together.'

'Your history book seems to have leapt into the future,' Levinger said dryly.

'You did not invite me here simply to talk about academe, Zvi,' Jacob said equably. 'I am a dove, a peacenik, you know that. By Israeli standards I am *very* dovish. But I am also *right*. The problem is not going to go away. It is getting worse. The history of Israel is a history of war against foreign nations. We happen to have won them all, albeit at great cost. Now we have a different war, a civil war, an ulcer which will devour the vitals of our nation. For what are we destroying ourselves? The Occupied Territories . . .'

'Rabbi Weiss calls them Judea and Samaria.'

'We may call the land what we will, although this use of Biblical expressions does not help the situation. Rabbi Weiss is himself a most alarming symptom of the disease now afflicting Israel. What are Weiss and the Numbers 33 Movement but Israeli Fascists?'

Jacob shook his head in disbelief.

'That I should live to see Jewish Nazis . . . But what he calls Judea and Samaria and you and I the West Bank and Gaza are what? The one 80 miles long and 26 wide, the other a mere 5 miles by 29, both among the least desirable pieces of real estate on earth. We do not want Gaza, nor the West Bank. We do not even have any moral right to them.'

'Your point about civil war is a good one,' said Levinger. 'But shall I tell you what General Shahak, for example, would say? He would say that the intifada conducted by the Arabs has proved that coexistence is impossible. We've been in bed with them for forty years. There hasn't been any love and nobody's got pregnant. We don't like them and they don't like us. Let's get a divorce. The question is, of course, who gets the house?'

He glanced at Jacob.

'But you aren't going to suggest that. Are you going to suggest what I think you are?'

'Yes,' Jacob said firmly. 'Let's deal with Arafat and the PLO. We have no title deeds to this land, only a temporary lease stolen from the landlord. That is why we must make a deal with Arafat. Arafat is like me. We are both old with all our venom gone. We know how the world is. If we do not make a deal now with Arafat, who is as moderate a Palestinian leader as you will get, then in a few years – or less – you will be trying to make a deal with some younger man who is not moderate at all. Let us talk to Arafat. Let him come, like Sadat. Give him these scraps of land. We returned Sinai to Egypt. It can be done again. Let us have an end to this thing.'

'There are those like Shahak who say that the nightmare within Israel is the Arab population. By next century, if we allow it, they'll outnumber us. We'll be like the Afrikaaners, ruling over a bigger native population. We have to get them out. That is what Shahak is saying, and he has a lot of support.'

'Let us give them Gaza and the West Bank.'

'Shahak is thinking of giving them Jordan.'

'Is he serious?' Jacob said quietly. 'Another war?'

'We could do it, you know. The little king knows we could do it. He could do it voluntarily, or we could do it for him. We can have it done in a week, if we go in. Then he can catch the first flight out to London and we'll start shipping in the Palestinians. That's what Shahak is saying, and there are people who agree with him. There'll be the usual wailing and wringing of hands in the West while we get on with it, but they'll soon forget about it. Everything has a heart. A person, a movement, a state. And a heart pumps. Zionism pumps. It pumps in, and it pumps out. We pump in Jews from the nations of the diaspora – mostly the Russian Jews, today – and we need to pump out the Palestinian Arabs. The two actions are interrelated, and indispensable. This is Shahak's philopsophy, Jacob, that's what he says.'

'What do you say?' Jacob asked levelly.

'I think we would be mad. I think we need to talk to Arafat.'

'We do!' Jacob cried out. 'Let him come to Jerusalem to address the knesset. He will sing the *Hatikvah* and salute the Israeli flag. He will kiss General Shahak on both cheeks. He will speak, and I will speak. We will address the fears of the other side, ask forgiveness for all the terrible deeds done. When we have both made our speeches, he and his staff will stay, to begin the formal talks.'

'Not so fast, Jacob!' Levinger said, smiling.

'Out there there's maybe ten per cent who would give the Palestinians the land anyway. There's twenty per cent who'd never do it. We tell the rest what we're doing and they'll buy it, because they understand that this place we live in, this Middle East is a wilderness of wolves. We're offering an end to forty years of hate – on our terms. They'll buy it.'

'I happen to believe you're right,' Levinger said quietly. 'We cannot risk Shahak's option. And the Americans want something to happen. They won the Gulf War, and now people are saying well, what about the Palestinians? You fought for the Kuwaitis. So we have to talk to Arafat. But you know how it is here. We cannot do so in the light of day. We have ... some back channels set up. There is the Madrid line, the Oslo line ... Once any get blown, we cannot use them. You met Arafat once ... We would like you to talk to Arafat.'

## Tunis

The Mercedes limousine had darkly tinted glass, it protected Jacob's eyes from the glare of the sun-baked hills and their white villas, and kept him from the eyes of the inquisitive.

The driver's eyes, framed by his black and white chequered *keffiyeh* in the mirror darted from the road to the image of the old politician in the rear seat.

'When I was a boy, sheikh, we would play a game. You stood facing a wall, while your friends tried to reach you. When you turned there was no one moving, and yet they were not where they were before.'

'I have played that game,' said Jacob. 'Many years ago, in Poland.'

'You know of what I speak,' said the man, pleased. 'We Palestinians, we have moved a long way these past years, towards a peace, and yet the distance between us and you Israelis has remained the same, for every time we came towards you you went further away.'

The eyes were still tinged with the amazement Jacob had seen, as he came down the steps of the private turbo-prop that had brought him across the Mediterranean.

'And now . . . here you are, talking to us.'

'When you talk to a man you realize that he is only a man, and not a demon. I sit in your car with you and you realize I am not a member of some master race, but an old man, a member of a race with long memories of persecution, a race that remembers the Holocaust and is fearful, and therefore aggressive. I talk to you and I realize you are not a blood-stained murderer of women and little children but a member of a people who have grievances, memories of humiliations and a feeling of the injustice that has been done to them that is without bottom. Without talking to each other I give you nothing, and you attack me, because you have no other method of getting through. Which confirms my belief in you as a blood-stained murder of women and children.'

'You are here,' the man said again, and there was still amazement in his voice.

He slowed the car as some high, wrought-metal gates appeared, set in a long stone wall. The guards had seen the armoured limousine coming and they were swinging back. The tyres crunched on gravel, and they stopped outside a tile-roofed villa, its plaster-stucco walls drenched in purple bougainvillaea.

Jacob got out, his eyes squinting briefly in the harsh sun. A blaze of scarlet hibiscus. The shade of the porch, and a long hallway, Persian rugs soft under his feet, men and women frozen by the walls, only their eyes moving as the enemy came by, a little girl in a blue dress clutching to her father's trouser legs, to keep safe from demons.

A big room, sofas and chairs scattered about, flowers on the tables. Men and women.

He is taller than I, Jacob thought in surprise, I had forgotten, but his beard is grey, as my hair is white.

He embraced Jacob in the Arab fashion, kissing him on both cheeks.

'It is the fabled Salem a-Din,' he said. 'Whose wealth is so great it cannot be counted in a whole week.'

He laughed, and as Jacob did likewise it spread across the room.

'You see,' he said, 'I never forget a face. Come. There is someone here who would meet you.'

He came out of the crowd, and he looked like his father.

'Jacob,' said Hamouda. 'I have waited long for this day.'

He reached in his pocket, and took out a small purple box. He held it out towards Jacob.

'I think this is yours.'

'Mine?' Jacob asked, puzzled.

'Open it. Please.'

It was a jewel box. Jacob took it, pushing up the lid with his thumb, and inside, set in silk, was a ring, a golden ring of great craftsmanship.

'This is not mine, surely?' he said, smiling.

'Look inside,' Hamouda urged. 'There is a mark.'

Jacob looked, and there it was, the menorah with its stem a capital A.

'It is Cousin Avraham!' he cried joyfully. 'Where did you find it?'

'I heard of this famed Jew in ancient times, this man who was related to you. I asked, and eventually, this was brought to me. But look below the A. Is there not a new sign?'

Jacob peered intently into the hallmark.

'It is Arabic,' he said in surprise. 'It says . . .'

'El-Din,' said Hamouda. 'A part of the great Salah el-Din's name. It originated in the court of Saladin. It means . . .'

'Peacemaker,' said Jacob, quietly.

'Yes, peacemaker. Is that not strange? For you, too, bring peace.'

# PART XIII

## Jerusalem. Today . . .

INSIDE the hall, it was quiet. Rabbi Gideon Weiss had turned down the sound on the small television, he and the young man sitting next to him on the cheap plastic chair simply watched the pictures. On both their faces was an expression of loathing.

The building was one of many, bleak, dirty concrete in a bleak dirty concrete sprawl. At one end of it was an altar, and on it shone a golden 33. The building itself was distinguished from the others in the slum by a neon 33 that flashed bright, day and night. It attracted the young Sephardic men of the area, who came for free combat classes and heady infusions of belief. Weiss had a number of such cheap halls that doubled as a kind of *shul* and sent numbers of the slum-dwellers out to the settlements in the West Bank.

The young man sat quiet, watching the pictures on the screen as his master had bid him. The jubilant men on the screen were olive-skinned and swarthy, with curly black hair, they looked like he did. Only they were Arabs, he was a Jew. Around his upper arm, like a holy badge, he wore a band, bearing a gold number 33 on a scarlet background.

They were carrying Arafat through some slum or other. Old and battered cars littered the streets, along with the rubbish and effluent running from the broken drains. It looked like the street outside. Weiss leaned forward and switched off the televison.

'You know them, don't you, Amos?' he said softly.

'Yes, Messiah,' the boy said.

'Arabs,' said Weiss, his mouth forming the word as though tasting something rotten. 'Filthy Arabs, vomited on us by the Devil and his agents, the Gentiles. Here we sit, polluted with vomit.'

'Polluted . . .'

'Smell the stench, Amos . . . did you not smell it when you lived amongst them? Did you not come to Israel to be clean?'

'Yes, yes . . . ,' Amos murmured. 'I know them . . .'

'God is waiting, Amos.'

'Yes . . . yes.'

'God is good to us' Weiss said clearly. 'God has given us his pledge. How else do you think we Jews have won victory after victory? I, you know, fought in the war that established us back here in the Holy Land. God told me to come. Millions of Jews have come home. You have come home from your suffering in an Arab land. How do explain the victories of us Jews against overwhelming odds? Because of God's divine hand. Have we not liberated Judea and Samaria? Did we not liberate Gaza and the Golan? Do we not have sovereignty over the Holy City and over Temple Mount?'

He paused, and the young man watched him with dark eyes, as alert as a rottweiler.

'What do all these things mean?' Weiss asked.

'They are parts of the divine pledge, and its fulfilment,' Amos said with certainty.

'Yes . . . the divine pledge, God's own word to us. Not to anyone else! Only us, for we are the people of God himself, and no other. We are a Chosen One and a Special One, selected for our purity and holiness, to rise above all others . . .'

Weiss reached forward and switched the television back on. Arafat was standing on some battered balcony, making a speech.

'Vomit . . . ,' Weiss whispered. 'Vomit spewing from the devil's mouth onto the Holy Land . . . How shall we make it clean?'

'They must go,' Amos said certainly.

'They must go . . .,' Weiss crooned.

He turned to look at the young Sephardic Jew, and his face became stern.

'Amos, Amos,' he said, and his voice was almost chiding. 'They are *not* going . . . do you not see them? Because of the Devil, they have taken back a pure part of the Holy Land . . . there they are, they hop and caper like demons violating the pure and chaste body of Israel. See how they finger her! See them defile her purity! And have they not also Hebron? Has the Devil not in his infinite cunning given them a foothold in Judea-Samaria? There shall they not be but the little thief put in at the window of the synagogue, to let the Devil in?'

Amos nodded, mesmerized by Weiss's voice, and by the sight of the agents of the dark power on the television.

'Yes, yes . . .,' he muttered, beginning to sway back and forth.

'How can God come, how can he walk through the open door and give us our redemption, if we let the Devil in first?'

'He will come, he will come . . .'

'No . . . he cannot come unless we are pure.'

'I am pure . . .,' Amos protested.

'Yes, yes . . .,' Weiss murmured soothingly. '*You* are as clean as holy snow, as clear as cold spring water. When *you* come to the gates of Heaven, God will be waiting for you with outstretched arms, he shall fold you to his bosom with Abraham and David, true soldiers all . . .'

Weiss looked deep in the eyes of the boy.

'But what of *Israel*, Amos?' he asked intensely. '*You* will be with God, but how shall God come to Israel, to give her his redemption?'

He gestured at the Palestinians on the television.

'How can we be pure?' he asked.

Amos twitched, as though connected to a current of electricity.

'They must go,' he said, with utmost certainty. 'We must drive them out.'

'Yes . . . we must drive them out . . .,' Weiss repeated, hypnotically.

Amos reached for a sports bag at his feet.

'Take off the arm band,' Weiss ordered softly. 'You shall not need it, on the shining white steps of Heaven. God will know you.'

'He shall, he shall,' Amos repeated, his head bobbing. 'Great gifts I will bring to him.'

'Great gifts, great gifts indeed.'

Weiss took the gold and scarlet arm band.

'Bless me, Messiah, for I go to do his will.'

Weiss took holy oil, anointing the young man's forehead, and chanting softly.

'Do the will of God,' he ordered. As loose and fit as a hound, the young man picked up his large sports bag and loped for the door.

He looked like one of them. He took off his shoes as he went into the mosque as they did. He went quietly up the stairs, reverently and respectfully, for he was performing an act of worship to his god, as those in rows below on their mats were doing to theirs.

The ullulating yowl of the mullah penetrated his consciousness, but for the first time he was calm as he heard it. From the balcony he could see them all below. He put his bag down on a bench and opened it. First he took out a number of long, oblong magazines, taped together, and arranged them in a neat row. Then smooth grenades the size of goose eggs. Finally, he slipped the Uzi sub-machine gun from inside the bag and slapped a magazine home with a practised movement.

He picked up the grenades, pulling the pins quickly and skilfully, tossing them over the balcony into the mosque below. The explosions went off in a booming sequence of explosive and screaming people.

Amos leaned over the balcony and began to shoot in short, expert bursts.

In the empty hall, Rabbi Weiss switched on his small television set. He watched patiently and without interest as American soap opera stars went through their routine.

Without warning and in mid-scene, the serial vanished to show the news desk. A grim-faced presenter was staring out at him.

'News just coming in is of a massacre in an East Jerusalem mosque. A lone gunman is believed to have killed over fifty Muslims before turning his weapon on himself. We go live to . . .'

Weiss switched off the set. Walking like a drunk man, he went to the altar and bowed down in worship.

# PART XIV

## Beersheva

IT was a small room, simply furnished. From the window Jacob could see white sand raining from the sky in the distance, falling on the scrub from sandstorms in the desert. She sat by the window, but he could tell that her dulled eyes saw only inside her mind. He'd acted too late to save her he thought again.

'Hullo,' he said softly. He spoke in Polish, as he knew to do, and her gaunt face came alive.

'Ahh . . . where are you from?'

'Warsaw. You?'

'Krynica.'

'That's a spa town, isn't it. Pretty.'

'It was before the bastard Germans came.'

Jacob smoked cheroots, but bought duty-free cigarettes to give to people as gifts whenever he travelled. He had a pack in his pocket, as he recalled that she had smoked when she was young.

'Would you like a cigarette?'

Terror contorted her face. 'Do you want us both to be killed?' she hissed. 'They caught the girl next to me in the work party yesterday. She was smoking something she'd made from dry leaves. They set the dogs on her. One big boxer tore off one of her breasts . . . we had to stand and watch until she died . . .'

She looked about her.

'I've got myself in here in the *revier*,' she said cunningly. 'Maybe I'll survive. What about you?'

'Not bad, kitchen detail.'

'Oh, that's good. Listen, I'll try to get a few medicines for you.'

'I'll get you some food.'

'Yes. Let's help each other. Here, I always keep something.'

She got up and went over to the simple bed. Under the pillow she had some dry bread. She broke off a piece.

'Here. Eat.'

'Thank you.'

She watched as he chewed and swallowed the bread.

'Good. Don't forget, try and get me something. We Poles have to stick together. Look out for the doctor. He's a bastard.'

'They're all bastards.'

Outside, there was the sound of people moving, and her face suddenly blanched.

'They're coming for me . . .,' she whispered. She was contorted, her hands wrapped about her emaciated body, bent over as though waiting for blows to rain down on her.

'No, no . . .,' Jacob said, trying to reach her. 'Ruth, Ruth, it me, Jacob. Nobody is coming for you . . .'

'He did it with the knife . . .,' she insisted. 'I stood and watched, he butchered her with the knife . . .'

'Ruth, Ruth, you are safe here. It is not the camp . . .'

She looked up at him sharply.

'You know my name.'

From somewhere, he suddenly felt a glimmer of hope.

'I am your husband, Jacob,' he said, taking her hands. 'Don't you remember?'

'Jacob . . .,' she said wonderingly. 'Yes, yes. Where were we?'

'Israel, darling. We are in Israel . . .'

She shook her head.

'It was not Israel . . . I remember, you promised.'

Suddenly, she seized him with hands of incredible strength, looking unblinking into his eyes.

'Yes, yes,' she insisted. 'You promised. You promised if they came for me you would make me free.'

He struggled to release her grip.

'We are in Israel,' he said desperately. 'Nobody is coming for you.'

'They are here!' she screamed. 'They come for me every night! There is a girl, on a chair. They make me hang her from a wire noose, every night! I push her off the chair and . . .'

'I cannot . . .'

'You promised! You promised you would make me free!'

'Doctor!' Jacob shouted, and she began to howl like a dog.

The door was thrown open, and a man and woman in their white coats came rushing in. She shrieked in terror, rolled up tight, but her eyes never left Jacob's.

'They are here! You did it! *You* did it!'

The needle glittered in the doctor's hand, she thrashed on the bed and the nurse flung her full weight on her to hold her down. She shrieked again and again as the drug flowed into her. Jacob heard her for ever.

The doctor was sweating when he came out of the room He had blond hair and blue eyes. He was a Dutch Jew, about forty.

Jacob was by the window. He reached into his pocket for one of the little plastic bottles he had taken to carrying, the ones they gave you on the airline, he unscrewed the top and tipped the neat liquor down his throat. He looked around, and the Dutchman was watching him.

'I'm sorry,' he said. 'It is a while since I saw her. I thought she might be better.'

The doctor shook his head.

'She is back in the . . .'

'*Kazett*,' said Jacob. 'The *Konzentrationslager*. The camps.'

'Yes. The camp. She will never leave, in her head.'

'Will she survive? Life among the memories is terrible.'

'I understand,' the doctor said sympathetically. 'I too knew someone who . . . survived. A relative. She fell from a window in Kensington, London, where she lived, last year. She'd had a lot to drink, they said it was an accident. I knew it was not. I knew of the things that had happened to her. You are yourself a survivor, are you not? How is it for you?'

'It's like a house. You build a life for yourself, and you live in it. Because you've been in the KZ the walls of your house are in fact cracked. They may look solid, but they're not. You may be the only one who knows they aren't firm. But while they stand, they will keep the storm out, keep the guilt and memories from overwhelming you. There are things it is best to avoid. I have a friend now in New York who cannot go to barbecues. Myself, among other things, I cannot walk on gravel. The ovens produced human ash by the ton. It's not like wood ash, it's got bits in it – teeth, fragments of bone. The Nazis used it for many things – to fill in swamps, as phosphate fertilizer – but before I was sent to the rocket factory I was part of a detail that took it by the cartload and spread it as gravel over the paths of the SS village near the camp. You just hope there's no earth tremor that will bring these walls crashing down around your ears. Levon survived Mauthausen. The last Christmas the SS put up a tree, a big pine, and they hanged six men from its branches, like ornaments, and had the others watch. He dreaded the festival after that. He shot himself on Christmas Eve two years ago – a wealthy businessman with three children.'

'Does anything help?' the Dutchman asked, professionally curious.

'It helps if there is something you very much want to do,' Jacob said wearily. He reached in his pocket and opened another of the little bottles. 'I thought that there would be justice, and peace, when we gave the Palestinians Gaza. I now see all we did was lock them and Arafat up in a new jail. The Arabs still hate us, the Muslims bomb us, we hate them, it will never end . . .'

He tipped the little bottle back.

'Now I find these small packets of liquor help me. My own personal concrete for the cracks.'

He looked at the doctor.

'What are you doing here?'

'I'm a Jew.'

'Ah,' said Jacob. 'How long have you been here?'

'I took temporary citizenship two and a half years ago.'

'And?' Jacob said softly. 'After three, you decide.'

'I'm going home. Back to Utrecht. Like you, I thought that giving the Palestinians Gaza would work. It hasn't. I do not want to take my little daughter for a walk carrying an Uzi, or keep a pistol on the dashboard. I do not want to hear Rabbi Weiss or General Shahak or any of the other madmen on the television talking about the Arabs the way Hitler used to talk about us. I don't want my wife hearing the militant Arabs howling for our blood, and I don't want my son growing up and having to spend sixty days reserve duty beating the Arabs. Living here is not unlike living in some sort of camp, where everyone around you wants you dead, and where you behave, not like the victims of the camps, but like the guards.'

Jacob got to his feet. Through the wall came the noise of a tinny radio. It was playing 'Me and my Surfboard.'

'You know that tune?' he said. 'It's the first Hebrew surfing song since Moses went through the Red Sea with the Children of Israel singing behind him.'

The doctor didn't smile.

'No, it's not a very good joke, is it?'

He got up to go.

'I have to say this,' the Dutchman said. 'I have read her notes. It would be better if you did not come to see her again. Every time you come she becomes very upset. She has attempted suicide . . .'

'I know. I . . . promised her I would not leave her so, and yet I cannot deliver on my promise. She knows.'

'How do you mean, leave her so?'

'She made me promise I would kill her. And I cannot do it. My son Saul blames me for her state. And is probably right. I was once an optimist, I survived, my wife survived. We had two sons, we founded a new nation. There was nothing we could not do. Now I am an old man and I see it was all untrue. Yet I still wish for peace . . . If there was peace it would make all of it, even this, worthwhile. But I cannot see how peace will come.'

He rubbed his hand over his face, tossed the empty miniature of brandy into the waste basket.

'They are sending me abroad again,' he said. 'I am to sanctify some new arms deal. I shall think about what you have said, doctor.'

The Dutch doctor watched from the window and saw Jacob walk slightly unsteadily to his car, a long silver Cadillac. The limousine lurched away, knocking over a line of plastic red cones, and went off along the street.

# PART XV

## Damascus. Tomorrow ...

THE small group of officers were waiting for the president; Hamouda at their head went to open the door as the Lincoln drew up. Over a decade of Syrian summers had aged the intelligence building, now small cracks had appeared in its facade, the paint was flaking here and there, the sun had bleached the wood to grey.

Asad too had aged. It was said that he played the game by Hama rules, after the great city of Hama which he had razed to the ground. Hama rules meant rule or die, and Asad still ruled. He came in as they held the sun-bleached door open for him, and followed Hamouda into the lecture hall.

'We are honoured by your presence, Mr President,' Hamouda said, and the other intelligence officers murmured their own approval.

'We hope that you will enjoy our little exhibition. It has a certain historical flavour.'

Asad nodded. Few leaders of any country were better equipped with historical understanding.

'And what is this exhibition called, Colonel Hamouda?'

'Weapons, warfare and technological advantage.'

'An interesting title.'

The room had been laid out with tables and exhibits. Asad reached out and picked up a crude wooden club.

'Is this a technologically advanced weapon?' he asked drily.

'It was, yes, to the first Stone Age person against whom it was used who did not have one and so suffered the consequences.'

Asad pursed his thin lips in acknowledgement of the point and put it back.

'However, sir, true warfare is a social, corporate and political activity, and therefore it was only once men became farmers and not hunters, and lived within cities not with their tribes that the true march of technological progress in war began. In walled, moated

and towered cities like Jericho or Catal Huyuk the high technology
of the day was metalworking, which provided the standard weapon,
the bronze-headed spear.'

Hamouda picked up an arrow-headed weapon, hefting it in
his hand.

'Still effective,' he said, 'provided your enemy doesn't have anything
better. Sargon, king of Akkad, did. Sargon, a most able general,
defeated all the spear throwers through technological superiority.
He created the first great empire by the use of a secret weapon, the
hunting bow, allied to new tactics, which included mobility, together
with a radically new structure for his army, which was built around
a corps of five and a half thousand professional troops, fleshed out
with levies. His empire ran from what we now call the Persian Gulf
to the Mediterranean, and included what we now call Syria. Sargon
was your ancestor, Mr President, he created *bilad al-Sham*, the lands
of Damascus.'

'And where are the Jews in this?'

'Sargon died in the twenty-second century BC, and Abraham, Isaac
and Jacob are at best not considered to have been born for another
five hundred and more years.'

'A good time to have lived – in a world without Jews!'

'Very true, sir. Sargon is important not only because he was the
first to use technological superiority to achieve great victory, but
because he introduced new and correct tactics for its use, and the
two must always go hand in hand.

'The centre of the world then was Syria, with its important trade
routes. Control for Syria was fought between the Mitanni, Egyptians
and Hittites. It was won by the last-named, largely due to their
possession and effective use of a superior weapons system – the
horse-drawn chariot with its three-man crew and bow and javelin
missilry.'

On the next table was a fine model of a light chariot and its
fighting team, and Asad paused to admire it.

'We can see a modern army in prototype here. The Hittites
trained and deployed special forces for pioneering, scouting and
intelligence. They had siege experts and shock troops. They exploited
the specialized skills of their allies or defeated states, such as the
archery of the Nubians and the horsemanship of the Hurrians.
The chariot, their equivalent of the Main Battle Tank – do not
the Israelis have a tank they call the *Merkava*, or Chariot? –
was so important that laws were passed concerning it. Its crew
took three years to train, according to a detailed manual on its

use, and it required support troops of grooms, armourers and woodworkers.

'If the Hittites had the first modern army, they also suffered the fate of over-extended states in any era. Such a war machine could not be supported by the economy of the day. Furthermore, technology was marching relentlessly on while the Hittites perfected their bronze weaponry. Iron provided stronger and cheaper weapons and protection. When improvements were made in smelting, it became available in quantity, and after that it was iron-equipped soldiers who wrote history.

'We can note many further examples of war-winning technological and tactical innovations in the centuries that followed,' continued Hamouda, moving down the tables. 'The phalanx of Philip of Macedon and his more famous son, Alexander, who conquered the known world. The war elephant. A smaller, but more effective weapon, the Roman pilum with its flexible head.'

Hamouda picked up one, showing it to the president.

'You throw it at your enemy's shield. The head sticks in, but bends, dragging the shield down, and you follow up, stabbing your foe with your sword. The Romans found it most effective, it helped give them *their* empire.'

A model of an armoured, charging knight, gaily apparisoned, fearsomely equipped.

'The heavy armoured cavalryman. The Frankish knights, the Crusaders who founded the kingdom of Jerusalem. They were technologically superior to the Arab peoples who opposed them and constructed mighty fortresses like Kerak and Margat to control and defend the land they had taken. However, their reign was brief. Under one hundred years later the great Syrian general Salah el-Din, known to them as Saladin, tempted the Latin King Guy into battle at Hattin, and slaughtered or captured the entire force. Guy had not properly realized that the defence of the Crusader state depended upon soldiers to man the garrisons of the castles. With these gone, the fortifications could not be defended and quickly fell.

'Alas, the Arab peoples soon fell into a kind of sleep, from which we have only recently emerged. The centre of the world moved to Europe. There, too, we can find many examples of technological superiority providing decisive victories, from the British longbow – a kind of medieval machine gun – to the much later 1870 Krupp steel artillery that pulverized the French. Slowly, slowly, we approach our own time. By the First World War the pace of technological change with which we are concerned was increasing.

'In 1939 the Germans put the whole package together and overran most of Europe, beginning with Poland, and came within an ace of defeating the Soviet Union. It was called *Blitzkrieg*, or Lightning War. Its elements hold good today – technological superiority, strategic surprise achieved by elaborate and skilful deception and overwhelming local superiority. In 1967 the Israelis did it almost without flaw and won in six days. When we attack the Israelis next time it will take us less than that.'

Asad's eyes widened slightly.

'With what?' he enquired. 'As president of Syria and commander in chief of the armed forces I assure you that it is the Israelis who possess the technological superiority, and who will be the ones conducting lightning war upon our prostrate form should we stupid enough to give them the opportunity.'

'Wrong,' said Hamouda. 'Zahal – the Israeli Defence Forces – are obsolete.'

'My army commanders tell me that the Israeli Defence Forces are, courtesy of both their American supplier and their own indigenous armaments industries, one of the most technologically advanced military forces in the world.'

'They are,' said Hamouda, 'but not enough. Their strength is based on the Armoured Fighting Vehicle, the AFV, and on Tactical Air Support, TacAir.'

'We, too have large numbers of advanced tanks, together with squadrons of tactical aircraft of the latest type.'

'All obsolete and unable to survive in a modern battlefield,' said Hamouda. 'Although still useful, if you could knock out the enemy's tanks and aircraft.'

'I would point out that far from abandoning the production of ever more advanced aircraft and tanks, they are being produced in great numbers. I ask you, would they be made if they were obsolete?'

'Yes. The generals responsible for the procurement of tanks and manned aircraft are all former tank men and former fighter and bomber pilots. History is repeating itself. The First World War proved that cavalry were completely outmoded. The mounted warrior simply could not survive in an environment dominated by the bursting artillery shell, quick-firing rifle, automatic machine gun and the armoured fighting vehicle. But the *really* interesting thing about this is that 1914 was not the first time the cavalry were shown to be obsolete. *That* was conclusively demonstrated in 1853, during the Crimean War, at Balaclava. Both sides, the British and the Russians, were made the objects of this lesson. The British Light Cavalry Brigade made the error of charging Russian artillery, and lost one third of their men and over two thirds of their horses in a matter of minutes. When in their turn the Russian cavalry charged later in the battle they were decimated by the fire from just five hundred infantrymen of the 93rd Highlanders. A technological jump had been made, and instead of muzzle-loading weapons the Scots were using breech-loading Minie rifles. They were able to reload sufficiently fast to stop the charge dead. The lesson should have been clear, that cavalry could not survive in such a hostile environment. Instead, there they were sixty-one years later. Indeed, the Poles actually fielded some in 1939.

'I say that history is repeating itself. The Israelis are as wedded to the AFV and TacAir as the cavalry general to his horse. Both the tank and fighter bomber are festooned with devices to improve their chances on the battlefield. Sophisticated stuff, from Blazer reactive armour to electronic counter measures. This is not to disparage the Israelis, who are without doubt at the forefront of the high-tech military revolution. It is simply that they cannot bring themselves to go through with what is required, which is the abandonment of manned systems.'

'So what is the wonder weapon that has rendered the entire military forces of the world obsolete?'

'There are two, actually, sir.'

Hamouda reached into the pocket of his smartly cut army jacket. He tossed something small on to the table.

'This is one of them.'

The president held it in his hand, a small black plastic square with a fine tracery of silver lines on it.

'What is it?'

'It's a Very High Speed Integrated Circuit, more commonly known as a microchip. The one you have in your hand has the power of a computer which twenty years ago would have filled this room. In that time, technological improvement has been such that the number of components per circuit has increased one thousandfold. The pace of technological change is stepping up. There has been a thousandfold increase in the cost performance of computers in the last decade. That is, a state of the art computer in 1992 had one thousand times the cost performance of one available in 1982. This means that all the old rules have gone out of the window.'

'So what is it that you would have me do?' asked the president quietly.

'Reduce the armed forces from the half million we have to about half that size. This will reverse the dilution of quality and provide us with the trained technicians that we need. Make the quantum jump that ensures technological superiority and lighning victory by investing in automated, intelligent weaponry not yet in production – acquire it in total secrecy. Start preparing. Psychologically prepare the Western public for a war by discrediting the Israelis. Use deception. Divert their attention elsewhere. Attack from a standing start. Drive them into the sea in four days. *Win beforehand.*'

'And what of the West, while we are doing this?'

'Here we are at one with Menachem Begin, we do not care what the *goyim* think. And once it is done, it'll be too late for them. They will forget about it soon enough. As the dominant power in the Middle East the Americans will quickly come to terms with us.'

The president stood quiet, and Hamouda and his intelligence officers waited watchfully. Asad collected his thoughts and then spoke.

'I thank you for a most lucid and learned exposition. I am struck by something you said.'

He picked up the VHSIC chip from the table.

'The cost performance of this and the computers it drives have improved one thousandfold in a decade.'

'Yes, sir,' said Hamouda.

'And that pace of change is accelerating.'

'It is, sir.'

'A thousandfold or greater rate of change does, as you say, mean that the old rules are thrown out of the window. This surely means that it is impossible to predict the outcome of a future war.'

'It means that Zahal is not the invincible power that everyone believes it to be. It means that in a war of technological imbalance a future war would be very, very short. Israel is a small country. We can overrun her and slaughter her population practically before the first United Nations delegate has got to his feet to call for a cease-fire.'

'But as I said, such a pace of change makes accurate prediction almost impossible. I wish, as you do, that the Israelis had never come, that we could drive them out. Once I believed it possible, now I fear it is beyond the realm of practical politics. If we adopt your plan what will happen? What if instead our choices of weapons are incorrect? Then the Israelis will overrun *us*. Striking through the Bekaa into central Syria, or through Kunietra or Rafid towards Damascus, using their air force and regular army as a first echelon, my understanding of the situation is that they could decisively defeat us within six to eight days, by which time they would have overrun most of Syria bar

the major cities, destroyed at least eighty per cent of our armed forces
and occupied all of our major military bases, all for the slight cost
of some two thousand fatalities. A pre-emptive strike against Syria
has always been considered politically impossible, however militarily
possible, but if we provide the *casus belli*, then may they not do to
us what they will? I too read history. Did not the Roman general
Julius Caesar say: "It is the right of war for the conquerors to treat
the conquered according to their pleasure?" There are those in the
Israeli cabinet like Rabbi Weiss and General Shahak who dream of a
greater Israel stretching from the Nile to the Euphrates. Would not
our attack provide them with the very excuse they need? I would
not care to experience the kind of things that would give Weiss or
Shahak pleasure. History pays no heed to the claims of peoples and
nations to exist forever. Where are the Hittites today, the Spartans?
Where is the state of Armenia? Do the Red Indians own America?
I would not have the Israelis do to the Syrians what Vespasian did
to them in the first century, I would not have the Syrians become
the new people of the diaspora. If there is one lesson I have learned
from my long years in a brutal world it is never to ask what you
may win from a particular course of action, but to ask what you
may lose.'

The president tossed the VHSIC chip back on to the table.

'So, no, we shall not gamble the existence of the Syrian people
upon a piece of plastic. Unless . . . I think you said there were *two* new
weapons. Perhaps the other can be guaranteed to bring victory.'

'It can, Mr President,' Hamouda agreed politely. They had come
full circle and were back at the beginning of the exhibition.

'Here it is, sir.'

Asad looked at the stone age club in irritation.

'This is some kind of joke?'

'No, sir,' said Hamouda.

He picked up the club, his fellow officers held Asad, and Hamouda
beat him to death.

# PART XVI

## Guatemala, Central America

THE man in the olive uniform accompanied Jacob from the presidential palace to the limousine. The deeds of protocol had been arranged, the memorandum of agreement was signed. Jacob Ben-Levi was leaving Guatemala to go to the UN.

'I thank you for all your help, Mr Ambassador,' General Aguillar said formally, and the two shook hands. Jacob's gaze did not seem to focus accurately on Aguillar's face.

'It has been my pleasure,' Jacob said, however. 'I shall leave you in the capable hands of my colleagues.'

'Thank you.'

Aguillar watched as Jacob climbed into the back of the limousine and the guard shut the door. His intelligence officers had told him what he needed to know about Jacob. He had arranged for a photograph of the two to be taken together in the lush presidential garden that morning, and for the on-board bar of the limousine to be suitably filled. As the car rolled forward down the driveway to the ornate gates he saw a gleam of light from inside as Jacob opened the little refrigerator.

He turned precisely on the heel of his boot and went back inside, to the large presidential office, where he shut the tall gilt door behind him.

'Fucking Jews,' he said morosely.

'That's what I say, general,' a voice said casually. 'Fucking Jews.'

Aguillar turned around. Two men were standing waiting for him, one tall and strong, in fatigues, the other small, with the face of an intelligent weasel. The Israelis. Aguillar made himself smile, showing very white, even teeth.

'You don't mind me saying fucking Jews.'

Shaul Shiloah smiled back pleasantly.

'No, general, we don't mind you saying fucking Jews. When

I'm stuck in a Tel Aviv traffic jam I say fucking Jews, most of the time.'

General Aguillar laughed, reluctantly.

'I've never been fond of Jews,' he confided. 'Slimy, cringing bastards. We had a Jew lived in our neighbourhood when I was a boy. Black hat, black coat, long black ringlets of hair, you know the sort. Hell, man, we got the bastard one day when we were bored, we rubbed kerosene into his ringlets and set fire to them! You should have heard him howl! He went up the street like a comet!'

Aguillar chuckled to himself.

'Ah, happy days,' he said. 'You got no worries when you're a child. Now, me, I have worries. Some slimy cringing Jewish congressmen whine about what we're doing down here and suddenly I got no arms contract, no CIA men, no special forces to help me. How am I supposed to fight communism without help? And now I got you! *More* fucking Jews! I mean, do I need more?'

Haazev Shahak stretched lazily, with the grace of the supremely fit.

'We can help, general,' he said. 'We understand your problem, we have solutions.'

Aguillar looked at the tall, lean young man rather malevolently. Haazev was olive-skinned, with jet black hair sticking up in the latest style, and he wore a gold-tipped lion's claw on a gold chain about his neck.

'I used to look like you. Only I didn't dress up like a punk. I looked like a soldier,' he said. 'Now I'm going bald, got a belly from sitting behind a desk, got worries coping with the fucking Indian communists. At least I still got a decent name. What sort of a name is Haazev, for God's sake? The old Jew we set on fire, he was Solomon Goldberg, you knew who a Jew was then. What is this Haazev?'

'The Goldbergs, the Goldmans, the Goldsteins, they all walked into the gas chambers in millions, general. Didn't fight. My daddy's changed his name to Shahak. That means pulverize. He called me Haazev. Being a soldier.'

Haazev smiled at Aguillar, soldier, commander in chief and president all rolled into one.

'That means Wolf, sir.'

'Wolf . . .,' Aguillar muttered.

'I'm a hunter. I eat people.'

Aguillar grunted. He looked at Shaul.

'Fine words,' he muttered. 'So what have you sent me, Mr Mossad man? A fashion-model who calls himself Wolf and a drunken ambassador.'

'Jacob Ben-Levi is an old-fashioned European liberal Jew, general,' said Shiloah. 'An endangered species in Israel, general. I have to say he is not at all typical of us, although very useful as an image. He survived the Holocaust, he believes in the possibility of changing human nature. I am somewhat more cynical.'

'I know what people are,' Aguillar said darkly. 'Bastards, most of them, who'd cut your throat for a dime, and give a penny back to dance on your grave.'

'Anyhow, fine country you have here, general,' said Shaul. 'Very beautiful.'

'Better if we could get rid of the communists.'

'That's what we're here to help you do,' Shaul said urbanely. 'I went out sightseeing a few days ago. Went fishing. I took my camcorder along. Care to see my video?'

'You're here to work!' Aguillar cried. 'Not to go sight-seeing.'

The room was supplied with consoles, telephones, VDU screens. Shaul Shiloah eased a video cassette into a machine and the television lit up.

'It won't take a moment,' he murmured.

'Look at that sky, Haazev,' said Shiloah. 'Clear as could be. Lovely sea, white sand. It's a tourist's paradise, this place.'

The wooden fishing boat rolled on the glittering water. Over on the shore hibiscus bushes splashed scarlet, orange and yellow. The fishermen heaved on their ochre-red net and glittering drops of water flew in the sun.

'Must be a good catch,' Haazev commented. 'Look at them pull.'

'Oh, yes,' agreed Shiloah.

The net bulged, with a final jerk they brought the catch on board. A man, bloated by his time in the sea, lay on the deck. He had no toes. There was a ragged hole under his chin where his tongue had been. Rusty pins stuck out of his eyes, and Shaul pressed freeze on the recorder.

'The Yanqui tourists want to catch swordfish, general,' Shiloah said reprovingly. 'They catch this sort of thing they won't come back.'

'We're fighting a war!' Aguillar cried resentfully. 'How are we supposed to find out what the enemy is up to. Are we just to ask nicely?'

'You can ask nicely, and *then* crush his balls, and he'll tell you. But only if you have the right man. *You* are just torturing people

at random, in the hope that they're involved with the insurgents.
It makes you very unpopular. It means you won't get all the lovely
tourists, with all their lovely money.'

'The fucking Indian communists breed like rabbits. There are so
many more of them than us.'

'We have to deal with the Palestinians, and the Arabs. There are
more of *them* than us,' said Haazev. 'We have acquired a certain
expertise in dealing with them. We make them afraid.'

'How?'

'Because we know who they are. And when we know who they
are, we strike, like the hand of God Himself. We know, for example,
where there is an insurgent cell, right here in this city.'

'You do?' Aguillar burst out in surprise. 'How, damn you, how?
You have only been here a month.'

'Back home, I work for intelligence. I have done tours with
Mossad, and Shin-Bet,' said Shiloah. He tapped a sleek, white
computer console next to him. 'When I arrived I put certain
surveillance routines into operation that have proved effective in
controlling the Palestinians in Gaza and the West Bank. One of
them has just paid off. You have a building here in the city that
consumes more electricity than it should, and it does so at night.
Why? Haazev here has gone round and watched it. There's a cell
in there, making bombs and arms.'

Haazev Shahak stretched himself like a cat and stood up.

'I've been training up some of your boys, general. We're going in
in an hour's time. Care to watch?'

Aguillar looked at the two Israelis with the glimmering of admiration in his eyes.

'Shit,' he said. 'I'll come along.'

It was over in seconds. The dark house suddenly lit up from within,
fierce yellow splashes of light blasting out from the windows, and
the quiet was broken by the flat crump of the exploding stun
grenades. Screams, and harsh shouts of command, smoke gushing
from the shattered windows. When Aguillar went in it was all over,
black-clad figures hustling bleeding men out to the black vans that
were drawing up.

The smoke was clearing. In the room where the Wolf was standing
was a long table laden with explosives and electrical equipment.
Underneath it in a pool of blood lay a dead man.

Haazev pulled up his black balaclava.

'Here it all is, general.'

Aguillar beamed with satisfaction. And then he died.

On the floor, an eye gleamed. The man in the pool of blood came alive, springing up and forward at him, a long knife in his hand.

'*Murderer!*'

Aguillar was middle-aged and slow, he had forgotten how fast young men could move. As the Indian sprang, Haazev caught his knife arm, almost lazily. A boot swept his feet from under him and the man tumbled over, high in the air, to crash against the wall. He came off the floor still fighting, but the Wolf was on him, his hands somehow vanishing into his very face. There was a hideous crackling and bubbling, blood fountaining in scarlet spray, and Haazev tore the man's face away. He dropped something like a gory rubber mask to the floor, and put his foot on the thrashing meat. The knife was there, he thrust it in, and it was quiet.

They were all drunk. The girls, the general, Haazev and Shiloah. The table was a ruined battlefield of feasting. Aguillar rose, pulling up two of the pretty, half-clad girls with him.

'Hey, I got to go to bed. Got the country to run in the morning,' he rumbled. He raised a glass, and Shiloah squinted past a naked breast at him. Haazev raised a glass from under a pile of giggling girls.

'I want a fucking Israeli name too,' Aguillar bellowed extravagantly. 'You boys are my kind of people. Shit, I thought you were fucking Jews. Slimy cringing bastards. *But you're not!*'

He roared with laughter and staggered out of the room, the women holding him up.


# New York


Jacob woke, his heart pounding. He stared at the ceiling, then at the room around him, trying to remember where he was. A hotel room. Somebody knocking on the door. He got up, pulling on a dressing gown.

'Who is it?' he called.

'Me, Dad. David.'

'David? *David . . .*'

He hurried to the door, removed the chain and opened it, to find his son beaming on the other side.

'Come in, come in,' he said, embracing him. David held on to him, composing his features so that his father could not see his shock. Jacob seemed old, he was not the strong man he remembered. And he smelled of stale liquor, like a drunk.

'Let me make us coffee, there is a kettle here somewhere . . .'

He shut the door behind his son, still holding on to him with joy.

'It is a long time . . .,' he said, 'a long time we have not seen each other.'

'We have both been travelling,' said David. 'So many foreign countries.'

'It's true . . .,' Jacob said, pressing the button of the cordless kettle. 'Instant all right for you? Little did I think all those years ago when I brought the refugees in on a landing craft that I should spend so many years abroad . . . I had a dream, that I should grow oranges, and get fat. Instead I have gone about the world like an itinerant pedlar . . .'

An attentive gleam came into David's eye.

'A pedlar! What have you been selling, Dad?'

'The good name of Israel, I suppose,' Jacob said. He spooned coffee into cups from a jar. A row of small plastic bottles were on the shelf, miniatures, and he cracked the seal on one.

He caught his son looking at him.

'I . . . usually put one of these in with my coffee,' he said. 'It helps.'

'I'll join you,' David said, as though it were the most usual thing in the world.

'You think I'm a drunk,' Jacob muttered. 'I find it helps, that is all.'

'Helps to do the job?'

'It is not easy,' Jacob admitted. He poured boiling water over the coffee and a sudden scent of brandy perfumed the air. He wiped his watery eyes with the back of his hand.

'The old days were magic . . . back when there was me and Golda and Abba, and dashing generals like Moshe and his eyepatch, and the world knew we were the good guys. But after that there was Begin and Sharon, the Lebanon, Sabra and Shatilla . . . bombing and shelling civilians . . . And now we have Shelesh Shahak and Rabbi Weiss, and nobody even makes a pretence that we're the good guys, since we so obviously aren't, *and we don't have any friends.*'

'And Mama's in hospital and will never come out.'

Jacob stared at his son with haunted eyes.

'You blame me too?'

'I don't blame you, Dad. But is it not the same story? Your own early days, and now this . . .'

'Saul blames me.'

'We had ideals. You used to talk to me of ideals. What's happened to us?'

'We have no friends. Except those we can find, like anyone going down a dark alley.'

'Like General Aguillar of Guatemala?' David asked, quietly.

'General Aguillar . . .,' Jacob muttered, and shook his head, in disbelief. 'Who could have imagined the day would come when we would climb into bed with murderers.'

'I know,' David said, and sipped his hot drink. 'Aguillar is doing to the Maya Indians – the indigenous owners of the country – what Adolf Hitler did to us. The Mayas are a fine race – magnificent and beautiful, when not malnourished or dying from disease as so many are – with their own culture, going back thousands of years. They work as slaves on the land of the descendants of the *conquistadores* – a few hundred families own all the arable land – and live in concentration camps.'

He looked at his father.

'Do you know this, Dad?'

'I . . . try not to think about these things,' he muttered.

'Guatemala is a hideous relic of Spanish colonialism that should have been eradicated decades ago,' David continued remorselessly. 'There is a brave, pitifully under-funded and ill-armed resistance movement that keeps alive the flame of hope amongst the Indians. General Aguillar and his like have been trying to stamp it out for years. Now, if my facts are right, and you have just returned from that country having signed an agreement with General Aguillar, we are adding our considerable expertise in this area to his efforts.'

'Do not parade your liberal conscience in front of me!' Jacob cried. 'I have to live in this world.'

'Is that why you need a brandy in your coffee, before you can go out and face the world?' David asked cruelly. 'If I remember rightly, once you would not join Saul's company in South Africa, because it exploited Africans. Now you dine with murderers.'

'You do not know how it is!' Jacob said bitterly. 'You do not know how diplomatically isolated we are. Once we had South Africa as our ally, us and Taiwan. Do you know what they called us, those waddling comfortably about in the corridors of the safe? The League of the Desperate! Now South Africa is no more, not as our strong ally, and Taiwan will be gobbled up by China, one of these days. *We have no friends.*'

'We have some friends,' said David carefully. 'All like General Aguillar, all equally unsavoury, equally brutal, and dictatorial. They all have one feature in common, we side with the few, the very few, who with technology and arms oppress the many.'

'I know,' Jacob said quietly.

'In Israel we are obsessed with keeping the past alive. But soon we shall run out of old Nazi war criminals to put on trial. We are interested in no one's history but our own. It is a great mistake. Israel is filled with war memorials — all those jagged, inscribed pieces of rock commemorating yet another bloody battle. And yet the most important battle of them all is not marked at all. It is near Tiberias, which was once Tyre. There another alien civilization that tried to transplant itself into the Middle East came to grief. They were the Crusaders, the Frankish knights, and all you may see of them are the giant castles they built. The battle they lost was the Battle of Hattin.

'It is the Palestinians,' he said quietly. 'We dispossessed them to make Israel. If the Battle of Hattin is not to come for us then we must find a way to give them back a home to live in.'

'I know this!' Jacob said indignantly. 'Did I not go and talk to Arafat? I am a liberal, I am the same as you. I want peace, I just do not know how to find it.'

David put down his cup.

'Talk to me,' he said intensely. 'I'm writing a book, I'm making a television programme. About Israel. The *real* Israel. Not the mythical one. If we can bring out the past, then maybe we can come to terms with it. If we can come to terms with it, us and the Palestinians, us and the Arabs, then maybe we can have peace.'

'They will hate you, at home,' Jacob said soberly.

'I am loathed anyway, by the madmen. I can take it.'

Jacob sat silent.

'Dad . . . you *must*,' David said quietly. 'Exorcise the past. The past has made Mama mad, she lives in a cell, imprisoned by the past, just as thin, as skeletal as she was in the past. The past will destroy *you too*. For all our sakes, you *must* talk to me.'

Jacob sat up straight, and took a deep breath, like a man preparing to set out on a journey.

'What is it you want to talk to me about?'

'You were there,' David said simply. 'You know it all.'

Jacob peered into his undrunk coffee.

'We shall have a drink later,' he said. He poured his coffee and brandy away, and turned on the kettle.

'While that boils, I shall wash and shave,' he said decisively. 'You have a recorder, a notebook? Very well. There is much to tell.'

He had been talking for a long time. It had poured out in a one long, clear stream. The places he had been, the things he had done, the people, the deals, the weapons and plans. David had listened, and his tape recorder had turned silently on the table.

There was a knock at the door, and Jacob broke off.

'Who can that be?' he asked. 'I am not expecting anyone.'

He went over to the door.

'It is the *shabbat*,' he shouted. 'I am busy at prayer. What do you want?'

'I need a lesson in firing a Sten gun,' a man called out, and Jacob suddenly grinned opened the door.

'Elie!'

Elie smiled. He was standing in the corridor, a young woman, black-haired and olive-skinned at his side.

'Hullo, sergeant,' he said.

'Come in, come in,' Jacob beamed.

'You're sure we won't interrupt your prayers?' Elie said slyly.

'It's the only day I get off,' said Jacob. 'I always tell people I don't want to see I have to pray. Who is this beautiful young lady, Elie?'

They went inside and David stood up to greet them.

'Rifka, meet my *mef-kaf*, my combat sergeant, Jacob Ben-Levi, and also, I think, his son David. Jacob, this is Rifka Berry, who is an Israeli too.'

'Everybody knows Israel's ambassador extraordinary,' she said smiling, and offered a small, smooth hand. 'How do you do?'

'Very well, thank you,' Jacob said.

She turned to David, shaking his hand too.

'I love your articles,' she said fiercely. 'I never miss one.'

'Are you sure you're an Israeli?' David asked quizzically. 'Back home there are plenty who'd like to see me shot.'

'Not me,' she assured him.

'David and I have been working all morning,' said Jacob. 'On a new project of his . . . but I think we can now pause for a drink.'

He took glasses from a cabinet, and a bottle from his refrigerator, pulling the cork with a practised hand.

'Australian semillon,' he said. 'I am not only a poor Jew because I do not pray, but a poor Israeli too where wine is concerned. I love

what the Australians can do to a grape. So Elie, who do you want
to shoot with your Sten gun?'

'Rabbi Weiss,' Elie said, and suddenly he wasn't smiling.

'Weiss,' Jacob said soberly. 'Yes, better for us all if he had met
with some accident, all those years ago.'

His expression became bitter.

'I am old enough to have seen Nazi stormtroopers attacking Jews in
the streets. Others too saw it, but I am one of those who survived . . .
I never thought to see Jewish Nazis attacking Arabs in the streets.'

'You would call Rabbi Weiss a fascist?' Rifka Berry asked. They
had sat down, she held her wine glass on slim knees.

'What else?' David asked.

'Of course,' Jacob said bluntly. 'He is a demagogue whose speeches
are a torrent of war, violence and triumphalism. His movement,
Numbers 33 takes genocide as its main platform. The Arabs are
compared to the Amalek tribe murdered by the ancient Hebrews.
Their genocide Weiss justifies by the commands of a primitive god of
vengeance who if he comes will do so only to a landscape drenched
in blood. We do not need Rabbi Weiss, nobody does. Yes, if only
someone had shot him all those years ago or handed him over when
the authorities were on to him. But why does he concern you?'

'He's here in New York,' said Elie.

'Then this is good for Israel, if bad for New York. But he goes
to America often since the FBI dropped their charges, taking money
from the Jews there, for his organization.'

'He's raising a lot of money this time,' said Rifka. 'He's campaigning
for Senator Behr.'

'Senator Behr . . .,' Jacob said thoughtfully. 'He is running for President, is he not? And you, Elie, you are still with Governor Kane?'

'Campaign manager. Chief of staff, if he wins. Which,' he said
slowly, 'is beginning to look unlikely.'

'Why?' Jacob asked in surprise. 'Kane's the best candidate. The
Americans have finally got lucky, they have someone running who's
genuinely capable. He'll make a good president.'

'Weiss is delivering the Jewish vote to Behr. It's close. It's a bad
stage in the race. If we lose New York the donations will dry up,
the campaign will fold. If we win, then we get the nomination.'

Jacob poured more wine. David stood by the window, watching
and listening carefully, sensing something in the wind.

'Why have you come to see me? On this *shabbat* we are not
observing.'

'We want you to take out Weiss,' said Rifka.

Jacob looked at her interestedly.

'Why?' he asked. 'Why do *you*, Rifka Berry, want me to take out Weiss?'

'I am an Israeli, as you are,' she said. 'I want an end to it.'

'An end to what?'

'What we have now,' she said quietly. 'I want peace. When I have children I do not want them to be killed in yet another war, I do not want them to grow up hating Arabs. I want peace, I want the Palestinians to have some land to call home, I want it all to stop. It will never stop unless Weiss is stopped. Unless Weiss is stopped then soon, one day, he will get what he wants, which is thousands and thousands of Palestinians murdered, and then no one will ever forgive us, and it will never stop.'

She looked at Jacob with passionate intensity.

'It must stop,' she repeated. 'And New York is the place to start.'

Bright tears suddenly glittered in her eyes.

'I have a father who has no legs, I have two brothers with six feet of earth to call their own. If it does not stop it will be my husband, my children who are maimed and killed in their turn, and on, and on . . .'

'Yes,' Jacob said gently. 'We have all lost . . . I, too, am a peacenik. I have seen evil at close quarters and first hand in my life, and for good to triumph the good have to fight.'

He looked down at his hand, where he wore the golden ring Hamouda had given him, the ring of Avraham, the ring of peace, and then he turned to Elie.

'But tell me, how can I help in this battle of yours?'

'Because he reckons that Weiss can deliver him the Jewish vote, Behr is identifying with him. Weiss has managed to sell himself as something he is not in America, don't forget. For me, as for you, for Rifka, Weiss is a megalomaniac psychopath, a religious maniac of lethal potential. Here in America, they see him as a religious leader, a war hero, a man of vision and principle. His Hebrew Defence Corps, which was an imitation Nazi SS group, a kind of Kosher Klux Klan, that went about making trouble with the blacks, a lot of people saw as a holy vigilante force keeping the streets clear of crime. The fact that he was charged with attempted murder for the bombing of the Soviet culture impresario has been translated into anti-communist patriotism. Behr is willing to be associated with this. Blacken Weiss, blacken Behr.'

'Why would I count?'

'You're a hero, Mr Israel,' said David.

'That's right,' Rifka said, nodding her head. 'In America, you *were* Israel. You epitomized everything that was good about Israel. A survivor of the Holocaust, war hero, secret agent, statesman, man of principle.'

'I have long thought that the Americans love Israel for her body,' Jacob said, sounding tired. 'And for certain, we love America for her money. My colleagues knew what they were doing when they sent me about the world for 20 years while they changed everything I knew about home. Israel is part of the Middle East now, but unfortunately we still need a European solution to our problems.'

'You mean the Palestinians?' asked Rifka. She had brushed the tears from her eyes, and smiled in sympathetic agreement as he nodded.

'What Rifka says is right,' said Elie. 'To most Americans you're Mr Israel. If you weigh in against Weiss, they'll listen.'

'I cannot just throw mud. I have to have something specific to say.'

'You have,' Elie said softly. 'You were in Deir Yassin. You saw Weiss commit mass murder.'

David saw Jacob put up an arm defensively.

'We cannot talk about these kind of things,' he muttered. 'And not in public. Here, we are becoming low on wine, the tide is going out. Let me open another bottle.'

He drained his glass, and went through into the tiny kitchen again. He opened his refrigerator. A light footfall was behind him and he turned.

'Let us have a change. Let us swap hemispheres. A bottle of English wine. It is surprisingly good.'

'I like the way you have it all chilled and ready,' said Rifka.

'You see a hero, this man of principled titanium,' he said. 'I see an old man who wakes up in the night and is afraid he may be back where he came from, who has to take a drink before going back to bed with the lights on. Every day, I am afraid that the roof beams may come down, or the cracks in the walls will make them crumble about me.'

'That's heroism, to me,' she said quietly. 'And you still go out and fight for what is right.'

Jacob went back into his living room.

'I am in your debt,' he said. 'Since many years, when I slipped and fell under Arab guns, and a young man saved my life. If you call in debt, I will do what you ask.'

Elie shook his head.

'Saving a life in wartime is not a debt. You were our sergeant, you looked after us, you kept *us* alive. I just want Kane to win, and Weiss to lose.'

'That has to be some sort of triumph of good over bad,' said Jacob. 'Very well. I will come.'

Rifka gave a sudden shriek of joy, and putting her arms about him, kissed him. Then she stood back with her hand over her mouth, blushing. Jacob smiled, in surprise and pleasure.

'I'm sorry . . .,' she said. 'It's just so important.'

'You may do it again some day, should I please you,' Jacob said. His face was slightly flushed, it had colour in it. David grinned at him. Jacob held up the bottle. 'English wine, now. Grown where the ancient Romans grew it. Let us try.'

They raised their glasses, and drank.


# New York


He could fill a hall. They'd come to see Mister Israel, Jacob Ben-Levi, and they'd bring their cheque books with them. They sat in their comfortable chairs, Jews who had done well out of America, ready to have their consciences made to smart a little, ready with a salve of money.

'You know me,' said Jacob. 'And I know you. You're friends of Israel.'

They settled in their seats, happy to watch an old film. She was there with them, in the front row, big luminous eyes staring up at him.

'Well, you're more than that, aren't you? You love Israel.'

He smiled at them, and they smiled back. Rifka did not smile, she with her big eyes on him, waiting to hear him describe the future. Somewhere near the back, David listened carefully.

'But what is love? It can take many forms, can't it? On one level, Israel is easy to love, for a Jew who lives here in New York. *Kibbutzim* riding tanks into the fiery light of a battlefield sunset, swaying commandos *davening* at the wailing wall, hot Uzis still in hand, selfless soldiers climbing the long trail up to Masada. A whole people, reunited in the land of David.'

Slight frowns were appearing. He thought he could see Rifka nodding, short, tiny nods of her head that made her black hair sway.

'Loving Israel is easy when it's like this, it's like making love to a beautiful, sexy woman, and when we get to cream the Arabs one more time you get to have an orgasm.'

They were watching him very closely, this wasn't how it was supposed to be. Their eyes flicked to the big poster that was spread on the wall behind him. Triumphant, their hands linked and raised, Rabbi Weiss and Senator Behr were marching into their future together.

'Having to live with the beautiful woman is different to making love to her. You get to know more about her. She may have a nasty side to her character. She may have some terrible secrets in her past. It's when you experience that unpleasantness, when you know the things she has done that you find out if you love her.'

Rifka's father had no legs. Ruth sat imprisoned by the past, every day.

'You still love Israel, otherwise you wouldn't be here. I love Israel too, otherwise I wouldn't be here, making my pitch. I know things that you know, yet we still love her. We know what happened in Sabra and Shatilla, that Israeli commanders let the Phalangists into the camps to murder Palestinian civilians. We know that there are those in Israel bent on massacre even today. We know there is a dark side to the bright face of Israel. There was a time when you used to listen to anyone from Israel quite happily, just like looking at one more pretty girl passing in the street, but I have to tell you, those days are long gone. We Israelis haven't dropped down from Heaven, freshly minted and pure. There are those of us who try to do good, and I hope I am one of them. But you should be aware that there are others, those in whom the forces of evil reside. They will try to persuade you to support things you should not. They are plausible, they are eloquent, they have charisma. Evil has taken up residence in their hearts, and you must shun them.'

His eyes swept slowly over the audience. Rifka's knuckles were white, her small hands clenched into fists.

'The Rabbi Weiss is one such.'

They shifted in their seats, someone had changed the movie. Rifka's face was suddenly flushed with colour.

'I have known him much longer than you, long before he turned himself into a rabbi, long before he put a name to the forces that drive his dark soul. It has a name now, he calls it Numbers 33. He'll tell you it calls for the expulsion of the Arabs from the lands of Israel – and they seem to be getting bigger all the time, in his mind – and he'll tell you that when it is accomplished, God will come to his people, in all His glory. I, Jacob Ben-Levi, lost my belief in God a long time ago, in places called Auschwitz and Dora, but I can tell you that what Weiss means by expulsion is genocide. He wants the Arabs killed. Not merely the soldiers of the Arab armies, but the civilians who live within Israel. There are those of you here who look upon Rabbi Weiss as a hero, because he claims to be responsible for the *aliyah* of the Russian Jews to Israel. I think the failure of communism had more to do with that. But you seem to have forgotten that his campaign involved the bombing of offices, it involved murder ... A young woman and her little daughter died in an inferno started by a fire bomb. No charges were ever brought ... Why? Rabbi Weiss has powerful friends. There is a dark side to Israel's soul. There are those who do not mind having crazy, murderous Jews, because they frighten people. They frighten the Arabs ... There are those who want Rabbi Weiss where he is, just *how* he is ...

'How can I tell you this with such certainty? It is because I know that there was a dark side to Israel from the very start. There were those who wanted to use massacre and genocide to drive the Arabs from Israel from the start. An ethnic cleansing, if you will. They were there right from the start. I know, for I saw them at their work. By accident, as a soldier of the *Haganah*, I entered a small village outside Jerusalem one April morning at the beginning of the War of Independence. The name of the village was Deir Yassin.'

He looked over at them and saw Rifka's eyes glittering in the darkened hall.

'I see that some of you have heard of this village. There I saw men of the Irgun slaughtering unarmed Arabs who lived there. I was witness to one particular massacre. A man who I had expelled from my own fighting squad for committing atrocities came out of a house. In the alley, huddled against the wall were the women and children of the house, those who had been dragged from it by force. I was unable to prevent what happened. With the Sten gun that he had not used to fight the Arab soldiers, our opponents in the war, he shot the women and children dead. I saw their blood, I heard their death agony.'

Jacob turned and pointed his finger at the poster behind him on the wall, pointed it like a pistol barrel.

'That man was Rabbi Weiss.'

He turned back as the rumble quietened.

'It is painful for me to tell you these things. I had just come from a time and a place where six million Jews had been systematically murdered by an ideology of evil. I never dreamed I'd meet Jews who planned to do the same thing to another people. I see that it is painful for you to hear them. When I escaped from a death march out of Auschwitz I had a huge phlegmon on my chest, a vast boil. A Red Army doctor lanced it for me. He had no anaesthetic. It hurt, but when the sickness was let out I was better. It is the same with this. You should know what kind of people they are, who talk of expelling the Arabs from Israel.'

He turned again to look at the poster.

'I know one thing. You do not want a man as president of this great nation of America, who holds hands with a murderer. In the past I have come to you asking for your money. Today I want no money, just your support. Vote for Governor Kane, and keep this evil from your hearts, and your country.'

When they came to their feet she was there with them, her face shining, as though with love.


On the television they were talking from Behr's campaign headquarters. Paper, bumper stickers, flyers and buttons lay about like the debris of a lost battle. A campaign worker was clutching a cold cup of coffee and crying into it.

With his shirtsleeves rolled up Kane turned from it.

'There it is. It's official,' he said, and beamed.

Jacob smiled back. He was tired, but like Kane, the pleasure of victory was keeping it at bay.

There were just the two of them in the little office, the tall, handsome, blond American and the small, dark Jew. Outside they could hear the euphoric buzzing from the staff.

'I just wanted to thank you here, the two of us,' said Kane. 'Before you came on board we couldn't do right with the Jewish vote, after you were with us, we couldn't do wrong. I'm going to make it now, Jacob, I can feel it, and the pollsters do too. Listen, is there anything I can do for you in return?'

'There is nothing I can think of at the moment,' Jacob said politely. 'I helped out of principle, not for reward.'

Kane looked at him thoughtfully.

'What you did, as I understand it, may have hurt you at home.'

'I am an old man . . .'

'Not that old. You worked the hustings like a young guy out of college.'

'I survived the KZ, too. But I am older than I was, I have little personal ambition left. I would simply like to see peace.'

'Well, maybe we can do something about that. Who can tell, when I'm in the White House.'

Kane suddenly seized a flat book of campaign matches, and wrote on it with his pen.

'Here,' he said, and passed it to Jacob. 'That's official.'

Jacob read it. Inside Kane had written: IOU one election.

'That's a debt you can call in, any time,' Kane said sincerely.


The hotel elevator doors hissed, and held themselves open for Jacob to get out. As they closed and the lift hummed in search of more customers he walked along the corridor to his room. The corridor was wide, sofas and chairs scattered along its length, as he approached a young woman got up. It was Rifka. She held up a dark green bottle.

'Buy you a drink, mister?' she grinned.

'A drink!' said Jacob. 'I have been offered more Perrier water tonight than I would care to bathe in. A drink would be wonderful.'

He unlocked the door and they went in. He fished in an antique cupboard for some glasses.

'The *Pierre* expects you to drink champagne,' he said approvingly. There was a pop and he held out a flute as the creamy wine foamed at the neck of the bottle, glistening with condensation.

Rifka held up her glass in acknowledgement.

'Congratulations,' she said. 'And thank you.'

'Thank you and Elie for giving me the opportunity to get involved. I actually feel I've done some good.'

'You have. Oh, you have.'

Jacob examined the bottle.

'Perrier-Jouet! You are clever, it's my favourite. They say, you know, that it was the famous unsweetened vintage of 1846 that started the fashion for dry champagne. A good thing too, sweetness masks all kinds of faults.'

He tipped back his glass, and refreshed both hers and his.

'Dealing with politicians in public gives one a hell of a thirst,' he said. 'They're so concerned to be politically correct. All that blasted fizzy water . . .'

'Jacob,' Rifka said quietly. 'Doing what you did means so much to me. For the future of all of us. Would you do something else, just for me?'

'What can I do?'

'Make love to me.'

The champagne in the flute slopped dangerously in his hand, as he looked at her in amazement.

'But my dear ... I am old enough to be your father. You are young and beautiful, what would you want with me?'

'I have never admired a man more than I admire you,' she said steadily. 'There isn't anyone in Israel with your courage, who would have stood up and done what you did. And you are not too old for me.'

He drank some champagne as he looked at her.

'You are very beautiful,' he said. 'Pardon me for staring at you, but one sees differently, under these circumstances ... Rifka, my dear, I don't even know if I *could*. My poor wife, Ruth, was taken away so many years ago, and I have not pursued women since ...'

'I have heard,' she said, 'that in the concentration camps – what is it they were called?'

'The KZ, the *kazett*.'

'In the KZ, that men never felt desire.'

'No,' he said soberly. 'Fear and hunger drives it out.'

'And yet it returned. When you were free.'

'Oh yes. Like a magic, like flowers suddenly blooming in spring. It happens. It was the great boil on my chest, for me. When the Russian doctor lanced it.'

She looked at him quizzically.

'When it was lanced?'

'Well, yes. You see, they had no anaesthetic. The pretty nurse who was with him, she unbuttoned her blouse, and put my hand inside. I felt no pain at all.'

She put her glass down on the table, standing close to him. Carefully, she undid the buttons of her white shirt, one after the other. She took his hand, and placed it inside.

'See,' she said, as the heat joined them. 'It still works.'

# PART XVII

## Kiryat Arba, Israel

'KILLING is not always killing,' said Rabbi Gideon Weiss, and the men and women in the hot hall listened to him, their eyes fixed on the thin, bearded, intense figure with the silver hair striding up and down the stage. Behind him was a huge banner with the gold 33 on it, and the command of God from the Torah: 'You must drive out all the inhabitants of the land as you advance. Any whom you let remain shall be as barbed hooks in your eyes. And what I meant to do to them I will do to you.' Outside it was dark, the cicadas groaned incessantly as though in pain.

'When you take a piece of unwanted scrub land, and turn it into a beautiful garden, this is creation.'

His gaze swept over them, urging them to look into his eyes, to feel his strength and they did.

'Creation,' he said again. 'That is a very important word, it is the word of God. When you create your garden, there are things to do. You cultivate, improve and fertilize the soil. You plant seeds and put in shrubs and trees. You arrange for a steady supply of water. And, of course, you must destroy the weeds.'

He suddenly stopped on the stage, and the crash of his boots echoed back from the wall.

'Weeds,' he whispered, 'are not allowed in the garden of God. He has said so. He commands us to remove weeds from His garden. Is this killing? No, it is the command of God.'

A strong, low rumble of approval ran through the packed hall, that smelled of sweat and orange juice, petrol, leather and gun oil. Bright eyes glittered from behind beards as thick as furze bushes, lipsticked lips tightened in agreement and flattened with belief.

'You are here, I am here, simply as the instruments of the will of God. He has created us for a purpose. To deny His will is to deny Him.'

He stood under the hot lights, and spread out his arms.

'What is it?' he cried. 'What is it that God has created us for? No slight thing, surely. No, we are here for nothing less than the final redemption of the Jewish people. *We are here to prepare the way for the coming of the Messiah!*'

They roared savagely, they could feel God in the very air about them, He was close, He was coming.

'He won't come if His garden is not perfect,' Weiss whispered chillingly, his eyes as cold as ice chips above his beard. 'If it is not perfect, He will make us suffer some more, for being so stupid as to disobey Him. The garden He wants us to make for Him is in the Biblical lands of Israel, for we are His people, and this is His land. He only wants Jews here. Everyone else is a weed, a blemish on His creation. He wants us, His chosen people. He wants us to make His garden perfect. We need answer to no one but Him.'

He paused, and they could see his chest rising and falling. They felt, like him, the heady mixture of blood and sex and the Almighty, and it rushed about their veins like a fiery liquor.

'There are some who see the uprooting of weeds as wrong.'

His voice broke the silence he had made, and they snarled. He held up his hand.

'No. It is true. There are those who would deny the will of the Lord our God. Have you not heard the words of Jacob Ben-Levi? He has called me a murderer. Yes, yes he has. He was in a clump of weeds called Deir Yassin, a long time ago, when God first called us back to His land. He says he saw me kill some Arabs there.'

He looked over them, his eyes very bright, and he nodded furiously, his hair flying.

'I shot them with my gun. But I ask you again, was this killing? No. For two thousand years Jews have woken up with the question in their minds: Who is going to attack me today? I was the first of the new Jews. We wake up each morning and ask: Which unbeliever am *I* going to attack today? What I did was pure, it was clean, it shone like a fine swordblade in sunshine. I was God's instrument. *What I did was God's will!*'

He put up his hands to brush back his thin hair.

'Jacob Ben-Levi's voice is as of a raven, croaking amongst the weeds, where he feels at home. For Jacob Ben-Levi is not a Jew. He does not believe in our God, the God of David and Moses. *We* throw weeds onto the bonfire. When his day comes, Jacob Ben-Levi will burn in that greatest of bonfires, the Lord's bonfire in Hell, made especially for all of those who do not believe in our Messiah. We are making the lands of God beautiful. Here where we live, we are making His garden amidst the thickest of weeds. All around us, rank, stinking, ugly, filthy weeds.'

Weiss looked over his flock and shook his head admonishingly at them.

'God won't come,' he said reprovingly. 'Not to a garden of weeds.'

He began to walk off the stage.

'I'm going to the temple to pray,' he said, looking over his shoulder. 'I want to hear the voice of God.'

He waited in the room outside like a showman, wanting to be sure of his timing. As he emerged onto the dark street, with his badge, his M16 rifle slung over his shoulder, the first heavy 4 X 4 pickups were moving, their batteries of lights carving open the night, the big off-road tyres whipping the dry dust into the air. The gates of the compound were open, he watched the lights rushing away through the heavy guard wire, and he walked to the temple, made, like everything else, from whitened slabs of concrete.

It was cool in there. A single candle burned by the altar. A young girl knelt praying, dressed all in white. Weiss closed the door behind him, and went quietly up to the altar.

'Have you come to find God?' he asked softly. She looked up at him. She was young and beautiful, untouched.

'Yes, I have.'

'Do you know who I am?'

'You are God's emissary, who speaks for Him here on earth.'

'That's good.'

He smiled down at her.

'We're going to blow out this candle. It will be dark. And then soon we will see the light of God, coming clean and pure through this window. Do you believe me?'

'Yes, I do,' she whispered certainly, excitedly. He bent, and blew out the candle. In the darkness he could smell the sudden smoke, the hot wax, the scent of the young girl, the gun oil on his rifle. In the dark he could see the other young girl, the Arab, on her knees, begging in the little room, feel the cold metal of the Sten gun, smell its oil. Suddenly, urgently, he fumbled with his trousers, and the M-16 clinked on its strap.

'Open your mouth, child, and feel the strength of the Lord.'

He felt her warm and slippery all about him. He stared at the window. Its darkness was suddenly brushed with a faint light.

'The Lord is with us,' he whispered.

He heard her moan frantically with passion, the crisp white dress rustling in the darkness.

As they torched the village on the hill the window burst into violent yellow and orange.

'See,' he howled triumphantly. 'See the hand of God.'

# PART XVIII

## Damascus

LIFE for the American ambassador had become easier. He had been most gratified that President Kane, upon his election, had reappointed him to his post. But he was, as Kane had been advised, a man with deep experience of the region.

Ambassador Warner was a man who believed that the early bird did indeed get to have first rights at the worm, and liked to be at his desk, working, by six in the morning. The habits of the old president had interfered with this admirable aim. The remoteness that had led his subjects to see him only upon television had not extended to the ambassador. Come ten in the evening, once and sometimes twice a week, the phone would ring with a polite summons to the presidential offices. As the ambassador's most important task was to achieve the most difficult of feats, the divination of the intentions of a solitary and all-powerful man, he would hurry round in the long black Cadillac. There Asad, who had suffered from insomnia, would inflict his disability upon the ambassador, who didn't, by subjecting him to a polite, learned but definite harangue on the state of the world and of the Middle East in particular. Permission to leave was granted by the arrival of a cup of thick, jet black coffee, which had to be drunk. The ambassador ran on decaffeinated and the impact of the real thing upon his nervous system was such as to deny him sleep totally until the next evening.

Despite his blood-stained entrance to the highest post, the ambassador approved of Hamouda. He kept office hours.

For what he had to say, however, Ambassador Warner would have gone out at midnight in a hailstorm and drunk a jug of the old president's best brew.

Hamouda had celebrated his first year in power by holding an election, and Warner formally congratulated him.

'I heard that ninety nine point eight per cent of the people voted for you, Mr President. You can't ask for more than that.'

Hamouda smiled pleasantly. 'I have. The names of those who did not.'

Warner worked at keeping the smile on his own face. He recalled that Hamouda embodied the Lebanese proverb, he had killed his predecessor, and then walked in his funeral.

'However, let us move from internal politics. It is time to put an end to this thing, al-Nakba, this disaster that has wasted so much treasure, spilled so much blood,' said Hamouda. 'The Jews must have their security, and somehow, the Palestinians, who are the Arabs' own Jews, must have al-Awada, the return. We must all, Arab and Jew, have peace. Someone has to begin it. I do not believe that the Israelis will unilaterally do so, so we the Syrian people have begun it. Our armed forces are being cut in a programme that will result in them being slightly over one quarter of a million strong.'

'The troops you have then will be highly trained, technically competent and able to use their weapons to maximum effect, and psychologically highly motivated,' Warner ventured. 'You'll be able to keep your best and get their best out of them.'

'*Exactly!*' Hamouda beamed. 'And what weaponry will they be using? What we have are large quantities of heli-, vehicular-and infantry-borne ATGWs, anti-tank guided weapons, and large quantities of surface-to-air missiles, from little ones fired from a soldier's shoulder to SAMs in a battery able to knock down an aircraft one hundred and fifty miles away. We intend to acquire and make more of the very latest type. But, please note what kind of weapons these are. They, and our entire military posture, are defensive. You cannot invade a country waving an anti-tank missile! We do not intend to invade Israel but, equally, we do intend to make it impossible for them to invade us.'

'You still retain your modern tank force.'

'We have taken the turrets from over three hundred of our T-55s. You yourself went to see them. Is this not a gesture of goodwill?'

'You still have your T-72s. What will you do with the T-55 chassis?'

'We are putting a variety of anti-aircraft turrets through trials. There is an interesting British one, known as Marksman, that fits the T-55.'

'The Israelis wil argue that your considerable investment in high technology – I realize that many of the systems themselves you prefer to keep secret – represents a great threat to them.'

'We have indeed invested deeply in the very latest technology. The Israelis themselves are not backward in this area, I will remind you. And there is something most interesting about the weaponry now being produced by the emerging technology. *It favours defence.* Ask the Israelis. It favours defence, not attack. So their fears may be allayed. And we may begin the peace process.'

'I shall convey what you say to President Kane,' Warner assured him. 'I know that he will be delighted with these moves to bring peace to the Middle East, and will want to do all he can to bring this process to fruition.'

'I am most pleased to hear you say that,' Hamouda said suavely. 'For I do require the president's assistance.'

'What is it that you want?'

'Mr Warner, like any competent chief executive I have made a close study of those who pose the greatest threat to my country. These are of course the Israelis. I very much fear that their government is sufficiently dominated by those whose response to our historic initiative will be to accept our force reductions and still stand where they are, upon the status quo. Men such as Defence Minister Shahak will not respond in kind, but will instead take advantage. I would remind you that General Shahak was in their Unit 101. He and his kind blew up villages, using those tactics pioneered in 1948 to drive the Palestinian Arabs from the land the Jews now call Israel. They would mount an attack on a village, and after the survivors had fled would set it afire, then march to the next village, to inform its terrified inhabitants of the fate that awaited them if they chose to stay. Was it not most effective? Did not their first President, Weizmann, say that it was, "a miraculous simplification of our task"?'

Come to the Middle East, get a history lesson, thought Warner to himself. All, Jew and Arab alike, constantly invoked outrages that had to be avenged, crimes which when investigated proved to have been committed by Joshua upon the forms of the five kings of Canaan, or by Saladin at Hattin.

Warner looked up at the wall, and noticed that the glorious ancient scroll commemorating the Syrian king's smashing victory over the infidel invaders had been taken down. Perhaps the guy's sincere, he thought.

'What is it that you would have me ask President Kane to do?' he said.

'I fear that General Shahak and his allies will derail my plan for a permanent peace with a plan of their own that will – as always with the Israelis – buy them a short-term solution at the cost of

eternal war. I believe that what General Shahak and his ilk intend is a
programme of terror designed to drive the Arabs from the Occupied
Territories. Once more to clear the land they call Israel of Arabs.
They even have a destination for them, Jordan. Let Jordan be the
new Palestine, they say. It will not be as neat and tidy as that. That
way, the war goes on forever. What I offer is a chance for peace.'

Hamouda paused, gathering his thoughts into line.

'What I need is an Israeli that we can deal with. A man of reason.
Not a bigot. Someone skilled at the presentation of a case. Not a
Weiss or a Shahak. They would not even sit down at the same table
with an Arab.'

'Who do you want?'

'Jacob Ben-Levi. He was their special minister, their envoy for
years. He is an immensely skilled diplomat. If he were Foreign
Minister, the process would at the very least be considered, would
get under way, not be killed off at birth. Prime Minister Levinger
knows him from a very long time back, and I believe that President
Kane does as well. In fact, I believe that President Kane owes him
a rather large favour. It could be presented as a suitable position for
a distinguished Israeli diplomat to occupy at the end of his career.'

You're well-informed, I give you that, thought Warner.

'I shall be communicating our conversation to the president
as soon as I return to the embassy, sir. I obviously cannot
guarantee that the president can interfere in the sovereign affairs
of another nation.'

A dry smile cracked Hamouda's face.

'You surprise me,' he said. 'My reading of history is that the
United States and its leaders have spent most of this century doing
little else.'


## Israel


The gritty path widened where the olive grove was divided, and
Jacob turned the Cadillac, parking it there. The road to Hebron lay
back through the trees, but there it was quiet.

'We are here,' Rifka said quietly, and Jacob looked about him
in puzzlement. The little valley of the wadi was pleasing to the
eye. Springs and storage pools for the sweet water glittered in the
sunshine, kitchen gardens and grapevines and olive groves formed

a patchwork of every shade of green. The smell of thyme was on the air.

A man was coming along the path, a checked *keffiyeh* with its black *igal* on his head, a dusted mattock in his hand.

'This is where my family live,' said Rifka. She had turned on the wide seat to look at him. Her eyes were very large under her dark hair. Her face seemed paler than usual.

'But this is an Arab farm,' said Jacob. 'Palestinian.'

'That's right,' she said, quietly and clearly. 'I have deceived you, darling. I am not an Israeli. I am not a Jew. I am a Palestinian.'

Jacob sat looking out over the little valley.

'Why?' he said finally.

'Because I love you. Because I admire you. Because I believe you will bring peace. That you are the only man in Israel who can bring peace.'

He was still silent.

'I will get out,' she said. 'I am sorry for what I have done, for deceiving you. You may leave me here.'

She was reaching for the door handle when he suddenly seized her hand.

'No,' he said. 'I cannot think of life without you. Not now.' Now she had become everything that Ruth once was to him but could never be again. And he could not bear to lose her too.

He looked at the man, standing patiently under the tree.

'So long ago,' he said, 'when Vespasian drove us out. And some remained. Now those who went call themselves Israelis, and those who stayed call themselves Palestinians. But what are we but brothers and sisters long separated. It is time we greeted each other with smiles, and not with rocks.'

He got out of the car, and went slowly forward.

'*Allah yikhalik*,' he said, and the man bowed in greeting. 'May God be with you.'

The man was in his forties, with a face seamed and tanned from a lifetime in the sun.

'This is my uncle,' said Rifka, behind him.

'I am Fayez Khader. I am going to my house, to drink a glass of tea. Perhaps you would like to drink tea.'

'Very much,' said Jacob.

As they went down the path they passed a small, carefully tended graveyard. Five graves were there, all decorated with flowers, three very fresh. Rifka paused, indicating the two older ones.

'My brothers,' she said sadly. 'Both shot by the army.'

She indicated the three new ones, and then pointed to Fayez Kader, her uncle.

'His son, his daughter, his wife.'

Jacob stood by the pathetic row.

'Were they shot too?'

'Fire killed them,' said Kader, and they went up to the house.

They sat in a shady courtyard open at two sides, looking out over the little valley, the house at their backs. There seemed to be a lot of people in the building, for its size. Just outside the yard a kitchen garden began, aubergine, lettuce, courgette, tomato and mandrake were growing. Behind them a woman was scooping the insides from some fat green courgettes, meat and onion and rice for its stuffing at her elbow. On the wall by the window hung sheared sheep wool airing before it was spun. By the corner of the house, in the spring sunshine, an older man was dozing, his greying moustache blowing in the breeze of his snore. He had no legs.

'My father,' Rifka said.

A young woman brought tea in tall glasses, and sat a little distance away, watching Jacob warily.

'You have guests staying with you?' said Jacob. The tea was hot, and scented.

'This is not my house,' said Fayez. 'I have lost my home, as have my relatives here, so we have come to live with my brother Khalid.'

'What happened to your houses?'

'They were burned. Our whole village was burned, by the *mustawtanin*, the settlers of the Rabbi.'

'The Rabbi?'

'Weiss,' Rifka said quietly, squatting next to him. 'Rabbi Weiss has Numbers 33 settlements near here.'

She glanced up at the hill.

'There is one just up there.'

'They came in the night, with fire. There were many who died.'

'You were not able to protect yourselves?'

'The army makes searches of everything. To own more than a mattock is an offence. To own a gun is to be taken away, and not seen again. The settlers of Rabbi Weiss had both fire *and* guns.'

'What of your village now?'

'The land is confiscated. *Mustawtanin* build *their* houses there now.'

'You could not get justice?'

The Arab looked at him as though he were simple.

'From whom?' he asked derisively. 'Many are those who support the rabbi in what he is doing. Have they not voted for him in their thousands, does he not sit for him in the government of Israel? They *want* him to kill us, to drive us out.'

'They are building above on the mountain,' said an older woman. The little courtyard was slowly and quietly filling up with people, come to see the strange Jew who would sit with them. 'They stole the spring from us, and said they were sharing it.'

'Dogs came in the night,' said a little girl.

'They blocked the road so that we could not go in the bus to school,' said a boy. 'We had to walk.'

A young man came up from the kitchen garden, where he had been working.

'My son, Hazem,' Fayez said. The boy had a face Jacob recognized. Hazem was *shebab*, one of the guys. One of the ones who threw rocks and got bullets in return. He had obviously been listening from the garden.

'*Falastin bladna wa-al-yahud clabna*. Palestine is our country and the Jews our dogs.'

'Not so loud,' his father said. His eyes flicked nervously up the mountain. There like a scar spread the new buildings of the settlement. 'The *mustawtanin* will hear you, and then it will be our house that vanishes under the bulldozer.'

'We have a saying, Mr Minister,' the young man said intently. 'We say, a man without land must shit in his hand. I do not intend to shit in my hand, not once.'

Rifka's father, Khalid, had awoken from his nap. Rifka went over to him, and Jacob followed.

'This is Jacob, the one I have told you about, father.'

Clear, intelligent eyes looked at Jacob.

'My own father could remember when the Turks ruled here,' he said. 'And after them, the British. When the British were gone, the Jordanians. Then the Jews. And one day soon, the Jews too will be gone, and we shall inherit once again the land that is rightfully ours.'

'You may be right,' said Jacob. He reached for his finger, and turned the ring on it, the golden ring of peace, round and round.

'I am right. Let me tell you how it will happen.'

The people, young and old, in the courtyard drew slightly closer to hear the words of comfort. In the kitchen the woman paused with rice ready to mix, outside the window her daughter stopped the teasing out of the wool, holding it in her lap.

'See the flowers,' said Khalid. Thistles and yellow wild flowers were blooming all over the valley. 'Soon there will be a wind. Hot. From the east, it will blow from the gate of Hell, *rih asfar*, hot and fearsome, come to seek out the wicked.' He nodded his head at the settlement, sitting like a carbuncle on the side of the hill. 'They, *walad-el-mita*. The Children of Death. They will hide from it in caves and tunnels, but even there it will find them. All those who have been unjust, have done cruel things, these it will find, and burn them to a cinder. The land outside will become yellow from the heat of the wind. And then the gate of Paradise will open, and from the west will come its cool, sweet wind. There will be showers that will clean the land, and the yellow flowers will bloom as we come forth from our hiding places, untouched and unharmed, to take the land that is our own.'

They sighed with pleasure, all of them, and as one, their eyes looked up at the scar of the settlement on the mountain. The blue sky above was scratched with the white trails of the fighters that were always in the air.

'Soon,' whispered the little boy sitting by Jacob's foot. 'Soon the wind will come.'

'I think this is it,' Jacob said slowly. They were sitting in the Cadillac, with the beautiful little valley once more spread out before them.

'One last chance to get it right,' he said. 'I don't know how I will do it, but I will.'

'You do not hate me then?' Rifka said, almost timidly, and he reached out and took her hand.

'I love you more than ever.'

'You do not want to send me away?'

'I would rather cut off my right hand.'

She paused, seeming suddenly afraid.

'What is it?'

'I am having your baby,' she whispered.

They wept, they were still clinging to each other when the car telephone of the Cadillac rang. Jacob took out a big white handkerchief, and wiped his face and blew his nose before answering.

'Hullo?'

'Jacob. I've been looking for you everywhere.'

'It's Zvi Levinger,' Jacob whispered to Rifka.

'What can I do for you, Mr Prime Minister?'

'Jacob . . .'

'I'm here.'

'Jacob, we got Franz.'

'Franz?'

Jacob sat in the car, hearing the words from a great distance.

'Karl Franz. The Butcher's Boy,' said Levinger. 'Mossad kidnapped him last night. We got him. He's right here in Tel Aviv.'


## Tel Aviv


'How did we get him?' asked Jacob. 'After all this time . . .'

'The last we saw of him was a blurred photograph in Cairo, back when Nasser hired all those Nazis . . . a trail goes pretty cold after all that time,' said Levinger.

It was quiet in this building which had been built specially to hold just such as the man they had in the room next door. It had lain empty for a long time. Old age was culling those who had murdered the Jews decades before. But now they had another.

'He was in Syria,' Levinger continued. 'He had a small villa outside Damascus, he was retired. He'd worked in their prison service.'

'Yes, he'd know about that.'

'The operation went really well. Without a hitch. We put a commando team in as tourists – inserted them from Hamburg. They snatched Franz in the night and we made an airborne pick-up out in the desert. Now there's just Hertz wanting to know where their Toyota Land Cruiser is!'

'But how did you find him in the first place?'

'Well, look. We're going to play the whole thing as a modern example of flawless intelligence and derring-do on our behalf, like we used to – you remember, when we stole the Egyptian radar with the helicopter, captured Eichmann, all the rest of it. We need a polish to our image. We'll put him on trial. The works. Live television, we'll have the old footage of the KZ-Auschwitz, Dachau, Ravensbrück, the lot. We *need* it, Jacob, we need it really badly. We need to remind the world why Israel needs to exist. Then we'll hang the bastard, so the world will not forget why Israel needs to exist.'

Levinger was uplifted. Jacob remembered him another way. On the day he'd asked for Ibach's trial and been refused. Politics, opportunism. Nothing to do with justice.

'It couldn't have come at a better time. Our image hasn't been so good of late. It'll be just like the old days. But you asked how we found him. Just between you and me, the information simply fell into our lap. Franz obviously made some enemy or other who knew who he was and decided to fix him. We got photos, past history, address, all in one envelope. We checked him out before we snatched him.'

Levinger reached out and put a black vinyl photograph album onto the table.

'When our guys found this we knew we had the right man. It was in a drawer of his desk in the villa.'

Levinger opened it. The first page bore no photographs, only an inscription in silver ink, flanked by hand-drawn SS lightning runes: *The Best Years of my Life*.

Jacob found his mouth completely dry, and his heart thumping in his chest. Levinger glanced at him.

'All right, Jacob?'

'Yes . . . I suppose so.'

They were all there, those from his past. The ones without expression, their faces like skulls. The ones grinning. The uniforms. The filthy ones with stripes. The elegant black ones. Watchtowers and wire. Chimneys. Huts. Dying and dead.

'There he is,' said Levinger, and tapped a yellowing rectangle.

'Yes,' Jacob whispered. 'There he is.'

Glancing at him, Levinger flipped the book shut.

'It's the only one of him, funnily enough. But there he is. You wouldn't recognize him now. Bald, piled on the beef, old. But then, I have a photograph of myself at home, and you wouldn't recognize me either. I was quite good-looking as a young man.'

Jacob had taken out his handkerchief, and was wiping the palms of his hands.

'Want to see him?' Levinger asked abruptly.

'If I must.'

'He's right here,' Levinger said quietly. 'Next door.'

The room was plainly furnished. The man in ordinary blue trousers had no belt to hold them up, his white shirt had no tie. The cup of water on the table was polystyrene. The Jewish people did not want to lose their captive before it was his time. He glanced up as Jacob came in.

'Another Jew,' he said brutally. 'I am clearly in Hell.'

'Do you know me?'

'Should I?'

'I was in *kazett Dora*,' Jacob said quietly. 'I worked in the assembly gallery, making the rockets. You were there, too, you hanged us from the crane.'

The man looked up at Jacob from around the folds of fat about his eyes.

'I did not,' he said indifferently. 'I did not work in the camps.'

'You are Karl Franz, and you were in the SS,' Jacob insisted.

'I do not like Jews,' said the man. 'I liked working in Syria, for they too hate Jews. But I did not work in this rocket factory.'

'We have your photograph album.'

'I have no photograph album.'

He sneered at Jacob, for Jacob had begun to tremble all over. His knees were trembling, his hands, his whole body, like a weak sapling in the wind.

'You killed my brother,' Jacob said, his voice quavering.

The German ignored what he was saying, simply eyed him contemptuously.

'I had a friend who worked in the camps,' the man said suddenly. 'He used to talk about it. He told me things.'

His voice suddenly barked.

*'Remove your cap in the presence of a German!'*

Jacob's hand snatched at his head, grasping for something that was not there, and the man laughed.

'Yes,' he jeered. 'You were in the *kazett* all right.'

The smile slowly slid from his face.

'But I was not.'

He was very hot. It was very hot in the little room. They sat at their tables, he and his companions, in silence. There was only the faint sound of the slim-bladed knives slicing away the skin of the limbs, torsos and skulls on the tables in front of them. The room smelled of meat. It was hot.

He trimmed away the skin in flat sheets. There was no fat underneath the skin, it clung to the wasted muscle beneath and his flat knife sliced it away.

Someone came and carried his sheets of skin off into the next room. Through the open door came the acrid smell of tanning.

He looked up and the Butcher's Boy was standing in front of him, grinning. The silver lightning runes gleamed at his throat, the death's head shone on his black hat, and he grinned.

'I have a very fine skull for you,' he said. 'It's quite perfect.'

He was holding something in his hand, by the hair. He lifted it up and placed it on the dissecting table. It was Rifka's head.

*       *       *

Jacob woke screaming, and Rifka cradled him to her in the Jerusalem night. The fan was on to keep him cool, but sweat was running from him in rivulets.

'It is only a dream, darling,' she said softly, as though to a child. 'Just a nasty dream. Here I am, here I am.'

They had brought him home in the car, white and silent. The doctor was with him, he had put him to bed, made him swallow the tablets he had brought. Now as Jacob gasped for breath she shook two more into her hand, and sat him up like a child.

'Just a dream,' she repeated. 'Here I am, darling. I am here with you, we are in Jerusalem.'

He took the tablets docilely, washing them down with the water she held for him in the cup, and the heaving of his chest calmed. As the sedatives washed over him he looked up at her.

'It isn't him,' Jacob said clearly. 'I shall have to tell them. It isn't him.'

The bed next to her was empty, in the early sunlight coming through the window. She awoke with a start, but then she heard the sound of the shower, and in a few moments Jacob appeared in his dressing gown, drying his hair with a towel.

'Good morning, darling,' he said brightly. He picked up a brush and ran it over his hair.

'Are you all right, Jacob, darling?'

'Yes,' he said. 'I am well. I am going in to the Knesset. Tonight I shall come home. Would you like to go out to the Italian restaurant?'

'Yes,' she said slowly. 'That would be nice. Are you sure you are well enough to go to the Knesset?'

He was selecting a shirt, a tie to wear.

'Oh, yes.' he said. 'I am well. I shall keep myself well. I am a boat. It is a nicely-painted boat, with shiny brasswork and white sails. Its structure under the nice paint is riddled with rot and woodworm. But it still floats, and sails. The trick in sailing my boat is to keep it away from bad weather. The past is bad weather. I am sailing it into the good weather of the future. If I can find the good weather I can tie up safe in harbour.'

He reached out with both hands and gently cradled her round stomach. His golden ring shone. Inside, the baby kicked, and he smiled.

'*That* is the future. That is what needs to happen. Israelis marrying Palestinians. Then there will be an end to it.'

She watched from the window as he got into his Cadillac and drove away in the bright morning, a strange expression on her face, one of calculation and knowledge.

# PART XIX

## Damascus, Syria

'ALL of us revere Yasser Arafat, who calls himself Abu Ammar,' said the man in the white *gandura* robe, sitting opposite Hamouda.

'Like Ammar bin-Yasser of old, the companion of Mohammed, he has fought for the cause, long after ordinary men would have given up. Let me say, without him there might not have been a Palestinian nation in exile. But what do they call him? The *gala gala* man. You know? The conjurer, when he makes coloured cloths appear from thin air, he says *gala gala*. And all we have is a nation in exile, camping out on this pitiful patch of land, a Jewish-made prison. Arafat is an illusionist.'

A servant, summoned by a hidden bell from Hamouda's desk, entered silently, and placed cups of strong, sweet coffee in front of both men from a silver salver, then left, as quietly as he had come. The aroma of the beans floated in the air.

'We know what haunts Arafat,' said the Imam Hussein. He wore no *keffiyeh*, symbolizing his distance from the old order, the paunchy old *jalabah*-clad PLO men in their Tunisian villas, smelling of cigarettes and coffee. He wore the robes of an Imam, a religious leader.

'Arafat feared the fate of Haj Amin al-Husseini, once Grand Mufti of Jerusalem and leader in exile of the Palestinian people after we were driven out. He died, after his years of struggle, with what?'

Black, intent, patient eyes looked at Hamouda.

'With *nothing*. Which is the fate Arafat feared. And so his persistence finally came to an end, and like the man in the Jews' Bible, he was willing to sell the birthright of our people for a mess of pottage.'

'Gaza and the West Bank towns are hardly nothing. For the first time since 1948, the people of Palestine have a homeland.'

'What homeland? Not *the* homeland. My family comes from Haifa, Mr President. I wish to go home. We Palestinians accept a slice off the Jewish roast, then it is over. Do you see that? If we accept that, then we have accepted the right of Israel to exist – *on our land*. What is this right of Israel to make a state on our land because they once – two thousand years ago! – had a state on part of Palestine and part of what is now Jordan. They only had it for eighty years! Then they split, and forty years after that they were finished. And yet they call this their historical right to return! The Romans were in Palestine eight hundred years, you might more easily say the Italians have a right to it. Or the Arabs to Spain, because they were there eight hundred years. Or the British to half the globe because they ran it for a hundred years.'

The Imam leaned forward so that his arm was on Hamouda's desk.

'The Jews belong back where they came from, in the diaspora, and that is where they will go, when we take the land that is ours. From the Jordan to the sea, and live in our own state, a state founded upon the teachings of God. For no one else is competing with us for it – not the Romans, not the Ottoman Turks, not the British. Only the Jews.'

'I am, as you know, a Christian, but we Christians and you Muslims have had no quarrel with each other, not since the days of the great Salah el-Din and the Frankish king, Richard. We are both Arabs. Our enemy is the same, the Jew. I command the resources of a great nation, you the minds of men within Palestine.'

Iman Hussein nodded in assent.

'The day will come when we shall rid ourselves of these invaders. Israel exists because of foreign, that is American support. One day the Americans will not need the services of the Israeli army, and the state of Israel will dry up like a big palm tree planted in a small jug. Then will be our time.'

'I have been told that your infrastructure within the people of Palestine is extensive.'

'Abu Ammar, Chairman Arafat, has sold out to the Jews. Now men turn to God, who will never sell them short. Among the people of Palestine, I represent God, I carry out his commands. The people come to worship, and through me, and through my servants, they hear the word of God.'

Hamouda smiled in sincere admiration and approval.

'Will they do what God asks of them?'

'*Allahu akbar!* God is great! They wish only to be instruments of his will.'

'Unto death?'

'They know that I have commanded – as I am but the mouthpiece of God – a *jihad* against the Jewish oppressors. Those who die in a holy war shall go straight to the arms of God in paradise. I assure you, they thirst for death.'

'Is your organization capable of ensuring they rise as one?'

'They await the sign from God.'

'Will they wait for it?'

'They will wait, whether it be them, their sons or their sons' sons who rise to slaughter the Jews. They will wait for a hundred years.'

'I assure you,' Hamouda said, and the Imam Hussein knew he spoke the truth, 'they shall not have to wait that long.'


# Haifa


Prime Minister Levinger had a house in Haifa, where he tried to go at the weekend, and where he planned to retire to. He liked it for the wonderful view he had, placed on one of the wide terraces cut into the steepness of Mount Carmel. His villa looked out over the curve of the bay leading northwards to Akko, which the Crusaders had called Acre, a slim line of white and grey against the deep blue of the Mediterranean.

He liked it also for its cosmopolitan *élan*. Of all the Israeli cities Haifa was probably the most relaxed and mixed in culture. The Galilee, its hinterland, contained over half of the country's Arab population, and they and the Haifa Jews lived together in a state of reasonable harmony. He had an addiction to the fragrant, oily, herb-scattered pizzas from the Arab bakeries.

When working late at the weekend when he could sneak away from Jerusalem and Tel Aviv he would often send his driver down to the port area for a bagful, and munch them while he got through the multitude of papers that was his necessary reading. His *batash* security men surmised that that must have been how the intruder gained access to the villa, by hiding in the boot of the car while the driver was buying the pizza and being taken in.

They knew that someone unauthorized was there when the

electronic alarm that protected the perimeter of the grounds gave warning. It was only when no one was found within that they realized that it had been activated by someone getting *out*.

Levinger was up out of bed, and when he checked his study he found a filing cabinet broken into, and the old Samsonite briefcase that was his political trademark stolen.

The man from Shabak, that had been Shin-Bet, was there by that time.

'Is there anything important missing?'

'I don't bring any secret papers here, and what I bring I put into the safe. The filing cabinet has routine material. The briefcase is valuable only to me.'

'Any ideas who would want to get at your papers?'

'Our enemies, obviously. Or, maybe, it's Haifagate. There are a lot of different groups in the Knesset, you know.'

A *batash* man came through the French windows, holding up the case in triumph.

'It was by the wall, sir. He'd opened it.'

'There was nothing in it. When he saw that there was no need to take it.'

Levinger took the case, and blew some dust off it.

'This case once held secrets meant to destroy our country,' he said. 'Now it holds secrets to protect it.'

'I know that, sir,' said the man. 'I saw your election broadcasts.'


# The White House


Elie moved a steam stripper so that he could sit on the window ledge. The little room was empty of its furnishings, dust sheets were on the floor and the red, brown and beige fabric on the walls was all that remained of the decoration.

'Mrs Clinton had the Lincoln rooms done out,' he observed. 'When Mrs Kane heard about it she ordered them done again her way. I guess Governor Lovestone's wife will be choosing her type of wallpaper in four years' time.'

'What do you mean? Kane won. He can do it again.'

Elie looked morose.

'Look, we have endemic political problems that seem to be creating one-term presidents. But in addition, Kane has a *specific* problem that looks like it could hand the next election to Lovestone, who'll be the candidate, if you ask me. He's running already.'

'So what *is* the problem?'

'You listen to black music, Jacob?'

'No.'

'No, it's not my thing either. Something funny's been happening over here, the blacks are thinking of themselves as a separate people – a nation, if you like. Being American hasn't done them much good, they're thinking of themselves as a people. If you're a people, you have to have a past, a history. Okay, they have the *Roots* thing, and now they've taken it back further than that, to the beginnings of human society as we know it. The first people recognizably the same as us were to be found living in the Nile valley. And the oldest continuously inhabited city is to be found not far away in the form of Jericho. Well, that's pretty good, when you're a poor black guy who's out of work. He can say, white honky motherfuckers, you're decended from me, I'm better than you are, don't give me this white supremacy shit.

'The black consciousness thing has taken off. It's reflected in the music. They talk about themselves as a nation in exile. And I don't know if it's chicken or egg, but someone smart has latched onto the fact that there's another nation in exile out there, a dispossessed people, and that's the Palestinians. Isn't Jericho in Palestine? So aren't the Palestinians and black peoples the same?'

Elie held up his hand with fore and middle fingers squeezed closely together.

'The result has been that the blacks have adopted the Palestinian cause for their own. The Palestinians, they say, are their brothers. Okay, where did this lead, back last campaign? We had to choose a running mate, and the pollsters came up with a very exciting hot button that indicated that if Kane selected a suitable black running mate he would be able to mobilize an exclusive black vote which, allied to his natural support, would deliver a fifty-three to forty-seven victory. Okay, so it was just a question of choosing the right man, and there really was only one, the Reverend Jonas Jones. Colourful, a great orator with his own community, but not so inflammatory as to upset the white folk. We held preliminary talks and he was ready. There was only one thing, his price was a commitment from Kane that after the election the establishment of a Palestinian state on the West Bank would be the top priority of the new administration. The reverend has a fairly king-sized ego, and the idea of going down in history as the saviour of the Palestinians appealed to him. Kane reckoned that the military security options could be worked out, and it looked like we were on. Until we received videos of the Reverend Jones screwing a thirteen-year-old girl.

'There was no way he could deny he'd done it, and to give him credit he didn't. The thing was his public and private images differed somewhat. In private, he liked to drink liquor and screw young women. But several at a time. The old guy was something of a stallion. He says he had no idea who the girl was, nor that she was under age. Fortunately for us we kept it under wraps, and it didn't come out – *provided we didn't go ahead with our choice*.

'Now, while it is clear that the reverend's career as vice-president was over before it had begun, to anyone with any political nose whatsoever, accompanying these videos comes a most appalling stink. The man had clearly been set up. By whom? Well, who had most to lose from all this? You did.'

'But would we do anything that crude?'

'Sure you would. *You did it before*. Andy Young was our ambassador to the United Nations and close friend of then President Carter. Mossad got word that he was going to start talking to the PLO about a possible settlement of the Palestinian issue and they fixed him. When Young resigned it was entirely because of the position he had been manoeuvred into by Mossad.'

Elie tapped a video cassette he had on the window ledge beside him.

'It's all in here. We had a guy on our staff here, Ben Bloom. Close to Kane. He didn't turn up for work and they found him hanging from a hook in his bathroom. The feeling is that he was what you call a *sayan*, a friend of Israel. They found evidence that he was the one who tipped off Mossad that we were negotiating with the Reverend Jones. It's all coming out, Jacob. Mossad's been running agents – *katsas*, they call them – within America for years. Pollard, buggings, dirty tricks, and murder. Kidnapping some old German and accusing him of being a war criminal. And then having to let him go. And I'll tell you something else. American Jews are beginning not to identify with Israeli Jews.'

'Different people,' Jacob said quietly. 'We Israelis are not good at accepting criticism. Either people are for us, or against us. Anything negative said about us is immediately classified as anti-Semitic, and therefore untrue.'

'Even when it is true?'

'The Jews have come back to the Middle East, and now we are Middle Eastern. The Middle East is a wilderness of wolves. To

survive you must at all times not only be strong but be seen to
be strong. You bare your teeth at anyone who might threaten you.
You must have what the Lebanese call the "eye". There's much
that's unlikeable. It's like living in New York, only more stressful
and uptight. But we live out on the edge. We live out in this
wilderness of wolves. You won't get anyone saying we did wrong
to fix the Reverend Jones. There's only one question to ask. Was
he for us or against us? Against. Fine, fix the bastard. You're talking
about morals, Elie. Nobody talks about morals in Israel, they're too
busy surviving.'

'To survive you need friends. You're losing yours. And you're
wrong. People do talk about morals.'

'Who?'

'You do.'

'Yes, that's true . . .,' Jacob said quietly. 'Not that it has got me
or my morals very far.'

'Ah,' Elie said, with a hint of triumph. 'Now you just might be
wrong there. Let me tell you our position. As you know, we had to
take Ellison as Veep, with the Reverend destroyed. Fortunately the
opposition didn't pick up on our black hot button, or if they did
they were not themselves in a political position to do so. I have
information that Governor Lovestone is not so slow, and is actively
garnering the black vote. If we are to win next time around, then
we must win on this Palestinian issue. It could be that close.'

'And I can help?'

'I think so . . .'

Elie looked at him curiously.

'You have an unusual admirer, Jacob.'

'Who?'

'President Hamouda. We have received a message from him, that
indicates he is willing to restart the Middle Eastern peace process.
On a condition. That in Israel he deals with a man he can trust.'

'And?'

'That man is you.'

'Me . . .'

'He wants you appointed foreign secretary. But will you take
the job?'

Jacob was quiet for a long time, twisting his talisman, his golden
ring, round and round on his finger. Then finally, he spoke.

'Yes. I will.'

# Tel Aviv

General Shahak's study was decorated with a mix of military mementoes and shards of history. His burly figure stood up behind his desk as Jacob came in, and he waved him to a chair.

'Jacob. I know it's the sabbath, but I use it to catch up on things. Levinger has put you in charge of foreign affairs. I think he's gone senile. But since you are now, and since Hamouda is making peace noises, I want you to hear a briefing on the state of Syrian military preparedness.'

'You want me to believe there can never be peace,' Jacob said obstinately.

'Well, let's hear it anyway,' Shahak grunted. 'I think you know our briefer.' From the corner, a middle-aged man Jacob hardly recognized stood up.

'Hallo, father.'

'Saul . . . ?'

'Saul is a colonel in the reserve. He has access to the latest intelligence. I thought it might help if you were familiar with the person briefing you.'

'Very well,' Jacob said stiffly.

'This is a complete package on the military preparedness of the Syrian armed forces,' Saul began. 'The full paper begins at the blue tab and covers some 76 questions in detail from the state of alert readiness as apparent from soldiers in the bases, training routines, operational fitness of equipment and quantities of armaments, through their current training programme, theory of battle and fundamentals to officers and manpower available. There's a lot of it, so you'll find a bridging document on the yellow tab.

'The Syrians have come a very long way from the days of the War of Independence, when with the exception of the Lebanese they were the least fitted of our opponents for warfare of any kind at all. Under the late President Asad they were probably the most formidable Arab nation, and his successor President Hamouda has built upon that legacy. Since taking office, Hamouda has taken measures which improve his country's capability for making war, while saying that his only desire is to improve his country's defences against us.

'We find a number of measures especially worrying. Firstly,

intelligence. Hamouda was Asad's head of external intelligence. His *memuneh*. He is responsible for Syria now having a modern, organized information intelligence service. In the eighties Asad hired ex-CIA, ex-MI5, ex-DST experts on Israel. He is known to have had some Chinese Central External Liaison Department officers working for him. His relations with the PRC are good; they launched his Korean-built dedicated surveillance satellite for him from one of their Long March rockets. He doesn't employ foreigners now, he has his own men trained up. Hamouda has real-time surveillance of Israel, gentlemen. He also has RPVs – remotely-piloted aircraft like our own Scout and Mastiff. We find this development of an effective intelligence facility worrying because intelligence is nothing less than the crucial second half of strategic planning.

'What, then, do we think Hamouda is strategically planning? You have to remember that predicting the intentions of a country like Syria is far more difficult than with, say, Great Britain, or even the PRC. Syria is totally controlled by one man, and it is *his* intentions that we must fathom. Here we find further cause for alarm. Since taking office Hamouda has paid numerous visits to his fellow Arab leaders. To the Saudis, to the Mullahs. To the Egyptians, to King Hussein. To Iraq. Iraq, the Syrians' term enemy. He has even seen Qadhafi of Libya, generally considered by heavy-hitters like Hamouda to be little better than a mad dog. And people come to see him. He has had meetings with the Muslim leaders amongst the Palestinians. So what is he up to?'

'He wants a lasting and just peace,' Jacob said. 'He cannot, for obvious reasons, take unilateral action, he must assemble a coalition of opinion. That is obvious.'

'Maybe.'

'Or, he is assembling a coalition for a future war,' grunted Shahak.

'Maybe,' Saul said again. 'If he is planning a war he has a far greater capability to wage it than his predecessor had. He was the instigator of the Syrian move in the eighties to send the brightest of their students abroad to the West, to receive their training. He may have got the idea from the Chinese, who did it in the seventies, and are now reaping the harvest of a highly educated and experienced scientific corps. Hamouda's are *all* military scientists, in fields as diverse as electronics, aeronautics, computer science and genetic engineering. He has the best of them in the *al-Sham* weapons complex. Security is very tight there, we haven't been able to get in, but we've checked on his men, and they're good. We're too used to thinking of Arabs as inferior, we forget that Arab scientists were once, a long time ago, the best in the world.

'We have managed to trace where some of the stuff is going. Hamouda's storing some things in the shell of the Zabadan military hospital outside Damascus. Since it's on a military base it's suitably guarded. We have a most revealing satellite photograph. They had an accident with one of the trucks and tore the side of the trailer open. I have the image here.'

He passed copies to Shahak and Jacob. There was not much to see, greyish, smooth metal, a part of a fin.

'Our analysts assure us it's a cruise missile.'

'The bastards can make cruise missiles ...,' Shahak growled, angry.

'They can. For what they want. Something like the American ALCM is highly sophisticated, able to travel maybe two thousand miles over unknown terrain at very low altitude. But they don't need that. Their requirement is for a missile able to travel no more than two hundred and fifty miles at most to hit any target the length of Israel – even less than that if launched close to the borders, flying to its target over a pre-planned and known route at low altitude. Our analysts say that it is certainly not beyond their abilities to put it all together. The airframe and propulsion unit are no problem – don't forget the German V1 was a cruise missile, and don't forget, too, Dad, that your nemesis Heinz Ibach works for the Syrians still. You took him from the Americans and gave him to Syria. He set up much of their missile technology.'

Jacob said nothing, but his mouth tightened still further.

'It's the terrain following and avoidance that you have to work on,' Saul continued, 'but with their satellite they can have their route pre-planned and fed into the guidance computer, fit it with FLIR, forward-looking infra-red for navigational updates at pre-selected checkpoints on the way and you have a weapon that can go from Damascus to Tel Aviv at fifty feet and five hundred miles per hour with a good chance, if not of coming through this front door, certainly of hitting the building, which is a CEP good enough.

'To summarize. The Arab forces have been getting better for a long time. As Dayan observed after the Yom Kippur War, they do not run away any more. Hit hard enough they retreat, but do not run. The way they fought when we invaded Lebanon was really first class. Hamouda's programme for the improvement of the professional NCOs of his military appears to have paid dividends if the recent exercises are anything to go by. The average Syrian soldier is now considerably more capable of getting the best out of his equipment than he was even three years ago. In short, we find the Syrian military forces far better prepared for war than they have ever been. This is not to say that they are capable of inflicting defeat upon Israel, they are not. However, President Hamouda's fine words about defensive postures and seeking a peace with Israel would seem to need to be taken with more than a good pinch of salt.'

'Just how offensive a posture are they adopting at the moment?' said Shahak. 'I want you to tell him. I already know.'

Saul hesitated. 'Do I take that to mean in terms of our reaction, general?'

'Yes. Exactly.'

'Were the reaction of the international community, and more especially the USA to be left out of account, given our necessity to respond rapidly and positively to *any* military threat, there would obviously be a very strong case for a massive pre-emptive strike.'

'Which would set the chances of any peaceful solution back to nothing,' Jacob said bitterly. 'And I have just returned from America, where I assure you, our standing has never been lower. May I remind you that the Americans have very large stocks of materiel in both Egypt and Saudi Arabia, and have proved their ability, as the conflict with Iraq showed, to act decisively on their own within the Middle East. We have traded long on being their surrogate soldiers here, the day may come when they decide they do not need such difficult allies. Starting a new war will bring that day much closer.'

Jacob had gone very pale, the folder slipped in his hand, spilling on the floor.

'You all right, Jacob?' said Shahak.

'Yes, yes. I am a little tired, I have been travelling . . .'

'Saul, get your father back home, would you? Jacob, think about this briefing if you insist on staying in the job,' Shahak said grimly. 'I know what I am talking about.'

Jacob got up, and Saul helped him to the door.

'Quit,' Shahak said brutally. 'You aren't up to it, you're a menace to us.'

'How can I go when the work is unfinished?' Jacob lashed out. In the afternoon sun his hair was pure white. Saul shut the door of his Volvo and got into the driver's seat.

Shahak went back into his house and to the study where they had convened. He took the satellite image and sat at his desk, staring at the grey body and fin of the missile.

Saul took the Jerusalem road, making for the pretty village of Ein Kerem, tucked away in the hills, where Jacob had his cottage. They passed a small group of Palestinian children and one bent for a stone. Saul gunned the engine before he could throw it.

'Father, the threat from Syria is real.'

'*Qui desiderat pacem, praeparet bellum.* Let him who desires peace prepare for war. Hamouda wants a settlement for the Palestinians. He is half Palestinian himself. He wants peace. He knows we will not give one inch if the Arab states are weak. We have to be forced to the bargaining table.'

Saul slowed the car to take the turn off the ring road up into the hills. From out of the bushes came a swarm of black-coated and hatted ultra-orthodox, ringlets a-swing, shouting imprecations at the secular desecration of the sabbath. A shower of stones rattled the limousine like gunfire. The windscreen starred, sending light splintering in all directions.

'Bastards,' Saul muttered, looking in the mirror.

He glanced across at Jacob.

'Father, I have to say this to you. This woman that you are living with, Rifka Berry.'

'The woman I love,' Jacob said quietly, determinedly. 'The woman who is bearing my child.'

'Father she is a Palestinian.'

'How do you know that?' Jacob said quietly.

'I've done some digging,' Saul said sombrely.

'I thought you were too busy planning a new war,' Jacob said savagely. 'Yes, Rifka is Palestinian. What of it? She is the very best thing that has ever happened to me.'

'She has inflamed you with this unworkable dream of coexistence between us and the Palestinians, of an eternal peace.'

'There is nothing unworkable about it,' Jacob said softly. 'Is this not the land of miracles? That is what we used to say. Well, I am going to perform one more miracle before I die.'

'Don't you see, father, you have been got at. This woman posed as an Israeli. She joined Kane's presidential campaign with her own political action committee, she gave them a lot of money, that's how she was able to get close to Elie. That's how she was able to get at you. Now she's at your very side, guiding your very thoughts and actions. *You've been set up.*'

The car pulled up outside his cottage, with its garden. Jacob stared at his son, white with anger.

'What have I done to deserve a wicked child like you?' he demanded.

'Rifka Berry is an Arab agent,' Saul said steadily.

'I have met her family. Farmers from Hebron. I have seen the graves of her brothers. She is what she says, an honest Palestinian, desperate for peace. And so am I. Desperate for peace.'

'Father, of all the men who hate us out there I fear Hamouda most of all. I believe this woman is the agent of Hamouda. Who is planning war. Who is using you to lower our defences. Father, how much more harm will you do us.'

Through the window he saw Rifka, talking on the telephone. He fumbled with the door handle.

'War, war,' he muttered. 'All you can see is war. I want peace.'

He went inside, without looking back at his son, shutting the door on him. Rifka was putting down the phone. She came hurrying over to him.

'What is it, darling?' she said anxiously.

'Shahak, Saul . . . warmongers, fascists . . .,' he choked, almost speechless with rage.

'Here, sit down, darling, it is not good for you . . .'

He heard the clink of glass, and she came from the kitchen with a goblet of golden wine.

'Drink this, it will calm you.'

He took a deep swallow and twisted his ring, calming himself.

'They will do anything to avoid making peace,' he said, his voice still angry, but under control. 'I have had to listen to an entire exposition on how Hamouda and the Syrians intend making war upon us. It is not so!'

'Of course, it isn't.'

'The old trick of every last tyrant in the book. A foreign threat. Whip up the masses into a frenzy of hate and hysteria, and hang on to the presidential palace . . .'

Jacob pounded his caseworn fist on the table.

'I shall have peace, I shall, I shall,' he muttered. 'I will not be stopped, it is only a question of how.'

She knelt down in front of him clasping his hands with hers, looking deep into his eyes.

'You will,' she said solemnly. 'If you say it, it will happen. Look, drink your wine and let's go. We must talk to David while this is all fresh in your mind.'

His face brightened.

'David! Yes, yes, let us get it down.'

He drank his wine with a flourish, and they went back out to the car. Rifka got into the driver's seat, and they drove out towards the hills, where David had his house.

'Here,' said Jacob. 'Park it here.'

Cars were scattered along the little winding road. Bougainvillaea splashed purple and red on the walls, petals drifted on the tarmac. Orange and scarlet flowers erupted from thick-leaved plants. Rifka placed the car neatly by the kerb and they got out. David's garden was overgrown, the grass in need of cutting. The butterscotch-yellow of the house was beginning to age.

The front door was ajar, Jacob pushed it open and went in, Rifka behind him.

He paused in the hallway, his nose suddenly wrinkling.

'What's that?' he said in alarm. 'I can smell petrol. David, David! Are you all right?'

He hurried forward into the house. On the floor of the living room he saw his son face down. His head was bloodied, it was seeping from his temple and running over the brown tiling in a pool.

A man was there. Short black hair, olive skin. Savage.

'*Jacob* . . .'

Rifka's voice shouting a warning.

He was getting old, his arm was slow to protect himself from the short black sap in the man's hand. He fell sideways against the wall. The slap of rubber on flesh, Rifka moaning in sudden pain. A harsh voice, shouting in Ivrit.

'Get on with it, Dov! Get that petrol spread.'

'Okay, okay!'

'Burn these fucking traitors!'

A sudden, hot, huge gasp of air. The smell of burning petrol in his nostrils. A fierce crackling, clattering, running feet.

'Get up, get up!'

Rifka was shouting at him, pulling him to his feet, blood running down her face. The kitchen was ablaze, flames stabbing up into the ceiling, David's desk, his bookshelves, his video and audio recordings were burning fiercely. They seized him by the shoulders, dragging him out through the hall and into the road.

He groaned, coming round, rubbing a hand over his face. A car came screaming along the road, its tyres howling, two men inside.

Rifka grabbed a pencil and paper from their car, scribbling furiously.

'Bastards!' she yelled. 'I have the number. I have their number.'

Fire and black smoke erupted through the roof of the house, staining the sky.

'Shin-Bet,' David said thickly. 'They told me who they were. They said they'd see to it I never did harm to Israel again.'

# PART XX

## The White House

ELIE came hurrying into his west wing office. Jacob was sitting quietly in a chair by the window, where there was a view of the Rose Garden.

'Since when does the Foreign Minister of Israel walk in off the street like someone doing the guided tour?' said Elie.

'I need to see the president.'

'This have anything to do with Shin-Bet trying to knock off your boy? Man, the journalists have had a field day with your lot. Even Nixon didn't try and assassinate them.'

'Yes. That brought it to a head for me. Fifty years of looking for peace. Now I'm going to do it. I need to see him now.' Jacob fished in his jacket pocket. 'Here, give him this.'

He handed over a book of matches.

'Ask him if he'd like another.'

Elie was gone a few minutes. When he returned he smiled cautiously.

'He says he's interested. What do you have up your sleeve?'

'When Levinger was head of the Institute – Mossad – they said he always had something up his sleeve,' Jacob said, getting stiffly to his feet. 'And he did, he's prime minister. They also said you had to deal with him, you hoped it wouldn't be your balls. What I'm going to do to him and the other madmen they'll all want mine, but it's too bad.'

Elie was as close to the big boss as he could get, and it was a short walk down the corridor to the Oval Office. Kane was at his leather-topped desk, the presidential and national flags at his back. He got up as Jacob came slowly over the huge, pale gold rug.

'Elie, pull out the chair for the foreign minister. Jacob, it's good to see you. But have you been ill? You don't look so good.'

'It's the KZ,' Jacob said simply. 'We don't wear too well. You, Mr President, you look very fit.'

'Maybe. But I'd feel a sight better if I knew how I was going to win the next election,' he said directly. He sat back down in the green leather, spoonbacked chair and picked up the book of campaign matches from the desk.

'IOU one election,' he read. 'But I thought I'd paid that debt by getting you your present post.'

'I'm grateful to you, for I could not do what I am going to did I not hold this office. However, the request was not mine, as you know, but that of President Hamouda of Syria.'

'You reckon he's sincere?'

'He wants what I want, which is an end to this thing that poisons all our lives in the Middle East. And I, with your help, am the only man who can do it.'

Jacob held up his hand.

'I know. How does this help you win the election? If as a result of what I do this fifty-year-old problem of us and the Arabs, and the Palestinians in particular is solved, once and forever, and it is known that you, the president, played an instrumental role in bring that about, would it not mend your fences with your black, pro-Palestinian constituency?'

'It would,' Kane said carefully. 'It is what I hoped might – just might – happen. What would I have to do to get into this advantageous position?'

'In Israel as in the rest of the Middle East, Mr President, it is necessary to get a man's attention. If when you go into his office you don't credibly threaten to break up his furniture in pursuit of your ideas he won't take you seriously. Prime Minister Levinger has to deal every day with people like Rabbi Weiss and General Shahak whose idea of a morning greeting is to kick you in the balls.'

'How should I threaten to break up some of Prime Minister Levinger's furniture?' said Kane.

'Make just one phone call,' said Jacob.


# Jerusalem


Rabbi Weiss peered malevolently through the tall arrow-slit window at the jumble of old buildings in the distance. From the top floor of the Knesset, built like a blockhouse, he could look across the park at sleek, modern West Jerusalem, all faced or built from the local creamy stone, across Ben Yehuda and the Jaffa Road to the old quarter of East Jerusalem. A knitted blue and white *kippot* was firmly attached to his thinning scalp.

'Something wrong with the view?' said a voice. It was Shahak. The defence minister sat down at Levinger's conference table, tossing a file down with a hand like a bunch of bananas.

'Arabs,' Weiss said in disgust. 'The place is crawling with Arabs, like lice.'

'You need a blowtorch to get rid of lice,' Shahak said, almost genially. Weiss darted a suspicious look at him, but he was not mocking him.

'Arabs,' Weiss muttered. 'All lusting after Jewish women.'

The door opened and Levinger and Jacob came in. Levinger sat down at the top of the table.

'Let's get on with it,' he grunted.

In the Knesset, as elsewhere in Israel, social discourse was conducted at the level of the snarl.

'What is it you want to talk about, Jacob?'

'I want to talk about the only thing that actually matters in this country, which is what we are to do about the Palestinians. No fine-tuning, no changes of emphasis, but a solution. A final solution to the whole problem.'

He looked at them in turn with challenging eyes, an angry, white-haired old man.

'I'd like to talk about that,' said Shahak, and he smiled pleasantly. 'You see, I happen to agree with you. What we do with the Palestinians *is* the most important issue.'

Weiss looked sharply at Shahak and instead of speaking shut his mouth, and sat staring at Jacob, hostile and waiting, his thin arms folded.

'It's a democracy,' said Jacob. 'You are entitled to your say, and I mine.'

'Israel must never be a democracy!' Weiss spat. 'Israel is a theocracy, she answers only to God.'

'I've got him here to remind you of the consequences of *not* going along with what I'm going to tell you,' Jacob said to Levinger and Shahak, without looking at Weiss.

'Get on with it then,' Shahak said malevolently.

'I have assured Jacob that neither Shin-Bet nor any other arm of the government of Israel had anything to do with the attack on his son David,' said Levinger. 'However, he does not believe me.'

'These details are no longer important,' Jacob said firmly. 'Nor are appeals to the six million dead who stand behind me. We do not have to listen to the plans of General Shahak, who wishes to drive all the Arabs out of Israel and Gaza, nor to the foul dreams of the Rabbi, who wishes to slaughter them all. All you have to do is stay quiet and listen to what I am going to tell you.'

'We will listen,' Levinger said, his voice cold. 'But I have the feeling that you will be leaving here no longer our foreign minister.'

'I have travelled, all these years,' Jacob said, ignoring him. 'How I have travelled. For Israel who guards the gate to Africa I have been all over this continent and others. I have been to South Africa at the tip, I have been kidnapped in Rhodesia. I have been in Algeria, Zaire, Mozambique, Angola, Uganda and the Ivory Coast, just to mention a few. I can remember when Africa was made up of countries with different names, different colours on the map. I actually have an old map, in my home, of Africa years ago, and it is coloured differently. We are there, only we are called Palestine.

'Colonial Algeria isn't there any more, by the way. The settlers have gone back to France. Rhodesia isn't there either. Curiously enough, I saw the Irishman who held me captive, I saw him on the television, he was a part of the IRA team negotiating with the British. The British are leaving the last part of their empire. I saw someone else I met – very briefly – in Rhodesia, he was a guerrilla, he killed my old friend Seamus Flynn. I met him when I was invited to the independence celebrations in South Africa by President Mandela. He was a member of the ANC, he's in the government down there.'

'This is sounding more and more like the retirement speech of an old bore,' Levinger said acidly. 'Does it get anywhere, or become even slightly interesting?'

'Oh, it does, Captain Zvi, it certainly does. What is it, that has swept away all these names from the map? It must be British Prime Minister Macmillan's famous force, that 'wind of change'. Can't you feel it? We have no windbreaks in front of us now, no imperial allies to hold us up. That wind is howling about us, for we are standing alone on the plain. The plain is black basalt, it is where the Crusaders fought the Battle of Hattin, the wind is the wind of history and it is going to blow us away, the same as it blew for the French in Algeria, the British in Rhodesia, the Afrikaaners in South Africa. We shall be at one with Nineveh and Tyre. Unless we can avoid their fate. Can we? We have no more right to live here than they did there. What can we do? Partial deals do not work, you know, and nor does force. Bringing Bishop Muzorewa into the government as a puppet did not work for the Rhodesians. The best paratroops in the world did not work for the French Algerians, and nor did state-sponsored torture. Possession of nuclear weapons did not work for the Afrikaaners, just as it will not work for us. Belief in God being on one's side does not work for anybody.'

Jacob glanced at his watch. It was nearly time.

'There is only one solution, and we are going to take it,' he said briskly. 'Locking the Palestinians up in Gaza does not work, nor does exiling them in refugee camps. We are missing the point. They have as much right – they have *more* right – to be here as and than we do. I hope they will let us stay.'

They stared at him in disbelief as his voice rang out, strong and certain. He held up his clenched fist and his gold ring gleamed.

'On behalf of the government of Israel I have this day informed the heads of state of all our Arab neighbours, of all Palestinian leaders, that all those who are proud to call themselves Palestinian are welcome to live amongst us. The state of Israel will cease to exist. The new state will contain Jews and Arabs as equal partners, equal in rights. We already have proportional representation. The Palestinians may have their own parties. They will form a government with us.'

'Jacob, you have gone off your head,' Levinger said in a low voice. 'I think we're going to have to put you in an asylum.'

The telephone rang on the table.

'Are you?' Jacob demanded. 'Pick up the phone, it's for you.'

Levinger picked it up, he listened without saying a word, only turning very pale. He put it back in its cradle, very carefully.

'That was President Kane,' he whispered. 'He has informed me that unless we begin talks with the Palestinians as Jacob has told us he will cut off all aid, political, economic and military, as of today.'

Gideon Weiss screamed to God, invoking him to strike the Agent of Satan down. Shahak got on to the Air Force, ordering them to do it by more earthly means. He left the Knesset and got into his waiting car, ordering the driver to take him direct down the mountain to Tel Aviv.

The car took him to the compound of Air Force headquarters.

Saul Ben-Levi was waiting for him there, having hurried from his lawyer's office, a flight bag in his hand.

'Your father has gone off his head,' Shahak said bluntly. 'Hamouda and the Syrians are planning a war against us and he is proposing

the elimination of the State of Israel in order to go to bed with the
Palestinians. We'll probably want to have him shot later. But for now,
we need to stop the whole thing in its tracks. Are you ready?'

'Yes,' Saul said. 'I am always ready.'

'Good. Then begin Operation Joshaphat.'

## Tripoli, Libya

Paul Kale had lived in many places since leaving Sydney aged twenty
with a Nikon and a set of tiger-stripes to cover the Vietnam War.
Whenever he moved he went back to Sydney, only to leave again
shortly afterwards. An ability to pick up diverse languages by ear had
taken him through Mozambique, Cambodia, Angola and Beirut, so
he concluded that he simply could not adapt to anywhere that was not
violent, irrational and dangerous. The Libya of the General People's
Congress was all three. Applications by experienced reporters to
become stringers for such a place were rare, and for a couple of
years Kale had eked out a living filing reports for such diverse
outlets as the British weekly *Observer* and its tabloid opposite the
daily *Sun*, tailoring both viewpoint and syntax to suit.

Kale had been arrested by secret police in eight countries, he
knew who the men at his door were even before they dragged him
out to the waiting car. To his surprise, he was taken not to some
noisome cell or interrogation room to be beaten up, but to the hall
of the People's Congress, where a sea of lack-lustre people in old
cinema seats suddenly came to their feet, waving small green books
and shouting slogans, as a man in a flowing white gown came onto
the podium above.

He held out his hands, and the trained cheering ceased.

'I speak to you, my people, and I speak to others. I speak to all
Arabs, and to all Muslims. I speak to my fellow Arab leaders. It is
the sacred mission of all Arabs and of all Muslims to destroy Israel.
We in this country have remained faithful to this ideal. We train for
the day when our armed forces will lead the final assault on the
regime of *Shaytan* that his slaves call Israel.

'My fellow Arab leaders have strayed from the true path. Even now
they prepare to talk with the Jews. Chairman Arafat of the Palestine
Liberation Organization prepares to go to their very heartland, the
Holy City, and be among them.'

The skin on the back of Kale's neck prickled. Something was wrong. The man on the podium sighed sadly.

'They are all mistaken. They will be betrayed by the Jews. Then they will come to their senses, and see what they have done – given away the historic land of the Palestinian people to the agents of the Devil. Then they will turn to us. For us, the war against Israel remains Holy.'

It was a short speech by the standards of the General Secretary of the General People's Congress. Kale had stood in similar halls shifting from one aching foot to the other while wild Arabic rhetoric had bounced from one crumbling concrete wall to the other, hour after hour. This one was over in 40 minutes, and the secret policemen took him home.

He wouldn't use Reuter's for this one. He had the copy typed up within the hour and got on to the telephone. Somewhat to his surprise, it worked. Within minutes, he was talking to his sub-editor on the *Daily Telegraph* in London.

'I have Qadhafi's official response to the Arab/Palestinian peace initiative with Israel.'

'Okay, go ahead.'

'He has declared war on Israel.'

There was a short silence.

'Isn't the official Libyan position that it has been at war with Israel since Qadhafi took power in 1969?'

'Yes, but he hasn't actually done much about it in serious military terms, aside from providing support and training for the PLO, and numerous other terrorist groups. Anyhow, he claims the Libyan Holy Army will lead the battle against the forces of Satan in Israel. His revolutionary fighters will attack Jewish targets on land, his submarines will blockade the country and his air force rain destruction upon them from above.'

'He's off his head,' the Englishman said decisively. 'The Israelis will swat his lot like flies if he makes trouble.'

'I know,' said Kale. 'But that was the funny thing. When he was making the speech. He was calm. Matter of fact. To the point. Sane, if you like.'

# PART XXI

## Koach Joshaphat

IT was Israeli Air Force custom that important operations be given suitable Biblical names. One of the most famous, the 7 June 1981 raid on the Osirak Iraqi nuclear reactor outside Baghdad had been called Operation Babylon. 'Before your eyes I will repay Babylon and all who live in Babylonia for all the wrong they have done in Zion, declares the Lord.' Joshaphat had been a warrior in the army of King David, distinguished by his bravery. His name was Hebrew for 'God has judged.'

The six pilots of the *koach* or team and their two back-up men had practised intensively for the raid. As with Operation Babylon, the decision had been made to use General Dynamics F-16 fighters, carrying 2,000 lb MK 84 'slick' bombs. Rockwell GBU-15 'smart' bombs were available, but for one hundred per cent accuracy on the first pass bombing it was considered safer and more effective to deliver the explosive by hand and wing rather than use the stand-off method. All eight pilots could place their BDU-33 white phosphorus practice bombs in the centre of the sixty-foot-diameter target on the Negev training site, one after the other, in 30 seconds. Saul Ben-Levi was the only reservist amongst them, but Shahak had wanted it that way.

Operation Babylon had been the longest raid ever attempted, 1,200 miles into enemy territory, but Operation Joshaphat was short – it was only 68 miles from the northern Israel base of Ramat David to the 'hospital' outside Damascus. Travelling at 450 knots over the Golan plateau, with the heights behind him, Saul was seven minutes out from Ramat David. Like all Israeli fighter pilots, he was used to turning on his armament switches the moment he went wheels up in a combat situation.

Saul was number three in the attack. The so-called hospital was in the shape of a capital I, with two wings crossing the main body of the building, top and bottom. Saul had been assigned the top wing. The MK 84 bomb produced blast, fragmentation and deep cratering. Its fragmentation envelope extended upwards and outwards for about 3,000 feet, and to get all six aircraft in and out before the defences could become effective delayed-action fuses had been selected. All twelve bombs would explode at the same moment, ripping the cruise missiles stored inside into so much tinfoil, and bring the shell of the building crashing down on the remains. They had been meticulously checked for any small bump or dent that might affect the airflow and throw off accuracy.

The flight commander had quoted from the Psalms before leading them out to the sleek fighters waiting at the end of the runway. 'His Excellency is over Israel, and His strength is in the clouds.' Saul had prayed before take off, he wore *tefillin*, a fragment of the torah strapped to his wrist, that God might guide his hand.

The small lake in the scrub came up on time and Saul put the waypoint cross on the HUD head-up display on the tower on its south end. The INS was accurate to a hair.

It was time. He pushed himself back in the seat as far as he could. If he was hit by AAA fire or a SAM he didn't want the ejection seat to break his back. The Arabs would do that for him if they caught him. With his right hand he set the flare and chaff switches, and called up the stores control in the panel above his left knee. He selected the thumb pickle button for the two bombs. Once gone he would change function to his Sidewinders, in case they got jumped by Syrian MiGs on the way out.

The six F-16s were in formation. At 450 knots and 50 feet the ground was a sandy blur. Damascus came over the horizon, breaking the smooth curve of the earth.

Four miles to the target and the white building gleamed in the sunshine. Ben, the pilot in front, pulled up in the first phase of the attack manoeuvre and five seconds later Saul followed suit. Chaff was spitting from Ben's dispenser at the rate of two bundles a second and it shimmered briefly as the sun caught the tinsel. He had full afterburner, and went to 5,000 feet in four seconds, with the sun at his back. Then it was hard left, nose down, wings level, and afterburner off as he came down the chute with the bomb pipper of the sight tracking onto the target. With peripheral vision he checked the radar warning receiver. The RWR was silent. No SAMs.

The two F-16s in front had pulled away and were heading for the deck on full afterburner. The bomb fall line on the HUD was tracking right onto the top of the I. The 'hospital' was marked with huge red crosses on the roof. The red dot was in the centre of the wing. Tiny antlike figures were running from the building. His thumb pressed the round red pickle button and the bombs were gone.

He pulled up hard and left, the G-suit bladders filling with air and squeezing the lower half of his body to keep the blood in the top. As the G-forces slackened he selected his fire control radar, ready to fire his Sidewinders.

Looking back he saw the last fighter pulling away from the target, and its bombs vanish into the building. As it went for the deck the 'hospital' vanished in a huge blast. Pieces of debris came tumbling high through the smoke and flame.

'*Baruch hashem*,' he heard the flight leader's voice crow in his earphones. 'Blessed be God.'

There was a CNN news team in Damascus and as soon as they heard of the raid they grabbed their cameras and got in the car. They were stopped at the gate to the military base, where smoke was still pouring from the rubble of the building. Ambulances and lorries were racing in and then out with the wounded and the dead.

The short-haired blonde reporter in her action-girl outfit stared stonily through the wire at the devastation.

'Certainly gives new meaning to the expression "surgical strike",' she said.

President Hamouda had been among the first on the scene, whisked in from the palace in his helicopter. When he heard they were there he issued orders that they be allowed in.

The bombing had been pin-point. There was no damage outside the building, the bombs had sliced cleanly into the wards and operating theatres. Bits of the dead lay everywhere, lengths of entrails hung from the trees, offal was strewn over the grass. A child's head, unmarked, lay in the gutter of the street by their feet. Hamouda came from the ruins, plaster rubble on his clothes and in his hair, blood on his hands where he had led the frantic efforts to free the trapped.

They had heard the Israeli radio on their way.

'Mr President,' said the blonde. 'The Israelis are claiming that this hospital was the site of a cruise missile storage depot. What do you have to say to that?'

Hamouda gestured mutely about him at the carnage.

'Please go and search for one,' he said huskily. 'All you will find are my dead and dying.'

The air was filled with the stench of blood, ordure and explosive.

The woman swallowed hard to push back the bile rising in her throat.

'What of Colonel Qadhafi's declaration of war on Israel?'

'General Secretary Qadhafi understands, as we do, that the Israelis are a race peculiarly prone to acts of violence. However, we seek peace, and not war.'

'Will this mean that the Peace mission announced by Foreign Minister Ben-Levi is now off?'

Hamouda stared full into the camera. The wailing of the trapped and the dying was all about them.

'There are many in Israel who do not want peace, who would murder women and children to prevent the Palestinian people coming home. These dead here are martyrs of that struggle. We shall not be stopped at this late hour. Chairman Arafat will go to Jerusalem, and we shall be with him.'

## Fac Nitzhon

The grey 'Reshef' class fast attack craft was 30 kilometres off the coast near Ashkelon, moving through the early-morning light sea mist at a steady 18 knots. In the control room under the bridge Moshe Rafael was at his equipment console, headphones on, a circular PPI plan-position indicator in front of him. The patrol had been uneventful, the only electronic noise coming through to him being the regular squawk of the two tankers heading up to Haifa from the west as their scanning navigation radars illuminated the 420-ton missile boat a few kilometres off.

The ESM electronic support measures system aboard was familiar with the Racal/Decca TM-series radar; it was in its library, electronically tagged as friendly. Like the computer, Rafael's ear was sufficiently well-tuned to be able to recognize frequency, pulse rate and repetition frequency as easily as a friend or acquaintance's voice.

The first indication that something was wrong was a soft, but regular chirrup. An unknown voice.

The ESM suite knew it, and pulled it out of its library. No tagging of friendly, *designated* potential threat. It threw it up onto Rafael's VDU and the control room went on to full alert.

The captain, Ariel Yaakov, came over tugging on his fire-proof gloves, as Rafael worked the PPI to give a bearing.

'J-band surveillance radar known as "Crow". Fitted to Sukhoi Su-24 attack aircraft. It's very low, it's popping up over the horizon to illuminate us and dipping back down. It's got the tankers between us and itself.'

'Who has them?'

'The library says only the Libyans, this part of the world.'

The *Nitzhon* come up to full speed, slicing through the water at 32 knots, the Argo NA 10 fire-control system bringing the bow-mounted *Barak* SAMs and stern-mounted 76mm guns onto the threat.

The soft chirruping suddenly changed to a harsh scraping, like a windscreen wiper in top gear.

'He's switched his tracking radar on,' Rafael said urgently.

'Action stations,' ordered Yaakov.

There was silence for a few moments, and then his headphones picked up a coarse whistling sound.

'Missile attack.'

'Launch chaff.'

The countermeasures suite was automatically searching for jamming measures. As the intermittent whistling changed to a steady tone as the missiles locked on, it threw up their identity on to Rafael's screen.

'AS-10,' he said. 'We still have no lock on the Sukhoi. He's below the horizon.'

Within a second, there came two immense, deep explosions. Yaakov lifted his eyes from the console and went, for the first time, to look outside.

Three kilometres away on the smooth swell of the ocean two pillars of black smoke boiled up into the sky.


## Kirya, Tel Aviv


'Thank God for Qadhafi,' said Shahak. 'Crazy Arabs we can deal with.'

Seated around the top end of the cabinet table were just four men. With Levinger and Shahak were Ehud Yoram, the tall chief of staff, and Yosi Barak, his opposite, the small, wiry former fighter pilot, and head of the air force.

'He's got his "war" off to a flying start,' said Shahak. 'First the two tankers this morning, and now news has just come in that an El Al office in London has been blown up, and a Moroccan airlines 707 has been hijacked on the ground at Casablanca by a group calling itself the Movement for the Liberation of all Palestine.'

'The king's asked for our help with that,' Yoram interjected. 'I have a CRW team fitting out right now.'

'Terrorist bombings and hijackings are pinpricks. The Sukhoi attack aircraft are more serious.'

'Qadhafi has more equipment than he can ever use,' said Barak. 'Mostly, it's in store. The Su-24s are not. He has one whole operational squadron, based at the September Revolution Air Base outside Benghazi. Again, most of his troops are a joke – the *Egyptians* can beat them up – but the attack on the tankers was thoroughly professional.'

'We need to take them out,' said Shahak. 'I'm moving the satellite to give us real-time imaging of the air base. How long will it take to prepare an attack? Yosi?'

'As you know, any future war with Syria will begin with a massive aerial attack on her three main air bases – plan Green. We are thoroughly practised and versed in this sort of operation. Once the satellite gives as the requisite information regarding the air defences of the base we can mount it within a day.'

## Casablanca

At ten that night it was still hot. It had been hot all day, and the terrorists aboard the 707 glinting in the arc lights had finally broken down and requested supplies. The women and children were gone, there were just a dozen men inside, plus the four hijackers.

A lone man wheeled the oblong trolley across the ramp towards the stairway at the front of the aircraft. As he came up a masked man poked his head out of the door. He was armed, with a sub-machine gun, and he gestured for it to be left. When the man had walked back across the pool of light into the darkness he came down the steps. Another man appeared in the doorway, covering him. From the other side of the airfield there came the sudden deafening, crackling roar of a fighter aircraft taking off on full afterburner.

Splashes of gold light sparkled suddenly on their chests, and they fell silently to the ground. There was a thump on the wing and a black parachute drifted away into the night as a dark figure slapped the escape door, dropping flat above the inboard engine.

The side of the trolley fell flat as three figures burst out. The explosive on the door slammed like a sledgehammer, and three more black figures thudded down out of the sky, to dive and roll through the open door into the empty fuselage.

They came through at the same moment, the team at the front capable of taking out either of the two terrorists left in the cockpit or front galley, the second team taking control of the centre and rear.

The aircraft was deserted. The first parachutist pulled off his black, goggled respirator. It was Haazev Shahak.

'Very good,' the Wolf said approvingly to his team. 'Now if Mr Arafat will just go to Jerusalem then tomorrow we'll do that for real.'


## Tel Aviv


Yitzhak Ben-Levi, son of Saul, brother of Eli and Shemaah had seen the 737 as it came in on final into Lod, he'd seen the colours it bore, colours that had never before flown over Israel, the white and red and green and black of the Palestinian flag. Now he stood next to his white Lincoln outside the building and waited for the Boeing's owner to come out.

The press were there, behind the line of soldiers, and the shade sparkled with the eruption of flashbulbs as he came through the automatic doors. His carefully unshaven chin gleamed with silver stubble, his trademark black and white *keffiyeh* was crisp. He beamed at them all, and Yitzhak held open the door of the limousine for him and his bodyguards. Then he got into the driver's seat in front, the policeman on his white and blue BMW nodded, he shifted the automatic into gear and they hissed out of the airport with the blue lights twirling in front and in the mirror.

A tapping.

He jumped, a little. Behind was the grey Chevrolet, stuffed with armed guards. The state of Israel had expended some effort, in the past, in trying to kill the man in the back of the armoured limousine. Now he was here, they had to expend even more to see that he stayed alive.

The tapping again. Pebbles? No, it was on the partition glass. He glanced behind him, and saw Arafat leaning forward, patting the glass with his pen. Yitzhak thumbed the button and the partition slid down.

'Hullo,' Arafat said. He sounded friendly. 'You drive very well.'

'Thank you, boss,' he said. 'It's my job.'

'I am fond of cars,' Arafat confided. 'I once had a Thunderbird, as a young man. Such power! Now that I am old I'd like a limousine, like this one.'

'Maybe they'll give you it,' Yitzhak suggested. When he had said it, he wondered why he had. It was very strange, to be driving up the road to Jerusalem, talking to the Captain of Murderers, to the man he had been brought up to believe was his people's arch-enemy.

Arafat beamed.

'Why, yes! They are to give me a country to live in with them, why not a car to drive about in it?'

'Why not, boss,' the young Israeli murmured.

The limousine and the convoy were gaining speed, now that they were out of the airport. Up on the hill, there was Jerusalem.

'Is this what you do? You are a driver?'

'That's it. This sort of driving. Except on reserve duty.'

'Ah, yes. Reserve duty,' Arafat said affably. 'For the army?'

'Yes.'

'And what do you do?'

'I was a paratrooper, but I wanted something more interesting.'

The Palestinian's eyes gleamed in delight.

'And what, pray tell me, could be more interesting than being a paratrooper?'

'I'm a driver,' Yitzhak said slyly.

'Aha. But *what* do you drive?'

'Hummer, boss. Like an armoured dune buggy. Got TOW missile, got grenade launcher, got heavy machine gun. But really, I'm a cat. I creep about ahead of the others, seeing what's ahead.'

'Who are the others?'

'Spearhead of the *Ugdah*. I'm the tip of the tip. I tell them what's there, then they go in and smash it.'

'Ah, yes. I'm so sorry to be putting you out of work.'

'Out of work?'

'Now we are to live together, there will be no more fighting between Arab and Jew,' Arafat explained gently.

'I hadn't thought of that.'

'I don't suppose you would want a job.'

'A job?'

'If they gave me this car, perhaps you would drive it for me?'
Yitzhak's throat was suddenly dry.

'Okay, boss,' he said, and it was hoarse. 'I'll drive for you.'

Arafat sat back on the soft grey leather upholstery, and Yitzhak
left the partition down. He drove up the road, feeling stunned and
somehow strangely happy.


## Casablanca


The Wolf, Amos Haazev, was in the bus that drove over the tarmac
apron towards the 707, together with Haim and Avi. The driver did
exactly requested, putting the nose into the corner where the wing
abutted the fuselage, and they were out and underneath without
anyone inside seeing them.

The door of the bus opened with a hiss of hydraulics and the
stairway vibrated to the anxious thudding of the hostages' feet.
Twelve men, all unharmed. They got in, the door hissed shut, and
the bus rumbled quickly away.

Then they came down, the four. From behind them, and to the
side, Haazev saw them, walking down steadily, their hands held very
high, palms open. The three soldiers were upon them fast, they gave
no trouble, lay down upon the tarmac spread-eagled in a row, just
like trained troops.

With the Heckler und Koch MP5 sub-machine gun in his hand
that he would have used to kill them, Haazev looked down upon
them in puzzlement.

'Now what the hell was the point of that?' he said.


## Jerusalem


Shaul Shiloah pushed his way through and got to Shahak. The
defence minister was wearing the trousers of a well-cut suit,
long-sleeved shirt and *Heyl Shirion* Armoured Corps tie. Shahak
looked up, seeing the little ferret-faced man from Mossad coming.

'Can I talk to you for a moment?' Shaul said, and they went over
and stood under the shade of the tree in the square.

'I have to sit next to Arafat while that old lunatic makes his speech,' Shahak said. 'Ben-Levi, I mean. It's my punishment for bombing the hospital. For years we've held a gun at Arafat, and said, eat horseshit, Yasser. Now he has the gun and he says, eat horseshit, Shelesh. So there, we're having lunch together.'

'Why do you think Hamouda fooled us into bombing the hospital, thinking it was a cruise missile store?' Shaul asked quietly.

'So we couldn't stop this thing that is now happening. We bomb a hospital, and the Arabs *still* come, what can we do? The world now hates *us*, and loves the Arabs. How things change . . . But let me tell you, we can still stop this thing.'

They were gathering there, up on the mountain; Mount Moriah raised high at the eastern end of the city. It symbolized the endless conflict between Jew and Muslim. As Temple Mount it was the site of the first and second Jewish temples, destroyed in 587 BC and AD 70. As Haram al-Sharif, the Noble Sanctuary, it held the Dome of the Rock, the lovely structure built over the rock upon which Abraham had been prepared to sacrifice his son Isaac. Just to the south of its gold-leafed dome was the third holiest site in Islam, the black-topped al-Aqsa mosque, the very spot from which the Prophet Mohammed had ascended into Heaven. Both built upon the ruins of the Jewish temples.

Haazev, not long off the aircraft from Casablanca, stood in the street with the others. It was as always, the Israeli soldiers with guns and riot sticks, the young Palestinians with hard hands ready to grasp a catapult or a stone, but somehow, the venom was going out of it. A young boy of fifteen caught his eye, poking his head cautiously around the alley wall at the tall Jewish soldier.

'I'm going to fuck your sister,' he announced, in passable Hebrew.

'I have already fucked yours,' Haazev replied.

'I shall fuck your mother.'

'Curse your mother that brought you into this world,' Haazev said using the Arabic.

They paused, both eyeing each other, and slowly the faintest relaxation of their fixed expressions appeared.

'What if it was more than just that?' Shaul said intensely. 'The forces of Jordan, Iraq and Egypt are all at a state of alert far higher than is warranted by their leaders being here to oversee the beginning of talks for a Palestinian homeland.'

'I know,' said Shahak. 'They have quite candidly explained that it is as a reminder, to place pressure upon us to keep the momentum up. You didn't mention the Syrians.'

'The Syrians yesterday began large-scale manoeuvres. They are quite sufficiently close to our borders to seem not unlike their pre-Yom-Kippur posture in 1973. What if they tricked us into bombing the hospital not to keep the peace process going, *but in order to achieve strategic surprise?*'

'But all the Arab leaders are here, except Qadhafi. Don't they believe they are getting what they want? What on earth would they want to start a war for now?'

'There is nothing in the past record of President Hamouda to suggest that he is happy with the idea, despite his championing of it. Don't forget, he is part Palestinian himself. And what about Qadhafi? It makes no strategic sense for him to "declare war" on us. But sinking the tankers and hijacking the airplane in Casablanca has sure got us looking the wrong way. *General, it's Yom Kippur again.*'

They were gathering, the leaders surrounded by their underlings, going into the al-Aqsa mosque to pray.

'Where *is* Hamouda?' Shahak said sharply.

'I saw him a minute ago there . . . he's talking to Ben-Levi.'

'Why isn't he with the others?'

'Don't forget, he isn't a Muslim. His father was a Christian, it's been one of his advantages, he hasn't got a constituency, he's been able to reconcile the Muslims and Alawis.'

Saul saw the grey hair on the back of Shahak's head rise up stiff.

The gritty path widened where the olive grove was divided, and David turned his car and parked. The road to Hebron lay back through the trees, but there it was quiet.

David got out. He reached in for his camcorder in the back. The little valley of the wadi was pleasing to the eye. Springs and storage pools for the sweet water glittered in the sunshine, kitchen gardens and grapevines and olive groves formed a patchwork of every shade of green. The smell of thyme was on the air.

There was nobody about. He went down the path towards the farmhouse with its courtyard, that looked over the valley. He passed a small graveyard with five graves, all overgrown with weeds. He frowned, looking at them in puzzlement, then hurried on to the house.

It was deserted. He went round to the shady courtyard, open

on two sides. All the shutters were closed. There was a kitchen garden there, weeds had sprouted, it was filled with the bolted heads of lettuce, with overgrown mandrake. Courgette had grown into marrow, tomatoes split on the vine. There was nobody about.

He went back down the path, his camcorder hanging from his hand. A man was coming towards him, an Arab in a checked *keffiyeh* and black *'igal*, a mattock in his hand. A farmer.

'*Allah yikalik*,' David said politely. 'May God be with you.'

The Palestinian eyed the Israeli with his strange technological equipment warily.

'Whose god?' he grunted.

'I am looking for the family of Fayez Kader, that lived in the farmhouse.'

'Gone,' the Arab said shortly.

'Gone, gone where?'

The Arab shrugged. 'Back where they came from. They were foreigners.'

He swung his mattock onto his shoulder and pressed on up the hill.

'What do you mean, back where they came from? Were they not from here? I have come to interview them. Today in Jerusalem the Jews and the Arabs are making peace.'

The Palestinian looked at him with contempt, and spat before moving on.

David looked about him in sudden alarm, his heart thudding. He was standing by the small graveyard, that had been so lovingly tended with flowers. He went in. A gnarled olive branch was on the ground, as dry and hard as iron. He picked it up and dug into the weed-encrusted earth of the nearest grave. When he had gone down a foot he hit solid earth that had never been turned.

He straightened up, the breath caught in his throat. From up on the hill he heard a sudden shouting, a kind of howl of mingled rage and joy. He did not understand it. A man was running along the path towards the Palestinian farmer. His arms waved in an an explosion of passion. The two men turned and stared at him.

'*Itbahu al-yahud! Itbahu al-yahud!*'

He heard them scream, scream words that had not been heard in Israel for fifty years. He saw them coming down the hill, their mattocks in their hands and he ran.

He could hear them behind him as he panted up to his car; he turned and hurled his camcorder at them. He scrambled frantically inside, fumbling with the keys. He fired up the engine and the window by his ear burst in a shower of glass.

Blood sprayed from his head, he crunched into gear as the Arab drew back the mattock for a second blow. The wheels spun furiously, the car slithering round in a circle like a trapped animal as the two men rained blows into it. Then he was lurching down the track, half out of control, with his attackers running after him. The windscreen was crazed and shattered, bloody fragments of glass flew everywhere. He crashed onto the tarmac road in a howl of tyres.

He was safe. He stared wildly back down the path at the two Arab men.

'Itbahu al-yahud!'

'Your father is an Arab,' said the boy.

'Your sister fornicates with dogs,' said Haazev.

They paused. Something faintly resembling smiles appeared on their faces.

From the hill there came an immense roar. The black dome of the mosque erupted into a ball of fire. The walls came crashing in, and flame and smoke climbed high into the sky.

The boy's face was suddenly contorted with familiar hate.

'Itbahu al-yahud,' he screamed. 'Kill the Jews.'

He came around the corner with a knife in his hand, and Haazev emptied the clip of his Uzi into his chest.

Thair Hasan's nose was flat. His first name meant 'Revolutionary', for he was *abna almuhayamaat*, one of the sons of the camps, a *samidin*. When Shin-Bet, the secret police, had had control before the *intifada* they had known how to handle such as he. After a night spent holding a chair in the air in *maslah lashahah*, the slaughterhouse of the youth, they had put a bag over his head and made him run as fast as he could in all directions. Once he didn't know where he was they had him run into a wall.

Now he worked for a man called Shlomo, who owned a restaurant on Dizengoff Street with his son Yisrael. Yisrael had been a fighter pilot in the Air Force, and the restaurant was a popular haunt of pilots on leave among the bright lights.

Thair worked six days a week, from noon until four in the morning, for 500 shekels a month. To travel from Gaza was a life *al-farshe al-warshe* and back, from the mattress to the workplace and back to the mattress, so he slept on a pallet in a cockroach-infested storeroom in the knowledge that if the police found him it was a beating, jail and a 2,000 shekel fine for staying within the green line overnight.

On his day off he went home, passing the citrus groves that had belonged to his grandfather, to the Jebalya camp in Gaza, where his mother made *bantalon kaboi*, cowboy jeans, for a Jewish factory owner in Tel Aviv. It was in the camp that he had discovered the comfort of religion. The man in the green and white *keffiyeh* had promised him that he would know when it was time, that God would send a sign, and since then every day as he performed his myriad tasks he would repeat what the man had told him, *Allahu maa asahirin*, Allah helps those who are patient.

When the streets erupted with noise he was in the tiny kitchen, preparing *shuarma* for the spit, alternating chunks of bloody turkey meat with a slice of fat from a lamb's tail. The fat gave the cheap meat the illusion of mutton. He worked expertly, his long, razor-sharp *halaf* cutting and trimming.

There was a television on in the bar, and he put his head around the door. What he saw told him that Allah had sent his sign. He went back into the kitchen and continued to prepare the *shuarma*.

He heard Yisrael coming in at a run, heard him exchanging fast words with his wife, who ran the kitchen and liked always to keep Thair busy.

'Who knows who did it? Some of the crazy ones. Gush Emunim, if you ask me. It'll mean war, that's for sure. I must get out to the base.'

Thair heard the thudding as the pilot ran up the stairs to the apartment above, and continued skewering the meat. He knew how long it took his employer to get into his pilot's suit and boots, and to grab his flight bag, always kept at the ready. It was the advantage the slave always had over the slave master. The one ruled without interest of the other, who by necessity became a keen observer of those who held power over him.

He moved quietly out of the kitchen. He was filled with the joy of *jihad*. There was a store cupboard there by the stairs leading up to the apartment. Yisrael came crashing down the stairs in his olive flight suit. The long *halaf* flashed in the dim light and Thair gutted him from crotch to throat.

Hidden in the bushes by the dirt road Hasan had his red and white *keffiyeh* wrapped over his head and around his face, with just a slit for his eyes. He was PFLP, his radio always tuned to George Habash's station in Damascus had told him. He had left the little plot of

land where he was weeding and hoeing, and slipped quietly into the
undergrowth by the road that led to the settlement the *mustawtanin*
had built on the old village, where his parents had lived. His catapult
was always with him. When supper was lacking with a smooth stone
he could knock down a bird on a branch at forty paces.

He heard the thrumming of the BMW motorcycle coming down
the dusty road. He knew that one would be first. He knew them
all, the *walad el-mita*, the Children of Death on the hill.

Where the road turned sharply he waited. The big machine with
its two jutting cylinders came hurrying down the path. The soldier
was wearing his green flying suit, he was a pilot. Hasan gripped
the leather between finger and thumb, the twin lengths of elastic
stretched back to his ear.

The aviator had to bring the machine almost to a halt to negotiate
the bend. Hasan let him have the stone full in the face from a range
of ten feet. The bike jerked forward, riderless, and rolled into the
bushes, where it fell, thumping steadily, on to its side.

Hasan ran out and dragged the dead man into the undergrowth,
where he stripped him of his Uzi and ammunition. His heart was
pounding with joy.

'*Alhamdullah*,' he whispered to himself.

The bike stopped thudding, and he could hear the revving of an
engine coming. A red Volvo came drifting round the bend. Dust
puffed up from the tyres as the driver slowed for the corner. It was
packed with men in army uniforms.

Hasan stood up in the bushes, almost close enough to touch the
car, and emptied the magazine into it.

By the time he had got the bloody weapons out others had arrived,
others of the *sumud*, those who had held fast so long. Some had
knives, some mattocks, some improvised wire nooses. Now they
had guns.

They went up the hill to where the rest of the *walad el-mita*
were, slipping through the olive and citrus groves their fathers and
grandfathers had owned.

The blood was sticky on Hasan's hands.

'*Alhamdullah*,' he whispered in joy. 'Praised be the Lord.'

Saul Ben-Levi stopped outside his office in a screech of tyres.
He jumped out, and Hussein, the Arab doorman, held the door
wide for him. He ran in and went up the stairs two at a time.
In his office he kept his uniform on a hanger. Like tens of
thousands of reservists all over Israel, he changed as quickly

as he could from his civilian lawyer's suit into his Air Force
uniform.

Still buttoning up his jacket he went back down the stairs. The
door was shut, the lobby empty. He paid little heed, shrugging the
door aside and going out on to the street.

His car wasn't there.

Furiously, he looked left and right.

Yes *there* it was.

Hussein, the doorman was sitting in the driver's seat, the engine
revving.

In the second that he stood there, trying to come to terms with the
fact that his doorman had somehow stolen his car, Hussein dropped
the clutch and the Volvo shot towards him, tyres screeching, its
engine howling.

He threw himself desperately to one side, felt its wind, felt a
thump as his foot caught some part of the bodywork. Hussein
slammed on the brakes and crashed it into reverse. As Saul
crawled to his hands and knees, all the breath knocked out of
him the big car hurtled back towards him. He had no time
to rise, he rolled over and over in the road, frantically trying
to escape.

Hussein swung the wheel violently, the front of the car swinging
like a giant metal club. It caught Saul as he was rising and flung him
across the street. He shoved himself to his feet as he heard the gears
engage and ran for the safety of his office, the rising scream of the
engine in his ears.

He fell through the door and his legs kept pumping, tumbling
and falling through the lobby. With a bang like a bomb going off
the Volvo smashed through the brick and plate glass behind him,
burying itself in the wall.

Saul scrambled on hands and knees up the stairs and heard
Hussein scream as he came out of the car.

'*Itbahu al-yahud!*'

He made his desk as Hussein came through the door. He had a
meat cleaver in his hand. Saul had the drawer open and his pistol
in his hand, he shot him until there were no more bullets left in the
gun. He collapsed into his chair, staring wild-eyed at the man he had
just killed, his chest heaving, blood streaming from cuts and grazes
all over his body, his ironed and creased uniform torn, stained and
bloodied.

Fifty thousand Palestinians left the Gaza strip every day to work in Israel. They flooded out before dawn to go to their jobs, or to stand in the places they called the slave markets, where they waited for Jews to offer them work. In the evening they came home. In between that time the traffic was slack and the border police at the wide Erez barrier had little to do.

The reservist could not believe his eyes when he saw the horde of ramshackle buses, cars and converted *Bazbena* gypsy cabs coming towards him. They all bore flags and scarves and pieces of cloth of red and white and green and black, the Palestine flag. He began shooting when it was too late, and they ran him down. They killed the policemen, took the pistols and rifles, and the machine gun out of the watchtower and poured towards Tel Aviv.

On television the frantic news programme was abruptly cut off. Rabbi Weiss was shown, standing in a studio without backdrop. He had his blue and white knitted *yarmulke* on his head, a Bible in one hand and an Uzi in the other.

'*Citizens of Israel*,' he yelled, and out on the street they could hear his voice coming from every window. 'The Arabs are killing our soldiers as they go to defend our Holy Land. Your son, your husband may be dead, may be in danger. The Arabs are coming to rape the women, to kill the children.'

His voice dropped, and everywhere men and women leaned forward to hear what he had to say.

'God is coming. Let us make his home clean for him. Redeem, O Israel.'

Then his voice rose once again to a howl.

'*Kill them*. An Arab on the street is on his way to rape a Jewish woman, to kill a soldier. Redeeem! Redeem! *Kill them. Kill the Arabs.*'

The streets were filled with swirling mobs, yelling the slogan that came most easily from the tongue.

'*Kill the Arabs. Kill the Arabs.*'

They found an old forty-eighter, an Arab with Israeli citizenship, a group of them who'd spilled out of a big reception hall on the Ben-Zvi road. He couldn't move fast and enough they tore him apart on the very street.

Then a strange convoy came hurtling by, ramshackle old vehicles a Jew wouldn't be seen dead in; some of them screeched to a halt when they saw the group of blood-stained businessmen and their wives, and they poured out of the old buses and off the trucks, dressed in ragged black trousers and dirty white shirts, in their hands spades and mattocks and kitchen knives and stained *keffiyehs* on their heads – and they howled the words that came most easily to their lips.

'*Itbahu al-yahud*. Slaughter the Jews. *Itbahu al-yahud*.'

They hacked them all into lumps of meat scattered on the gore-spattered street.

Looking out of the second floor window were the men from Gaza who worked the reception hall. When they saw what their brothers and sisters were doing the fear of years left them. They rushed the owner, rich and fat behind his bar, and they threw him through the window. They set the building alight, and went out on to the street.

Through the window the three men could see the smoke rising. The thick column from the ruins of the burning Mosque had been joined by numerous other fires as the Arabs torched Jewish properties in the West.

'Are you getting your men on the street?' Shahak asked irritably. 'Wait much longer and there won't be much of the city left.'

'We're deploying,' said the tall man. He wore the insignia of chief of staff of the IDF, he was Ehud Yoram.

'Shoot to kill.'

Levinger was listening on the phone.

'Okay,' he said, and put it down. 'They have Hamouda safe. All right, you two had better tell me what we should do.'

'It's war whatever we do,' Shahak said shortly. 'You don't imagine we can have most of their leaders blown up in Islam's third holiest site without them doing something about it.'

Yoram nodded sombrely.

'Since it's war, the only thing that makes sense is to win it as quickly as possible,' Shahak continued.

'The Syrians are the most immediate threat,' said Yoram. 'The Air Force has contingency plans to take out their air defences and aircraft. If we begin this afternoon then within 36 hours our aircraft will be ready to support the ground forces. Our mobilization is faster than theirs, our reserves will be with their units and we can go ahead and smash the Syrians before we have any trouble from the others. If the Egyptians mobilize we'll be in time to cut them to pieces in Sinai, and swat the Jordanians too.'

Levinger looked depressed. 'Very well. There is no time to waste. Let it be done. Call a meeting of the general staff.'

The MiG-25M flying at 80,000 feet over the Mediterranean had been designed to intercept and shoot down the proposed American B-70 Mach 3 strategic bomber. That vast machine was never put into production, but the MiG-25 was, along with the missile it would have used, the enormous AA-6 *Acrid* air-to-air missile. Two modified versions of these were clasped under its wings.

The MiG-25, what NATO had called Foxbat, was a pig to fly, hard to get up to speed, and even harder to maintain there. The Syrian colonel flying it had nursed it like a baby all the way to 80,000 feet. The Mach-meter showed 2.4. He eased the nose down, accelerating to Mach 3.2 for a loss of 20,000 feet. Then he pulled back on the stick, zoom-climbing at full afterburner. At 110,000 feet, ten miles into the stratosphere, he ignited the two *Acrid* missiles.

Seconds later the twin Tumanskii R-31 turbojets flamed out and the great interceptor tumbled out of the sky. It took Mustapha Jundi 60,000 feet to re-ignite them, by which time the missiles had performed their task.

As he landed back at the Nayrab air base in Northern Syria a Syrian Tupolev transport was coming in over the Mediterranean to Damascus. Under its wings were four RPVs, slender-bodied, delta-winged. Made from composites and powered by a single turbofan, they were transparent to radar. One after the other, the transport released them as it descended from 35,000 feet to its base, and they began to fly, cruising slowly up in the cold air holding racetrack patterns, waiting.

Saul Ben-Levi staggered through the door of the operations room. Through the window he could see the fuel bowsers and armament trucks and dollies preparing the sleek F-16 fighters. The tyre-streaked white concrete of the runways and taxiways shimmered in the heat.

The duty officer turned to look at him, grim-faced.

'What happened to you?'

'My doorman tried to kill me! He tried to run me over with my own car! What the fuck is going on?'

'You got lucky,' the man said savagely. 'The Arabs have killed as many of our boys as they can get at. You can throw away that uniform. Go put on your flight suit and go to briefing. We need everyone who's qualified up in the air.'

'Another war . . .,' Saul said, in disbelief.
'Let's make it the last. Let's slaughter the bastards forever.'

Luigi Riva fitted in. The tourists lining the beach along Hayarkon
had come for the sun and a good time, not to have anything to do
with the political goings-on up in Jerusalem. Luigi had got off the
Alitalia 737 at Lod and caught a taxi straight to the Carlton. He had
a room high up on the eighteenth floor, at his own request, looking
out over the city. He was a fan of loud rock music, as befitted a young
man, and spent his evenings in the clubs on Dizengoff. When in need
of a fix he turned on his own big ghetto blaster, that he had brought
with him. He gave no trouble to anyone, and the management were
glad to have him and the lire he spent.

Like the other tourists he quickly realized that the natives –
both Jew and Arab – were suddenly more than restless, and the
beaches cleared as they ran for the shelter of their hotels. From
his eighteenth-floor balcony he had a clear view over the city. He
saw the numerous thin columns of smoke spring up as buildings
were set afire, saw a mob capture an Arab down near the Hilton
and murder him.

He went inside, and for the third time that day tuned his powerful
ghetto blaster to the frequency he had been given and memorized.
He had the machine plugged into the mains. He was going to need
the power.

There was a scraping of chairs, and a shuffling of papers, the
clink of a glass being filled with water. Then he heard the voice of
the prime minister of Israel.

'We all know why we're here,' said Levinger. He took his papers
from the famous old briefcase on the table in front of him. 'Shall
we begin?'

The senior commanders of the IDF seated around the table
together with Levinger and Shahak were a unique breed. Every
single one had begun his career as a private soldier or pilot, an
official policy weighting combat experience as the most important
criterion for promotion meant that as a group they had more
personal experience of fighting than any other general staff in
the world. Frequent wars, involving accelerated promotion for
the survivors and high casualties among officers because of the
other official policy of leading from the front, meant that they
were all also young, all in their forties. The IDF had consumed
their entire lives, they knew nothing outside war, and planning for

war. If they had to do it, they could do it faster than anyone else in the world.

They sat around the long oval table in the house in Kirya where their predecessors had engaged in the same task. Here had sat David Ben-Gurion and Yigael Yadin, Golda Meir and Moshe Dayan, Menachem Begin and Ariel Sharon. There were very few of them. Fearsome casualties and rigorous selection process had left a mere twenty men, fourteen regulars and six major reserve commanders, who were responsible for wielding the sword of David under the ultimate authority of Levinger and Shahak.

'We expect to attain strategic surprise over the Syrians,' said Yoram, the chief of staff. 'A factor in our favour is that as is traditional, President Hamouda has invested ultimate control over almost everything in his own person. His generals will not start a war without instructions from him, and as you know, he is our guest, so to speak. Aman informs me that their intelligence is that while the Syrians are buzzing like a hive of bees they are not making preparations for an attack on our eastern front.

'We will use our air force and regular army as a first echelon. We expect to decisively defeat the Syrian forces in about six to eight days. We will destroy approximately eighty per cent of her armed forces and occupy all major bases. What we do after that will be up to you, Mr Prime Minister. You want to say anything, Yosi?'

'The air force will begin operations this afternoon,' the Air Force commander said. 'We will attack the Syrian air defence assets and will be able to support the ground forces to only a limited extent for the first 36 hours. After that, we are all yours. Menachem?'

'Thirty-six hours from now the second-line reserves will be in their pre-prepared positions along the Jordan valley and in the Golan Heights,' said Menachem Or, in charge of the Northern Command. 'We plan to concentrate our armour into "mailed fists" and thrust through Kuneitra and up the Bekaa in Plan Joshua.'

'Casualties should be low,' said Yoram. 'Around 2,000. We can interdict any attempts by the other Arab states to aid the Syrians, and plan to acquiesce with whatever peace initiative the UN throws up only after we have conclusively destroyed the Syrian capacity to wage war.'

Yosi Barak, commander of the air force, glanced at the old Breitling he wore.

'The first wave's going in now,' he said.

On the eighteenth floor of the Carlton Hotel, Mohammed al-Aswad, registered under the name of Luigi Riva, extended the long aerial of his ghetto blaster. He re-tuned it to a second frequency, and depressed the 'play' button.

Powered by the electricity supply of the hotel a strong signal was emitted from the electronics concealed within the shell of the machine. Fifty miles away the four steadily circling RPVs responded to its call. Dropping their noses, they dived south.

Much closer, on the eastern side of town, a relay within the body of Levinger's briefcase silently closed under the instructions of the signal from al-Aswad, and its beacon began to transmit. The approaching robotic aircraft sensed its beam, and locked on.

Shahak's stomach was churning. It was always the same when the war was ready. He had hoped to make it through the meeting, but the pressure within his intestine was imperative. He pushed back his chair.

'Excuse me a moment,' he said. Yoram, chief of staff grinned, not unsympathetically.

'Tummy trouble, Shelesh?'

'Uhuh,' said Shahak, on his way to the door.

'It's always the same with him,' Yoram grinned to the others. 'I was in his *Ugdah* at Yom Kippur and we were ready to move out against the Egyptians, only no General! Five minutes later he came hurrying out of the desert, spade in hand!'

'I only have to go once,' said Shahak. 'Then I'm good the whole war.'

They laughed, anxious to have anything to laugh about, and he hurried down the long corridor. For reasons best known to the architect, the lavatory was on the other side of the building from the cabinet room.

The closet was small, built for the older generation, and he was big and burly. In the confined space he bent with difficulty to pull his trousers up from around his ankles and belt them. There was an enormous explosion, and the door blew into his face.

The battle was going to be fought in four distinct stages. Firstly, the enemy forces had to be found, then identified and tracked. The idea of this was to ascertain where he was going to attack, with what, and when. Since they knew the enemy well, and knew perfectly well what their own major assets were this was more a question of watching to see the attack building up, which confirmed when.

The second stage involved evaluating the threat posed by the attack, and deciding what to do about it. The third stage put the decision into effect by selecting the appropriate weapons and firing them at the enemy.

The final stage meant assessing the damage done to the enemy by reconnaissance to determine whether his forces had been made ineffective. If they had not, one repeated steps one to three until they were.

The first stage was carried out by military intelligence, using a variety of sensors. Prior to the attack Aman, Israeli military intelligence, had identified the mix of anti-aircraft artillery and surface-to-air missiles that defended the three major Syrian air bases, using the sophisticated sensors of their dedicated satellite, and at a shorter range, stealthy drone aircraft – RPVs – equipped with both television and radar sensors. Since the aim of military intelligence was to provide information about the Syrian forces in real-time these RPVs were despatched as the operation began. The information they received was transmitted to a E2C Hawkeye airborne warning and control aircraft by secure data link.

The three Hawkeyes running things were protected by having them orbit well away from the battle area off the coast. In addition they had the electronic armour afforded by the dedicated Boeing E3A – a 707 equipped for electronic intelligence and countermeasures, as well as the more physical protection of F-15 fighters equipped with Sparrow and Sidewinder missiles and 20mm cannon.

The attack began with the use of Mastiff and Scout RPVs emitting the signals of manned attack aircraft to get the Syrians to switch on their missile-tracking radars. These signals were relayed to the Hawkeyes and to the E3A and analysed by the crews on board.

Behind the RPVs came the first wave of F-4 Phantoms, using jamming radars to blind the Syrian missile-tracking radars and flares and chaff. Behind them the F-4s were to take out the Russian-built self-propelled anti-aircraft guns and the F-16s carrying their Shrike anti-radiation missiles to destroy the radar-tracking vans. Behind them came the waves of Kfirs with both smart and slick iron bombs. The Israelis had their entire complement of front-line aircraft in the air that afternoon.

The enemy forces had been found, identified and tracked. For the first time, the Syrians knew. The Syrians knew where the Israelis were going to attack, with what, and when. The threat posed by them had been evaluated, and the decisions as to what to do about it made. The appropriate weapons had been selected. It was only a question of firing them at the enemy.

The first weapons used were the two modified *Acrid* air-to-air missiles fired by the MiG-25M of Colonel Mustapha Jundi. The dedicated satellite of Israel, based on the technology of the US KH-11, followed an elliptical polar orbit, as was the American way. They called it *Ofek*, meaning Horizon. Shahak had moved it back, the planned attack on the Libyan Sukhoi squadron was now a side issue, to be taken care of after the war was won. It passed over Syria east of Damascus, on its way over Jordan and peer deep into Iraq the proximity fuses of the two missiles ignited the warheads. The masses of delicate circuitry, lenses and mirrors became a collection of loosely-connected, multi-million-dollar orbiting junk in a matter of a few nano-seconds.

The first shot of the battle had been fired. The enemy commander in his airborne $C^3$ command control and communications post was not yet aware of it, as the intelligence provided by the satellite was being handled by Aman on the ground. For his real-time surveillance he was reliant on his RPVs, now over the target airfields.

The second group of weapons selected were the four RPVs released by the Syrian Tupolev as it descended towards Damascus. Each had a warhead of 500lb of explosive. It was not large, but since the delta-winged pilotless aircraft were guided to their target with such precision that they came through the window, this was irrelevant.

The high command of Israel had been taken out, but the airborne commander still did not know it. The defences of the airfield were beginning to burn as the attack developed momentum. As he watched, he saw Syrian attack aircraft begin to creep out of their hardened sheds. As they manoeuvred down the taxiways he reckoned he could count over 120 MiG-27Ms and Sukhoi-25K ground attack aircraft, the hardpoints of their wings hung with laser-guided glide bombs and cluster-bombs.

The F-4s were starting to chew through the ZSU self-propelled anti-aircraft guns. Behind them were the F-16s and their Shrike missiles. The Kfirs, laden with similar weaponry as the Syrian attack aircraft, should arrive just in time, he thought.

Like most of his fellow officers, General Mordechai Aharon had spent time in the USA. Crouched over his battery of VDUs and television screens in the orbiting E3A he grinned delightedly. It was a commander's dream to surprise his enemy in the act of moving out of barracks.

'It's going to be like the Fourth of July down there,' he murmured.

According to the plan of battle decided upon by Hamouda and his commanders it was now time to launch the third set of selected weapons. The sea below boiled white as strange rafts like enormous barges rose to the surface. They were grouped together like a daisy. Floating on the surface, the centre raft opened its roof. In the sky to the north were aircraft radiating vast amounts of electronic energy as they controlled the battle beginning to rage inside Syria. Control signals, electronic counter-measures, radar emissions, spoof signals, commands poured from the E3A and the orbiting Hawkeyes in a deafening electronic cacophony. To the sensors looking at them from the barge, they were as bright as searchlights. Other barges lay around the command centre like petals of the daisy. They were fitted with huge protective bins in the Soviet manner.

Explosive charges blew the lids of the bins from them, and the tips of the missiles inside gleamed in the sunlight.

Narrow, intense laser beams sprang from the command barge, stabbing through the air to paint the E3A and its three Hawkeyes to the north. They were coded $CO_2$ guidance lasers. They were locked on to the four aircraft, unjammable. The barges around the control centre were wreathed in gushing white smoke as they fired their enormous nine-metre missiles, in salvos. Cruciform-winged, quadruple-boosters blazing fire, the SA-4s climbed north.

For the first time Mordechai Aharaon knew that he was under attack, as the laser warning receivers howled. The pilot of the E3A was an old F-4 jock, he had been fired at by missiles before. He banked the big Boeing steeply, looking for the approaching SAMs.

In the clear air he could see the blazing red dots of the ramjets rising to meet him. They were big bastards. As he was being illuminated by laser the ECM equipment behind him was of no value. The only way to escape them was by means of violent, high-G manouevres, more easily performed in a fighter than an aircraft originally built to carry airline passengers.

He waited until the last moment. At a speed in excess of Mach 2.5 the ability of a missile to make its own last-second corrections to its course was limited. In an eighty degree bank he hauled on the yoke, the stall warner howling, and stick shaker shuddering in his hands. There was a tremendous blow as the proximity fused warhead exploded, and then he was rolling it hard back the other way, nose down, diving for airspeed, another blazing torch filling the screen, and he pulled hard. A second vast impact smacked into the airframe.

The target was rolling left. The third missile exploded directly beneath it, where the wings joined the fuselage, and pieces of alloy rained down into the Mediterranean like chaff.

At one hundred feet and 500 knots Saul felt as though he was flying through a tunnel. There was a segment a mere fifteen degrees wide to the front of his F-16 that was clear, everything else was a sandy blur.

'Aleph two six.'

It was his Hawkeye controller.

'Two six,' he affirmed.

'Twelve miles from target. Expose.'

Saul twitched his right hand and the F-16 popped up five hundred feet into the air. The RWR blared, and he took the bearing of the Syrian missile-tracking radar as he eased back down into the safety of the shallow valley.

'Got it,' he said laconically. He armed one of the Shrike anti-radiation missiles hung under his wings.

On the other side of the craggy brown hills were the arrayed missile batteries and their radars. He broke cover fast, climbing steeply and half-rolling. The RWR blared again and he squeezed the pickle button, launching the Shrike into a high trajectory using the 'over the shoulder' manoeuvre devised for the task and pulling the F-16 into a half-loop to bring it back down into the valley hurrying back in the opposite direction, weaving all the way until the radar warning receiver went quiet.

'Aleph two six is ready for trade,' he said. His radio was silent.

'Aleph two six.' He checked his radios for some battle damage he might not have noticed, but the frequency numbers shone brightly in their windows. He changed channels to talk to the boss upstairs in the E3A.

'Aleph two six.'

He entered a racetrack holding pattern while he attempted to find a controller. He waited as long as he could without success. The area was probably becoming unsafe. Wondering what had gone wrong – whether it was his own F-16 or the complex, highly-coordinated attack itself that had fallen apart – he set course home for Ramat David, his home base.

In the clear air, he saw it forty miles away. The column of black smoke roiled tens of thousands of feet into the air.

He called approach control and it was dead. The tower was dead.

Standard instructions were to divert to his secondary dispersed

base at Araba, so he altered course, checking his stores control
panel as he did so. He still had one Shrike hung under the wing
together with two Sidewinders on the wingtips and full ammunition
for his M61A1 20mm cannon. He changed frequencies again.

'Araba approach, this is Aleph two six out of Ramat David, twenty
miles out for landing.'

'Negative, negative Aleph two six,' an agitated voice crashed into
his headphones. 'We got nearly 150 airplanes here already. Guys are
landing on the taxiways. Divert to Lohamei Hagetaot.'

Saul snapped a glance at his fuel state. He was still a long way
off from running out.

'Lohamei Hagetaot, Roger,' he said. He knew the field, a small
training base up towards the Lebanese border, close by the coast.
Looking out through the clear bubble canopy from three thousand
feet as he changed course again he saw the Araba field packed
with fighters – F-15s, F-16s, F-4s, Kfirs. They were squeezed
in everywhere, it was going to be a nightmare refuelling and
rearming.

*What the hell are those.*

The sleek MiG-27s that followed the wave of Sukhoi Su-25s
skimming over the ground were like a shoal of deadly fish moving
together.

He half-rolled, diving back the way he had come. There were
over 60 aircraft in the strike formation.

'Araba approach, 60 plus Syrians coming at you. Ten miles to the
north-west.'

There was no reply. It was all wrong. What was *happening*?
With full afterburner he was catching the formation up fast.
He selected his first target, one of the heavily-laden MiG-27s.
The tone sounded in his ears as the Sidewinder locked on, and
he squeezed the pickle button. Then the next. The two missiles
streaked from his wingtips in long stems of fire, and the brown
land below blossomed into brilliant gouts of flame as they found
their targets.

He pulled up, barrel-rolling the F-16 to make a pass along the
line of Su-25s leading the attack. Balls of white light were pouring
from their tail dispensers as they scattered flares. Pieces flew off the
brown and grey Sukhoi in his gunsight but it still continued to fly.
The 25 was built to take damage. The missiles hissed from under
its wings.

He was hanging under a parachute.

*What had happened . . . ?*

Something was burning over there, it had set alight to an orange grove. He thought it might be his F-16.

The parachute turned him round as he floated down. Araba was burning. A myriad of explosions sent coloured fire arcing high into the air.

It looked like the Fourth of July.

He hung from his harness and screamed out at the heavens in his agony.

*'Lord, Lord, why have you forsaken us?'*

# PART XXII

W HEN Jacob opened the door the first thing that he saw was Hamouda, standing with his back to him. He was looking out of the window into the dusk falling over Tel Aviv, to the south.

'We're keeping you here,' he said. The toe of his shoe caught on the carpet and he tottered, holding onto a table to keep his balance. He felt very tired and old, he was unwell.

'I am in Palestine,' said Hamouda pleasantly. 'I have no plans to leave at all. I am simply waiting for my countrymen to join me. May I ask what this comfortable place is?'

'It is the *midrasha*, officially the prime minister's summer residence,' Jacob said wearily. 'Mossad uses it as their training school. It's very secure, which is why we thought it would be best for you to be here. You would not last long, on the street.'

'And what is over there, where all the smoke was?' Hamouda asked innocently.

'That is Kirya. Where you were looking. You know what that is, and what happened to it. They're all dead, Hamouda.'

'I have enjoyed the view this afternoon,' Hamouda agreed.

'Why?' Jacob asked. 'Why? We were going to give you what you wanted.'

'Sharing something with Israelis is not what we wanted.'

'What *do* you want?'

'Am I speaking to the new prime minister?' Hamouda enquired courteously.

'Yes. I am the senior minister left.'

'Then you may come to discuss terms with me whenever you want. I shall not be going anywhere.'

Jacob was suddenly angry, the fury of betrayal penetrating the fog of shock that had enveloped him.

'We shall win the war first,' he snarled. 'Then I'll come and tell you what we're going to do with you.'

'Win the war?' Hamouda said musingly. 'No, Jacob. Not this time. This is the Battle of Hattin. This time, *we* get to decide.'

Jacob went out. The limousine was waiting for him, and he got into the back.

'Where to, boss?' asked the young driver. It was his grandson, Yitzhak.

'The command post. Metzada.'

The Lincoln hissed into the darkness, just the twirling blue lights of the police motorcyclists ahead of them. The underground command centre was named after the Herodian fortress, and protected by metres-deep ferro-concrete.

'Arafat sat there,' said the driver. 'I drove him to Jerusalem. He offered me a job, when the Palestinians came back.'

'Well, they won't come back now, not for a very long time,' Jacob said grimly. 'And we all have different jobs to do.'

'Yeah,' said Yitzhak. 'I'm off to mine, when I've taken you. I'm recon man, I find out what's ahead.'

Jacob smiled, very faintly.

'If you find out, I wish that you'd tell me.'

The great stone entrance to the tunnel was marked with an inscription, carved deep in the rock. METZADA SHALL NOT FALL AGAIN. They went through and the armoured doors hissed shut behind them. Jacob had a sudden sense of being inside the mountain at Dora, marching in to build the German rockets, and he shivered, involuntarily.

The Lincoln came to a soft halt where they were waiting for him.

'Best of luck with the war, boss,' said Yitzhak.

'Yes,' he said. 'You too.'

The tunnels were lit and air-conditioned, but somehow he felt the cold rock behind them. He was taken into a long room, a commander's room with a long table down the middle, with a situation screen lit upon the wall, and battery of telephones at one end. When he turned around, he was alone. He stood at the head of the table, his hands shaking. He rested them on the wood of the table and tried to gather together his whirling thoughts to take charge.

'It's all right, Jacob,' said a voice. 'You aren't going to have to do it.'

He turned, and Shahak was standing in the doorway. The defence minister was in army uniform. Bloodshot eyes looked out from within a frame of bandage and sticking plaster, one arm was in a sling, the hand encased in plaster.

'They didn't get me,' he said.

Jacob pulled out one of the chairs, and sat down, his legs weak. He was aware most of all of an overwhelming sense of relief.

'Glad?' Shahak asked.

'Yes,' he admitted.

'Me, too,' Shahak said cruelly. 'If you can start a major war with a peace treaty, I'd hate to think what you could make from running the conflict.'

'I'll go, then. You will be busy. I saw Hamouda.'

'I know.'

Shahak had sat down next to him, wincing with the pain from his injuries.

'I wanted him to believe that you were in charge, as he meant you to be.'

'Why?'

'With *taboulah*, with stratagems shall ye wage war. And I want you to do something.'

'Of course,' Jacob said humbly. 'What can I do?'

'We committed the ultimate sin. We became predictable. Hamouda knew what we would do. This afternoon for the loss of a quarter of his own aircraft Hamouda has destroyed two-thirds of our Air Force. And even worse, pilots. It takes two years to make a combat pilot, and this war is not going to last that long. I want you to go to Washington. We need new aeroplanes, and new pilots. They'll give you a list of our guys over there, *yordim*, who are ex-IAF. You know, there are about a million Israelis out there. In the USA and the rest of the diaspora. *Yerida*. We're trying to track as many down as we can who aren't too old to get into a cockpit. But they'll need some retraining on whatever the Yanks give us. That's your task, Jacob. Planes, and pilots.'

'I'll go. I know all the right people over there.'

'I know you do,' said Shahak. 'That's the only reason I'm not sending you out to be point man on the Golan. Go on, then. I have a plane waiting for you at Lod.'

When Jacob had gone Shahak remained seated. His new commanders were waiting to come in. He picked up a phone.

'Shaul? This is Shahak. No, I'm not dead, I'm in charge. In the morning, I want you to get the Rabbi. Yes, that's right. Weiss. He's out at Kiryat Arba. Take a helicopter and bring him here first thing.'

## *Koach* Yanosh, The Golan Heights

The aluminium hull of the *Ta'gad* APC was burning like a torch. Artillery was starting to fall; with the shock of the explosions chunks of basalt and metal fragments of the shells were flying about. Yanosh Aviram pulled his head down inside the turret. The tanks of *Koach* Yanosh could be seen as clear as day at their firing positions silhouetted against the light of the bonfire raging in the dark behind them. The *koach* took its name from their commander; if Yanosh died it would become *Koach* Yair.

He got back onto the battalion net.

'This is the battalion commander. Artillery got the medevac *Ta'gad*. We still have a number of casualties on the Boster Ridge.'

'I'll send another.'

The gun of the far Centurion drooped, the turret was at a strange angle. If they were still there come the morning and the Syrians let up, he would try to pull it to the rear. He wished the medevac APC behind him would burn out. If the Syrians had their MiG-27s in the air it would attract them like wasps to jam. Where *was* the air force?

'*Yanosh* tanks in front of the *Ta'gad*,' he said on the *Koach* net. 'Deploy away from the light.'

The team of Centurions began to move, re-deploying about the undulating, rock-strewn ridge to get away from the glare. They moved forward into new positions with the ridge shielding them from the light, and once more they were hidden in shadow Yanosh ordered them all to shut down their engines.

Getting back down into the turret Yanosh swept the area with his thermal observation system. Avi's platoon was in Ayn-Vivon. The kibbutz was deserted. The Syrian artillery had pounded the area in depth and his night sight was filled with the glare from phosphorous fires. It was like trying to see through a rain-filled windscreen against the headlights of on-coming cars.

Something was moving.

'Avi, are your tanks shut down? There is something moving there.'

He spoke on the tank intercom. 'Gunner, load sabot.'

'I am trying to see. The phosphorus is obscuring my view.'

Yanosh got on to the battalion net.

'Zakar, this is the battalion commander,' he said, calling the fire direction centre in the gun line to the rear. 'I want illumination four hundred yards north of the kibbutz.'

'Twenty seconds, Yanosh.'

'All *Koach* Yanosh tanks, there is something moving in front of the kibbutz. Illumination in ten seconds.'

The flares burst brilliantly, hanging from their parachutes. The slope behind the blinding phosphorus was covered with moving vehicles. More were pouring over the far ridge.

'T-72s and infantry. *Esh*. Fire. Fire at will.'

There was an immense explosion as Gideon, the gunner, fired. Standing up in the turret the muzzle flash blinded Yanosh momentarily. Dust was in his eyes and he wiped them as he issued commands over the net.

'Get the paras into position, the enemy has infantry support.'

At close range, the dismounted infantrymen were deadly with their RPG-22 anti-tank rockets.

As he was calling for artillery he saw the *Nag'machs* spilling out the paratroops who had been waiting in their hides. They were armed with Galil assault rifles and TOW missiles. Hull down, taking advantage of their ability to depress their barrels to 9 degrees, the Centurions were firing at the high rate the crews of *Heyl Shirion* had made famous. Fires were erupting on the slope. In the light of the falling flares he saw two Mil helicopters flying away from the high ground towards Tel Hermonit. They vanished into the darkness and suddenly a fresh wave of flares burst over them.

'*Zakar, this is Yanosh. You're illuminating us.*'

'We're firing commander, as ordered.'

Yanosh heard the first MiG as it screamed above the swaying flares, saw the cluster bombs discarding their casings, scattering their submunitions along the ridge as he scrambled down into the turret. A rain of blows slammed into the tank as though it were being attacked by men wielding sledgehammers.

'*The sight's gone*,' Gideon screamed.

'Reversionary mode,' said Yanosh. 'Aim visually.'

'I can't see shit through all this dust.'

The firing of the heavy armament was kicking up huge clouds of dust.

'Driver, prepare to jockey.'

Yanosh stuck his head out of the turret again. The paratroops had been caught in the open, the slope now covered with their bodies. The Centurion next to him erupted into flames. From the turret hatch a blazing figure came tumbling, falling to the ground, where he ran like a madman among the rocks, lighting them with his passage.

He looked north toward Tel Hermonit, where the Mils had landed. A shaft of fire brighter than the sun brushed his eyes and the battle in front of him vanished.

He was trained. In *Heyl Shirion*, you fought to the last.

'All *Koach* Yanosh tanks, beware of laser. Get into cover if you can. Yair, this is the commander. I am blind. Take over command.'

The net was silent.

'Driver, we are being illuminated by laser from the north. Get behind rocks if you can. Elan, this is the battalion commander, I am blind. Take over command.'

'Roger, Yanosh. The fighting is heavy here. Have your tank take you to the rear.'

'Disregard that,' Yanosh said over the intercom. 'Gideon, assume command of the tank. Keep fighting.'

Yanosh heard, but did not see the second wave of MiG-27s. The gliding bombs came out of the darkness, seeking the big splashes of laser radiation that marked the frantically-moving tanks below, their fins moving effortlessly as they tracked the moving beams.

Yanosh's Centurion slammed to a halt. His ears rang, blood was in his mouth. Fire licked about him as Gideon shoved him up out of the turret. The air was filled with the screaming of shells and of men, the roar of burning machines. The air was suffocating, made up of diesel and explosive and blood. There was the heavy grinding of Soviet-built tanks as they pushed through the wreck of the battalion, heading into Israel.

The sea boiled white as they came to the surface. The long, clamshell casings burst apart and the boosters turned the night to day as they blasted the missiles clear of the waves. At cruise speed and altitude they fell away, sinking to the bottom like the protective casings, and it was as if they had never been.

The missiles came over the coast at 50 feet, cruising at 300 knots, their ducted turbofan engines almost silent. To their sensors the environment ahead of them was a blaze of electronic signposts telling them where to go, and they used them to update their INS inertial navigation systems on their way to their pre-programmed destinations. Over there the transmission tower of the Israel Broadcasting Authority, to the other side the glide slope at Lod airport, ahead the Ramallah VOR. Electrons racing around their circuits made the correct conclusions, noted as the bearings changed, and the machines knew where they were.

They were all the same, except in what they carried. The two that went to Beersheva split the dusty, sleeping town between them. They popped up on approach to 500 feet. Over the outskirts of town the outer casings of the missiles were discarded in flight, displaying the hundreds of submunitions arrayed around their bodies like nuggets of sweetcorn on a cob. As they flew over the town the missiles emitted a high-pitched, demented shriek. The little cluster bombs blew off in sequence, scattering over a wide area. As they began to fall they exploded, covering the whole town with a blanket of aerosol vapour.

Ruth Ben-Levi awoke. There was a scent of oranges in her nostrils, which she did not fully understand, and a screaming and a sobbing in her ears, which she did. In the KZ there were many reasons for fear, all justified. She pushed back the sheet of the cot and dressed in her hospital smock went out of the room. In the corridor outside a girl was scrabbling frantically on the ground, attempting to burrow into the very carpet. Ruth recognized her, it was the Russian girl. She screamed constantly in terror.

The old woman bent down, and taking her by the elbow helped her up. The young nurse hid her face in her hands against the things of horror all around her. Ruth pulled her into the room, where only a night light burned, then sat her down by the wall.

'You are safe here,' she whispered in her ear. 'The Germans will not find you.'

The girl pulled up her knees like a foetus, wrapped her head with her arms, still sobbing.

Ruth went out into the corridor. The hospital was filled with the screams of men and women burning in a hell. She moved along, looking for others to save. In the house of the mad, only the madwoman was sane.

The wings that were pinned to the uniforms hanging by the beds in the flying school's dormitory were new. The class was passing out early. In the morning the uniforms would be put away in the closet, and their green flight suits put on. Their elder brothers were dead, they were to pick up the sword of David.

The missile covered the whole length of the sleeping blocks in a single pass, the chemical that floated down had no smell.

*        *        *

The voice of God awoke Rabbi Weiss. The Lord spoke to him in his house next to the temple, inside the compound, and he awoke. Pale moonlight from the eyes of God lit up the room, and Weiss listened as the Almighty told him what was to be done.

He dressed, picking up his M16 automatic rifle, and went outside to his pickup. He was strangely unafraid. He drove down, unlocking the gates in the wire fence then making them secure once he was through.

The Lord told him where to go. He parked the pickup down in the olive grove, where the settlers did not normally go. On the hill was the Arab village.

He got out of the vehicle. Nearby, a stream gurgled through the rocks. He stood in the quiet, waiting. In the quiet of the night he heard something coming in the air, a soft, hoarse, mechanical rasp. It grew in intensity, rising to a peak before passing by. He saw something against the white of the moonlit clouds, whipping through the air like a great bird.

It was quiet after the machine had gone. Slowly, the night gave way to the approaching dawn. Somewhere from the poor village he heard a cock crowing, then the soft rattle of a stone tumbling on the rocky path, the clink of metal.

The little stream slowed and widened into a pool. A young girl came down the path in the half darkness, pail in hand.

God instructed the Rabbi. His commands rang in his ears. As the girl bent to dip the bucket in the water Weiss came out of the dark bushes from behind her. He muffled her cries with a length of cloth as he held her down. He tied her limbs, and threw her into the back of the truck.

He made haste to carry his prize away, for the Lord's work would not wait.

In the gathering dawn the four-wheel drive raced along the dirt road and up onto the tarmac. The settlement of the righteous glowed from behind its wire fencing on the hilltop, as the first rays of the sun struck it.

No one came to open the gate. In the cab Weiss frowned, the gate should be manned as dawn broke. He got out of the cab. In the bed of the pickup the Arab girl looked up at him, her eyes wide with terror; her shawl had slipped away and glossy black hair tumbled about her face. Weiss suddenly remembered the one in Deir Yassin, so many years ago, and his breath quickened. He went to the gate, and as there was nobody there he unlocked it himself.

The holy settlement was quiet, and nothing moved as he drove in down the main street. The tower of the temple glowed in the morning sunlight as he parked outside. Leaving the girl in the truck he went to the nearest house, and let himself in, for the community had to gather to take part in the ritual he was to perform.

They were dead. They lay still in their beds, as though asleep, but they did not move.

He was not afraid. He knew, suddenly and completely, that the hand of God had moved in the night, to prepare the way for His coming. He had awoken His servant in order that he might be saved, had taken away the small flock in order to give him the greater part.

It was time, his hour, his day had come; the redemption of Israel was nigh. There were only the final rituals to be observed.

Weiss went out, and now the sun gazed upon him, flooding him with the warmth and approval of God. He carried the girl inside the temple, where he took off her clothes and laid her upon the altar.

'Nobody's answering.'

The pilot of the Huey glanced across at Shaul Shiloah as they sat next to each other, the turbine whining behind them. Through the windscreen they could see the fenced settlement below, and the huge Numbers 33 set upon the marked out helipad.

'Put her down, then,' said Shaul, and the pilot lowered the collective, letting the helicopter drift down as he circled on to approach.

He left the Huey behind him on the hard earth pad, whining softly, the long blades swinging above the canopy, and walked down towards the main street in the morning sun. Nothing moved.

'Hullo!'

He called out, his voice eching flatly from the breeze-block of the white-painted buildings. He saw a lizard on the dirt, green and grey, sunbathing. When he stamped his foot, it did not move; when he prodded it with his toe, he saw it was dead.

He was close to the squat, ugly temple with its gold 33 above the door when suddenly from within came a hideous, gargling shriek shattering the silence.

The doors of the temple were open and he crashed through into the circular interior. Close to the altar a fire burned bright in a gleaming brazier, upon the altar was the body of a young woman and bent over her was a figure in white robes. It started to turn and Shaul saw it was Weiss. Scarlet gore spattered him and he had a long, bloody knife in his hand.

He addressed Shaul.

'I am ready,' he declaimed fervently. 'The Lord's task is done, now let me go forth for His people. God asked but a lamb of Abraham, for His time was not yet come. Now He is ready, and I have sacrificed for Him his enemy.'

A glittering bowl was on the altar, Weiss took it and tipped its contents onto the glowing coals. Gouts of blood flew, spattering the marble floor, and harsh, acrid smoke rose crackling to the roof.

'I am ready to lead the people of Israel in their Holy War,' he howled.

## Tel Arad

Paunchy, balding men were gathering at the vast grey hangar outside the town. To the east past Masada lay Jordan, to the south Sinai then Egypt. The men with glasses and bad feet knew Sinai. They looked unlikely heroes, but once, when young and handsome, they had fought for six days in the grim sands down there – and won.

The doors were stiff. Other middle-aged men were arriving with toolkits in their hands. They all went in, with the young *Heyl Shirion* Lieutenant-Colonel from *Ugdat* Gideon who had summoned them from their places of work.

'You'll all be familiar with these,' he said as they looked at the lines of Centurion and Soviet-built T-55 tanks standing cold in rows.

'This is a museum, maybe, Colonel?' an old company commander from 1967 called out hopefully. There were some chuckles.

'Zahal doesn't throw away things that might be useful. Not tanks, and not men. There's been heavy fighting on the Golan, the Syrians had ten to one in some places and our boys have taken heavy casualties. The situation's stabilizing and we're preparing to counter-attack once the *miluimnicks* are mobilized. We're moving regular forces north – the 162nd Division – to take part in the attack. You're to hold the 162nd positions south of Sede Boqer. You'll be supported by elements of the Southern Command's reserve, and be commanded by staff from *Ugdat* Gideon.'

'Hey, Danny,' the company commander called.

A burly man who had done well from the Israeli desire to own Volvos turned from staring gloomily at a T-55.

'I'm having a Centurion,' he said. 'The Soviets made their tanks for little guys. What is it, Avraham?'

'You used to be slim, back then. You remember what you said, a few weeks ago? You said when the peace talks were done we ought to invite those guys we fought back in 67 to have a reunion with us.'

'Yeah, I remember that.'

Avraham Einan stared out past the guard wire. In the distance the grim wrinkled brows of the Jordanian mountains were just visible.

'They're coming,' he said.

A car that looked as though it had been in a war pulled up on the hard standing outside. The windows smashed and starred, its bodywork slashed and battered by repeated blows. A man got out, leaving the door half-open behind him. He walked over to them, dressed in a tanker's coverall. Danny Cohen watched him come and asked, 'What are you doing here?'

'I've come to get a tank,' said David.


## Ramat David AFB


The major limped. Hit by ground fire while bombing Beirut in 1982 he had ejected, only to float down among the people upon whom immediately prior to that he had been raining high explosive. The experience had very largely caused them to lose their sense of humour and they broke his legs in 17 places.

Saul limped too. He ached and was stiff all over from the effects of the ejector seat and his passage through an orange grove on his way to the ground.

They both shuffled to a halt as they inspected the shiny fighter in the hardened dispersal shed. From outside came the intermittent crump of delayed-fuse area-denial munitions going off. The F-16's paintwork was brand new, its alloys smooth and unmarked.

'This one they didn't get,' Major Geva said. 'The latest twenty F-16Ds arrived from the USA last week. This is yours. If, heaven forbid, you break it, we may even be able to give you another.'

'How's that?'

'We have a total of 34 F-16s of varying marks. We plan to assign two pilots to each to keep them in the air as much as possible. The Air Force currently has 66 pilots trained and current on the F-16, so there's one left over. Yesterday they got the guys who had been in the air on the ground – right here and at Araba, mainly, although all six major bases were hit as well as four other secondary fields where the aircraft had piled up. Some 300 pilots in the Reserve were murdered by Arabs yesterday. Before yesterday we'd lost under 50 aircraft in combat since 1948. Shot down 700 of theirs. The bastards knew they could never beat us in the air. They even murdered the kids in the training school last night . . . This fucking war's no accident, Saul. Someone had it all thought out in advance.'

Fitters and armourers were hauling in their yellow dollies laden with ordnance.

'The army's going in to smash the Syrians,' Geva said. 'We'll be supporting them. The engineers are clearing a path to get these out. It'll be three days before the runways are back in use – you'll have to take off from the road.'

# PART XXIII

## Metzada

THE underground command headquarters north of Tel Aviv took its name from the Herodian fortress overlooking the Dead Sea where the Zealot Jews had made their final stand in their rebellion against the Romans some 2,000 years before.

The call for Shahak came through after midnight, but he was still awake.

'Jacob. What do you have for me?'

'I've just come from the UN. Syria's Foreign Minister, al-Kawasme, has just finished addressing the Assembly. In order to send us a message, naturally. He claimed that the Arab peoples had demonstrated their ability to rain death upon Israel, they had inflicted terror upon them in kind for the terror inflicted upon the Arabs since 1948. they had executed the madmen of Kiryat Arba as retribution for the murders carried out by the Jews at Deir Yassin. Should Israel use any of the nuclear weapons she possesses against the Arabs in the course of this Holy War, then the Arabs will smother Israel with poison gas.'

'We found one of the missiles in the desert outside Beersheva. It's a sophisticated piece of equipment – not unlike the US Harpoon in its guidance system. It had a GPS receiver-processor unit, FLIR and a guidance interface to link all components. A genuinely autonomous intelligent missile. Hamouda's investment in that German Ibach paid off. His team did it.'

'I know,' Jacob said quietly. 'I know, I should have shot him years ago, when I had the chance.'

'You've never understood where we live, Jacob,' Shahak said brutally. 'You've got as much sense as a snail. The RPVs which smothered the air defences were relatively simple. Aman doesn't think the Syrians can have that many of the sophisticated model Ibach designed, it must have taken a major expenditure of resources to build the eight they fired last night. They were effective, though. They used two to kill at Kiryat Arba and the Air Force flight training school. Though they missed the Rabbi. The others hit three towns and induced panic among the civilians. Psychochemical agents.

'The air force has mounted a standing combat patrol, with 24 hour AWACs cover over Israel itself. They reckon that they can handle any more cruise missiles. Having got hold of one they can configure their radar to pick them up. They aren't very quick. The Brits shot down V1s with propeller-driven fighters, so an F-15 should have no problem. We've still a few left, fortunately. You'll be glad to hear that we're counter-attacking. We should be able to evict them from the Golan in two days, then we'll drive to Damascus. One half of the pincer is already cutting through to the Bekaa around Yanta and Kfar Quoq. Do you have anything else?'

'Some good news.'

'We can always use that.'

'It's partly what's been happening with you that's helped me. I've been able to persuade Kane that this time I'm yelling wolf for real. Our people here have been working 24 hours a day to trace former Israeli Air Force pilots – not just in the USA, but literally, all over the world. We found one ex-Phantom jock running a bar in the Seychelles. He's on a 747 into Los Angeles as we speak. We haven't had one turn us down so far. We have a bag of about 400 with experience in F-15s and -16s, Phantoms, Skyhawks and Mirages. They're getting current as soon as they get here. Kane's giving us 50 F-15s, 100 16s, 50 Skyhawks and 100 Phantoms. He's getting them from storage, and from the Air Force and National Guard. Most of the pilots will come on a chartered 747 at the end of the week.'

'We need them.'

'What about the missiles that got the AWACs planes, the ones sunk in the sea?'

'We've been using minesweepers. We're clearing a lane 50 miles wide to get the fighters and the 747 in safely. We'll deploy Patriot batteries to cover the approach.'

'Kane's going to have the 747 escorted in by F-14 Tomcats off a carrier. Oh, the National Security Agency have their computers working through all the electronic emissions. They should have a location for the Syrian high command post soon.'

'Good,' Shahak grunted. 'I'm going to move up to the front soon, I'm taking over overall field command.'

'Is that wise?'

'Did Joshua lead the Israelites into battle from an underground bunker?' Shahak snarled. 'I'm the best general in the country. And besides, the Syrians might have thought of doing it too. If I'm going to slaughter their generals in their beds they might try and do the same. But they won't find me in the middle of a battle group.'

## *Ugdat* Gideon, Hasbaiya, Lebanon

'Some of us have been here before,' said the general. Dawn was an hour away. Outside the most modern fighting vehicles in the world waited, abristle with sensors, electronics, counter-measures and C³. Inside, the barn smelled of 200 years of goats, olives and chickens. Major-General Gideon Tal was briefing his *Ugdah's* brigade, operations and Intelligence officers.

'This is thoroughly bad country for armour, as we found in 1982. There are few roads and it is filled with ravines and wadis. The terrain is in fact ideally suited for defence. The size of the manoeuvre elements that can advance is limited to a brigade at best, often a single lead platoon. Without the engineers to span the rivers and repair the culvert bridges it can't be done at all. However, it is all worth while because of *this*.'

Gideon Tal slapped his pointer onto the broad highway leading south to north across the map.

'The Bekaa Valley, which is as good tank country as we could hope to fight in.'

The Lebanon was suffering the fate of any weak country surrounded by strong, belligerent neighbours – its prostrate form was being used as a useful avenue for one to march along on its way to bloody the other. Through the dingy shutters came the dull crumps of the combat engineers cutting a road.

'Those of you who were with me in the 188th *Barak* will remember that in 1982 the Syrians fought very well up here.'

A few grim smiles flickered through the faces of the men clustered about the easel. The 188th had been devastated in combat with the Syrians twice, when holding the Golan Heights in the Yom Kippur War, and again nine years later.

'We hadn't trained for mountain warfare then and they had. We expect them to fight much the same, using small groups of tanks and commandos equipped with sniper rifles and anti-tank missiles – RPGs, Saggers and so forth in ambush situations, fighting well and retreating to the next bend or next selected site to do it again. They will use their anti-tank helicopters – Gazelles with HOT last time, and very effective they are too. Their air force will be in the air this time and we can expect some use of laser-designated stand-off weapons.'

Tal stood up straight, tall for a tanker, not the usual short, burly model.

'Most of you know that after the Lebanon war the conventional thinking of most Zahal commanders involved was that our war there was not typical of wars we might have to fight in the future, and so there was no need to rethink our armour doctrine. They may have been right. Once we're into the Bekaa and slicing into Syria it'll be classical tank warfare. *But we have to get there.* I always believed we'd have to fight in the mountains and here we are. *Ugdat* Gideon is specifically tailored to fight our way through as quickly as possible, for the least loss.'

Outside, the first blush of colour was appearing in the far sky. A Merkava started up and the twelve cylinders of its AVDS diesel settled down with a lumpy beat.

'The Syrians have produced some surprises since Wednesday. Now it's our turn. One last thing. We are Jews, our tradition demands moral conduct in war. In 1982 our concern for civilian life cost us heavily in terms of our own casualties. *I do not intend it to happen again.*'

## The Wilderness of Zin

The grit of sleeplessness was in Danny Cohen's eyes, made bloodshot by the smoke. Grime, stubble and sweat laminated his face. I'm being paid back, he thought grimly. God got tired of hearing me tell now I got five Egyptian tanks in as many minutes back in 1967.

At least I've got a Centurion now, he thought. A fat guy like me couldn't get in a T-55. He took another shell from Shlomo, who had brought them up in the half-track and swung it up to Manny standing by the turret. They hadn't forgotten the importance of grabbing ammunition and fuel whenever they got a chance.

On the far ridge mangled and burning T-72s, Centurions, BMPs and half-tracks told the story of the counter-attack. The officer had read the books; they said get in close, close with the enemy and make his air superiority nugatory – so they had.

'That's it, Danny,' Shlomo called. Manny, who had the gas station, tossed him a plastic bottle of water, and stood on the back of the half-track for a moment, looking at the scene.

'They've got better,' he said. Danny took a swig, he was so parched the water seemed to vanish into him before even hitting his stomach. He passed it up to Shlomo who took his quarter then sent it down inside the turret.

Where they had stopped some purple muricandia was blooming, a splash of colour in the grim landscape. There was a tiny wheatfield planted by Bedouin; he picked an ear and chewed it. The winter rains must have been good, it was plump.

'Commander's on the net,' Shlomo called heaving himself up onto the deck. Another attack, he knew. As he squeezed into the turret he looked along the dell. The line of Centurions and infantry half-tracks was thin. David Ben-Levi was half out of the turret next to him, staring at the far ridge line, waiting for them to come. He hoped the boys up north would whip the Syrians soon.

## Ugdat Gideon

The *Ugdah* was the basic combat unit of the Israeli army. It was a *Kampfgruppe*, a combined arms task force group, tailored to the task at hand.

Tactics decreed the brigade to be the basic manoeuvre element of the *Ugdah* and the 188th *Barak* was spearheading the advance along the steep, winding road that led to the eastern foothills of Kfar Quoq. General Tal had a platoon of Merkava tanks on point, supported by paratroops armed with Galile assault rifles and anti-tank rockets, riding in APCs. Then came the combat engineers in their bulldozers, armoured recovery vehicles and counter-obstacle vehicles, abristle with blades, digging buckets and cranes, mine rollers, markers and a host of extra tools, not to mention their weapons. Combat engineers going into combat. Behind them came tracked anti-aircraft gun systems with six-barrelled cannon, and Stinger AA missiles.

Then there were some funny ones. There was one with something like a circus cannon mounted in a tall, long turret like a howitzer, followed by its own resupply support vehicle.

Behind that came an M60 carrying the turret of some kind of anti-aircraft gun system. Unusually, it had but one barrel. Attached to the 118th *Barak* it was clearly brand-new and like the lead Merkavas manned by a crew of *Hesderniks*, the Jewish equivalent of Jesuits or Knights Templar, fighting priests who combined religious study with military service. In the sure knowledge that they were but the sword of the Almighty, and instruments of His will they made formidable, totally-motivated soldiers. Known as fine tank crews, Tal had as many as he could in the brigade.

In complete contrast to normal doctrine, he had placed a 'leg' infantry screen in front of the point tanks, in the British or American way of mountain warfare. The sensitivity of the IDF and the Israelis as a whole to casualties led them to protect their soldiers in machines, using infantry as mobile shock troops. Tal believed from analysis of Zahal dead and wounded in the 1982 invasion that infantry survived far better on a modern battlefield when engaged with such a combined arms team than had been feared, and that as such, he could afford to use them to protect the point tanks and deny the enemy the first shot. His thesis was about to be examined by experts.

The attention of these experts was bound to result in some casualties, and the mobile surgical team from the medical battalion rode right behind in their APC. In addition to scalpel and forceps, they carried weapons.

And behind them the 100 plus other tanks, the battalion of M-109 and M-110 SP artillery, the intelligence, engineers, transport, maintenance and medical troops. Tal in his command vehicle with its high roof for the $C^3$ equipment and map boards was up with the spearhead platoon, along with the *Barak* brigade commander in his personal Merkava. *A'harye* meant leading the charge personally, whether it was a squad attack or *Ugdah*. The doctrine had played a large role in the success of Zahal against its enemies, and a greater one in massacring its officer corps.

The road was narrow, steep and winding, but the stretch ahead around the bend carried straight up the side of the valley for half a mile. The column was stopped while Tal climbed up onto the lead tank to talk to the young commander, his turret-mounted .5 machine gun covering the infantry ahead.

'All right, Shemaah. Remember what I said. This is where you want to look out for it.'

The driver below sitting behind the engine was looking apprehensively up the road. Older than the commander, in his mid-twenties, he had the paler features of one of the Russian immigrants, and Tal bent to slap his shoulder.

'*Krahsseevah*, Ivan,' he said grinning and waving them on up the hill.

The young man smiled faintly, pleased to hear his native tongue, but unwilling to believe that anything beautiful was going to come down the mountain.

But it did. As the column moved on a lorry came around the corner, hung with streamers of coloured cloth. Two pretty women hung out of the cab windows, waving, while some children were standing up in the back. Their teeth were white in the sun as they laughed.

The drumming of the heavy machine gun in Shemaah's hands obliterated the grumbling and squeaking of the tanks. Bullets struck the front of the lorry, slicing into the tyres and smashing the engine compartment. The windscreen exploded into shards of bloody glass and the savaged vehicle veered off the road to crash into the pines. A woman lay twisted on the road, her long legs sodden with blood, and the morning air was made horrible by the screaming of children.

The gun was still in Shemaah's hands. He stared, momentarily stunned at what he had done. A voice was shouting in his ears.

'*Get down man, get down.*'

It was Tal, over the platoon net.

The paratroops ahead were down in the ditches, Ivan had vanished. Shemaah drooped down inside the turret just as the lorry exploded. Jagged rain lashed the outside of the tank. An immense hole had been blown in the side of the hill where the truck had crashed.

'*Esh*,' commanded Tal. 'Open fire.'

The sides of the valley were winking with red light and the road ahead and very hills exploded as the hidden commandos and RPG teams opened up on the column. The paratroops were already firing from their positions of cover and the Vulcans opened up on the valley sides with their anti-aircraft cannon, mowing the trees like grass, their incendiary bullets setting them afire.

The RPGs bounced off the armour of the Merkavas, exploding in the trees behind. A *Nag'mash* with its troops dismounted took a hit and began to burn furiously, its driver hurling himself out, rolling over and over to extinguish the flames.

Then the shooting became one-sided and ceased, and there was just the crackling of the flames as the trees and shrubs burned with a white smoke and the screaming of the wounded Syrians as they were licked by the fire.

Shemaah, son of Saul, brother of Eli and Yitzhak, looked at the hole in the side of the hill where the lorry he had destroyed had blown up. The love of the Lord welled up inside him, and he knew that He would be guiding him throughout this Holy War.

'Driver advance,' he said and his voice was firm. He touched the *tefillin* in his pocket containing the word of God and felt His presence.

As the column began to move Tal poked his head out of the hatch of his M-577. Beyond the ridge, in the distance, marched the Jabaal Barouk Mountains, overlooking and controlling the western half of the Bekaa Valley. As he watched, the slope nearest to him glowed with a pinpoint of light.

Eli Ben-Levi considered himself a lucky man. Off duty, he got to surf. On duty, he flew a helicopter. Not just an ordinary one, but an AH-1S Cobra helicopter. What was more, while most helicopter pilots were required by law to fly high and away from obstacles, the regulations made for him would usually have him severely reprimanded for being up there at all. The designation of his helicopter stood for Attack Helicopter One, the letter S being the latest of a long line of modifications to make it better at its job.

When Eli and Benny the gunner were in their Cobra they were tank hunters, although happy enough to chew up soft-skinned vehicles and troop concentrations with their folding-fin rockets and 20mm cannon. For tanks they used their tube-launched, optically-tracked, wire-guided TOW missiles, or the superior fire-and-forget Hellfire, of which they had up to eight depending upon mission configuration. However, being queens of the battlefield, tanks did not travel without suitable escort, and those guards had the kind of weaponry able to turn an AH-1S helicopter into so much tumbling junk. In order to hide from them, Eli spent his working life flying nap of the earth, and if his rotor wash didn't strip the bushes of their leaves and the blast of his passage scare chickens, dogs and old women half to death he wasn't doing his job properly.

Today, for once, he was up at 5,000 feet in the clear blue sky. He hoped he wouldn't become dizzy or get a nosebleed.

He was watching the slope of the first ridge of the Jabaal Barouk Moutains, as they climbed towards Masser el Shouf. With him in loose formation as they circled was his wingman, Yossi. A speck was tumbling down towards the mountainside. A helicopter, a little one, an MD 500.

There were three in the Purple team, Eli and Yossi, the Blue platoon, and Micki, with his crew chief Dan in the back in their 500, the Red platoon.

The Red platoon pulled out of its dive right over the trees, and began to work the area in tight circles, clattering and whistling. It was officially known as 'recon by target', but Micki knew better than that. He was a lump of meat on a hook, that was all. Bait.

They bit. Red tracer erupted from the trees. There was the sudden glow of a man-portable SAM and Micki hit his flare dispenser and dropped the collective, swooping into the shelter of a little clearing as the missile punched a hole in the incandescence of the flare and flew off over the valley. Popping up and kicking his rudder he laid a line of white phosphorus rockets along the Syrian position. Then with the 7.62 M60 machine gun banging away from behind him he put the cylic forward and at full power scooted away.

High in the sky, they were watching. The Cobras were configured for their mission. No tanks up there. Their stubby wings held a mix of 20mm cannon and pods of 2.75 inch folding-fin rockets. They rolled in on the target.

'Purple One and Two going in,' said Eli.

'Purple Three is running in to the target,' confirmed a voice.

The Cobra was nose down, the white phosphorus smoke growing in the armoured windshield. Something skimmed across the valley below him. Two fat barrels tumbled from its wings and the hillside erupted into flame. Napalm.

'Right on target,' Eli said with approval.

The F-16 half-rolled, corkscrewing away from the mountainside to loop over the valley. His next approach would bring him at ninety degrees to the line of attack of the helicopters.

The Syrians were running like ants.

The two Cobras pulled out of the dive and slowed to 40 knots as they opened up with their 20mm cannon and 30mm Gatling guns. There was some sort of command post there and Eli tore it into brick dust and plaster with a salvo of rockets. Troops were clustering about an artillery piece commanding the valley below and he wiped them off it with some more flechettes.

Willy-pete puffed a quarter of a mile ahead and the two Cobras pulled away for a reverse pass as the site exploded into fire under the impact of the napalm from the F-16.

The fires had gone out by the time they had rearmed and returned. Red phosphorus marked the site of the LZ and they sanitized the surrounding area with their cannon before the big CH-53s came lumbering in. The Cobras stood off, slim, narrow and vengeful, ready to take action, but the Syrians were dead or gone. The paratroops debussed from the CH-53s, taking control.

# The Wildernesss of Zin

David Ben-Levi had once been on the tank commander's course, he knew how it was done, it was all coming back to him. High-speed offensive action was the method used to defeat the enemy, and to achieve it certain essential principles had to be adhered to. You sought surprise, and achieved mass in decisive areas, breaching enemy defences in weakly defended positions. You employed artillery and tactical air suport, were willing to accept heavy losses, and conducted operations 24 hours a day.

The M-2 half-track on his flank scurried for cover as the slope erupted. The Egyptian artillery had their range. It suddenly slewed, pieces tumbled from its nose, a tyred-wheel flew high in the air, its axle oscillating furiously – and a T-72 came through the smoke on the far ridge.

They were hull down as the turret swung smoothly on target.

'*Fire.*'

The gun kicked up the usual huge cloud of dust. When the blast effects began to clear, the Egyptian tank was burning and its crew hurried for cover. The enemy commander was probing for a weak spot through which to insert his attacking forces, and David knew that he had read the book too.

The MiG-27 came over so fast he had no time to spray token machine-gun fire at it. The thud of its passage and slam of its bomb were one, the breech of the gun came back and smacked him in the face.

He found himself lying on the side of the turret, broken teeth had cut his tongue and he tasted the blood. Shlomo was dead and Moshe, his driver, was heaving the hatch open. The Centurion was almost on its side, tracks blown off.

The artillery barrage had lifted. Avraham's tank fired and David saw the T-72s coming down the slope. He felt a sense of rage. I am not anyone's weak point, he thought furiously, it was a matter of pride. He ran through the dusty scrub towards the M-2 half-track. Middle-aged infantrymen lay around it like discarded logs and he recognized Menachem, the lawyer. RPG-22 anti-tank rockets were there too. He grabbed a launcher and dragged a box of rounds towards a small gully, where he fitted a rocket into the launcher, crouched down and waited for the fire-breathing monsters to come closer.

Inside his command vehicle Tal was watching television, courtesy of his Scout RPV. The unmanned aircraft was being 'flown' by its air vehicle operator in an APC half a mile behind Tal. What it saw was transmitted down to Tal by secure data link. The panoramic camera aboard gave him a view sixty degrees either side of the miniature aircraft, now cruising over the valley at 3,000 feet. Or he could command the television camera aboard to give him close-up views via its telephoto lens of anything that took his interest. In addition it had other sensors and equipment aboard.

Whirring machines hid on the reverse slope.

'Helicopters on the west ridge,' he warned.

Behind the point tanks moving up the road the Vulcans raised their cannon. It was bad country for them, for even when the VPS radar caught a target, the gunner had to acquire it visually and track it. In direct contrast, it was wonderful country for tank-hunting helicopters, whose noise of approach was hidden by the deep ravines, which also provided them with the cover they needed to shoot and scoot.

Behind them, the barrel of the strange new anti-aircraft gun twitched like gun-dog's nose, its turret moving to and fro as lightly and quickly as a ballet dancer, the electro-optics scanning the ridges. It paused as one of the engineers' armoured D-9 bulldozers pushed the blazing *Nag'mash* into the ravine, where it tumbled over and over, throwing blobs of flaming alloy into the air like a catherine wheel.

They popped up over the ridge, a line of bobbing dragonflies, and white fire erupted from the pods that bulged either side of them like eyes. The strange new gun with its crew of priests moved as fast as a champion boxer, the turret whipping down the line, bolts of white flame stabbing, uncurving and ruler-straight, onto their targets. The Gazelle helicopters tumbled from the sky, cartwheeling over and over to hit the thin trees clinging to the rocky slopes, pieces of fire flying away from them, tumbling through the air. Unguided, the HOT missiles they had fired swerved about the valley, criss-crossing it with trails of white smoke.

The plasma gun poked up at the sky, its acquisition and tracking radars turning gently. Helicopters were always teamed with attack aircraft.

Tal saw them coming, moving like barracuda down the channels of a reef. They came in down the valley, the wingtips streaming white trails as they condensed the damp morning air, pulling around the elbow of the land with their target strung out in a long line along the road. They were MiGs, the troops below could see the bulky cluster-bombs hanging below the high-set wings.

The plasma gun twitched again, the barrel simply pointed like an index finger at the target and the plasma, travelling at hypersonic velocity, struck the two aircraft 800 metres out. It blew them apart – they because balls of tumbling white fire trailing smoke, dripping flame onto the valley floor. They hit the rocks, smearing them black, starting fires. The noise rocked down the valley, bouncing from side to side.

A Merkava commander had been shot by one of the Dragunor-armed snipers attached to the ambush squads. The high neck of his flak jacket had partly deflected the round, but it had entered his throat and they hurried him to the surgical APC. As the column resumed the march the doctor aboard began to perform an emergency tracheotomy on the choking soldier, Tal called for the medevac helicopter from the rear.

On his television screen he could see the forward screen of infantry moving up the road. It had begun to twist and turn once more, and they reconnoitred with care. The point man was in a ditch, peering down the road to the next bend. The following moment, he came on to the net.

'Do you see me, General?'

'I see you, Amos.'

'There is a terrific ambush site on the next bend. Thick trees and scrub, enough to hide some tanks. Looks like they can exit to the rear, too.'

'I'll check it.'

Tal asked the RPV's mission payload operator, riding in the APC behind him beside the air vehicle operator to target the site using thermal imaging. The picture on his television screen changed to shades of green and red.

'You're right, Amos. Three large heat sources and a scattering of small ones.'

He switched to the artillery net. The circus-cannon-armed M60 came under their control. The artillery battalion major rode in a command APC, his television screen giving him the same picture as Tal. Using the laser of the RPV the mission payload operator gave him the distance and bearing of the centre of the ambush site from the circus-cannon accurate to a hair. He fed the information into his fire control computer system, which transmitted it via secure data link to the artillery piece.

The cannon swivelled and elevated deliberately. There was a heavy, flat bang and it was wreathed in white smoke. Soaring high over the valley the troops could see the huge black shell, fat as a barrel, curving down to fall onto the ambush site.

It came apart in the air, they saw the casing like a starfish and the spreading aerosol cloud white against the sun, like pouring water into ouzo. White fingers thrust through the canopy of the trees. Then the secondary shaped charge went off. The explosion was like tossing a match into a burst gas main – the fireball rose orange into the sky, and right back to the middle of the advancing *Ugdah*, they felt the overpressure squeeze on their lungs.

The column resumed its march. As they passed, the soldiers saw the site blown clean of trees, with only torn stumps remaining. The soldiers in the open had received the same fate. The three T-72 tanks, with their barrels pointed along the line of the narrow road, were unmarked, but their crews were dead. The blast of fuel-air explosive killed inside vehicles, within houses, in bunkers.

The 118th *Barak* moved forward, advancing towards the Bekaa and Syria.


## The Wilderness of Zin


They were holding on to Sede Boqer and were dug in about the *kibbutz*. It was as good a defensive position as any, and besides, Ben-Gurion was buried there. They all felt he wouldn't approve if they fell back any further. The *Ta'gad* was burning from the air strike that morning, with the doctor crisping inside it, so they had made a field station close by Avraham's T-55, hull down behind the terrace by the stone amphitheatre.

Smoke was drifting over from the fighting on the west side of the position, there was the banging of the tank guns, the crump of anti-tank missiles and the staccato rattle of small arms fire. A stench of garlic and onions and burning pork drifted in with the smoke and made David gag. The noise of the battle died away without the sight of Egyptian T-72s, and he assumed that for now the attack had been repulsed.

Two old boys came hurrying through the smoke bearing a blood-soaked form on a makeshift stretcher, puffing from the load. The man was fat, and Avraham got down from the tank, going under the stretched tarpaulin. Old Morris Carter, a gynaecologist, was tending the wounded. He took one look at Danny and continued working on the soldier whose life he thought he could save.

'David,' Danny whispered.

He bent over the dying man, and offered him a sip of water from his canteen.

'I was thinking, while we were fighting,' Danny said quietly, his mouth moistened by the water. His lips were black, and cracking from breathing in all the smoke of the battle. 'I couldn't help thinking, all the time we were laying fire, and reloading, and laying the gun again. I was thinking how they delivered ten new Volvo 940s last week, and how the hell I was going to sell them when three of the customers were right here and dead. Then I was thinking where we were. Do you know where this is, David?'

'It's the Wilderness of Zin.'

'Moses was here, David. He brought the Children of Israel here, and do you know what they said? "Why have ye brought up the congregation of the Lord into this wilderness, that we and our cattle should die there? And wherefore have ye made us to come up out of Egypt, to bring us in unto this evil place?".'

He looked across the bleak landscape where in the distance the dry granite mountains glowed beige.

'They weren't wrong,' he whispered. 'Say, why don't you write an article about it? Postcards from the Wilderness of Zin?'

'I will.'

'David, what the fuck are you doing here?' the dying man demanded. 'You're supposed to be a fucking pacifist.'

'I was wrong,' David said. 'I got it all wrong.'

# PART XXIV

## Metzada, Tel Aviv

SHAHAK looked Joshua up and down in his tiger-striped Syrian officer's uniform.

'You make a good Arab,' he said. 'Who are you?'

'Colonel Fu'ad al-Jazy. I'm in Special Forces.'

'You're ready?'

'We're ready. Saul Ben-Levi's leading the air strike, I'm in one of the Syrian BMPs, your son Haazev, the Wolf, is the commander of the other. We just want the Rabbi, now.'

'You'll have him, don't worry. Look, sit down a minute.'

Joshua sat down, crossing his booted legs.

'We're going to win,' said Shahak. 'What I want to do is win the peace too.'

'Okay,' said Joshua, and listened while the air conditioning hissed faintly in the walls, blowing rubber-scented air.

'Syria remains the front-line state in the Arab coalition against us,' said Shahak. The blood from his broken nose was turning his face purple, yellow and blue. 'Destroy Syria as a force and any centre of opposition to us, to which other Arab states might become attracted, is also destroyed. Syria's potential for development and modernization is regrettably high, especially since the replacement of Asad by Hamouda as president. Even when Syria loses this war she – and Hamouda – will receive enormous adulation within the Arab world for having led the fight against us and having fought well.'

'I'd agree with that.'

'In which case we face the unpleasant prospect of facing a stronger Syria, most probably supported by all the other Arab states, while we ourselves are economically weaker, perhaps supported by a weak America, in maybe six or eight years' time. However, this could be avoided.'

'How?'

'Do you have time for a short story? You do. Not very long ago the president of South Yemen called a meeting of his fifteen man politburo. When they were all there his bodyguards burst in and began shooting. However, all the cabinet ministers were armed too, and they all hauled pistols and sub-machine guns from their jackets and briefcases and began blazing away themselves.'

Saul grinned. 'That's the way to conduct a cabinet reshuffle.'

'The fighting spread out into the country, because of what South Yemen is – a collection of tribes, each of which had been represented by the various cabinet ministers the President was trying to knock off. Civil war resulted.

'In my opinion Hamouda is a political genius. He is able to switch roles between the three dominant political traditions of his region – one minute tribal chief, the next brutal autocrat, after that modernizing technocratic president. But . . . Kill Hamouda and the picture changes. Defeat for Syria and the death of Hamouda, the one person holding together the still-precarious internal situation, would trigger off concerted attempts to grab power between those various factions. Just as in Yemen. One might be quite certain that in those circumstances the internal situation would develop into a civil war, with the army itself taking part along sectarian lines. Under Asad and Hamouda the army has been regarded as the repository of whatever honesty, stability, order and progress there is within the fragmented Syrian society. Once let it become fragmented and tainted with the blood of civil war it will become useless as an external fighting force. All it requires is for Hamouda to die *suitably*.'

'Most attractive,' said Joshua. 'But Hamouda is in our charge, and if we put a knife through his throat he will instead become a martyr and a rallying cry for the next decade.'

'Not if one of *them* did it,' Shahak said softly. 'If Hamouda remains here he remains untainted by defeat. But let him return to Syria to participate in that defeat and then in the chaos following it he could plausibly be assassinated and the country be plunged into the anarchy of civil war.'

'Why are you telling me, General?' Joshua asked quietly.

'Because you're going to be there. You and your special forces outfit. There, in Syria, dressed and behaving as Syrians. You, you've been able to pass for an Arab all your life.'

'We're going in to take out the Syrian high command. We hope to do it and escape with our lives. Now you're telling me you want us to stay and assassinate Hamouda once the war's over?'

'Yes,' said Shahak.

                    *       *       *

Shahak took Tal into the briefing room off the main situation room itself. In the briefing room a smaller screen presented the positions and state of Israeli and Arab forces at that time. In a corner was Shahak's army cot.

'We're establishing a corps-level command as we did in Lebanon. I'm taking over overall field command and will ride with you in the west, with four *Ugdah*, 38,000 men and 800 tanks. Uri Gilboa will command a similar group in the east.'

Shahak had called up a presentation of forces in the north, and as he spoke pointed first to the western forces massing in the Bekaa valley, then to the forces in the east, and then to the Golan Heights.

'The Syrians made advances of up to eight miles here. The *miluimnicks* in *Ugdat* Haim and Albert mobilized with some difficulty, being under attack from the Syrian air force, and are currently containing the situation. However, the Syrians are continuing to bring more forces to the scene, to the extent of weakening their deployment in the Bekaa.'

Tal assessed the situation. The Israelis were concentrating their forces in both west and east into powerful mailed fists, supported by their organic self-propelled artillery and squadrons of tank-killing attack helicopters. On the Golan a relatively weak force was containing the Syrian advance, which was, however, gaining in strength all the time. He estimated that they had deployed some four divisions in front of the Golan, with approaching 2,000 tanks, 1,400 APCs, 1,600 self-propelled guns and artillery pieces and approximately 60,000 men.

'It looks as though the encirclement might be on,' he said. 'It's Plan Red. The Syrians have done what we hoped, now it's just a question of doing it by the book.'

Shahak looked at him sharply for a moment.

'Remember, nothing has changed, we need a swift and decisive victory. If we can wrap up the Syrians the others will lose enthusiasm quickly enough. The battle will begin with *Ugdat* Haim and Albert starting to fall back under Syrian pressure. This will have the effect of making them concentrate their momentum to the south. Using your two best *Ugdat* you should be able to drive east from Jabaal Barouk, passing close to Damascus, and fall on the Syrian rear, linking up with *Ugdat* Magen from Gilboa's command. The Syrians will have entered a killing ground. The pilots training in the USA will have arrived, and they will be committed to the battle. The F-15s will gain air superiority and we can devote the Phantoms, Skyhawks and F-16s to the ground attack role. The Syrians will be destroyed in detail. Especially as they will be without their high command. Traditionally Syrian field commanders have not been allowed to exercise much initiative – they were trained by the Soviets for years, have suffered from the effects of the internal security apparatus and Hamouda is no less likely to fear an armed coup than any of his predecessors. So they operate under rigid central control. Remove that control and they'll be running about like a lot of headless chickens.'

'How do you plan to take out the headquarters?' Tal asked quietly. 'We don't know where it is.'

'We do *now*. The American National Security Agency sucks in electronic emmissions from all over the world, using its array of satellites. The air attack on our airfields with which the Syrians began their war was operated under central control – the swarms of RPVs which managed to swamp our defences. The SAMs in the sea that ambushed our AWACs planes, and the cruise missiles that night – all operated under central control. We figured that somewhere among the electronic babel would be those commands, and that if you had them, you could find out where they came from. The National Security Agency out there in Maryland has computers nobody else has ever seen, and they cracked it last night. The Syrian command post is in the mountains, east of Latakia.'

When Tal had gone back up to his waiting Gazelle helicopter Shahak picked up a telephone.

'You can bring him in now,' he said.

A few moments later the door opened and a burly male nurse came in, pushing a wheelchair. In it, as trussed as a turkey in a grey straitjacket, was Rabbi Weiss. He stared at Shahak with insane eyes, a fleck of spittle at the corner of his mouth. Shahak bent down beside him.

'Not long now, Rabbi,' he said. 'You're going to lead the tribes of Israel into the Promised Land.'

# The Wilderness of Zin

The goats were taking very little interest in the fighting. A tank had gone through the wire of their enclosure and they were taking the opportunity to eat whatever they could wherever they could. One was thoughtfully chewing through an ornamental shrub outside the *kibbutz* dining hall. An olive Egyptian T-72 ground round the corner and halted, engine panting, on the neat green lawn. The turret swung and a burst of machine gun fire ripped into the building. The goat ran off and paused by the administrative building, casting the monster an aggrieved look.

David popped up from the irrigation ditch in the avocado grove and loosed off an RPG-22 rocket, aiming for the join between turret and hull. The weapon went off like an outsize shotgun. The shot went high and there was a loud bang as the reactive armour on the turret destroyed the rocket then the turret itself began to swing towards him.

He dropped down, running on all fours like a monkey down the ditch dragging the launcher and his bag of rockets as angry machine-gun fire raked the orchard, and a hail of leaves, bark and twigs fell about him.

He got to the temporary safety of the earth bank on the other side of the grove. Oily smoke was drifting from the positions over by the stone amphitheatre, and the crash of the anti-tank rockets and the rattle of small-arms fire came from the industrial buildings. Peering over the wall he saw further tanks moving through the *kibbutz*.

He felt incredibly tired. Irrationally it occurred to him that it was his father's birthday, he should have been at home helping with the celebrations. He was filthy, his face was a lacquer of grey stubble, sweat and dirt. His forearms hurt where they had been scorched as the Centurion went up and his knuckles were bleeding from his escape down the ditch.

He fished in the bag and fitted a new black rocket into the launcher. He had never been a very good shot, so he decided to wait where he was until one of the T-72s got close enough for him to spear it. There wasn't much point in moving, he thought, he was in the shade here, no point in going out there in the dusty desert for the last minutes that were left to him.

A giant door slammed over his head. Then another, and another in quick succession. Terrible clangs of sabot rounds striking armour came from over the other side of the grove, followed by secondary explosions. Peering over the wall he saw the T-72s ablaze. One had lost its turret, which lay beside it like a cup-cake. Infantry were running, some lying like tumbled logs.

The firing continued, fast and accurate, the hallmark of *Heyl Shirion*'s crack tankers. Looking behind him he could see the snouts of *Mag'achim* M60 Pattons poking over the low ridge 600 metres away, keeping up the deadly fire.

Then the T-72s that remained were pulling back, and the Pattons were racing over the scrub. They penetrated the *kibbutz*, he heard the rattle of machine-gun fire and the slam of the main armament. The dismounted tankers were fighting as infantry and as the tanks came in they moved up with them, dislodging the Egyptian soldiers from the buildings. One of the *Mag'achim* stopped close by, pushing itself into the avocado grove like some great beast to cover the approach to the *kibbutz*. He got up and went over, carrying his RPG, happy to be in its company.

The commander's hatch went up, and a small figure emerged, peering warily down the road. But the Egyptian thrust had been blunted, only burning and wrecked tanks remained, and the dead. On the shoulders of the commander's coveralls were the badges of a tank instructor, and David realized where the reinforcements had come from.

The commander looked down upon him, standing below. God but they look young, David thought. This one doesn't look old enough to shave.

The commander unbuckled the white helmet, and shoulder-length black hair fell about her face. She smiled.

'*Shalom*,' she said.

# PART XXV

## Washington, USA

JACOB sat on his hotel bed in his shirtsleeves, and wearily began to shake off his shoes. He did not hear the tapping at the door the first time. It came again and he made himself get up and go across the carpet to open it.

She was standing there, a small bundle wrapped in a white shawl, in her arms.

'I have brought you your son,' she said, and in the dim light her big eyes shone luminously. He looked into her arms in incredulous wonder, all the thoughts of the war driven quite out of his mind.

'My son . . .,' he whispered. 'May I hold him?'

He took the little baby with its wisps of dark hair into his arms, cradling him, and went into the room. Rifka followed him, closing the door softly behind her.

'Our son . . .,' he sang. 'Now we must find a name.'

He looked up at her and his eyes were wet with tears.

'Not a Jewish name nor yet a Palestinian one . . . one to bind the two together.'

He cradled him gently for long minutes.

'But I am forgetting myself. My darling, how wonderful of you to find me . . . and you both will need refreshment, clean clothes . . .'

She had just one bag in her hand.

'I had to come,' she said simply. 'We are your family, we cannot be apart.'

She took the sleeping baby, and softly placed him down in the middle of the bed.

'A cot,' said Jacob. 'I shall arrange it.'

She went up to him, and put her arms about him, resting her head on his shoulder.

'You are tired,' she said.

'Worn out,' he admitted. 'But it is done. We have them. Over 350 pilots who were once in the Israeli Air Force. We found one running a bar in the Seychelles! They have all been retraining at US air bases. They fly out tomorrow. We're putting them on a 747. Kane's giving them fighter escort, all the way.'

'That's wonderful.' On his shoulder, her dark eyes glittered. 'When the war is over, we can start again.'

He held her tight.

'We shall make sure of peace this time.'

His eyes travelled to the sleeping child.

'For all the little ones,' he said.

'The pilots, they will help finish the war,' she said. 'You must be proud. Will you see them go?'

'Yes,' he said. 'I'm flying there tonight.'

'Where do you have to go?'

'South Carolina. The Orangeburg Air Force Base. That's where they're going to assemble.'

'Flying out tomorrow.'

'Tomorrow morning. Nine o'clock.'

She came out of the embrace, and held his shoulders with her hands, smiling at him.

'Then we shall wait for you here. But ... we shall need a few things. A cot, did you say ...'

'A cot! And supplies. Look, let me go down and arrange things. It is no use picking up the phone. I know the manager here, he'll get some things up in no time.'

He kissed her.

'We shall never be apart, after this.'

'Never,' she promised.

She watched him walk down the corridor to the lift. As he got in, she waved, and went back into the room. The baby boy was sleeping quietly. She picked up the telephone and dialled, using an outside line. There was a quiet click as someone lifted the receiver at the other end.

'They are flying out tomorrow,' she said. She spoke in Arabic. 'At nine in the morning, from the Orangeburg Air Force Base in South Carolina. In a 747.'

## The Golan

The Syrian T-72 was burning, setting alight the row of wooden huts through which it had emerged. Ethan's Merkava had fired from a range of no more than 50 feet from its *Emdot*, hidden in the village grove of carob and poplars. The smoke was drifting across his firing position, carrying with it an unbearable smell of scorching pork, which made his eyes water. He scratched the dirty stubble of his beard. About him were strawberry plants, raspberry canes and vines. Syrian tanks were burning along the road, more were coming up. Israeli *Ma'gachim* M-60s and a couple of Merkavas burned in the village, where pigs and chickens and goats ran about snorting and clucking. The survivors wedged themselves further into their defensive firing positions and waited for the Syrians to come on.

'This is Yisrael One to all *Koach* Dror tanks.'

Yisrael One had a very powerful transmitter, it cut straight through some poor swine caught out in the open on the wrong side of the village with his tracks blown off and the Syrian commandos creeping up the hill with their tanks. Ethan had the feeling it was Amnon, who wanted to be chief of staff one day and needed a chestful of combat decorations to do it. Silly bastard, the Syrians would roast him like a chicken.

'This is Yisrael One.'

We know, general, we know who you are, but do you have the good news? It simply isn't healthy sitting out here.

'All *Koach* Dror tanks, pull back to your purple line *Emdot*.'

Thanks, General Shahak. Colonel Dror's dead and fried, but we'll pull back in his name.

Amnon was still moaning over the battalion net. Dust was rising as the M-60s and Merkavas wheeled, their turrets rotating to lay fire over their decks as they retreated to their pre-prepared defensive positions in the rear.

'Driver advance,' Ethan ordered. 'Through the village.'

'Gunner, load fin. Prepare for quick firing.'

The Merkava grumbled forward out of the grove, and Yoab, the driver, sent it crashing straight into the line of huts. Beneath him the carousel clanked as it selected sabot for Amir. They went through a hencoop and chickens and feathers flew everywhere. The road of the village was heavily grooved with the treadmarks of the tanks, and the grubby white plaster of the houses bore the scars of their jostling in the narrow street. As they came out of the smoke Ethan saw the ravine, where clear water was flowing, and the bridge that was marked on his map. Green Syrian T-72s were pushing across, and some BRDM and BMP armoured personnel carriers with infantry. He had passed control of the gun over to Amir, and the turret tracked onto target.

'Open fire,' he ordered, and the 105mm gun went off, shaking the whole tank. 'Fire at will.'

He could see what had happened. Amnon's *Ma'gach* was out on the slope, its tracks strewn behind it like guts. Amnon was in the turret, above the blocks of black reactive armour, firing with the .5 machine gun, still yelling over the net. Beyond him, down on the dirt road a Zelda *Nag'mash* was burning like a Roman candle, its infantry fighting from dents in the ground. They were the boys from the training school, got the map upside down, went the wrong way. Zahal believed in on-the-job training, whenever there was a war on they sent the students out to be taught by experts. It was open ground, the experts coming over the bridge would turn them into fertilizer the second they moved out of their meagre cover to stagger up the sixty degree slope.

Amir, the gunner, was keeping up a high rate of fire, the crashing of the gun beating on his ears, its percussion smacking him in the face every time it went off. In *Ugdat 36* they said, you fired more quickly and more accurately and you stayed more alive.

Amir, who wanted to stay alive, worked the laser range-finder and ballistic computer that controlled the cannon like a ballet dancer, raining fin-stabilized hypervelocity *Hetz* rounds down upon the tanks coming across the bridge.

'Amnon, shut up, you silly bastard,' Ethan yelled over the net. 'I'm coming, get your crew out and into the back.'

A huge gout of earth exploded in front of him, obscuring his view, as the Syrians began to react. His mouth and nose were filled with gritty earth. RPG rounds were flying towards him like enraged black wasps, there was a bang as one hit the armour over the suspension and something smacked into his helmet. There was a singing in his ears.

'Yoab, go alongside, with the rear doors away from the enemy.'

Amnon and his crew were scrambling down over their rear deck as the Merkava came down the slope, sliding like a sports car. Ethan had the rear doors of the infantry compartment behind him open, and they jumped in, falling over themselves, almost without the tank stopping. He noticed paint strips flying around the turret and realized that they were under heavy machine-gun fire. Ducking down into the cover of his armour he spoke again on the intercom.

'Keep going, Yoab. Down onto the road to the infantry.'

The slope was rough and steep, they slithered down it, the Horstmann suspension thumping, throwing Ethan about in the turret. Amir was still firing, using the twenty-power zoom lens that was slave-connected to the fire-control system to lay the cannon onto his targets.

There was a tremendous bang and something hit Ethan's helmet on the other side, blowing him into the turret. There was another explosion, and the beating of RPG rounds striking the armour. He struggled back up as Yoab locked the tracks, sliding onto the dirt road with a terrific thump. The impact sent his face crashing into the hatch cover, he felt bone and teeth break, and his mouth fill with blood.

They were stopped by the burning APC, the infantry running for the safety of the tank. The heat of the blazing aluminium scorched his face. Syrian infantry were moving in the black smoke, and he reached for the machine gun. His hands grasped air, something had wiped the top of the turret clean. Silver scars scraped its armour.

The boys were all in, and Amir gave it full power, burned diesel streaming from the side exhaust as the wide tracks bit into the dirt of the hill. A gun barrel poked through the smoke and belched flame.

White-hot knives sliced into Ethan's legs, and he screamed, falling inside the turret again. Choking black smoke filled his lungs, and the metallic gas of the fire-suppression system. As the fans cleared the smoke he saw Amir. The gun sight was buried in his face, and his asbestos overalls bloody ribbon.

He pushed himself back up into the air. The village was behind them. Syrian T-72s were halted, taking up defensive firing positions. His thumb moved, and he was plugged into the battalion net.

'The bastards aren't coming,' he said. His voice sounded as though he was speaking under water. The Merkava was hurrying over the dry ground, dust pluming high from its tracks. He saw the carob trees, and poplars, raspberry canes and vines. The air was fresh. He hung over the turret rim, wanting to see more before he died.

'You hear that, general?' he whispered. 'The bastards aren't coming.'

The setting sun shone in Ethan's eyes, but he did not blink until they took him down and closed them for him. To the north it flooded into the compartment of Tal's M-577, crammed and cramped with all its C$^3$ equipment. At the head of the Bekaa the early evening air was fresh, he had opened the doors to taste it.

Shahak's voice came through clear and strong through the secure data link.

'This is Yisrael One. They didn't take the bait. They've realized what's happening. They're holding their position on the Golan, and re-deploying to face you. If we wait until morning they'll be in a good defensive position. You'll not be able to get between them and Damascus.'

Tal had been watching the pictures from the RPV.

'If we go now we'll catch them on the move and destroy them in a meeting engagement at night,' he said.

'You won't have air power until the morning.'

'We'll still be fighting,' Tal said laconically.

Through the open doors came the grumble of the diesels, and the squeaking of the tracks, the distant thudding of helicopter blades beating on the skin, the whistle of their turbines and the low muttering and mumbling of men asking for the assistance of the Almighty in their task.


## Tel Aviv


The thing that wheeled high in the black sky above the city was a predator. It was a superior one to an eagle or a leopard, in that it could see in what was pitch darkness to an animal, or through dust, fog and cloud could hear its prey 50 miles away, and know what it was by its smell. It was not restricted to the narrow band of light waves visible to animals, nor those sound waves that could move an ear drum. Its sensors also operated on frequencies in the far infra-red and on radio frequencies, especially millimetre waves.

Like the best predators it was very unobstrusive, and its presence extremely difficult for its prey to sense. Its own sensors being passive it had no emissions of its own that could be detected. Its wingspan was no more than six feet, and its body and propeller were made of radar-transparent composites. Its engine was a shrouded 25cc kerosene-burning four-cylinder not unlike a large model aircraft engine. The exhaust gas was led down cooling baffles the length of its fuselage, which contained its fuel cells – it expended very little energy wheeling up there, like the best hunting birds – and around its centre of gravity the warhead, ten small pounds of explosive.

It was small, quiet, cool and did not reflect the kind of transmissions in which its battlefield was bathed. It was visible only to the Mark One eyeball, known to perform badly in the dark.

It heard its prey coming a long way away, and saw it too, a blaze of electronic transmission. It checked that the transmissions were the ones it had been told its prey would emit, and they were. It smelled right. It was accompanied by several other, smaller ones, and they, too, emitted the right signals. One of them was louder and brighter than anything in the sky, and told lies. The predator ignored it.

As its prey approached, unaware, it prepared itself. Its low-light television module locked on. Its wings folded back into a delta shape, like an arrow head, and it began to dive. The air around its prey was ablaze with lights and strips of foil and electronic noise thrown out by those accompanying it. The predator ignored them all. It kept its prey in the middle of its picture. Any deviation sent signals to the four control surfaces of its empennage to return the image to the centre.

It dived at 350 mph, the cockpit of the aircraft below filling its vision.

## The Bekaa

Yitzhak had been a paratrooper before he found a more interesting job. Ahead was the village, one of several, sprawled across the wide valley floor, its rich orchards and fields indicating the historical fertility of the soil, its location, its historical role as invasion route and battlefield.

The scent of crushed thyme filled his nostrils as he crouched in the carob grove, looking down from the top of the copse. The engine of the FAV ticked quietly behind him as it cooled. Through his thermal-imaging night-vision goggles the landscape was a strange world. He scanned carefully, methodically, looking for movement, for life.

Yitzhak was the very tip of the armoured spear moving up the valley. His FAV was no more than a plated dune-buggy. It was quiet and fast, as befitted its role, to reconnoitre by stealth, moving about ahead of the *Ugdah* like a cat. It even had claws to deter, a 40mm grenade launcher, .5 machine gun, a TOW missile launcher. But it wasn't supposed to be seen.

There. It was well hidden, pushed back in the barn, but his thermal imaging equipment penetrated the darkness and the foliage camouflage. He could see it, the long barrel of a 125mm smoothbore gun. A T-72. But how many more, what force was hidden there across the invasion route?

He went back to the FAV, on to the battalion net. Behind him were the vehicles of the combat reconnaissance patrol. His job was to investigate by stealth, without being seen. Theirs was to investigate by force. Lay fire on it and see what came back. Yitzhak knew exactly where he was. He had a GPS receiver in his thigh pocket. It took readings from the Global Positioning System satellites orbiting the earth. The size of a fat paperback, using MRGS military grid reference system it told him his exact position on the face of the earth, to within a foot.

He keyed his microphone, and quietly began to talk.

The president of Syria had finished supper. He had asked for chicken roasted in the Arab style with ground red *sumak* seeds, giving it a refreshing touch of sourness, served with *mujadara*, rice, lentils and onions mixed with yogurt, hot pita and sliced tomato, hot red pepper, washed down with cold dry Goldstar beer. The mossadniks who guarded him were more familiar with felafel and borekas, and had to send out. The Arab cook who prepared it never knew his distinguished guest. After his meal he sat back, smoking a Farid cigarette, which he enjoyed for its strong bitter taste.

There was a thump and a thud outside the door. Since being kept a prisoner in the *midrasha* the routine prescribed for him had not varied nor had it included violence of any sort, so he turned in alarm as the door was opened very suddenly and two armed men in black combat clothing and black camouflage face paint dragged in the guard. Blood was running from his head and he was unconscious.

The three stared at each other and then one of the soldiers beamed, exposing very white teeth against his warpaint.

'*Asalamu aleikum, ya sidi,*' he said and bowed his head.

'*Aleikum asalam,*' Hamouda responded in relief. '*Marhahtein, ya jamaat alhir.* Bless all those present.'

'Are you ready, sir? I am Kamil and this is Salim. Your servants have come to take you home.'

'I am ready.'

Salim opened the door a crack.

'The way is clear.'

'*Tishah bil heir,*' Kamil murmured humorously as he passed the unconscious guard. 'Wake well in the morning.'

Both commandos were in black one-piece coveralls, black flak jackets holding grenades and carried Heckler-and-Koch MP5 sub-machine guns. They hustled Hamouda quickly but quietly down the empty corridor and through a small door into the darkness. Gripping him by both elbows they ran fast over the grass. The air was fresh after the days of filtered air in his room.

'Here is the wire,' said Kamil. White cloth shone in the dark, indicating the cut ends, and they wriggled through into the lane on the other side.

'The car is waiting.'

They ran down the lane. The sky in the distance blossomed with orange lights, falling like a firework display. As Hamouda got into the car there was a brilliant white flash, and yellow and orange streamers of fire cascaded down from the air.

The team of six Cobras were at the holding RV rendezvous, facing inwards in a wide circle. All could see Mordechai, the commander, sitting beside Micki in the MD 500.

Eli was watching him through his night-vision system. Mordechai held up the code card, and one by one, the pilots picked up their helicopters, following him out of the RV, and down the road, hover-taxiing to make maximum use of the cover.

Ahead, the combat reconnaissance patrol was going in. The sky lit up red and white with the flashes of gunfire. A piercing white glow illuminated the copse of trees ahead, and faded to a dull orange. A tank had taken a direct hit.

The attack helicopters were lined up behind the wood. Mordechai had taken the 500 to one side, sheltering behind an olive grove. They were three kilometres from the target. Micki pulled up on the collective and, still hovering, the little helicopter poked its mast-mounted sight up over the trees. The TADS target acquisition and designation system grabbed an image of the scene ahead, reading everything emitting a heat signature and storing it on video. They popped back down under cover, and Mordechai reviewed the picture from safety. He selected a target sequence. Micki pulled collective again and the mast-mounted sight popped up once more. This time it emitted laser beams, 'splashing' the targets three kilometres away, cutting through the smoke and dust of the battle as though through clear mountain air.

'Purple One,' Mordechai ordered, and within seconds Benny, the gunner, had released a full salvo of Hellfire missiles. Eli did not even have to break cover. Turbines whistling, blades thudding, they hurried back to the RV to rearm and refuel. Through his night-vision system Eli saw the mass of the *Ugdah* vanguard pushing up through the valley, Zeldas and Merkavas, ZSUs guarding the command M-577, combat engineers with their COV combat obstacle vehicles and M-728s carrying their demolition guns. They shoved through the wreck of the Syrian battalion burning brightly in the villages.

Eli put it down in the safety of the RV and the ground crew began fitting fresh missiles.

The length of dirt road was empty, clear of telephone and power lines. The dark aircraft came out of the night as suddenly and quietly as an owl, they heard the thump of the tyres hitting the ground, the rumble as they rolled over the dirt and the howl of the propellers in reverse pitch. They went running after it, its rear ramp was down and a loadmaster was beckoning urgently.

They were inside, their boots clanging in the echoing interior, the loadmaster hit the button to raise the ramp and the twin turbines came back to 100 per cent power. Dust rose from the metal floor as the rough road kicked them through the undercarriage, then the nose rose and it was smooth. Peering out through one of the small windows Hamouda dimly saw the ground rushing by, not far below.

'We're still over Israel,' Kamil yelled, over the din of the engines. 'We have to stay low.'

The loadmaster was wrapping something around his body, pulling straps tight. There was a weight on his back.

'Parachute.'

When it was done they sat him on one of the hard, functional seats that lined the sides of the cabin. This was a transport, meant for carrying paratroops.

Kamil and Salim were taking off their flak jackets and their webbing, similar parachutes to his own propped by their feet. The loadmaster offered him a plastic mug of hot coffee from a thermos. It slopped over the floor in the turbulence of the low flight, but he gulped some gratefully.

Then the ride became smoother and looking out he saw small lights below, they were climbing.

Kamil grinned across at him, his teeth white in the dim light.

'We're over home territory, *ya sidi*,' he said triumphantly. Salim had gone up to the front, through the half-open door Hamouda could see the pilots in the soft glow of the instruments.

There was an electronic howl from the cockpit. Hamouda's head slammed into the side of the fuselage as the pilot manoeuvred violently. Bright lights streamed past the wing outside.

'*Fighter, fighter*,' Salim yelled, from the floor.

There was a bang and flames started pouring from the starboard engine, lighting the interior of the cabin with its glow. Gears were grinding, air roaring about them, the loadmaster had the ramp down. Salim and Kamil were hauling him to his feet, the loadmaster snapping a cord to the rail above, they ran him the length of the fuselage and threw him into the night.

The airblast tore his shoes from his feet, tumbled him like a cork in a torrent. Then there was a tremendous jerk as the parachute opened with a bang. He hung under it gasping for breath. A huge gout of flame billowed from the darkness, and to the south, he heard the howl of a jet turbine going home.

Below there were the lights of habitations. Hamouda wore paratrooper's wings on his Lieutenant-General's uniform, he had done the course. He took control, and began to steer himself towards the village.

The 500 came whistling and clattering into the field, where Yitzhak was waiting. A figure scrambled out clutching a map and carrying a radio pack over his shoulder. He got into the FAV next to him. The little helicopter was gone before Yitzhak was in gear. They shot down the track, good for goats and his recce vehicle.

He had found a good site for the artilleryman, on the reverse slope of a ridge among the rocks. They got out and scrambled up until they could see the land below.

'Okay, give me the SALUTE on this,' ordered the forward observation officer, peering down.

'Okay. Size, battalion strength at least. Activity, dug in and waiting. Note the fortifications. Location, here on your map. That's your grid reference. Unit, from the markings I can see they seem to be from the 76th Tank Brigade of the 1st Armoured Division. Tough soldiers. Time, I found them 20 minutes ago just as they are now. Equipment, 40 tanks that I can see, T-72s and 64s. Infantry in the fortifications. Anything else?'

The FOO was methodically working across the line, noting the features.

'No, I'll get on to the battery commander with the fireplan. Good position. Thanks.'

'Just here to help,' Yitzhak grinned, and scrambled down the slope to the FAV. He heard the FOO begin to talk quietly on the radio to the commander back in the fire direction centre. It was a simple but precise message: Where it was, what it was, what he wanted doing to it and for how long.

He had positioned the FOO off to the flank, where he could observe the effects of the indirect fire from the SP guns moving up into position in the rear. He sent the armoured buggy hurtling back down the track, travelling across the enemy line, but staying behind the slope of the hill. On the other flank there was a big hill, with open ground on both sides, and he had selected it for the commander as the forming-up point of the operation.

The BRDM and the *Mag'ach* of the combat recce patrol were there, having ascertained it had no enemy in it, and remaining to keep any out. With them was a lieutenant-colonel who would lead the assault, and a major in the engineers, who would be right alongside. Yitzhak took them up to the top of the ridge. The most important thing for the commander was to know where the enemy actually was – the recce crews like Yitzhak were the only ones to have actually seen the position. He wouldn't go anywhere or attack anything without his combat engineer however. Yitzhak pointed out the formidable obstacles, the fire positions that covered them. The engineer drew a swift but detailed sketch with an expert hand, and when they were satisfied they went back to the FUP. The first Merkavas and combat engineer vehicles were moving up, sprouting strange shapes in the darkness with their dozer blades, winches and cranes, piles of fascines. In the turret of the lead Merkava the commander was *davening*, swaying back and forth with his *tallit* prayer shawl about his neck. The lieutenant-colonel was using *hezderniks* as his spearhead.

There was one place Yitzhak and his speedy dune buggy were now not meant to be and that was anywhere within the combat area. But it didn't mean he couldn't be of any use. He got back in and burned off over the scrub, climbing up onto the flank. He set up a good observation point, and reported to the commander over the net. Then he sat and watched. He was hungry, so he took a bar of nut-packed chocolate and a can of coke from the locker.

No one near the target heard the M-109s fire. They were 15 kilometres back. The first anyone knew was when the first salvo of eight 155mm shells from the battery arrived. They were short, there was a pause, and the next salvo arrived on the front line of the defences, spewing flame and earth high into the air. The FOO had done his job.

The battle group was pouring out of the FUP. The artillery stonk was to last three minutes, they wanted to be in among the enemy as it stopped. Three M-60 chassis carrying bundles of stout plastic tube maxi-fascines were in the lead and they halted by the anti-tank ditch. Less than 200 feet ahead of them the artillery barrage pounded the fortifications, each side of them the Merkavas poured fire into the near positions. The fascines rolled into the ditch and the M-60s turned expertly away, allowing the two COV counter-obstacle vehicles behind to begin pushing earth over the fascines.

It was done, a bridge had been formed, the artillery ceased and the Merkavas poured through. Four hung back with the Zelda APCs to provide intimate support, the rest rolled through the position, vanishing into the darkness to form a defensive ring on the far side.

The troops debussed, pouring from the back of the APCs, and the smoking battlefield became a cacophony of noise and light, the rattling of machine-gun fire and the crump of grenades.

It was not all one-sided. One bunker at least was intact. White fire lanced out in the opposite direction and a Zelda went up, burning incandescent in the night. There was a dull boom from the combat engineers' M-728's demolition gun and the firing ceased. The huge low-velocity weapon fired a HESH high explosive squash head round designed to destroy fortifications and could do it with people in them just as effectively as without.

The noise of the battle was over, the soldiers were reorganizing and climbing back into their Zeldas. Two *Ta'gad* medevacs moved across the fascine bridge ready to handle casualties, and from the darkness came the clatter of a UH-1 helicopter to take the seriously wounded straight to the hospitals in the rear.

As the battle group reformed the engineers were moving earth, preparing firing positions for the M-109 SP howitzers coming up from the rear. Up on the hill Yitzhak munched his last square of chocolate and fired up the FAV. His blood glucose level high, he felt full of energy and accelerated up the hill, seeking the high ground to plan his new route. There was something up there too, so well-disguised it looked like rock; it was only because he was on top of it he noticed it. It had an antenna, it looked like some kind of FM repeater station, though for what purpose he couldn't imagine.

Part of the art of good recce was to let the commander know; intelligence was a mosaic, and some little piece could help build up the whole. He reported his find on the net to *Ha'mefaked* Tal. The battle group was moving, he had to get ahead of them.

He shot off down the hill, looking for trade.

*　　*　　*

The man from Aman had promised that the satellite imaging could not lie, that the wadi was smooth and wide and without obstructions. At 130 knots and ten feet in the darkness the men in the C-130 Hercules had to take him at his word.

The first BMP-2 rested on its pallet by the open rear cargo door. The cold night air swirled about them as the pilot, peering through his infra-red night-vision system let down the last five feet. Trailing back out of the door from the armoured personnel carrier on its strong pallet was a parachute. It was restrained from opening by a reefing line that held it to some four feet in diameter.

The dropping zone came under the nose and the co-pilot tripped the switch. A small explosive broke the reefing line and the parachute mushroomed to its full 48-feet diameter, ripping the APC and its pallet from the cargo hold to vanish into the night. As the C-130 climbed out to a cautious hundred feet they began winching the second BMP back on the rollers for the next pass.

Themselves, they went out in two sticks, the 16 paratroopers and their passenger. The C-130 pilot edged up to 200 feet for the job.

Joshua, called Fu'ad, was first out, following the weapons containers. The airblast turned him upside down, filled his jacket and his mouth, the parachute snapped him upright, swung him like a toy on the end of a string. He had time to take control and assess the landing sight through his night vision goggles before he hit the wadi floor with a thump.

They were all there, they discarded their parachutes and Haim shoved them in a hole in the wadi wall. The pallets had done their job, disintegrating in a controlled manner to absorb the tremendous impact of fourteen tons of armoured vehicle landing from five feet up at close to 150 miles an hour. The two BMPs rested some 400 metres from each other, looking merely badly parked, and the teams quickly unchained them.

Joshua and Haazev as commanders of the two vehicles had to be seen as Syrian soldiers, and they wore the appropriate combat uniforms of the 85th Infantry Brigade. The rest were dressed in the equipment they would wear for the coming battle. They were CRW, counter-revolutionary warfare troops. In time of peace they were trained to storm hi-jacked aircraft or rescue hostages from a building, in time of war, to go in and kill everyone inside.

They favoured the tough maroon jump boot of the paratroops. Their black one-piece coveralls were fire-retardant to provide protection from the flash blast and heat of the weapons they would use. From crotch to shoulders they wore armoured vests to protect themselves against the weapons their enemies would use. These comprised ceramic contoured plates front and back, combined with layered Kevlar and a blunt trauma shield to provide all-round cover, extending high under the arms to protect while firing. They had shielded leather-covered Nomex gloves to give them a sure grip of their weapons.

Before they set off, Haazev lined them up to check their equipment. Most of this they bore on their load-carrying assault vests, worn over their armour. The vests had a strap at the back of the neck with which a colleague could drag its wounded owner from the immediate scene of danger. A rich variety of weaponry and tools was on display. Haim, only five feet seven tall but with the shoulders of a weight-lifter, was the entry man, across his chest was a cut-down sledgehammer, on his belt heavy bolt-cutters, in his hand a short, handgripped Franchi PA-3 automatic shotgun, useful for blowing locks and hinges off doors and, with a wide variety of ammunition in his pouches, the heads off the occupants once inside. Ahron was the sprinter, the first man through the door in a hostage rescue, he used a Heckler and Koch MP-5 SMG, the most accurate sub-machine gun made. It allowed Ahron to place his shots with the accuracy of a surgeon.

Equipment was a matter of personal choice in teams like these. As befitted loyal Israelis, many carried Uzis. Haim had a mini-Uzi as a back-up weapon, Yaacov a Model 10 Ingram gun. He liked the .45 ACP bullet for its stopping power. All were heavily festooned with grenades, the British L2 HE fragmentation weapons proving the one of choice. All their primary weapons – and MP-5s, Uzis, shotguns – had powerful torches mounted alongside their barrels. The grenades inevitably blew out all the lights, so the torches were vital for target acquistion within smoke-filled rooms. They were operated by grip switch pads on the pistol grips for short bursts of illumination and firing.

With it done they strapped the man they had brought with them to the front of the lead BMP, using heavy wire. Joshua was dressed like the soldiers, now he had to put on his camouflage smock and trousers over his combat clothing. Before he did so he checked his personal weapons. His AKSU-74 was the weapon he used as a Syrian soldier, short, totally-reliable and strong enough to be used as a club when the ammunition ran out – it was a superb assault rifle. Under his smock he carried his sidearm, a Colt.

Haim grinned as he saw Joshua check the revolver, and his speed loaders of semi-jacketed hollow-points.

'God created men, Colonel Colt made them equal,' said Joshua.

Haim patted the 40-round magazines of his mini-Uzi, clipped together into L-shapes for swift reloading.

'I want to be more equal than that,' he said.

Haazev's men had finished and were climbing into the back of their BMP. Joshua went over to inspect their work. The front armour of the fighting vehicle sloped at 80 degrees, making a flat platform. Upon it, lying below the barrel of the cannon was a man, strapped out spread-eagled. He was held to the armour like a pinned butterfly, wired on at wrist, ankle, elbow and knee. His eyes stared vacantly into the dark sky. He was drugged. It was Rabbi Weiss.

The soldiers had squeezed themselves into their troop compartments, the doors were shut. The two drivers were in their seats, their heads poking up through their hatches. Joshua and Haazev climbed into their turrets, and the six-cylinder diesels grumbled into life. Dawn was still some way off, but it would come suddenly in these parts, when the morning kissed the night and brought with it the harsh daylight.

As they ground down the wadi to the road Joshua switched on his burst-capable MRR-50 radio.

'This is Fu'ad One. Condition Green,' he said, giving the codeword for moving out to the target.

The radio remained quiet.

'Fu'ad One, Condition Green,' he repeated, but there was no reply. He looked up into the sky. Saul, he thought, Saul, where are you?

The sea was smooth. At 50 feet he was using his PVNS night-vision equipment to see and it was running a light swell. On either side of him, as though running on that water, the two heavily-laden Phantoms rose and fell a few feet as they kept formation. Danny was a veteran, but this was Efraim's first combat mission. He was doing a good job of holding station.

A voice in his ears.

'Cyclops is out.'

What the hell? The RPV was forty miles ahead, flying their route, to warn them, ensure it was clear. What had happened? The headphones were silent, and he could not break his own radio silence. They would simply have to keep going. He felt strangely unbothered. The F-16 felt like an extension of himself, a partnership of man and metal.

A white line, flashing beneath at 450 knots. Behind them the sky was lightening, with the coming dawn. Down to the south, a battle raged.

The air in his mask tasted fresh and sweet, like the water in the stream where he had fished as a boy. He had had no more than eight hours of cat naps since it all began, but his hands were steady, his eyes unblinking. Through the infra-red he could see up to 15 miles ahead. There was a jagged crop of rocks above the olive groves that led into the valley. He put the waypoint cross of his head-up display on it to update the low altitude navigation and targeting system after the time spent over the featureless water.

In the valley, Saul felt sheltered.

The RWR howled, and the darkness suddenly bloomed red with the light of myriad shells. Through the infra-red they glowed as bright as coals, seeming to move slowly, and then, terrifyingly, accelerating straight into his face. All three pilots instinctively came up. The RWR told Saul that he was being illuminated by radar. The artificial complacency borne of combat weariness and the amphetamines prescribed for him by the air force doctor was suddenly ripped away. Crouched down in the cockpit with his elbows tucked in, he felt his arteries thumping in his wrists, his temples, under his knees.

To port the night blazed white. Danny's Phantom spewed burning fuel behind it lke a torch. The RWR above his knee told Saul that the anti-aircraft systems were tracking him, and had fired a salvo of SA-19 missiles. He hit the chaff button to leave a trail of centroids behind him. To port night became day, and then faded into darkness.

It was clear ahead, Saul put the stick forward to reacquire the safety of low altitude. He saw Efraim high above him, visible in the pale sky of dawn, saw the blazing red torches of the SA-19s.

Orange balls of fire floated lazily towards him from the side of the valley. He pulled hard, feeling his mask slipping on the sweat under the G-forces, his suit squeezing his legs hard.

*The ground.* He kicked rudder with the stick hard over and rocks flashed past his ear. There was a tremendous bang behind him and a mule kicked him in the head.

Yitzhak was nervous. Prowling through the undergrowth, creeping along tracks, peeping around orchards and over ridges he was happy. But gigantic forces were both ahead and behind him. The glow in the night sky was Damascus, in the darkness beneath were entire divisions of armour, aircraft and artillery. Behind him the *Ugdot* were deploying. It was time for small sneaky people to stop poking their noses into other people's affairs.

The FAV stood ready to go, to bug out before the sky was filled with white-hot rain, but he waited. Yitzhak was a good soldier, he'd found something and the commander had said to wait while someone came to look at it, so he waited in the dark, feeling nervous.

Another FAV came bounding over the scrub and a man got out, one of the radio-electronic combat types from the electronic warfare battalion that was busy working at radio and radar intercepts and direction-finding, targeting the enemy radio transmitters, radars, command posts and communications centres, monitoring their tactical communications; attacking him with electronic counter-measures and protecting their own forces with ECCM, counter-counter-measures.

'All right,' he said abruptly. 'Where is it? I don't know why I have to be out here, the battle's about to get going, I'm needed.'

'The boss said to look at it,' Yitzhak said. 'So we're looking at it.'

'It's probably just a trunk node for their C$^3$. They ought to teach you people to recognize such things then people like me wouldn't waste our time dragging out here.'

Yitzhak took the electronic warfare officer off into the darkness.

'Here,' he said. 'They aren't easy to see. It's just the aerial that gives it away.'

The man stared at it for a while, and then without a word went off into the darkness. Yitzhak saw his torch waving about as he poked around in the scrub.

Then he came puffing back out of the night.

'Where's your radio?' he said agitatedly. 'I need to get on to the *Aluf*.'

'What is it?' asked Yitzhak, jogging effortlessly beside the electronic warrior as they returned to the FAV.

'I think it's a REMBASS system,' he gasped.

Yitzhak looked at him curiously.

'What the hell is that?'


The pines lining the top of the valley were turning green in the light. Down on the road the two BMPs stopped in the gloom that hung over its floor. For the last time, Joshua tried the radio.

'Fu'ad One at condition Yellow,' he said. The outer gates were half a mile around the next bend.

There was nothing. He had been calling every two minutes since leaving the wadi. He climbed down from the turret and took a syringe from his jacket pocket. It was pre-loaded. Rabbi Weiss stared vacantly into the dawn. Joshua slid the needle into his arm and pressed the plunger in until it was home. He threw the empty syringe into the undergrowth, and climbed back over the metal decking. The mountain air was cool, he could smell the resin, the damp earth and took a big breath of it. Adrenalin was squeezing his stomach painfully, he was aware of his heart thudding in his chest. He reached down in the turret and felt the chill metal of the AKSU. The body armour about him felt stiff.

They had lights by the guardhouse, heavy concrete anti-tank obstacles to make them slow and manoeuvre. The BMP squeaked to a halt. A squad of troops came tumbling out of the post, Kalashnikovs in hand.

'Look,' Joshua bellowed, in Arabic. 'Look what we've got.'

Below the cannon barrel Weiss's eyes glittered. Saliva frothed at his mouth.

The lines of vehicles within the Damascus factory had been built there. The T-55 tank chassis had been driven in, all components pre-delivered over a period of time. The engineers who then assembled the completed weapon all lived on site while the task was being completed. Their quarters were comfortable, they had good food and entertainment, but they never left the compound.

The crews had never seen their fighting vehicles before. The 900 soldiers had trained intensively for six weeks in a camp set up for the purpose. Like the engineers, they were never allowed out. The drivers practised outside in T-55s, and inside learned routes so intensively they could navigate them in fog. The other two crewmen learned how to operate the built-in boom and hoist that picked up the pods and fitted them into the cage. The commander was trained to use the on-board computer. Linked by secure digital link to the fire direction centre, it received the fire missions. Using GPS it knew where it was at all times. Given the current meterological conditions it would automatically lay the launcher carried aback the T-55 on target.

The crews trained for their tasks over and over again. When the war started they remained where they were. Only three days later, with massive enemy 'mailed fists' advancing from both east and west, were they taken from the camp and driven to the factory in Damascus. Three hundred multiple launch rocket systems were waiting for them, fuelled and armed, twelve rockets per machine. Not all the rockets contained warheads that were immediately lethal; for the first salvo half contained expendable communications jammers. The crews were given a good meal and told to rest. That night they rolled out of the massive hide. The roads were empty, cleared of traffic by the military police. They drove along their pre-planned routes to their firing positions about the city, and waited for the fire order.

\* \* \*

Both Shemaah and Obadiah had laid *tefillin*. The little boxes contained portions of parchment inscribed with prayer from the Torah. When strapped to head and arm they agreed that the Lord was able to directly guide both their thoughts and deeds. The knowledge that they were working as direct instruments of His will cleared their minds of all extraneous thought. They became the perfect fighting team. Alexei, the driver, was the only blemish, declining the invitation to join them. Alexei had proved a disappointment, still not having chosen a proper name, and Shemaah had decided to have him replaced once the war was won. Fortunately, he was competent as a driver, despite his shortcomings as a Jew.

Tal was using his tanks expertly, concentrating them into fast-moving packets of ten and fifteen, exploiting the massive firepower in carefully-controlled moves to cut up the enemy in detail.

Shemaah was commanding the platoon. About him the turret was filled with the growl of the diesel in front, the constant droning of the cooling fans, electric motors and filtration units. In each ear different nets communicated simultaneously. His eyes scanned his arc, taking the far distance while Obadiah below took the close. While he did so he planned the firing positions for the platoon, organizing cover and routes, ensuring that they would not be against obvious background, could provide mutual support. While preparing to fight his own tank he issued a stream of instructions to the others over the platoon net, picking out landmarks, guiding Alexei over the intercom, the turret twitching to and fro under the command of the joystick under his thumb.

The turret poked up over the ridge line.

'*Target left.*'

Shemaah swung the gun onto the T-72 moving towards the trees so that Obadiah could acquire it.

'Fin, tank, ON,' he said, passing control. The Syrian tank was at about 1500 metres. The carousel clanked as Obadiah selected the fin-stabilized Hetz arrow round.

'ON.'

Through Shemaah's 20-power zoom lens the T-72 loomed large, the red ballistic aiming mark fastened by Obadiah to the join of turret and hull. Thrown up on the screen was information confirming the Hetz round in the breech, gun ready to fire and firing circuits live.

'Fire.'

'Lasing!'

The ballistic aiming mark shifted down on to the engraved graticule pattern as the computer calculated the elevation and aim off. Then the gun drove up on to the target.

'*Firing now!*'

The gun went off with an enormous explosion, the Merkava rocking on its heavy suspension. Through the huge muzzle flash they could see the tracer burn streaking to the target, and the blinding white blaze of light as it struck.

'Target!'

Shemaah was checking.

'M-kill,' he said urgently. The Hetz round had blown a track off, but the turret was turning on the slewed vehicle. 'Driver reverse.'

Alexei backed quickly down the slope and earth and rock flew high in the air as the Syrian tank returned fire.

'Driver advance.'

They came over the ridge line and Obadiah had the gun laid and fired. The round streaked across the dark night and the blaze of light became a torch.

'K-kill,' said Shemaah. The shallow valley was ablaze with fires from the shooting of his platoon. Twenty seconds had elapsed since the action began. He felt the presence of the Lord flowing in him through the boxes on his arm and head, felt it like a purifying flame.

'Driver advance.'

The Merkavas rolled down the slope under his command. He resumed scanning his distant arc. About 4,000 metres out he saw a number of dust clouds moving fast. They were pulling out of defensive positions, T-72s with their guns laid back over their decking. He called Tal on the *Ugdat* net.

'*Ha'mefaked,* this is *Koach* Shemaah commander. We have destroyed a force of ten T-72s. Some 20 more are in full retreat. We are following up.'

His *tallit* was about his shoulders.

Scanning his arc, planning the route for his force he began *davening*, swaying in his cupola, thanking the Lord for using him as His instrument to carry out His will.

The Cobra vibrated horribly as Eli made the transition from forward flight into hover. They had bits blown off everything, the main rotor was trying to come off the shaft so he put it down before it could do so. The port skid gave way at the front and the battered helicopter sat wearily down on one knee. Eli and Benny pushed up their canopies, unbuckled their sweat-soaked harness and clambered out. The night air was fresh and sweet. The Cobra bore the marks of a machine that had got too close to a ZSU, nobody would be using it for anything ever again.

A ground crewman was calling them and they trudged across the ground, helmets in hand, feeling the air cool on their sopping hair. The man had a bottle of mineral water that he gave them, they chugged it back in seconds, and climbed into the new Cobra that was waiting for them.

The ferry pilot must have been burly, Eli was slim, it took a few moments to tighten up all the straps.

'You'll have to go to your re-arming point for missiles,' the crewman yelled, as he put the damp helmet back on. 'You've got full fuel and a full load of thirty mil.'

'Right,' Eli said laconically, and his fingers began dancing over the controls. The motor whined, the rotor blades began to turn slowly, the rpm came up to speed and he gave it the fire.

The night vision equipment glowed, projecting its picture in front of his eyes, the rpm were top of the green and he picked it up. Nose down, the attack craft accelerated away into the dark. Benny selected the frequency to get back onto the squadron net and his headphones were filled with appalling white noise.

'Fucking radios don't work, Eli.'

'Try the other one.'

Eli had decided to go the long way round. With the battle becoming hot the troops would be taking hits and in the mood to fire at anything clattering about overhead.

'It's the same on all frequencies, Eli,' Benny said, sounding worried.

They whistled along at 50 feet and 130 mph, rising and falling as they crossed the ridges of the land.

'We're being jammed, Eli,' Benny said quietly.

'Let's get back with the others. We can communicate with the cards.'

'*Nine o'clock, helicopters.*'

Eli caught them and pulled it around in a tight turn to follow the shoal of Mi-17 troop-carrying helicopters hustling down the shallow valley to port.

'Must be two dozen of the bastards,' Eli yelled. The Mi-17 could haul nearly 30 armed troops, the squadron vanishing into the darkness would give someone a very nasty surprise when it arrived out of the night. 'Let's get them.'

'*Hinds at three o'clock,*' Benny screamed and they came down the ridge line like sharks. Fire rippled from under the stubby collective winglets and Eli dropped the collective. They went down like a stone, scarlet tracer streaming overhead. The three huge attack helicopters screamed past, Eli caught it before they made a hole in the ground and kicking rudder let off a burst of 30mm cannon fire. He scored some hits on the nearest one, and some glowing fragments flew off like sparklers.

The lead two Hinds vanished into the dark, following the Mi-17s, but they saw the distinctive tadpole shape of the third pulling round in a wide turn to come back at them.

'Slow it up, Eli,' Benny urged. 'Make him fight slow, he's made to go fast.'

Out of cannon range red flame bloomed from under a winglet and they saw the intense orange glow of the missile accelerating towards them. Benny popped a pair of magnesium flares as Eli turned sharply across the course of the missile, dropping back down into the safety of the land.

There were rocks down there, he arrested their descent with a handful of collective, working the controls like a skilful rider on a horse. They hid behind some boulders.

'I see the bastard,' Eli said. He had the top of his canopy peeping over the rock in front. The ground about erupted into dust and flying splinters. Things clanged and whined all about them, then the big ten-ton machine hurtled past. Eli had turned the Cobra with his rudder pedals and it flew directly into the stream of fire from the 30mm Gatling in their chin turret.

The dustbin-sized exhaust behind the cabin streamed flame, there was an explosion and the big machine hit the slope, pieces flying off it. It slid along for several hundred metres before coming to a halt, lying on its side.

Eli pulled the Cobra up out of cover. The Mi-17s and their accompanying Hinds had vanished. Down on the slope men struggled out of the burning helicopter, smashing holes in the plexiglass. Eli put the nose down and accelerated down the shallow valley, heading back to the battle.

The face of Damascus was marked like smallpox with the immense clouds of dust and smoke from the rocket sites. Their salvos launched the T-55 chassis carrying the big boxes of the multiple launchers raced away from their firing points. The naked eye and uncovered ear could identify where the rockets had come from, and so could radar and much more accurately.

The drivers roared down the empty streets following the routes imprinted upon their brains by intensive training. At their new firing positions fresh pre-loaded boxes awaited, and it took no more than three minutes to unload the empty ones and rack in the new.

The city erupted as Israeli counter-battery fire thundered down upon the sites they had left. People ran screaming from the disintegrating buildings. The launchers wheeled, the computers laying the rockets onto their targets outside the city.

Ahead the sky was glowing red, Eli came over the ridge line and the plain was lit with fires. Smoke and dust drifted across the battlefield, black and choking. Sudden coruscations of lights like a firework display indicated tank ammunition cooling off, and Eli pulled round to stay away.

'Where the hell are we?' he said. 'I thought we'd come up behind our armour.'

'They've gone through the Syrians already,' said Benny.

'So where are they? In Damascus?'

Benny was scanning the field ahead through the PNVS. Vehicles were moving, out there.

'Look, there they are.'

Eli was flying slowly along the ridge line, trying to make sense of the battlefield ahead.

'What are they doing? They're going the wrong way.'

Benny moved the projector in front of his eyes to scan the scene with his naked eyeball. Among the fires burning were ones brilliantly white.

'Aren't those Zeldas?' he said.

'What the hell happened?' Eli whispered.

They dropped down, and began moving to the rear to find a re-arming and re-fuelling point. Behind them a battle group was pushing through the wreck of the *Ugdah*. Below a handful of men were staggering out of the killing ground. Eli came down into a hover; they clung to the skids and he hauled them away.

It was the cold that brought Saul round, the aching pain of sub-zero air slicing through his flight suit. It roared in his ears, he could not understand it. A bright glare pierced his lids and he opened his eyes.

He was quite alone in a pale blue sky. The F-16 was wings level, climbing steadily. He was at 18,000 feet, where the air was chill. It blasted into the cockpit through a ragged hole to his right.

His right leg was at a strange angle. It did not hurt, and he

wondered why. Dark blood was congealing on the alloy floor around
his boots.

He trimmed it to lose altitude, he was asking for trouble poling
about up there like some tourist. He leaned forward to check
his position and stores, and pain stabbed through his neck and
shoulder. He sat gasping in the seat, and then cautiously used his
other hand.

The mountain range was rising up to meet him, its valleys dark
green with shadow, the sun kissing the ridges with gold. It was not
far to go home, he could be on the ground in twenty minutes.

The stores panel told him that his load of air-to-ground flechette
rockets and napalm was intact. In addition, he had his 20mm
six-barrelled cannon in the port leading-edge root.

It was warmer down there, the blood coating the floor pan began
to slosh about. His leg hurt now, he could feel a pulse pumping hot
in his knee. He needed to get to a surgeon.

This was the one. His eyes squinted as he dived into the gloom
of the valley, the bright sunlight above him.


The soldiers clustered around the front of the BMP, marvelling at
the sight of their enemy so displayed. They laughed and slapped
their hands together, they poked him with long bony fingers, and
tweaked his nose. Weiss raved about Arab men fornicating with
Jewish women.

'General Shahak we killed. We slaughtered him like a hog,' Joshua
bragged, 'and this one we took.'

The officer stood by the guardhouse gate, the phone by his ear.
The barrier was down.

'I have to have clearance,' he called apologetically to Joshua. 'We
were not told of this.'

Joshua forced himself to lean calmly in the turret, smiling pleasantly.
The back of his neck began to tighten into hawsers.

'They say to wait here,' called the officer. 'Someone is coming
to . . .'

One hundred feet away, the compound burst into flame. Two
vast fireballs hurtled in front of them. Above the gigantic crump of
the explosive came the crackling roar of a jet fighter on afterburner
and the F-16 shot overhead, no more than 50 feet up, the noise of
its passage beating off the valley sides on to their ears.

'*The Israelis!*' Joshua bellowed. 'They have tracked us here. Let us
in before we are slaughtered.'

High in the sky they could see the F-16 at the top of its loop.

*'He is coming back.'*

The gate was up and the two APCs burst through. The road swung to the right, it led into the side of the mountain. The fighter was coming down the valley at incredible speed. Some ZSU anti-aircraft guns on the perimeter were opening up, but they were 23/4s and the ECM pod of the fighter was configured to handle the Gun Dish radar. Fire blossomed from under the fighter's wings and the gun sites exploded. Joshua ducked down and splinters and pieces of shell rained about him. There was another huge explosion, and the noise of the napalm burning. The smell of hot kerosene gas drifted into the turret.

The F-16 came right over the two armoured personnel carriers as they ran for the grey concrete entrance, the blast of its passage smacking Joshua in the face as he crouched in the turret.

The great steel gates were shut. A man was looking out at them through a plate of armour glass.

*'Let us in,'* screamed Joshua. 'We have the criminal Weiss as our captive.'

He pointed frantically at the raving rabbi strapped to the armour, looking back over his shoulder. Saul was half-rolling at the top of the loop. He came back into the valley, and lightning sparkled white under his wing. Just behind the two APCs the ground erupted. He flashed by, and the gates slowly rolled open.

They accelerated in, the noise of their diesels drumming off the concrete walls.

'Keep going,' Joshua ordered Dudik, his driver, and the Syrian in front jumped frantically out of the way as the two machines thundered down the slope.

They emerged into a big underground park where crates and barrels and boxes were stored against the wall. It was lit by overhead neon lighting. A squad of troops was coming from a door, armed, and under the command of an officer. Joshua ducked down inside the turret, gripping the gunner's controls. As it swung he pressed the foot-mounted trigger of the machine gun, and a hail of 7.62 bullets blew them all down the wall, where they lay. The APCs came to a halt, and the troops in the crew compartments debussed. Joshua and Haazev jumped down from their commander's hatches, with the drivers scrambling out after them.

Leading off the park through wide swing doors was a white, lit corridor. A stairway led both up and down before the doors. They split into two teams of eight, Joshua taking the corridor, Haazev the stairs, going down.

Joshua had his respirator on, and did up the strap of his grey
ballistics composite helmet as Amos's team vanished down the
stairs. Haim was peering through the glass down the corridor.
Some unarmed men were coming out of a doorway, alarmed by
the noise of the machine-gun fire. He had CS gas grenades loaded
in the Franchi, he opened the door with his boot and fired two
down the corridor.

Joshua swept the area ahead with a burst from his AKSU and
led his team to the end as the others cleared the two rooms. There
was the crump of the L2 grenades, and screams. He poked his head
around the corner. It was clear. There were marked doors at the
end. He came round in a rush, followed by Haim and Ahron, and
something hit him in the chest like the hoof of a mule, blowing him
over backwards. He lay on the ground, and did not move.

The heavy machine-gun bullets slammed into the walls, punching
holes in the plaster. Following up behind, Yaacov stopped in the
shelter of the corridor, assured that the area behind him was cleared,
his team behind him. Haim and Ahron were dead, their respirators
torn from their faces by the impact of the .5 machine gun bullets.
Joshua lay in a crumpled heap.

Yaacov took a round mirror on a telecopic handle from the
equipment bag on his chest and poked it round the corner. The
doors at the end were guarded by hidden bunkers, from within which
someone was firing the machine gun through a gun port; he could
just see him peering through a slab of armour glass.

'Moshe, Moshe,' he called. They were all linked by the personal
radios carried on their assault vests. 'The M-72.'

Moshe Lahav carried three of the light anti-tank missiles; he
unclipped one from his vest and passed it to Yaacov, who was snapping anti-flash outsert lenses over the eyepieces of his respirator.

He had to fire left-handed around the corner, which they had
practised.

'Now, Danny.'

Danny Tamari was the second shotgun man, he carried a pump-
action Winchester. Poking it around the corner he fired two rounds.
They exploded against the wall by the bunker in a double flash of
blinding light. Tests had shown that anyone caught looking at it
could not see properly again for over an hour.

Yaacov leaned around the corner, and squeezed the trigger. The
corridor was filled with fire, and there was an enormous bang, shaking
the walls they leaned against as they waited to go.

In the smoke Joshua pushed himself onto hands and knees, and peered down the corridor. His breath rasped in the microphone as he dragged air into his lungs.

'Put another through the door,' he ordered.

There was a second blast, like the slamming of a great door and they felt the heat even through their fireproof clothing.

Joshua pushed himself to his feet. His AKSU had taken the first round and the receiver was so much torn metal. His wrist was broken, he could feel bone grate on bone. He pulled his Colt Python from his holster.

'*Acherei,*' he grunted. 'Follow me.'

Yaacov dropped the tube launcher, pulling off the outserts and followed Fu'ad. The corridor was filling with smoke, the bunker a torn area of concrete rubble and iron reinforcing. They paused by the blasted hole where the door had been. People were screaming, and they threw in grenades. Then they followed up, going into the darkness. The great room was filled with smoke, illuminated only by the fires breaking out from the ruined equipment and the brief flashes of light from the torches of the team as they illuminated targets.

Joshua stood by the door in the shadow, his own weapon ruined. From a far corner someone opened up with an automatic weapon, the high-velocity rounds screaming around the walls, attacking friend and foe alike. One-handed, Joshua fired all six rounds from the Python, the heavy revolver thumping, and the noise ceased.

Then there was nothing but the crackling of the flames.

'Let's go. Back to the vehicles.'

They came running out of the dark, Yaacov dragging Yoni by his neck strap, his hands trailing on the ground. The corridor was on fire as they ran through the flames, pausing to collect Ahron and Haim from where they lay. Nobody was left behind, wounded or dead. They ran down towards the doors, and into the park, heaving the dead into the crew compartment of Haazev's BMP, their breath gasping in their ears.

'Uncut the rabbi,' said Joshua. Yaacov was standing by the front of the lead vehicle, bolt-cutters in hand.

'No need,' he said, and Joshua went quickly over. Haazev and his men were running out of the belching smoke of the stair well, dragging three bodies.

Blood soaked the armour of the APC, running down onto the floor from Weiss's exposed crotch. His eyes stared sightlessly at the ceiling, his mouth stuffed with offal. Haazev heaved himself up onto the turret and set the timer.

Dudik had the engine running. Haazev had taken the surviving men of his team up the tunnel. They heard firing. The BMP crunched into gear and as they shot up the slope the great gates were opening. Haazev and the team scrambled aboard.

Outside smoke drifted across the compound, shafts of light spiking through from above. They raced for the guardhouse and a machine gun opened up. Joshua was deaf from the blast, the first he knew of it was the sight of the men on the decking being wiped off. A BRDM came through the smoke, green like a fish, Joshua slipped down in the turret, bringing his cannon to bear. He fired, and screamed with pain from the shattered bones in his wrist.

The BRDM sprouted black oily smoke, and a man scrambled from the turret. They vanished into the murk. Joshua fired one-handed into the guardhouse, and the small-arms fire ceased.

'Stop, Dudik, stop,' he shouted. The BMP came to a halt, engine grumbling. Out of the smoke came Haazev and three others, staggering and limping, dragging two more. Joshua had broken ribs from the impact of the .5 machine-gun rounds, but his body armour had saved him, as theirs had them.

They climbed up, and Dudik put it into gear once again. From behind them there came a tremendous, rumbling roar. From hidden shafts in the mountainside plumes of white smoke jetted high into the air. The very ground beneath the tracks of the BMP shook.

They jerked forward, moving past the wreck of the guardhouse, manoeuvring around the anti-tank obstacles they had passed, about a thousand years ago.

Joshua looked behind him. Black smoke covered the compound, drifting down the valley. Blood was dripping from the crew compartment, leaving a trail of red splashes on the dusty road as they accelerated away. His mouth was dry, metallic from so much adrenalin, his tongue like a piece of wood. He pulled off his ballistics helmet and his repirator and tasted the clean air.

Its IFF said it was friendly, but it didn't respond to the radio. It came from Syria, flying steadily on a course of 205 degrees. They had a Kfir out there supporting the reserve *Ugdah* fighting in Sinai and they gave him a heading to go look at it, since he was close by. He formated on it over the sea west of Gaza, up at 20,000 feet. It was an F-16, its blue stars gleaming in the morning sunshine. It had battle damage, there was a big hole under the canopy and its racks were empty, rocket pods hollow.

The pilot was sitting back in his seat, looking straight ahead. The Kfir pilot flew close by, but he took no attention. They flew together for a few minutes, then the Kfir broke away, fuel low in its tanks.

The F-16 flew on, out over the blue sea.

The coldroom in the *kibbutz* was still running, so they took out all the boxes and used it to store the dead. With Egyptian MiG-23s and 27s roaming Sinai it was too dangerous to send them on the road back north to Beersheva, and too hot to keep them in the open. As it was flies of all colours had already appeared from nowhere to feast on the blood.

In the dawn light David drove the light van about the positions. The Egyptians had attacked early, their BMPs were burning in the open ground to the south, where the Kfir had caught them with his cluster bombs. In the distance a column of dirty smoke stained the purity of the first light. The Kfir pilot had stayed to help, and had taken out a MiG with his cannon.

In the avocado grove the *Mag'ach* crouched like a gigantic feral monster, the armour of its front bearing a long silver and black scar. Only 100 metres away three Egyptian soldiers lay tumbled on the ground, half in and half out of a small gully. One held a bulbous RPG launcher in his hand.

The commander lay beside the track where the driver and gunner had put her. David had thought her small when she had first pushed up out of the turret; in death, she seemed no more than a child. He picked her up and she was light. Her black hair fell away, showing the terrible wounds the rocket splinters had made in her face. They called them *Gananimm*, kindergarten teachers on the tank commanders course. He put her into the back with the others, and drove to the store.

They had them stacked like wood in there, stiffening in the cold. He brought the ones from the van, both women and men, and laid them in a new pile.

Then he left the van, and walked back past the wrecked T-72s to the avocado grove. In the *Mag'ach* the gunner was sitting up in the commander's cupola, she looked like a child.

'I'll do that, if you like,' he said and climbed up. The machine gun was still sticky with the dead kindergarten teacher's blood.

They were getting low on ammunition. He leaned back against the hatch, and waited for them to come.

He waited all morning. Finally, something moved in the distance. A small column of white vehicles.

The young gunner had some binoculars, he peered through

them. There they were clear and clean, the big black letters on their sides.

United Nations.

## Latakia

The villa was in the old French style, the *colon* had built it to go with his orchards outside the then-sleepy town. There were still some left, the villa was still secluded from the development of the city, which was why Joshua had made it his own, away from prying eyes. He sat inside, and listened as his instructions came through on the radio.

The other commandos sat out in the morning sun, letting the warmth soothe their wounds and bruises. About them bees hummed busily, visiting the purple flowers of the bougainvillaea spilling down the wall. From the terrace they could see the Mediterranean, blue in the distance, and behind them the Alawi mountains where their dead lay buried, all in a single grave.

Pain stabbed through Joshua's chest as he breathed, his ribs heavily strapped. The radio stopped talking in his earphones, he put it down and went out to join the others.

'Hamouda's in Latakia,' he said. 'For the *Zafir* victory parade. We know that. The background to it is that he's been very careful not to give any one section of society here too much of an advantage over any other. Asad was an Alawi, they're a minority overall. He promoted them, poured a lot of money in, it made him very unpopular with the Shi'a and Sunnis. Hamouda stopped that. There's enough Alawis who remember the good old days of Asad's gravy train to be resentful. He knows that, which is why he's coming up here to give them the honour of their own *Zafir* parade.'

His wrist was itching under the plaster, he reached under with a teaspoon to scratch it. His ears were still singing from the explosions. He thought that they were probably permanently damaged.

'Hamouda is still the one person holding Syria together as a fighting unit. If the Alawis were seen to kill him a civil war would result.'

He breathed in. Haazev, Danny and the others all sat slumped about, in varying degrees of pain, but their eyes watched intently as they listened. The BMP was in the barn, their weapons in the room behind them.

'The parade's going to be televised. Loyal Alawi units, including us members of the 85th, will march and ride past. We'll take him out from short range with cannon and machine-gun fire.'

'Aren't they going to say *we* did it?' Haazev objected. 'We Israelis?'

'That was Shaul Shiloah I was speaking to,' Joshua informed him. 'There's going to be somebody else there at the parade. He's in Latakia now.'

'Who?'

'Jacob Ben-Levi. He's come to start talks with Hamouda. As a part of the so-called reconciliation he's going to stand with Hamouda – next to him – as he reviews the troops. Showing respect for the Arab cause, that sort of thing. Your father General Shahak has ordered him to do it.'

'And?'

'We blow him away too.'

# PART XXVI

H AMOUDA had the scroll behind him on the wall, it was the first thing Jacob noticed as he came into the room where Hamouda waited for him.

'You are the new Saladin?' he demanded, without waiting for pleasantries.

'I may be,' Hamouda agreed. 'My armies are regrouping at the frontiers. We hold the Golan Heights, we look down upon the ancient lands of *bilad al-Sham* below us, the rightful lands of Damascus.'

'Filastin,' Jacob said shortly.

Hamouda raised his eyebrows in exaggerated query.

'Where?'

'Filastin. The home of the inhabitants of Palestine, old and new.'

Hamouda laughed.

'Palestinians? Who are they? I stood on the Golan Heights myself yesterday, and all I saw were the lands of Damascus, that run from the Euphrates to the Nile.'

'You also saw the forces of the United Nations, that has drawn a line of peace about the new nation of Filastin.'

'I saw people in blue hats,' Hamouda said vaguely. His eyes suddenly snapped up at Jacob, like a dragon. 'How many divisions do the people in blue hats have?'

'They have more than divisions, they have moral force. The people of Filastin, old and new, shall not be deprived of their land. The people that Arafat led will find new leaders. We who called ourselves Israeli will find new leaders. We shall come together after all, and all your killing will have been for naught.'

'Moral force?' Hamouda jeered. 'You are a fool, a very old fool. Will you never know where you are? These are the lands of the old god, who drinks blood morning and night, and consumes mens' souls.'

He pointed a savage finger at Jacob.

'Shahak knows that. Weiss knew it too. Only you were so foolish, so naïve, so arrogant in your idealism to think that you could change where you were.'

Jacob turned the golden ring on his finger.

'What of this ring then, made by my ancestor, Avraham, in the court of Saladin?'

Hamouda sneered. 'Made by Hussein, a jeweller in Damascus, to my instructions. I know nothing of this ancestor of yours, I do not know what happened to him after the Battle of Hattin. What I *had* discovered was that rarest of things, an Israeli who believed that Jew and Arab can live together in peace.'

Sighing Jacob took the ring off and looked at the possession he had prized above all others. Then he put it back on.

'I still believe it can be done. I shall keep the ring anyway, even though it is not real it is a symbol. For it can be done. I, a Jew, have a son with one who is a Palestinian.'

'No,' Hamouda whispered dangerously. '*You* do not. *I* have a son. *My* son, by a *Syrian* woman. I tell you again, you do not know where you are. Here, winner takes all.'

Jacob went very pale, he was breathing hard. Hamouda *must* be lying to him now. Rifka? He fought to gather control, to suppress Hamouda's insinuations. *His* son?

'You do not have it all. Your armies do not occupy Filastin. They are halted. You have lost,' he countered, his mind racing. He would not give in to Hamouda's trickery. Not this time.

'Your commandos destroyed our command centre,' Hamouda said openly. 'But we have reformed. We stand poised. Do you not know who we are? We are the Assyrians, who will slaughter all.'

Martial music had begun to blare from loudspeakers in the square.

'Let us go out,' he said abruptly, standing up. 'Let us review the forces that will, if I so choose, destroy you all. Then when we return I will tell you under what conditions I shall allow this Filastin to exist. For the time being. Even the great Saladin did not expel the Crusaders immediately. It may be that like my ancestor, I shall have to slowly starve you to death.'

Jacob managed to smile. It was a victory, of a kind. There was hope yet. If peace was never to be achieved in his lifetime, his son must have his chance to do what he, Jacob had spent his life trying to achieve. Yes, there was still hope.

Together, they went out into the square.

The BMP grumbled slowly down the lane, its squeaking tracks

echoing off the old stone walls. Dudik was driving, Joshua standing up tall in the turret, the white of the sling around his arm a symbol of his part in the victorious war. The first trucks were rumbling through the street, Dudik pulled over into the kerb as they turned in. Haazev got out of the back and raised the front engine hatch, then hung over it as though making a repair. The trucks with impeccably-turned out troops rolled past on their way to the square with its French colonial buildings.

Looking behind him, Joshua saw some BMPs coming up, commanders smart in their blue berets.

'Okay, Haazev,' he called softly, and the soldier put the hatch down, and hurried round to get back into the fighting compartment at the rear. The BMPs went past, two abreast, and they slipped in behind them.

Hamouda was a Christian. He had a Sunni minister of defence, a Shi'a foreign minister and an Alawi as head of the air force. However, he entrusted his security to another Christian, for he would distrust them all.

Colonel Sayigh disliked parades as much as the shade of Anwar Sadat, and for the same reason. However, if his employer insisted on holding one, then Sayigh would see to it that it was the kind he approved of.

The parade vehicles and troops were clean, Sayigh's men checked them before they left the holding point for the parade. The guns were unarmed, the rifles conspicuous by the lack of magazines. As each left the holding point a soldier slapped on a magnetic device to the armour, a transponder.

Sayigh controlled the parade from his command helicopter that circled watchfully over the city. When the unknown BMP went through the electronic wall it lacked IFF, identification friend or foe, and was classified foe.

At the back of the column of BMPs Joshua stood up in the turret, passing down the street with its old buildings, hearing the cheering of the crowd that lined both sides in his ears. The great square was coming, he could see the modern statue of Hamouda in the middle where the one of his predecessor had been, thirty feet tall.

The parade poured straight across the square, but there was a road that led off to the left, going down towards the sea. As they came up to the red and gold podium from which Hamouda was conducting the review they would hose the whole thing with cannon and machine-gun fire from the turret, and from the fighting

ports of the troop compartment. Cutting sharp left they would race
across the square to vanish into the road leading to the sea, firing
as they did so. With luck a vehicle would follow them into the road
which they could knock out, using it to block pursuit. Out of town
a captured Syrian Gazelle would pick them up and whisk them out
to sea, where a fast attack craft was waiting.

Joshua realized that something was wrong when the heads of the
BMP commanders in front whirled round, to see who was following
them. A helicopter was clattering overhead.

'Dudik, over the pavement,' he yelled, as the nearest APC jerked
sideways, forming a roadblock. He dived down into the turret, taking
the controls of the guns.

The BMP went through the people lining the street, crashing
through the barriers. They shot past the wheeling BMPs. People
were running and screaming, tripping in front of the racing vehicle.

'Coming up to the square,' Joshua shouted over the intercom.
Gun muzzles were pointing from the ports behind him.

He saw the podium, saw the vast, hurrying shape of the *Hind*
helicopter gunship hurtling towards him over the rooftops.

'*Open fire!*'

He squeezed the triggers, and flame streaked out in a finger of
death. The podium erupted into flying gore. Over the rooftop, the
mouth of the gunship sparkled with fire and light.

When it was all over, they stripped the bloody corpses that they
dragged from the wreck, and put them on display naked under the
gigantic statue of Hamouda. They found most of the bits of Jacob
Ben-Levi, and tossed him on as well. His hands were there, but the
golden ring had fallen off, lying somewhere in the gore-spattered
wreckage of the reviewing stand.

The scream was so sharp, so loud, that the doctor came running.
Before he opened the padded door he peered through the viewing
slot, felt in the pocket of his white coat for the preloaded syringe,
full of sedative, for even ones like the old lady were possessed of
incredible strength when the madness took its hold on them. But
Ruth was standing in the centre of the room, her white hair hanging
down, staring into space. He opened the door, went in, and spoke
quietly to her.

'Is everything all right, Ruth?' he said in a friendly manner, fingering
the syringe.

'He is dead,' she said clearly. She looked at him strangely, her eyes seemed quite lucid.

'Who is?'

'Jacob,' she said articulately. 'Somehow I know he is dead. He was a good man. But, you know, good men kill more people than bad ones.'

'You've just had a dream, Ruth,' he said reassuringly.

'He was my dream,' she said. She waved her arms at the land they could see through the strong glass outside. 'That's all it was. A dream. Now he's dead.'

She looked at the doctor for a moment with old, certain eyes. Then they glazed over again. 'Are they coming for me,' she said. 'We shall all die now.'

The troops of the army drove past them, on their way to the front.

## Jerusalem

There was a tank out there somewhere. Young Amos heard it first, he looked up from the little fire where he was brewing tea and drying Arab ears at the same time. He had a necklace of them, all tanned like obscene crisps, which he wore round his neck.

'T-72,' he said.

Crouched under the piece of tarpaulin he had pulled over the gap between the two great chunks of smashed rock David Ben-Levi nodded. His home might have been a patch of Sarayevo, a crumbled ruin in Chechnya or any other place where the ending of the twentieth century had brought hideous phoenixes of hatreds long thought dead back to life. But it had once been the Western Wall, people had pushed folded prayers on paper between its cracks. Now fourteen-year-old Amos smoked enemy ears in it.

Jerusalem itself was smoked. The ruins were blackened with soot, grey with ash. They had been fighting in there for weeks, and both sides made a point of destroying the enemy's sacred places. They smashed up the Christian parts too, but nobody cared about them, only the United Nations, and they were long gone. Not even journalists hungry for film went into the old city; both sides made a point of killing anything that moved. David slept in as good accommodation as anyone else in the city, on rubble under a piece of old tarpaulin.

"T-72." he said. He supposed he could walk out, the United Nations had done. He didn't feel like it. Why? Everybody else he knew was dead somewhere nearby. Israel had been so small, if you died anywhere in it it was not far away. Only Jacob was any distance, thrown into a Syrian ditch for the dogs to eat. The Arabs had conducted wholesale slaughter as they came. He supposed he could join all those who had fled in panic, go back to the diaspora. But then, why? There had been brave talk of the Israeli nation in exile. If Arafat could do it, so could the Jews. But Arafat was dead, and the Palestinians as scattered as the Jews. It was Syrian territory that the tank was grinding its tracks on. It always had been. Saladin had come this way, when he drove the Crusaders out the first time.

David knew who he was. A crusader. They had all been crusaders wearing the star of David instead of the red cross of Jesus. He felt no remorse, not now. Shahak had been right, he wrong. He crouched in the rubble of a world played by Hama rules.

The Jews wore their weapons even as they slept, they slipped out through the filthy ruins like ghosts, themselves and their clothing encrusted with blood and grime. They were a small band, David was not sure how many, six or seven. Sometimes they acquired new members, survivors of other fighting squads that lurked in the wreckage, or hid in the tunnels and sewers, sometimes they left dead and dying in the sudden skirmishes that were a feature of the fighting.

They were somewhere near the old Dung gate. The souk was tumbled stone slabs and a crater. The casing of a cluster bomb stuck out of a crack.

David was carrying an RPG rocket launcher taken from a Syrian he had killed. He crawled on his belly through the rubble, the heavy thudding beat of the tank's diesel engine in his ears, the stink of its fuel and exhaust catching in his throat.

Rifka Berry had stood on a T-72 as she declared holy war on the Jews for killing her husband, he'd seen her on the television. Not that it had been her name. Hamouda. Rifka Hamouda, wrapped in a Syrian flag, an AK-47 held high as the troops rolled past to the fighting. Well here they were.

He poked his head up. Fifty yards away Syrian commandos were moving in short, quick rushes from one piece of cover to the other, the tank grinding slowly forward with them. A strange pole stuck up from its rear casing. It was decorated with some species of gourd, which swung about wildly as the tank lurched over the rough ground.

His comrades were waiting for him to fire. He edged up, so that the muzzle of the rocket launcher poked just above the edge of the rock slab.

He was so tired. He did not even feel adrenalin any more. He brought the simple sight down onto the join between turret and body, and squeezed the trigger.

The rocket flew from the launcher with a terrific bang that blew dust high in the air. The Israelis opened up with their weapons in a cacophony of sound and smoke.

There was a roar as the reactive armour exploded on the tank turret and the massive gun swung towards him.

He was lying on his back, dirty black smoke was staining the blue sky and it was quiet.

Two men were looking down at him, men in camouflage suits, stained from the fighting. One kicked him, he felt it as though under water.

'Arabs,' he grunted. 'Bastard fucking Arabs.'

Blood gushed up into his mouth and he spat at them.

'Filthy fucking Arabs,' he said again.

The Syrians hacked off his head with a spade and lashed it by the hair to their pole on the tank along with the others. It swung wildly, open sightless eyes watching as the Syrians pushed forward towards the sea, driving the Jews before them.